Broken Road

Broken Road

A Milltown Novel
Book One

Devin Sloane

vi

Dedication

For all those who suffer with anxiety and other mental health issues.

And, as always,

For A,

who has given me my very own

big, fat, Greek, family.

Playlist

Don't Forget About Me – Emphatic

Rubylove – Yusuf/Cat Stevens

Be Alright – Dean Lewis

What if You – Joshua Radin

Breathe Again – Sara Bareilles

What Might Have Been – Little Texas

Little Too Late – Default

Believe – Staind

Pieces – Red

Not Broken Anymore – Blue October

So Are You To Me – Eastmountainsouth

Best is Yet to Come – Red

It Only Hurts When I'm Breathing – Shania Twain

Alone – I Prevail

The Mess I Made – Parachute

Photograph – Ed Sheeran

Ready When You Are – Trapt

Come Home – OneRepublic

Shattered – Trading Yesterday

All I Want – Kodaline

What Hurts the Most – State of Mine

In My Veins – Andrew Belle, Feat. Erin McCarley

No One – Alicia Keys

Last Kiss – Boyce Avenue, Megan & Liz

I Can't Wait – Runner Runner

Burning Bridges – OneRepublic

Can't Forget You – My Darkest Days

Hold Onto Memories – Disturbed

Pieces - Tom Francis

Sorry – Aquilo

Arcade – Duncan Laurence

I Lived – OneRepublic

I'll Fight – Daughtry

Waiting Outside the Lines – Greyson Chance

Lost Without You – Freya Ridings

Shameless – Sandro Cavazza

Vocabulary List

Pappou – Grandfather.

Yiayia – Grandmother.

Koukla – doll – a common endearment.

Ela – come here, come on.

Nouno – godfather.

Nouna – godmother.

Thia/Thio – aunt/uncle.

Moro mou – my baby.

Psychi – soul. Pronounced Psee-he.

Koritzi/Koritzaki – girl/little girl.

Pouli/Poulaki – bird/little bird.

Agapimeni/o mou – my beloved.

Glykouli mou – my sweet.

Levendis mou – strong man.

Kala – Fine/Good.

Table of Contents

Chapter 1 - Promises

20 Years Ago

Ruby

"Promise me," he urged, his face tipped down, dark eyes searching mine. "Promise me you'll think this through. It doesn't have to be over."

Standing in the circle of his arms, I nodded, though I had no intention of doing what he asked. For the past several weeks, I'd thought about little else, and could see no alternative for us.

My grandfather, my pappou, was gone, and I'd made the only decision I could for my family. Better that Vander leaves now, while he still loved me. Better now than later, when what we have becomes a burden, and his eyes reflect resentment instead of love.

I gathered up the tattered remains of my resolve and moved closer to him within the circle of his arms, pressing my forehead to his lips. "Vander, I love you," I whispered. "But you have to go."

Six weeks had passed since my pappou had collapsed.

Five weeks and six days since Vander dropped me off at the airport in British Columbia.

Four weeks since I deregistered from university.

Three days since I called Vander and told him I wouldn't be coming back.

Two days since Vander showed up at my door.

Pure, unadulterated joy suffused my entire body when I opened the front door to find Vander on my doorstep. Dark, thick, wavy hair pushed back off his high forehead. Perfect lips curved in a smile, eyes alight. I stared gape-mouthed into his smiling face, certain I conjured him from my wildest dreams.

He grinned and opened his arms. I leaped, knocking him back several steps. He laughed and squeezed me tight as he stumbled to keep us upright. I wrapped my legs and arms around him, and tucked my face into his strong neck.

"What are you doing here?" I finally asked, leaning back in his arms, my heart in my eyes.

He tightened his arms around me, and his face softened. "I had to see you for myself, make sure you were okay." He took a breath, his eyes boring into mine. "I also wanted to talk to you in person. I think you're making a mistake, Ruby-mine."

I closed my tired eyes and pressed my forehead against his.

"How long can you stay?" I asked softly. I needed to mentally prepare myself to say goodbye in person. It would, I knew, be infinitely more difficult than it was over the phone.

"Two days, Ruby-mine. Two days to convince you to come back with me."

Over the two painfully perfect days we had together, I delayed the conversation as long as possible. It was not difficult, especially when I already knew the outcome.

Vander and I worked side-by-side at Spuds over the weekend. Spuds, the tiny restaurant my pappou and yiayia opened four decades before. It funded Amber's and my childhood since I was ten years old, when my father died, and my mother checked out. It clothed us, fed us, paid for our schooling and extracurriculars. In short, Pappou funded our childhood instead of his and Yiayia's retirement.

I knew, from looking through the paperwork, that there was no way the three of us who were left could survive without one of us manning Spuds full-time. Yiayia couldn't do it on her own.

Amber, being in the final year of her undergrad, had never wavered in what she aimed to do with her life. In fact, she had already applied for her Masters, while I still had little clue what I wanted to do. I couldn't let her quit when she was so close.

Vander and I laughed more than we worked, and I wondered if it had been like that for Pappou and Yiayia when they worked there together. Vander got a taste of the business, but he didn't clue in to all the financial ramifications of my decision to run it. I waited until Monday morning, while he got ready to leave, to explain it to him.

With my yiayia at Spuds doing the prep work for the day, and Amber already at school, I sat him down in our tiny kitchen and lay out the facts.

He could not deny my points, but stubbornly refused to accept my decision. At a stalemate, tired from arguing, and heartbroken over our looming separation, I stood and pulled him into my bedroom.

Standing at opposite sides of the bed, we undressed, our eyes locked on each other's. Goose pimples raced across my flesh. That old house never could hold the heat. Vander slid into the bed first and held the covers open for me.

I crawled in, and he immediately scooped me under him, covering me with his long, lean body. He parted my thighs with his and rested his pelvis in the cradle of mine. With his elbows braced on either side of my shoulders, he cradled my head gently between his big palms.

He dipped his head and kissed me. His kiss felt hesitant, unsure, a question, like the first time.

I parted my lips under his, inviting him in, and he slanted his sweet mouth across mine. His hands tightened around my head. He rocked his hips, sliding his erection through my wetness, nudging my clit.

Pulling my knees up, I hooked my ankles around his thighs. I dragged my hands up his sides and wrapped my arms around his strong back.

My mind flew once again through the facts, searching for a nonexistent loophole, so I could hold this beautiful man. Coming up with nothing, it hit me that this would probably be our last time together.

Grief wrapped her fist around my heart and squeezed. I sobbed into his mouth.

He pulled back, a heavy sheen covering his own eyes, and kissed the tears that escaped my closed lids.

"Ruby-mine," he whispered. "We'll find a way. I promise."

I couldn't see how, but I didn't argue. Instead, I pulled his dark head closer and kissed him with all the love I had in my heart. I tipped my hips to allow him entrance, and he plunged inside with a sigh.

"I can't give you up, Ruby-mine," he whispered, his lips trembling against mine.

The tears abated as our kisses became more desperate, and he ramped up his pace inside me. I curled my legs around his and cried out his name, shattering around him as my heart splintered into a million tiny pieces.

He tucked his face into my neck as he came, and my mind clung to the exquisite perfection of him pulsing with life inside me. I pressed my cheek against his temple and held him tight, counting the minutes until I had to let him go.

He quietly tossed his things in his bag, then threw his bag in the trunk of my little blue Mazda 323. We drove in silence to the Go-Station, our hands linked tightly on his hard thigh, the silence between us thick with sadness and dread.

I tucked my scarf snugly around my neck to ward off the icy November wind. He held me close against his warmth as we crossed the parking lot to the other side of the station, where I could accompany him no further.

The station was busy enough to help me hold it together.

Vander turned toward me and encircled me with his arms. His tall frame sheltered me from the wind while people passed us on either side, heading in both directions.

I could barely feel him through the bundled layers of winter clothing between us, but I pressed closer anyway.

"Promise me," he urged, pulling back slightly, his dark eyes searching mine. "Promise me you'll think this through. It doesn't have to be over."

I nodded. It was easier than arguing. In any case, grief on top of grief, from loss upon loss, squeezed my throat closed.

I pressed my forehead to his lips. "Vander, I love you," I whispered. "But you have to go. You're going to miss your train."

4

A shudder raced through his long body while he wrapped me up tight for one last moment. "Don't forget about me, Ruby-mine."

I hiccoughed. "I could never."

"I'll always be here for you." He palmed my face and dipped to look into my eyes. "We'll work it out. Somehow, we'll work it out. What we have is too special."

I swallowed hard but didn't answer. I knew what the end would be. Three thousand miles between us and not two pennies to rub together did not equal a viable long-distance relationship. We were over.

I knew it.

He must have known it, too.

He hugged me tightly one last time, his lips pressed firmly against my forehead, then he released me abruptly and strode away.

My stomach pitched and rolled at the sudden loss of his warmth. The bitter wind slapped my cheeks, and I prayed to keep my breakfast down, at least until he got on the train.

"Don't look back, don't look back," I whisper pleaded, my face chilled from my tears, my eyes frozen on his retreating form.

Halfway down the pathway that led to the train, he stopped. The sounds of the people and the tracks receded into the background. All my attention homed in on his back.

"Oh, God!" I sobbed. I slapped my cold fingers over my mouth.

Turn around. Please.

He was too far away to hear me, but if he turned, he would witness the despair I could no longer hide. If he turned, I wouldn't be strong enough to let him go. If he turned, our parting would be delayed, and our love would sour.

I witnessed firsthand what staying had done to my mother. Eyes that used to look at us with affection and dance with laughter, rarely took us in at all after we lost my dad. When I did catch her gaze, it reflected only grief, as if the mere sight of us magnified her pain.

Over time, her grief morphed into anger, and neither Amber nor I could do anything right. Anger faded to indifference, and that indifference allowed my mother to walk away from us, even as Amber ran down the driveway after her, screaming and begging her to stay.

Yiayia and Pappou were at work the day she left. I did not run after my mother. I ran after Amber.

I held her on the driveway as our mother drove away.

I wiped her tears.

I bore the crescents from her nails in my arms as she wailed out her despair.

Our mother never looked back.

Her absence in the days and weeks that followed, for me, was a relief. At the time, that relief shamed me, and I pretended a devastation I didn't feel.

It wasn't hard.

The look on Amber's face etched itself onto the inside of my closed lids, and I saw it every night as I drifted off to sleep. When the silence of the night descended, the echo of Amber's cries ripped my heart apart.

The thought of Vander's love fading to indifference and dismissal kept my mouth shut tight and cemented my feet to the concrete. I would not run after him and beg him to stay. He had to choose me freely.

He stopped and looked down at his feet, his hands fisted stiffly at his sides. He half turned his head. I held my breath in hope that he would turn all the way around and save me from myself.

Turn around. Please, please, please.

He paused, and I watched his shoulders heave before he shook himself, averted his head, and walked on.

Involuntarily, I called his name. Even so, my voice failed me, and my feet remained in place.

I watched until he reached the platform to the waiting train. He paused once more at the door, but a moment later, he was out of sight. I pivoted slowly on my heel and clumsily dodged the people blocking me on my way to my car, my mind and heart mired in a quicksand of my own making.

I opened my car door and slid behind the wheel, my breath escaping in panicked gasps.

Oh, God!

The sight of Vander walking away looped on repeat in my head. I turned the key in the ignition, drove to the back of the lot, and parked. I turned on the radio and blasted the music as loud as it could go to drown out the wet, garbled sound of my ruptured heart.

By the end of the third song, I could almost breathe.

Vander

We were out with friends when Ruby received the call from her older sister. Amber attended university in their hometown, so she could commute to school and still be around to help their grandparents with the restaurant and keep Ruby's flighty ass in line until she finished high school.

Or so Ruby laughingly told me.

When it came time for Ruby to apply for university, Amber encouraged her to go wherever she wanted, feeling sure she could handle whatever came up at home. Ruby took her up on the offer, applying to go to a school in British Columbia, not for any particular program, but for the milder weather. She hated the cold with a passion she was convinced was due to her Greek heritage.

She changed her program twice that first semester, and for her third year she enrolled in a general arts program, not yet having any clear idea of what she wanted to do with the rest of her life.

I met her the first week of our first year. She was sunshine and light and laughter. She drew me to her like a moth to a flame, a flame that enveloped me in gentle warmth, warming me with her ready smile.

It took time.

We became friends first, bonding over our shared Greek heritage, which I used shamelessly to my advantage. By the end of the first semester, we were inseparable.

She picked up her brand-new Nokia cell phone and punched the button to accept the call.

"Hey, koukla!" She answered upon hearing her sister's voice.

Her bright smile dimmed, and fear widened her dark eyes. I focussed on the emotions flitting across her face and stepped closer.

7

"What happened?" She whispered, then turned and walked outside to escape the noise of the bar.

I grabbed her purse off the back of her chair and followed her out.

Right outside the door, she came to a full stop, blocking the entrance. With a firm hand to the small of her back, I gently propelled her off to the side.

"What do you mean, 'Pappou is gone'? Where the hell did he go?" She snapped.

Her pretty face went slack with shock. She fell back against the outside wall, and I barely broke her fall before she hit the ground.

She sat with her legs splayed out in front of her. Dropping her head, she bent low over her knees, pulling air in through her nose and pushing it back out forcefully before dragging in another breath.

Hunkering down beside her, I listened shamelessly as her sister explained that their pappou had a heart attack at work.

Fuck.

I dropped my chin to my chest for a moment, not wanting this for her, then sat down beside her and gathered her up in my arms. I slipped the cell phone from her hand.

"Hi, Amber. This is Vander," I said softly. "I'm so sorry. I'll get her to call you back in a few minutes."

"Is she okay? What is she doing? Is she okay?" Amber panicked.

"She's shocked. I'll stay with her. Please email her any pertinent information, and I'll get her to call you back as soon as she can."

Ruby needed to see everything in print to process it. She couldn't retain information that she received verbally. It felt odd to ask her grieving sister to send an email, but we both knew Ruby needed it, and in her grief, Amber needed the reminder.

A full half hour later, Ruby climbed off my lap. She swiped her palms across her cheeks and released a shuddering breath.

"I'm going to head back to my apartment and call my sister back," she stated, her eyes red-rimmed and slightly glazed. She looked without seeing, seemingly having retreated deep into her head, and disconnected from everything around her, including me.

The change sent a chill down my spine.

"I'm coming with you."

She looked vaguely in my direction. "I don't want to ruin your night. Go back in with everybody else, and I'll call you tomorrow when I know what's going on." She nodded decisively.

She lifted her chin for my kiss, and I obliged her before pulling her in for a hug. She shivered. I pulled off my university hoodie and slipped it over her head.

Drawing her close under my arm, we began the walk back to her apartment. She held herself rigidly at first, but by the time we reached her place, she leaned, soft and yielding, against my side.

Twelve hours later, I slipped my cross from around my neck and looped it around hers, tucking it inside her t-shirt.

"Vander," she gasped. "I can't take this!"

It was my baptism cross that I'd had since I was a baby. It was sacred, holy, and I wore it every day. It represented my heritage, my family, and my faith.

"Wear it, moro mou. Wear it and keep me with you until you come back."

She placed her hand over the cross, and that action alone took away some of the chill of her impending absence. "Thank you."

She gifted me with the ghost of her smile, and I soaked up its faint warmth. I kissed her gently, then released her to catch her flight.

Six weeks later, when she made the decision to leave school, I got on a plane and flew to her. I had only two days to change her mind, and at the end of those, I'd made exactly zero headway. Standing in the minuscule vestibule of her house, before heading to the train station, she turned to me and started to slip my cross over her head.

"No, absolutely fuckin' not," I stated grimly.

She looked at me in shock. "It's yours. You need it back."

"What I need," I spoke gruffly and wrapped my hands around her wrists, stopping her from removing my cross, "is for you to be safe. For you to be with me somehow, someway."

"Vander," she whispered, her eyes wide. "I can't keep this. It's too important."

I needed her to keep it. I needed the connection. I dropped my head for a moment, then looked up at her from beneath my brow. "We'll see each other again, Ruby-mine. Don't take away my hope."

She dropped her hands, her face pained, and I breathed a sigh of relief. Pressing her lips together, she tucked my cross back inside her shirt, snaked her arms around my waist, and lay her cheek against my chest.

"Thank you," she whispered.

I splayed my hands over her back, and lay my cheek on top of her head, sharing her light.

Twelve hours and three thousand miles away from her, there was no promise of warmth or sunshine anywhere.

Chapter 2 – Hi-jacked

<u>Ruby</u>

Vander and I kept in touch daily. He worked on his campaign to keep us together by applying for several summer internships in Milltown and the GTA, but luck was not on our side. We were holding out hope for the last one.

He called Spuds shortly after the lunch rush. I left my yiayia at the front of the store while I moved to the back room to answer my phone.

"Ruby-mine," he greeted me softly.

"Hi moro mou," I answered sadly. I could tell by the tone of his voice that he didn't have good news.

He sighed heavily. "I didn't get it."

I swallowed hard and leaned against the back counter, my hand wrapped like a vice around its edge. "I know."

Silence weighed heavily on the line between us.

I heard him take a breath. "I can't keep going on like this, Ruby-mine." His voice broke along with my heart.

My grip on my phone tightened.

This.

This is what I'd been trying to avoid months ago when I said goodbye to him at the train station.

I worked to keep my voice even. "I understand," I said, even though I didn't. Why wouldn't he transfer schools? Why wouldn't he wait if he truly loved me?

"I can't ask you to wait for me," he explained.

"I think, what you're saying, is that you don't want to wait for me." Suddenly light-headed, my voice sounded far away to my own ears.

I wasn't being completely fair to him. I knew it. Still, I needed it to be his choice, free from guilt or obligation.

Neither of us said anything for the longest time, his silence an admission, the connection over the phone the closest thing we had to being together. The only sound from my side came from the ticking of the clock and Cat Stevens singing 'Ruby my love' over the store speaker.

"You've got our song on, Ruby-mine," he murmured.

My tears welled up and overflowed.

Our song.

Back when our friendship first showed signs of turning into something more, we went out for karaoke for a laugh with our friends. For his turn, he picked that song and sang it to me.

Badly.

I laughed until my sides hurt. He often said my laugh won him over completely. It is neither genteel nor ladylike. His terrible singing cemented his place in my heart. I became 'Ruby-mine' for him from that night onward.

I pressed the phone closer to my ear to get closer to his voice.

He sighed. Goodbye was all we had left.

The hope I couldn't resist harbouring deep in my heart turned to acid despair and detonated, sending bitter shrapnel slicing through my chest. The pain stunned me. My heart bled from the lacerations, the outer layer peeling off in bloody strips, leaving the entire organ a weeping, swollen, quivering mass of anguished flesh.

I sobbed aloud, and he cursed angrily, "Fuck!"

12

"Not yours. Not anymore," I choked out. "And you're not mine anymore, either."

"Fuck, Ruby!" He exclaimed exasperatedly. "I don't know what else to do! I've tried everything I can think of. Can't you come here?"

I could see him in my mind, his hand impatiently pushing his dark waves off his forehead as he stomped around the way he did when frustrated or angry. I paced back and forth in front of the prep counter, spinning on my heel to turn, as his words pinged around in my brain.

Moths took up residence where my heart used to be, their wings beating frantically as they ricocheted off my ribcage. I placed my palm over Vander's cross, the cross I wore every day in place of my own. I took a deep breath to steady my racing pulse.

"You know I can't," I said evenly.

"Do I? Really? Because it seems to me your sister could take over Spuds for the summer, and you could come out here to me," he challenged.

He had a right to be angry. Truthfully, Amber offered to run Spuds on her own for the summer.

Repeatedly.

She'd even lined up a possible part-timer just for the lunch rush. I ruminated over her offer constantly. Both she and Yiayia sat me down, trying to convince me to go.

Several times I attempted to buy a plane ticket but could not complete the transaction. I was fine until the agent requested my credit card number. The card quivered in my trembling grasp, while the pounding of my heart pulsed in my ears. Beads of cold sweat broke out over my forehead, and the rising nausea forced me off the phone every time.

Hours after hanging up the phone, I still felt as though my head was detached from my body, a floating ball of air bobbing untethered. At those times, I felt sure I was going to pass out, maybe even die, certain that Amber or Yiayia would find me on the floor in the same way Yiayia had found Pappou.

I lined up appointments to get my heart checked, convinced I'd inherited a heart condition from my pappou. All indications so far pointed toward some kind of panic disorder.

It made sense. Even the thought of leaving filled me with dread. The episodes weren't only limited to plane tickets, either. Going anywhere new provoked an attack, it was getting to the point that even my regular haunts were becoming problematic.

Yiayia constantly pushed me to go out, but the only places I felt truly safe were at Spuds and the little house I grew up in with Amber and Yiayia. Going anywhere else filled me with dread and the irrational thought that something bad might happen, and I wouldn't be able to escape or make it back home in time.

"I'm sorry," I whispered.

"Sorry," he scoffed, and I winced at his tone, hearing his frustration, his hurt, his doubt. "Is it that you don't love me enough, Ruby?"

Tears coursed down my cheeks.

Telling him about my panic wouldn't change anything. He'd still be there, I'd still be stuck here, and the pain of our parting would be further delayed. Eventually, he would move on with his life, he'd just do it with guilt, and I didn't want guilt to be what remained of what was us.

I answered him the only way I could, my voice thick. "I will always love you, Vander. We tried. It's not going to work out for us. At least not right now."

He sighed heavily. "You're not coming?"

"No." The bald word rang between us like a death knell.

He spoke softly as he promised, "I'll always be here for you, Ruby-mine."

"I love you, Vander."

I choked out the only truth I wanted to leave with him and hung up the phone. I stood with my hands tucked under my chin, my eyes squeezed shut.

My body went rigid with the shock of what I'd just done, and the loss of connection to him. Whatever was happening to me, it had hijacked my mind, my will, my heart, and my future.

I turned to see Yiayia carefully open the door to the back room and peek in, dressed in her signature elastic waist polyester pants, floral blouse, and a flashy pair of flats. Her ruby ring was the one piece of jewelry she never went without. Even at work, it hung on a cord around her neck. She was forever tsking at me for going out wearing 'beejamas' and without make-up. She believed in always looking your best and had tried, to no avail, to instill that in Amber and myself. Even this morning, she berated me for going to work in jeans and a t-shirt.

She opened the door fully as she took in my face and hers crumpled.

She opened her arms and called to me softly, "Ela, moro mou. Ela styn yiayia sou." *Come, my baby, come to your yiayia.*

I put my phone down on the counter and stumbled towards her.

She met me halfway and wrapped me up in her arms. Arms that had always been there for me steadied me once again, and she held me while I cried, streaking tears, snot, and mascara all over the shoulder of her pretty blouse. Several minutes passed before the comfort of her embrace bolstered me enough that I could pull myself together.

I released her and swiped my fingers beneath my eyes. She stood at exactly my height, but to me, she always seemed so much taller. "Sorry, Yiayia. I got mascara on your blouse."

She shrugged, her grasp firm around my elbows. "Ech. Who cares? I got it seventy percent off..."

We finished at the same time, "Five dollars only."

I smiled. She always said that to my pappou when he asked about her new clothes. It always made him smile.

"Psychi mou," she probed gently, rubbing her hands up and down my arms. "Why don't you go to him?"

I heaved in a shuddering breath and bowed my head. I spoke through the tightness in my throat. "I can't, Yiayia. Every time I try to buy the ticket, I feel like-" My voice broke. I swallowed hard and continued in a whisper. "I feel like I'm having a heart attack."

"Moro mou," she murmured, stroking my dark hair back from my face. "The world is yours, poulaki mou. O ti theleis, whatever you want, is yours! Don't be afraid, moro mou. Life is happening to everybody. Go to him."

I loved my yiayia's mishmash of Greek and broken English. Her accent and Greek endearments comforted me.

I dropped my chin to my chest. "I can't, Yiayia. I just can't."

15

Silence and worry shrouded her face before she suddenly clapped her hands together. "Okay! That's okay, koritzi mou," she said decisively.

She wiped the last of the tears from my face with her work-roughened hands.

"You go to talking doctor, yes? Do it for Yiayia. And Yiayia will light the candles at the church." Her words revealed the depth of her concern. Greeks didn't go for counselling; they went to church.

I nodded, and her face lost a fraction of its tightness. "Bravo, koritzaki mou. Vander is a nice, Greek boy and I want to see you pregnant before I die."

I barked out a laugh. "Yiayia!"

She shrugged her shoulders. "Ech, I'm old lady now. As mother, I dreamed of seeing my grandchildren. Now, I'm old and greedy." She nodded, a twinkle in her dark eyes. "I want to see my great-grandchildren."

Vander

I spent the summer in a quasi-zombie state, and I failed three courses the next semester. Barely squeaking by the grade cut-off to get into the fourth year of my program, I finally started to wake up. Friends pulled at me to go out with them, counselled me to give up on Ruby, and encouraged me to move on to someone new.

I couldn't bring myself to do it.

She hadn't contacted me, not once, but I could not bring myself to move on.

Not for months.

When I finally did go out on a few dates, I didn't allow anything to go up on social media. This told me like nothing else could that I hadn't yet given up hope. Occasionally Ruby liked my posts on social media, so I knew she, too, still occasionally checked in.

The morning I woke up to find a picture of myself, with my arm around my latest date, pinned on the Facebook page of a mutual friend of mine and Ruby's, Ruby shut down all her social media. I could no longer go online to see her sweet face.

My heart broke with the loss, and for what she must have thought.

16

Part of which was correct.

Wracked with guilt, overwhelmed anew with the sorrow of her loss, and angered beyond reason that I'd been exposed and had lost contact with her entirely, I immediately broke it off with the girl. Furious with myself for giving into the temptation of loneliness, I called Ruby, several times, hoping to explain, but she never answered.

Three days later, I received a padded envelope in the mail with Ruby's return address on it. My heart thudded in my chest as I carried it into my sterile rented room and opened it with shaking hands. My cross spilled out into my palm. I opened the envelope further to find a jagged piece of lined paper, ripped from a note pad, with the last words she spoke to me scribbled across it, the letters watermarked with her tears.

I tucked that scrap of paper into my wallet before my own tears made it worse and scribbled off my own note.

I prayed she would be safe and find her way back to me.

The next day I bought a padded envelope of my own. I kissed my cross, whispered my prayer, and mailed it back to her with my own jagged scrap of paper tucked inside.

I'll always love you, Ruby-mine.

I'm always here for you.

Don't forget about me.

Chapter 3 – Loss

Ruby

At first, rage and fear ran rampant. Neither Yiayia, nor Amber, could talk to me without setting me off. There were nights I lay in bed squeezing my hands in fists because I wanted to slap myself so badly.

I cried myself to sleep.

I lost weight.

I finally got an appointment for a psychological assessment and the doctor diagnosed me with agoraphobia and ADHD. All those months waiting, all those hours of assessments, and the work was only beginning.

My homework consisted of compiling a list of everything I would do if anxiety wasn't an obstacle, and then prioritizing each item according to its level of difficulty. Going to the mall made the list. That rated a three on a scale of one to ten. Going on vacation clocked in at ten only because that was the highest rating possible. B.C. did not make it onto the list.

Vander had moved on.

I stopped following Vander on social media almost immediately after our last phone call, but there were times I searched him, just to see his face. The day I saw a post of him with another girl, my heart skittered in my chest, then dropped to my stomach, leaving me with that sick feeling you get from the sudden drop of the rollercoaster, minus the thrill. I slammed my monitor off and stood, knocking over my chair in my haste to get away from the computer.

I spun away on my heel, my eyes wide, my mouth gaping with shock. "No, no, no, no, no," I moaned. I grasped my head between my palms and squeezed as I stared unseeing into space. Closing my eyes only made it worse.

The keening sounds coming from my throat scared me. The more I tried to suppress them, the louder they got, until my cries erupted harshly from my throat and my tears broke free in harsh, angry wails.

Nothing in my life prepared me for the loss and betrayal of seeing that picture: not the moment I'd lost my father, not my mother's abandonment, not witnessing Amber's grief as she ran down the driveway after her. Even the loss of my pappou could not compare to the wave of anguish that sucked me under when I saw the evidence of what I'd done.

Every great loss up until that moment in my life seemed to have served one purpose: to exponentially increase the pain of the subsequent loss. By the time I lost Vander, the pain was unfathomable.

I stuffed my feelings down into a tiny box at the pit of my stomach and shut down all my social media. I didn't want to see him happy with another. I didn't want to see him married. I didn't want to see him become a father, not without me.

I vowed not to look for him anymore after that. I cut myself off from everyone I knew from university, isolating myself to insulate myself from the pain.

The next day I mailed him back his cross, then I went to bed in his sweatshirt and stayed there for five days. All the anger I had thus far aimed at myself for fucking up my future morphed into grief. The fury that had been my daily companion gave way to anguish at what I had allowed to slip through my fingers. Grief trapped me in a bleak well of mourning from which I did not wish to be freed.

On the fifth day, Amber bravely slipped into my bedroom and sat on the edge of my bed. She stroked my hair back from my face, and I heard her sniff, when yet another tear escaped my closed lids.

She kicked off her shoes, climbed over me, and nestled in to spoon against my back. I cried as she rocked me, her arm banded tightly across my chest, her own tears soaking the hair behind my ear.

When I finally calmed, she dangled an envelope from her finger and thumb in front of my face.

"I opened it, Ruby." She murmured. "I'm sorry if I overstepped. I worried it might make things worse for you, and I was afraid to give it to you."

I recognized Vander's handwriting. I sat up and wiped my palms roughly across my face and dried them on my pajama pants. Amber swung her legs over the side of the bed and sat hip-to-hip beside me. I opened the envelope and pulled out Vander's cross and his note. Amber spoke softly beside me.

"It's not over, Ruby. Not by a long shot."

I nodded. I slipped his cross back over my head and tucked it under my shirt. I lay my hand over it and pulled in a shuddering breath.

"Okay." I nodded again.

"Okay?" she asked. "You going to keep fighting? Get better? Even if you and Vander are never to be, he has sent you a big piece of himself. He loves you. He always will."

"Me, too," I replied, my lips trembling.

She patted my knee. "Ela, koritzi mou," she coaxed softly. "Get up before Yiayia calls the priest to come. Do we do exorcisms?"

I snorted, but I felt bad, too. "I'm sorry I worried her."

"I hope you're hungry," she joked, bumping me with her shoulder. "She's been cooking up a storm."

I laughed, the sound wet and garbled, and bumped her lightly back.

Amber continued. "She's made all your favorites." Then she added mischievously, "Even roast beef."

"Roast beef is your favorite!" I accused weakly.

"Ech," she shrugged her shoulders. "I might have told a little white lie."

I snorted out a laugh. "You took advantage of my misery to get roast beef?"

Amber smiled at me and twisted to tuck my hair behind my ear. "In my defense, she offered to make it with lemon potatoes, and you know how I feel about lemon potatoes. She already made Yemista and Moussaka.

Neither of which are my favorite, as you know. The only thing left was cabbage rolls. Do you want me to die of starvation?"

She stood and pulled me up in front of her. Her face turned serious, and she gently palmed my cheeks. "You're going to be okay."

I nodded in agreement though it wasn't a question.

"Now, go brush your teeth. Your breath stinks like a dead badger."

I pushed her away and scoffed while she walked away. She paused at the door.

"Ruby?"

I turned to her with a small smile, my hand resting over the familiar, comforting weight of Vander's cross. "Yeah?"

"He's not the only one who loves you. I love you, too."

I nodded and swallowed hard. "I love you, too, Amber."

She was right. I had to fight, and I couldn't do that lying down.

So, fight I did.

While true travel remained an elusive goal, I worked hard for two years and managed to include all of Bridgewater, Bayview Village and Milltown in my bubble.

Every weekend I practiced. I filled my car with gas and drove to various places in the triangle of those three locales. I took myself out for lunch, went to bookstores, shopped for new clothes, and a few times I even met with old friends from high school who had returned from university. Those friendships quickly fizzled under the restrictions of my condition, but I told myself it was no great loss.

Mostly, I tagged along with Amber and her bestie, Minty. With them, I could go anywhere, and they often went with me when I ventured somewhere new for the first time.

Thankfully, financial troubles were not among the things I had to worry about. Spuds brought in enough money to cover our monthly expenses, including Amber's tuition fees. Yiayia took an allowance the same as she always had, and the rest went to me.

It was not a lot.

I learned in those first few years how much more went into running Spuds than I'd imagined. Pride for my pappou, for being able to navigate the tax forms, the banking, and all the rest of the paperwork involved, filled me to overflowing. It must have been difficult for him. He didn't speak English well when he first immigrated, and he had very little education. Not even high school.

I mean, I struggled with it, especially with my ADHD brain.

My therapist and I set up a simple but comprehensive system to keep my life in order. The system hinged upon me carrying my brain around in a day timer rather than expecting myself to remember everything, or anything really. I simply had to check it every morning and add items to it as soon as they came up.

It should have been foolproof.

Still there were times I forgot to check and double-booked myself. Some instances were funnier than others.

I lay back on the gurney, feet up in the stirrups, cold and exposed. My doctor, the same one I'd had since my tender tweens, who had seen me through my first period, my need for birth control, my heartbreak over losing my pappou, the decision to discontinue university, as well as the dual diagnoses of ADHD and Agoraphobia, perched on a stool between my feet, shining a bright light on my hoo-ha.

I cleared my throat. "Dr. Zywie, I'm going to need to take a call in the next 30 seconds. If I could avoid this, believe me, I would."

She looked at me blankly for a moment and then laughed, well-used to my foibles. "Okay, well let's get started and see if we can't finish before your phone rings."

She touched the inside of my knees gently. "Let your knees fall open... Perfect. Okay, two fingers..." She held up her two fingers to tell me what she would do next when my phone rang.

I cleared my throat again, nervously, and lifted my head to peak at her through my spread knees.

"Okay, uh, you can skip the play-by-play. I have to take this."

I hated screwing up, but I had learned to embrace my quirks. If I saw the humor in my missteps, others did, too.

22

Sometimes.

She sat back in her chair, amused. Bemused? I couldn't tell.

"I can wait," she assured me.

I waved my phone at her. "Please just go ahead. This will be a good distraction for me."

Still blabbing away when she gave me the thumbs up, I rolled my eyes at myself. She tossed me a smile and a wink as she slipped out the door.

It took two solid years, but I achieved maintenance status with my agoraphobia. By no means cured, my world was not big, but it was bigger, plenty big enough for what I needed and wanted to do. The best part being that I could move freely within its boundaries.

I still needed time and notice before leaving the house. I never simply rolled with last minute changes in plans, but with notice I could come and go as I pleased. Life was looking up a bit, and I even enrolled in an online university for business and human resources.

I had a new dream to replace the one I lost in Vander.

Chapter 4 – Hungry

11 Years Ago

Ruby

It took me six years to complete my degree online. In some ways, I straggled behind my peers who finished university by their early twenties. In other ways, I'd lurched ahead.

My grandmother, with Amber's blessing, signed ownership of Spuds over to me when Amber finished school and set up her practice. Because of that, I owned my own business, free and clear, and I finally started saving money.

Although he was always on my mind, I refused to look Vander up on social media, afraid of what I might find. When I missed him more than usual, I listened to Cat Stevens' 'Rubylove' on repeat and relived that sweet chapter of my life. Over time the pain of losing him lessened and reliving the two years I had with him sustained me when the loneliness hit me particularly hard.

I dated, occasionally, but no one could hold a candle to the fire Vander lit inside me. I never got over him. It took seeing him again for that to happen.

My love life resembled a barren wasteland, so I decided to focus on my career. I registered for a conference for small business owners looking to franchise. The conference was located a little over an hour away, thirty minutes outside my bubble, and I drove myself.

It took me six weeks of snowy, slushy weekend drives to work my way up to it, but I did it. The morning I checked in, I didn't even break a sweat. Being at that conference signified the successful culmination of all my work, both in school and with my mental health, over the past decade.

I booked the hotel for two nights, so I could attend both days without the added stress of driving home after a busy day. I clicked across the marble floors in my smart new heels, wearing a freshly tailored pantsuit that even impressed Yiayia when I left the house early that morning.

I felt like a woman finally coming into her own, clicking across the floor, pulling my roll-a-long behind me. I bought it expressly for the conference. I'd had no use for a suitcase up until then.

After checking in, the bellhop stored my heavy coat and luggage behind the counter. They assured me that they would later deposit it in my room, and it would be waiting for me at the end of the day.

I tucked my room key into my new briefcase and stepped through the double doors into the conference room.

I signed in at the long table near the entrance and collected my lanyard, then scanned the large room. The buzz of excited conversation added to the atmosphere of anticipation. These were people just like me. Small business owners wanting to take their ideas to the next level.

"What do you think, Pappou?" I whispered softly with a grin. I probably looked like a crazy person, but I didn't care. How proud he would be to see this.

I could hear his voice in my head. 'Food is life, koukla-mou. We eat together, means we celebrate together, means we mourn together, means we live, together.'

I walked the periphery of the room to peruse the displays that were set up but as of yet unmanned. Later there would be bank representatives, lawyers, business analysts and coaches, marketing specialists, and social media gurus attending each station. In short, every service and team member imaginable, ready and waiting to answer my questions.

I collected a few pamphlets. I needed to see information in print to be able to process it and collecting the pamphlets would give me time to organize which booths I wanted to visit later.

The odd sensation of someone looking at me had me twisting around to locate the source. There were dozens of people, not one paying the least attention to me. My breath accelerated and I felt a chill. My heart fluttered.

I attended to my breathing to ground myself and looked for a chair to sit on until the sensation passed. I repeated my calming mantra in my head. *I breathe and live and move freely in my world.* When my body settled, I looked around the room to get my bearings once again.

My eyes caught on the back of a dark head that topped wide shoulders and a long, lean frame. My heart pinged painfully. Something about him reminded me of Vander, or how he might have looked once he'd filled out. I could not pull my eyes away from the unknown man. I willed him to turn around. I wanted to see his face, so I could stop fooling myself.

Logically, I knew it could not be Vander. He lived three thousand miles away. Still watching the dark-haired man, I noticed when he straightened to his full height and stiffened. His head turned slightly to the side, and my heart pounded in my chest.

Even the way he held himself reminded me of Vander, but this man wore glasses. Vander didn't. His hair was cut much shorter than Vander had ever worn his. It couldn't be him.

Turn around, I willed him in my mind. If he didn't turn soon, I planned to walk over there to assuage my curiosity.

All at once, he turned one hundred and eighty degrees and immediately met my eyes.

My mouth fell open in shock, and I jerked back in my chair. Immobilized. The conversations around me receded to a low drone, and my blood pumped loudly in my ears. Vander didn't look at all surprised to see me, but his expression tightened as he held my gaze.

The blood rushed from my head and the room spun. I quickly bent over, tucking my head between my knees. I dragged air in through my nose. Someone lay a soft hand on my back and asked if I was okay with an equally soft voice. I nodded but couldn't sit up.

"Happens sometimes. I'll be okay in a minute," I explained.

Another voice, a deep male voice, cut in. "Do you need a drink? Something to eat?"

"No, no," I answered, mortified. "I'll be okay in a moment."

"She's okay," the deep voice from my dreams asserted. "Ruby, would you come with me please?"

I sat up slowly and stared into his beloved face. The glasses were new since I'd seen him last. Through the lens I could see that his eyes were harder, and the laugh lines etched around them were deep. His mouth, which had once been full and soft, now appeared firm and unyielding, deliciously framed by faint brackets in his cheeks. He held out his hand. I hesitantly reached for it, and he folded his strong fingers around mine, pulling me gently to my feet.

"Are you sure you're okay?" The soft-voiced woman asked.

"Thank you, yes, I'm fine," I replied, sending her what I hoped was a reassuring smile.

"She's going to need something to drink, Vander."

My eyes flew to hers and then to Vander's.

He answered my unasked question with an almost imperceptible shake of his head. I looked to his other hand, his left hand, and he tilted it to show me the absence of a ring. My eyes skipped back to his, and I flushed with embarrassment.

He shook his head slightly and gifted me with a small smile. "I'll look after her," he answered the soft-spoken woman.

He gently pulled my hand through the crook of his arm and led me away behind the screens, where only a few staff members lingered.

"Still wearing your emotions on your sleeve, Ruby-m-" He cut himself off abruptly and stopped walking.

My free hand flew to cover his cross under my blouse. His gaze sharpened on my hand, then flew to my eyes, his turn to ask a silent question.

In answer, I pulled it out to show him. He turned to face me and held both of my hands in his. I drank him in, making no effort to hide my eager perusal. It did not even occur to me to do so.

"I forgot how tall you are," I murmured when I made it back to his face.

He smiled. "What else did you forget?"

"Not much else," I answered honestly. He looked older than I thought he should, harder. I didn't know what to say to this Vander. This Vander wasn't my Vander. I began to pull my hands away, but his grip tightened.

"Did you marry?" He asked gruffly.

"No." I looked down. Did I want to know? I met his eyes. "Did you?"

Vander

She visibly winced when she asked the question. Guilt and sorrow, that I thought I'd finally shed, hit me anew.

"Divorced," I answered softly.

She took the hit with a sharp inhale, then nodded shortly, accepting the blow.

I studied her reactions harder than I'd studied anything before. Pissed with myself, I questioned, what the fuck I was doing? This woman nearly derailed my entire future. Instead of treating her like a prospective client, I grilled her for her marital history and her present availability. In addition to being stupid, it was utterly unprofessional, and it wasn't going to stop me.

"Are you seeing anyone?" I asked.

"I don't date," she murmured.

I think my eyes bugged out of my head. "Ever?"

Irritation narrowed her big brown eyes, and she tried again to tug her hands away, but I held fast. Nothing short of a crowbar would make me release her.

I spoke quickly. "I'm sorry. You're a beautiful woman, and you have so much to offer. I'm just surprised you're not taken."

She nodded and relaxed her hands in mine once again. I couldn't believe I wanted to open this door again, but I had to ask.

"Have dinner with me tonight."

She smiled bigger this time. "Dinner is included with the conference. You're kind of a cheap date."

I laughed outright. There, right there, was my Ruby. Full of life and fun. To my ears, my laugh sounded rusty from underuse.

"Not here. I'll take you out, and we'll have a proper meal with no toasts, no speeches, and no interruptions."

She smiled and began to nod before checking herself. She looked down for a moment and then brought her gaze back to mine. I noted the slight wince around her eyes again.

"Are you seeing anyone, Vander?"

"No."

Her shoulders relaxed and she nodded. "I'd like that."

I could not resist. I leaned over and brushed my mouth against her cheek. The softness of her cheek combined with her scent hit me at the same time, and I couldn't step away. Exhaling, I lay my cheek against hers, and she pressed her face gently against mine. When I finally managed to draw away, I noted her tightly closed eyes and the pained look on her face.

My God, had I been wrong all those years ago about how she felt? When she stopped fighting for us, I assumed, no matter what she said, that she didn't feel about me the way I felt about her. To think that I might have caused the pain on her face, gutted me.

"Ruby?" I whispered.

She opened her eyes and read the question in mine.

"Always," she whispered back, her eyes searching mine for an answer I wasn't sure I could give her.

I drew her into my arms, her small body, after so much time, soft and yielding against mine. She felt different. It irritated me. Had I been holding her all these years, the changes would have been so gradual that I would not have noticed.

"I would leave right now if I could," I admitted. "The conference ends at five o'clock. Meet me in the hotel lobby at six. Will you do that?"

She nodded against my chest and worked her hands between us. She pushed away from me, but I wasn't ready and refused to let her go. She laughed. God, I missed that sound. I smiled down into her upturned face and reluctantly released her.

"Six o'clock," I reiterated.

"Six o'clock." She nodded, backed away a few steps, then turned and clicked away on fancy heels that were so foreign to how I pictured her in my mind.

I tore off my glasses and roughly scrubbed my other hand over my face. What the hell was I doing other than torturing us both? I couldn't move to her anymore than she would come to me.

Still.

I looked at the floor, knowing I would regret what I was about to do. There was no help for it. A starving man doesn't quibble about where his next meal comes from, and I'd been hungry for a long, damn time.

Chapter 5 – Pandora's Box

<u>Ruby</u>

I gripped the back of his neck and curled up, my forehead hitting his collarbone, my thighs tightening reflexively around his lean hips.

His breath fluttered against my temple. The muscles in his back flexed under my hands as he slowly drove inside me. My eyes locked on the joining of our bodies.

I was so close.

"God, I love you, still," he muttered roughly against my temple.

With those words, I came apart in his arms.

As soon as the conference had ended for the day, I rushed to my room, freshened up, and changed into jeans and a soft, off-the-shoulder sweater. Being ready twenty minutes early, I found myself pacing the narrow length of my room. I forced myself to stop and take five minutes to practice my breathing exercises in a failed attempt to calm my nerves. The walls of my room closed in, and I couldn't stay there a moment longer.

Sitting in the lobby, my heart rate continued to flutter and skip from anticipation, and a splash of panic, but at least I no longer felt trapped.

What was I doing, opening this Pandora's box?

Pleasure and pain.

Sustenance and starvation.

Salvation and execution.

All and nothing.

I didn't try to fool myself into believing this would go anywhere, but I'd be lying if I didn't admit a tiny ray of hope shone onto a future filled with him. He had built a life. I had a life. I still wondered if he would be able to walk away from his, or if it would be fair to ask him to.

I chose a chair off to the side, half-tucked behind a pillar. This way, I would see him before he saw me, and take a moment to collect myself. I knew where this night was headed. Would I be a disappointment? After all these years dreaming about him, would he?

Like a magnet, his entrance immediately drew my gaze. I was struck again by his height. Funny. Of all the things I could have forgotten, it was that. His body had changed. His shoulders were wider, his torso thicker, and heavier muscles covered his arms and chest.

He'd changed into jeans and a cable knit sweater, his jacket folded over his arm. I preferred this to the suit. Like this, he looked more like my Vander.

He walked with confidence. Striding into the lobby, he scanned the room, looking for me. I knew I should stand, but I wanted to take a moment to take in the thrill of him searching for me.

His face appeared harder, his mouth almost stern. Throughout the day, his countenance rarely shifted. He hadn't looked like that ten years ago. I wondered what caused the change.

I hoped I hadn't contributed.

He stopped walking and stood with his legs slightly braced. He rubbed his free hand over his jaw while he scanned the lobby, looking for me.

The same woman as before, the one with the soft voice, came up on his left side and lightly placed her hand on his bicep. My stomach clenched as he dipped his head down towards her to hear what she had to say, then shook his head no. She nodded and moved off but not before revealing her disappointment. His eyes followed her for a moment, his face thoughtful.

I stared down into my lap. I could have done without seeing that.

32

I took a deep breath and prepared to meet him. I lifted my chin at the exact moment he found me.

His brow smoothed, and a small smile tilted the corner of his mouth as his long legs ate up the distance between us. He dropped his coat on the chair beside me, reached for my hands, and pulled me up from my chair.

He tugged my arms around his waist and pulled me flush against his chest. With one hand in my hair, he turned my head to press my ear against his chest over the soft cables of his sweater. His other arm came around and splayed across the middle of my back. He lay his cheek on top of my head.

His chest rose and fell with his deep inhale. I stood within the circle of his arms as if I'd never left. I closed my eyes, the rest of the world melted away, and I breathed him in.

His hand slid down to nestle under my hair at my nape. It trembled slightly before he gave me a gentle squeeze.

"Let's get you fed," he muttered gruffly.

He released me and picked up my coat from the chair, holding it open for me to slip my arms inside. He smoothed his hands over my shoulders then shrugged into his own jacket. Stepping forward, he gently pulled my hand through the crook of his arm and led me across the lobby to the doors.

As we walked, I slid my hand down the inside of his forearm and linked my fingers through his like I used to. He dipped his chin to look at me. His face regained the tightness I'd come to expect from him. It didn't soften even as he held my gaze and wrapped his fingers around mine.

In the car, he claimed my hand once more and held it on the seat between us. At the restaurant, he chose the chair beside me, butting his knee up against mine under the table. He didn't miss an opportunity to touch me, and my dry, parched soul soaked it up.

The restaurant he chose was far from fancy, but the low lighting and the spacing of the tables and booths gave us a modicum of privacy. Music drifted through the speakers, wait staff bustled back and forth, and the low murmur of dozens of conversations coalesced to a steady hum, intermittently interrupted by the occasional burst of laughter.

"This place has the best meatballs. You still love meatballs?" Vander asked, his eyebrows arched in question.

33

"I do!" I exclaimed.

We chatted easily about old friends until our order came. I wanted to keep him talking, fascinated by the workings of his mouth, the myriad expressions drifting over his handsome face, relearning his mannerisms anew.

The meatballs were as delicious as he promised. "I can't believe you remembered that I love meatballs!"

His expression sobered. "I remember everything, Ruby-mine."

He looked surprised momentarily, perhaps at the endearment that slipped past his lips before resignation filled his eyes. He sighed as he sat back and met my eyes.

"It's never been anyone else."

I stared back at him. "You married." I hadn't meant it to sound as accusatory as it did.

He nodded and sat back in his chair. He met my eyes dead on. "I had to move on."

I looked away. I felt sick. The old anger at my mental hijacking resurfaced for a split second. "I don't want to talk about her," I admitted, barely repressing my shudder. "Whoever she is."

He leaned towards me. "You really haven't looked me up all these years?" He asked, his eyebrows raised.

"Not since the last time," I winced. I shook my head to rid myself of the picture in my head, amazed at the power the image still held. How could a decade old memory still cause so much pain?

He looked away and sighed before turning back to me. His eyes were sad and slightly wary. "I have a son, Ruby."

I swallowed hard. My voice sounded raspy when I asked, "How old?"

His eyes assessed me quickly before he answered. "He's two." His voice changed, and a genuine smile lit his features.

He didn't offer more, and I waited a beat before asking. I wondered if I could handle it, but I wanted to see more of that smile, more of the old Vander that I remembered.

"Did you name him after your dad?" I teased with a small smile.

"I did," he admitted, laughing dryly. "Although I had to fight to get it."

I feigned shock, my fingers touching my chest delicately. "You married...xeni?"

He laughed outright. "Yeah, I married a foreigner. She was a mistake, but he is not."

We grinned at each other; we'd always snickered over the idiosyncrasies of our shared heritage. It bound us together in the beginning. His smile warmed me, making my next question easy.

"You going to show me a picture of Georgie?"

"You want to see?" He checked, his eyes wary but hopeful.

"I do," I replied firmly.

I realized I did want to see his child, more than anything I'd ever wanted in my life, next only to my desire to have his child. I pushed that thought away, deep into the dark recesses of my heart. It was easy to do after all this time.

He unlocked his cell, opened his photo app, and handed me his phone.

The most beautiful child I'd ever seen stared out at me from the small screen. I studied him. Large, dark, luminous eyes and a joyful smile graced his tiny round face. Dimpled hands held tightly to a purple elephant, and wild curly hair topped his little head.

I touched his face through the screen and swallowed my sorrow. "He's beautiful, Van."

"I should have had him with you." He muttered rawly.

The sound pierced my heart. I looked up from his phone to see his face pained, his gaze stark.

I answered softly, offering comfort. "But then he wouldn't be him. Don't wish him away."

He looked away, and his Adam's apple bobbed in his throat as he cleared it.

I sighed. I'd hurt him. I swallowed hard. An explanation was long overdue.

"I have agoraphobia."

35

His face blanked at the sudden change in conversation, then he swung his gaze back to my face. He suddenly looked pissed.

"What?" He bit out.

I took a deep breath and continued, watching him as I explained. "It's why I couldn't come to you. At first, I thought I had a heart condition, that I inherited a heart defect from my pappou." His eyes opened incredulously as he struggled to absorb the new information.

I continued. "Every time I went to buy a plane ticket for the summer, I got these crazy symptoms. I honestly thought I was dying. Somehow, losing my grandfather and going out, especially anywhere near an airport, got connected in my brain. Later that year, the doctor diagnosed me with agoraphobia." I forced out a laugh and joked. "At least I don't have a heart condition!"

His face suffused with red. "Why didn't you tell me?" He gritted through his teeth. "I would have moved heaven and earth to get to you."

I leaned closer and almost hissed the question that had burned inside me for ten years. "Why didn't you?"

We stared at each other, eyes skittering back and forth, assessing, reading, searching.

"I thought your feelings were different from mine." He finally broke the silence, his breathing heavy as he struggled to accept a different version of what he'd known as reality.

"I told you how I felt," I rebutted.

"Your words and your actions didn't match. What was I supposed to think?"

I nodded. That was fair. It was also time for a little more truth. I soldiered on, softer now, wanting him to understand the depth of my feelings for him.

"I rarely date. I haven't slept with a man since you. I have not moved on."

He sat back hard in his chair and looked away from me. His Adam's apple bobbed up and down, and the muscles of his jaw flexed with the gritting of his teeth.

"For the past year, I've been in a battle for partial custody of my son. I can't leave." He turned back to face me.

The tiny ray of hope I'd been nursing dimmed to a shadow. I looked down into my lap. "I understand."

I heard him take a deep breath, then looked up to see him with his glasses in one hand, his other hand rubbing over his handsome face. He put his glasses back on then turned to me, his voice grim.

"Will you give me this weekend, Ruby-mine?"

I swallowed. Did I really have a choice? When you're starving, you don't quibble over crumbs.

"Yes."

He threw his napkin down on the table and signalled the waiter for our bill. "Let's get out of here."

I thought we'd head back to the hotel right away, but he drove instead to a quaint area of the old downtown. "I want to walk with you. I've dreamed of exploring with you."

He held my hand as we strolled the cobbled streets. It got colder as the evening wore on, and we ducked in and out of stores, in part to shop and in part to escape the cold for a few minutes. We talked and laughed and held hands until the tension between us became too much for me to bear.

"Vander, please," I finally begged.

He took one look at my face and turned us back toward the car, walking fast and driving faster. Neither of us spoke a word, but he kept my hand tucked tightly in his.

Once in the room, he took my purse off my arm and dropped it along with his wallet and keys on the dresser. I slipped out of my coat, and he hung it up beside his. He turned on the bedside lamp, pulled the covers down, and flicked off the harsh overhead lights.

I stood, shifting from one foot to the other, assailed by nerves. Did I even remember how to do this?

Turning back to me, he took in my face, and stopped abruptly. He stood with his legs slightly braced, hands loose at his sides. He smiled.

"Are you scared, Ruby-mine?"

My eyes widened with the pleasure of a shared memory. It was exactly what he'd asked me the first time we made love. I smiled back and gave him the same answer I'd given before.

"Terrified."

It was as true now as it was then.

More so.

Back then, I only had an inkling of what he would mean to me.

Now I knew for sure.

He smiled at the memory and took the two steps necessary to reach me. Holding my face gently between his palms, he dipped his knees, bent his head, and pressed his mouth to mine. For the longest moment, he didn't move.

I closed my eyes.

His lips felt the same.

Thank God.

He moved to cradle the back of my head in one trembling hand, wrapped his other arm around my waist, and pulled me tight against his chest. Standing to his full height, he brought me to my toes, and I wrapped my arms around his neck.

With a deep sigh he tilted my head and licked the seam of my lips. I opened to him, and he gently sealed his mouth over mine, gently invading.

The mood had shifted from desperation to tenderness. He held me not like I was fragile, but like the bubble of time we found ourselves in was, its walls thin, ethereal, and liable to burst.

His tongue stroked slowly along mine, and a low, mournful sound came from my womb. He broke the kiss, dipped his knees, wrapped both his arms around me tightly, and stood up straight. He tucked his face in my neck as a deep shudder wracked his long body.

I stroked his dark curls in an effort to soothe his grief.

"Take me to bed, Vander," I murmured, my lips to his ear, my fingers tunnelling into his hair.

He didn't move, just drew in another deep breath. "I can't believe I'm holding you."

I laughed softly and hugged him around his wide shoulders. "It's a dream."

He lifted his head and met my eyes. "I wish it weren't. I don't ever want to wake up from this."

The pain in his eyes mirrored that in my heart. I pushed it away.

I closed my eyes and turned my face away. "Don't talk about leaving. Not yet. Please."

He nodded and ran his mouth along the side of my neck, then touched his nose to mine. Holding my eyes, he walked us slowly to the edge of the bed, and gently, reverently, set me down on my feet in front of him before placing his glasses on the bedside table.

Taking hold of my face in his hands once again, he tipped my chin up and stared into my eyes. His hands trembled, his eyes caught fire, and he dropped his mouth swiftly to mine, his kiss harder now. Demanding. He kissed me until we shared one breath.

I heard the breath catch in his throat. I tasted salt as his tears mixed with mine and ran down my face to my mouth. He didn't bother wiping the wet from his face. There would be honesty between us, finally, though there were no words.

He reached down, lifted the hem of my sweater, and yanked it over my head. The cool air danced around me, touching me in all the places he wasn't.

I slid my hands under his sweater, revelling in the feel of his skin under my hands. I'd missed him so much, loved him so long, but never dreamed I'd touch him again. I skimmed over his abdomen and pressed the palms of my hands against his bare chest. Closing my eyes, I concentrated on imprinting the feel of his body onto my brain.

He grasped his sweater at the back of his neck and pulled it over his head. His breath ruffled my hair as I moved closer and leaned my forehead against his collarbone, nuzzling my face into his wide chest. I rounded his wide shoulders with my hands and pressed my breasts against his ribs, skin to glorious skin. A shiver danced over the surface of my skin.

Oh, the connection! The pleasure seemed almost too much to bear. I hadn't been so physically close to another person in years, and for it to be this person, my person, was blissful agony.

We slowed, remembering and learning anew.

His hands swept up my back and separated, one to the back of my neck, the other to the top of my ass, and he gently pulled me closer. He was hard against my stomach. His chest hair tickled my cheek, and I turned my head to press my ear over the reassuring beat of his heart as he ran his hands smoothly up and down my back.

I felt a shift in the tension in his body. He dragged his palms up my back to open the snap of my bra, pulled the straps down my arms, and eased back to drop it between us.

He stood for a moment, staring at my bare breasts. The stillness was broken when we lurched for each other's belt at the same time. We laughed at our clumsiness as we fumbled and withdrew to undo our own instead. The laughter broke the spell of trepidation as he pressed a laughing kiss to my mouth, overjoyed in that moment at finding ourselves together.

I pushed my jeans and panties down my legs and stepped out of them. When I looked up, he had done the same. Neither of us wanted to take any time for teasing.

Standing naked in front of each other for the first time in a decade brought a sense of reverence.

He had changed. I'd already noted it, but without his clothes it was more pronounced. His body had thickened, his chest deeper, his arms more muscled. His abs that had once been so well defined were barely a hint, and the smattering of chest hair he'd once boasted about had since spread across his wide chest and trailed down his stomach to his very eager erection.

I wondered what he thought of the changes in me. I pulled my attention warily up to his handsome face. The heat in his eyes left no room for doubt that he wanted me. I pulled in a deep breath of air and held it in anticipation.

Broken Road

He dragged his eyes back to mine and held my gaze. Reaching out with one finger, he traced a line from my jaw to my throat, down between my breasts, and over my stomach until he lost contact.

"I'm going to worship every inch of you. There will not be a single place I haven't touched, licked, kissed, sucked, or tucked by the time I'm done."

My head dropped back weakly at his words.

He grasped my hips and pushed me back gently onto the bed. Climbing in, he hovered over me, then hesitated.

"What is it?" I whispered, my voice shaking with need and anticipation.

"I don't know where to start," he admitted, his gaze roving over my body. "I never imagined I'd ever have you again."

I curved my arms around his broad back and pulled his body down to rest on mine. I tunnelled my fingers into his hair and drew his mouth down to within a breath of mine.

"I'll start here," I murmured against his lips, and kissed him, pouring every drop of longing I'd stored up for him over the past ten years into the kiss.

Heart to heart, his instincts kicked in, and he pressed his erection against my very wet centre.

I gasped, then moaned, at the sensation of heat and hardness. His smell, the weight of his body over mine, his sweet mouth, the rasp of his five o'clock shadow, the silk of his skin under my hands, he filled my empty cup to overflowing. I wriggled beneath him, wrapped my legs around his lean hips and rubbed frantically against his shaft, desperate for release.

He drew back slightly. "Slow down, Ruby-mine," he murmured.

I pushed my fingers into his hair to bring his mouth back to mine. "Ten years, Vander," I gasped.

"Right." He immediately widened my thighs with his and slid his cock back and forth over my slit, bumping my clit with every pass.

The first tremor rippled through me. My neck arched back, and I dug my fingers into the muscles of his back. He pulled back quickly.

"Oh, god, Vander, no!" I cried.

41

"Condom, Ruby-mine. Ten seconds. Give me ten seconds," he assured me hurriedly.

Before I'd finished counting, he lay over me, notched at my entrance, and ready to ease his way in. I wiggled to accommodate his girth. He pushed in halfway, and I winced.

"I'll go slow, koukla," he soothed, his weight on his elbows at either side of my head. He eased in and out, inch by inch, until he was fully seated inside me. Sweat beaded on his forehead as he hovered over me. "You okay?"

"Yes." I nodded swiftly then ordered, "Move."

His eyes lit up and he smiled. "There's the Ruby I remember." He kissed the corners of my mouth, pulled my thigh up over his hip, pulled out almost all the way, then drove back in hard.

"Ah, yes... this is what I've needed..." I breathed, throwing my head back.

I ran my hands down his sides, feeling the contours and muscles of his body that were new yet still familiar and, oh, so loved.

He ground his hips into my pelvis, brushing against my clit, filling every empty place.

"Vander, I'm there, agapi mou," I warned him, and he kept up the same steady pace that I'd always needed.

I gripped the back of his neck and curled up, my forehead hitting his collarbone, my thighs tightening around his lean hips.

His breath fluttered against my temple. His back flexed under my hands; my eyes remained locked on the joining of our bodies.

I was so close, teetering on the edge.

He nuzzled his chin against the side of my face, dropped gentle kisses along my hairline, dipped to pull my earlobe gently into his mouth, all the while steadily maintaining his wicked pace, hitting every spot except the one I apparently needed.

I reached for an orgasm that remained stubbornly out of reach. I pressed my mouth against his chest, his shoulder, his throat.

I needed... something...

He kissed my temple and nuzzled his cheek against the side of my face. His breath quickened. "God, I love you, still," he muttered roughly against my temple.

With those words, I came apart in his arms.

He carried me through to the end, steadily maintaining his pace. As the last tremor died, he hooked his elbow under my knee and planted his hand in the bed at my side. He thrust in hard, and I tipped my chin back to gaze up into his face from under my heavy-lidded eyes.

God, he was gorgeous.

The muscles in his arms flexed as he pushed himself up, his shoulders shadowing me, my knee hooked around his elbow, opening me further and allowing him to go impossibly deeper. I watched his lips tighten as he chased his release, his eyes roaming my face like a man desperate to remember. His movements stuttered. He released my leg, wrapped his hand around my thigh, and curled into me as he came with a deep grunt, tucking his face into my neck.

I'd forgotten about that, too.

I wrapped my legs around him and cradled the back of his head. His chest heaved and I heard him audibly swallow.

"I'm so fucking sorry I didn't try harder," he rasped out.

I stroked the hair I missed so much. "Shh..." I soothed. "You wouldn't have Georgie."

"God help me, I don't know if-"

I tugged his hair. There were some things that shouldn't be said. "Don't go down that road, Vander," I murmured. "There's nothing good at the end of it."

He went to move off, but I tightened my legs around the backs of his thighs, holding him to me. He stared down into my face.

He was miserable, his eyes shiny with unshed tears. Even as I watched, one tipped over the edge of his lid and fell onto my chest.

"Vander," I whispered. "I love you, always."

He went down onto his elbows, crushing me slightly under his weight.

He sighed deeply. "The custody battle, it's going to last another year. At least. I can't do anything to screw things up or my ex-wife is going to nail me to the wall."

"Did you cheat on her?" I couldn't believe we were having this conversation while he was still buried inside me.

I don't know why I asked. Perhaps I could think of no other thing that would make a woman so angry.

"No. But she knew my heart belonged to you."

"How?" I challenged. I tightened my legs around him, holding him to me, my jealousy and disbelief evident in the tone of my voice.

"She found my box of pictures and tried to throw them out." He lifted his mouth in a half-smile, almost apologetically. "I never should have married her. I shouldn't have allowed her to tie herself to me when I couldn't love her."

He rose on his hands again. I protested and he laughed. "Ruby, I've got to get rid of this condom. I'll be right back."

I unwound my legs from around his and watched him cross the room to the bathroom for only a moment before I turned my face away.

I hated seeing him walk away from me.

Chapter 6 - Hindsight

Vander

This woman encompassed everything I ever wanted, she always had, and I still couldn't have her. Worse, she'd wasted ten years of her life, unable to move on. Seeing Ruby forced me to step back from the walls of my cage and notice the bars for the first time. Imprisoned by my choices, no matter how I tried to pick the lock, I could discern no way to free myself.

She lay half-sprawled over my chest while she slept. I ran my hand over her curls. I'd been hard on her last night, considering how long it had been for her, but I didn't regret a moment of it. I hoped she wouldn't either.

There was no doubt in my mind now that I'd dropped the ball ten years ago, wounding us both in the process. Hindsight was a vengeful bastard.

The sharp edges of frustration and regret needled my senses. I had grown into a man used to getting what I wanted. I worked hard to control every aspect of my business, planned for every possibility, and achieved the results I expected. I assessed, I planned, I prepared, I executed. Forcefully when necessary. Only where Ruby was concerned, I was hopelessly inept.

Helplessness was neither familiar nor comfortable, and the stakes were never higher than they were right now. I stood to lose my son, and it was a certainty that I would lose her.

Again.

If I started seeing her, and my ex-wife found out, it might harm my chances for custody. She would spin it in such a way as to damage my petition. Part of me wanted to give in to her demands, see Georgie when I could, and pick up my life, and my heart, where I left it.

With Ruby.

Behind my closed lids, two pairs of dark, luminous eyes beseeched me. Either way, I would suffer a broken heart. I had a responsibility towards my son. It wasn't an easy choice, but it was the clear one.

I wondered if it would be fair to ask her to wait until the custody battle ended. Not even knowing how long it would be, it didn't seem right. Could we do long distance and keep it under wraps until I resolved the custody issue? I'd keep in contact with her when I went home, take more business trips out here to see her. When the time came, we could find a way. Maybe by then she'd be ready to move to me.

She stirred in my arms, hugging me tightly as she woke. She nuzzled her face into my chest. For just a moment, I allowed myself to imagine waking up like this every day.

Her hand came up, and she lightly scratched my chest hair. "You have a lot more of this than you did ten years ago."

I chuckled. "Yes, and in ten more years, my Greek blood will ensure I have a matching pelt on my back."

She chortled.

God, I missed her laugh. Craziest fucking laugh I'd ever heard in my life. I chuckled and squeezed her.

"You wear my cross," I stated.

"I never take it off," she answered, her fingers automatically going to it. She pulled the long chain out from under her, placed the cross on my chest, and covered it with her palm. "Maybe you should take it to give to Georgie."

I shook my head. "No. Absolutely not. The only thing I've been able to give you is my prayers, and I want you to know you have them still."

She nodded. "You sure?"

"Positive," I said decisively, laying my hand over hers.

46

"What time is it?" She asked.

"Six."

Her body slumped against mine. Defeated.

"What time do you have to go?" She asked softly.

I ran my hand down her back to rest on the curve of her hip. "I can stay until tomorrow." I closed my eyes, praying she could do the same.

"I can stay until tomorrow, if you want," she responded slowly.

Relieved, I tightened my hold on her. "Yes, Ruby, I want that very much," I murmured and tipped my head to rest my cheek against her soft curls.

We spent one, whole, glorious day together, packing in as much as we could in a frantic race against the clock, as if, in our desperation, we might hold back time. After dinner, we headed back to the hotel, our lovemaking colored with grief and tinted with desperation. Would we ever again have each other any other way?

The next morning, her face was drawn, suffering from the same potent combination of despair and lack of sleep as me.

We lingered downstairs in the nearly deserted hotel restaurant over breakfast, but neither of us could eat. Sitting closely side-by-side, we nursed our coffees and clung to the minutes we had left.

A spike of anger straightened my spine. I couldn't allow my ex-wife to control me any longer. "Ruby," I ventured. "Is it possible you could move? Come to me?"

She raised tortured eyes to mine.

"I want to. Desperately. I can't move my grandmother. Amber's job takes her away sometimes, and Yiayia can't be left on her own for too long. She's got severe osteoporosis and she thinks she's invincible. Sometimes her decision-making is not the best and the doctor said if she falls it could be really bad..."

"What else, Ruby-mine?" I watched her closely as she spoke, noting the rising panic.

"It's really hard for me to go out and do new things, but I would try. I would go back to therapy and try for you. For us. I'd need to be much stronger, though. What if I got to you but couldn't get back? What if something happened to my yiayia? My sister? What if something happened, and I couldn't get home?"

She started to squirm in her seat and her eyes went glassy. Her breaths tumbled out in soft pants, while red tinged her cheeks and crept across her chest. She rolled her neck and clasped her hand over her chest.

"Ruby!" I exclaimed, surprised at the sudden escalation. I grasped the back of her neck and pulled her closer. "Breathe, koukla. Just breathe. You're okay."

I rubbed her back and her body slowly relaxed under my hands.

I held her hand, caressing her wrist with my thumb. "Is this what it was like for you back then?"

She laughed, the bitterness of it unexpected coming from her.

"Worse. So much worse. This is nothing. At least I can go out now. I'm good if I stick to my area. It took me six weeks of practice to work up to coming to this conference. But I got here. Back then, I could barely leave the house. I only went to Spuds." She shrugged.

I understood then, what really stood between us. My life would always be wherever my son lived. If Ruby couldn't move to me, how could we have a relationship?

"I'm so sorry," she whispered, her face and chest a mottled red.

"It's okay, Ruby-mine. It's not your fault, it's mine."

"It's nobody's fault. Not really."

There was no answer, which was the running theme for our relationship. I checked the time. "I have to go, Ruby-mine," I whispered.

She stood up quickly and averted her face. Her back expanded with her deep inhale. I helped her with her coat, grabbed hold of her hand, and walked her outside to her car.

At the driver's side door, I turned her into my embrace and held her tightly, protecting her as best I could from the cold. I tucked my nose into her hair and breathed her in.

"Are you sure you don't want your cross? For Georgie," she asked.

"Georgie has his own. You keep mine because you'll always be a little bit mine."

48

She sniffed and I held her tighter.

I didn't want to let her go. I couldn't. If we weren't meant to be together, why did we love each other the way we did? I cupped the back of her head, pulled her body closer to mine, and remembered another time I stood in the cold to say goodbye.

Tears burned the backs of my eyes. I nuzzled my chin against the side of her face. "God, I love you, always," I whispered brokenly against her temple.

With those words, she came apart in my arms, her body buckling with her grief. I held her as the sobs wracked her small frame. I tried to be strong for her, but more than one sob escaped my throat.

"Fuck, Ruby, we can never catch a fucking break," I snarled. I wrapped her up in my arms against the wind, imprinted the feel of her body against mine, a memory to warm me for a lifetime without her.

What the fuck did I ever do to deserve this? To fall in love with a woman I couldn't have. Worse, what did she ever do? She lost her parents as a child, lost her grandfather, lost years of her life to agora-fucking-phobia, lost me and never moved on from that loss. Not that I'd moved on from her either, not in any way that mattered.

The truth became clear. It would be unfair to hold onto her. I had to let her go to give her a chance to build a life for herself in her bubble, one that might include marriage and babies with a man who loved her and wouldn't leave her. I cringed at the thought, but I didn't want her to be living a painful half-life as I did. I dropped my face to her neck and could not quell the tremor that shook me.

I held her tighter, prayed I'd get my shit in order and be in a position to come back for her. For now, though, I would let her go. She might find love, but I'd risk it to give her the chance to find happiness. Condemning her to reside with me in my self-imposed prison was no life.

I dragged my hands down her back, imagining every inch of her back under my hands. God, I prayed, please don't let it be another ten years until I hold her again.

My resolve weakened. My heart argued that I could be like thousands of other fathers seeing their children when they could, and I knew if I didn't leave now, I wouldn't be able to. I stepped back and pulled her arms from

49

around my back. Holding her hands, I brought them to my lips and kissed the backs, then turned them over and pressed a kiss into each of her palms.

Firmly, I cupped her mottled, tear-streaked face and met her damp gaze. The hope in her eyes caused the words I wished I had the strength to say to lodge in my throat. Swallowing hard against the knot, I pressed one last kiss against her trembling lips, turned, and walked briskly away.

I did not pause, and I did not look back.

If I did, I would abandon my son, and I couldn't live with that.

Chapter 7 - Forward

Ruby

He didn't look back.

Turn around. Please, please, please.

I stood in the cold and watched him leave, praying that this time, he'd turn around, that we'd find a way, but he didn't look back. Then I watched him leave again, over and over, in my mind.

I sat in my car, and I cried, just as I had the last time. If possible, it hurt worse this time. The last time, I did not understand the full extent of my loss. This time I knew.

My tears slowed. I caught my breath and checked my appearance in the rear-view mirror. There was no way I'd get past my yiayia with my stricken face, swollen eyes, and reddened nose. I had thought to pass off my mood as stress from being away from home, but Yiayia was much too smart for that.

I knew she was at Spuds preparing the produce for the day. I told her I'd be there in time to do it, but she insisted and had Amber drive her in. At least, I didn't have to face her right away.

I made it home in record time and jumped back into the shower, hoping to wash away the evidence of my anguish. I closed my eyes and turned my face to the spray. Behind my closed lids I saw Vander's retreating form and the tears began anew.

I scrubbed hard at my face.

It might not be like last time.

He may have business here all the time!

You'll see him again.

Maybe even soon.

It won't be like last time.

You're older, he's older, you both know what you want.

He'll call.

You'll work it out.

It'll take time, but with the promise of him at the end, it'll be worth the wait.

I walked into Spuds, hoping Yiayia would be distracted by whatever Elisavet had filled her ears with that morning.

"Hi, Yiayia!"

"Ela, poulaki-mou! Ti kaneis? How was, koukla?"

"I saw Vander." What? Damn my bucket mouth.

Yiayia stopped chopping the vegetables and focused all the powers of her concentration on me, pinning me like a butterfly to a board. "Aw, poulaki-mou. It was good, but it was bad, yes?"

I drew in a shuddering breath and moved to help her with the lunch prep. Working side-by-side, talking through life, with Yiayia, comforted me. "Yes, Yiayia. Good and bad."

"You love him still, poulaki-mou?" She asked softly, turning her attention back to her work.

"I do, Yiayia. I don't think I'll ever love another," I admitted.

She stopped and I heard her sigh. "I think you must go to him, poulaki."

"I can't, Yiayia." I couldn't leave her.

"Amber is here, koukla. I am healthy, and I want for you to have your great love like I had my great love!"

"Yiayia," I paused, and my voice dropped to a whisper. "Please, can we not talk about this?"

"Okay. Okay, moro mou. I will say only one thing more. I think you make mistake right now."

I started to protest, but she cut me off.

"Oxi, no. No more talking, but you must think. I told you last time you make mistake and Yiayia was right. Think. Hard. That is all." She paused. "What you want me to make you for dinner tonight? You want roast beef? With lemon potatoes?"

I laughed. Amber really screwed me over ten years ago. I'd had to choke down more roast beef over the past ten years than anyone should have to tolerate in an entire lifetime. Amber had moved out with her fiancé a few years back, but she'd benefited greatly from her little white lie.

"How about pastitsio, Yiayia?"

"Roast beef tonight, pastitsio for tomorrow when Amber comes for dinner."

I smiled to myself. I'd take that deal. It would be worth it to watch Amber choke down the pastitsio after ten years of roast beef and roast beef leftovers for lunch for days.

All day long, Yiayia's advice replayed in my head.

She was right.

I called my therapist to set up an appointment. It would be several weeks before I could get in to see her, but at least I set the ball rolling. If I could conquer air travel, we might have a chance. I almost texted him to tell him, but I didn't want to create additional pressure for myself. If I told him, and I failed? I didn't want to be a disappointment.

I'd tell him when it came up naturally in conversation.

He didn't text that first night, and I wondered if he saw his son when he got home. Maybe he didn't have time to contact me. I'd ask him how often he got to see Georgie when I talked to him. I smiled to myself. I'd tell him Yiayia still championed him. I'd tell him about the roast beef. He'd laugh. He knew the struggle of being force-fed by a Greek yiayia.

53

Thankfully, the following two weeks were jam-packed with final preparations for Amber's wedding. It would give my brain something else to focus on. She planned a big, fat, Greek affair, and I looked forward to it. I loved Greek dancing, I loved the solemnity of the ceremony, the idea that God joined the couples and that what He joined could not be severed.

Realistically, I knew that made no difference to the divorce rate, but it warmed me in any case.

I checked my phone as soon as I woke up the next morning, but there was still no message from Vander. A small, hard knot of trepidation formed in my stomach. The thought that he might not contact me started to take hold, but I pushed it away as an impossibility. There was no way. He wouldn't let what we had slip away twice.

Would he?

During the day, I distracted myself with work and family and pushed thoughts of Vander deep down where they burned into the lining of my stomach. I popped antacids like breath mints and struggled to eat anything, even when Yiayia pinned her eagle eyes to my dinner plate.

Food prep at work became hazardous to my health. Sharp knives and tear-blurred vision did not mix well. I cut myself twice, and the second time I required stitches. I needed extra help that week from Yiayia for food prep for the first time in a long time, and her steady presence helped me to keep it together.

My pamphlets for franchising sat untouched in a corner of my small office, having lost their lustre.

I pretended excitement over the wedding preparations for Amber's sake. Only a fraction of it was real.

Every night, the blank screen on my cell, where his texts should have been, mocked me. I replayed our weekend over and over, wondering if I'd made it out to be more than it was.

Several times I started to type out a message only to put my phone back down.

He had to want us. I told him I loved him, told him there'd never been anyone else. I wasn't going to beg him to want me, but my pride did not warm the sheets. My pride did not ease the loneliness. My pride did nothing to stop the bleed beneath my breast.

54

From the outside, I gave every indication that I was fine. Yiayia didn't buy it, but I got past Amber, who, being wrapped up in the final push for her big day, was not as observant as usual.

Inside, I was utterly broken.

In the morning, I dragged myself out of bed, unrested no matter how many hours I slept. Sharp shards of rejection pierced my lungs, and the band of grief around my chest tightened by infinitesimal degrees with every passing hour. The sensation of being cornered never left me, whether I considered flying to him, or decided to stay, I felt like a trapped animal.

Thoughts of him stung my eyes and drew down the corners of my mouth. The remembrance of his unyielding mouth softening into a smile just for me, his tears when he made love to me, his shoulders shadowing me, his arm hooked under my knee, his hand keeping mine warm as we explored the downtown, the sob that escaped his throat in the moment before he walked away.

Without looking back.

By the eve of Amber's wedding, I'd heard nothing from Vander.

I stared at my reflection in the bathroom mirror. I had lost weight, the skin under my eyes dark from lack of rest. My olive complexion lost what little colour it had, my hair hung limply, my lips were dry and chapped from biting them. In short, I looked terrible, and the pain twisting my guts never relented.

Exactly like the last time.

"You need to move on," I murmured to my reflection.

A single tear escaped to roll down my cheek. I watched its path until it dripped off my jaw and fell on my breast. I rubbed it into my skin and promised myself that would be the last tear I would ever shed over Vander Vitalis.

It was time to accept some hard truths. Although Vander was very real, he wasn't real for me. He was a dream, a fantasy, one that I could never hope to attain or hold onto. Our lives were too complicated, our individual issues working together to keep us apart, and I wasn't important enough for him to make me a priority.

The weekend we had together revealed strong feelings on both our sides, but in the end, he walked away just as quickly as he had the first time. I guessed he loved me in whatever way he was capable of loving, but I deserved a man who couldn't walk away from me.

No matter what.

Unconsciously, I'd held out for Vander for ten years. I didn't waste those years. I expanded my safe zone to a thirty-kilometre radius. I worked at Spuds to support myself and my family. I earned my degree online, and years of therapy enabled me to leave the house, most of the time, by myself.

Life moved on. It had moved on for him. It had moved on for me. It had moved on for Amber as well.

In the past ten years Amber earned her PhD, met the love of her life, opened her practice, got pregnant, and now she was getting married. I needed to put my dead dreams aside and focus on celebrating Amber's big day.

Standing beside my sister at the altar, I held back all my tears save one. I told myself that one was a happy tear for Amber. I watched as the priest crowned Amber and Angus king and queen of their home. I watched as he blessed their rings, and the best man slid them onto their fingers. I carefully held her train as they took their first steps as a married couple, and I hoped that I'd one day stand where she stood, at the front of the church, our friends and family witness to what God joined together.

I wanted it to be with Vander.

If it couldn't be him, did I still want it? I considered the possibility that I did.

After the church, I threw myself into reveling in my sister's joy. I toasted the bride and only cried a little. I ate until I nearly burst out of my dress. I laughed and joked with Amber, Angus, and Angus's best man, Drew, all through dinner.

At the end of the meal, Yiayia stood beside me while I delivered her speech for her, the one she wrote in place of the father-of-the-bride speech. My tears flowed, and Amber bawled like a baby, until finally Angus moved her onto his lap and wrapped his arms around her tightly.

Near the end of her speech, at Yiayia's beautiful words, I had to take a break. Yiayia rubbed my back and scolded me. "Ela, poulaki mou! Fagame to gaidaro, mas emeine i oura."

Our Greek guests laughed, and there were several cheers of "Yiayia!"

I leaned into the mic to translate for the sake of Angus's side of the family. "My grandmother just scolded me. She said, 'we ate the donkey, only the tail is left' so I'll wrap this up." I looked back to Yiayia's speech and delivered her final words. "This last part is in English. I am proud. I am proud to be your yiayia. I am proud to call you my child twice over. I am proud of who you have become, and I am proud of the man you chose. God has blessed me. I pray He blesses you, too. Go make babies. Start tonight." I chortled into the microphone as the room disrupted into laughter, and renewed cheers for Yiayia rang through the room.

I hugged Yiayia tightly. She would be ecstatic when she learned that Amber was well into her third month. I looked over her shoulder to see Angus wagging his eyebrows at Amber while he wiped the tears from her cheeks. I watched as my sister pulled herself together and laughed at his antics. Angus pulled her face into his neck. The look of tenderness and concern on his face robbed me of my breath.

"Will be you one day, poulaki mou. Don't lose the hope."

I hadn't realized that Yiayia had pulled away and peered intently into my face. "I'm okay, Yiayia." I pulled in a shuddering breath and offered her a tremulous smile.

"You will be, poulaki mou."

When the Greek dancing started, I danced in circles with wild abandon, whirling around faster and faster. I laughed aloud when my sister grabbed me and placed me between her and Angus. I danced with the best man. I danced with Yiayia. I danced with my aunts and uncles and all the cousins who were not really cousins, but that's what we called them because when you are Greek everyone is family even when they are not.

The night passed in a blur of music, family, food, dancing, and far too much drinking as I steeled myself against the pain of my broken heart and determined to propel myself forward.

I may have overshot a little.

Chapter 8 - Beauty

<u>Ruby</u>

I looked at the tests lined up on the bathroom counter. After the first test produced a positive result, I bought three more. They lay side-by-side, four tiny crosses all in a row.

I sat down hard on the closed toilet.

Pregnant.

Huh.

I didn't think that would ever happen for me. I didn't feel like I could properly look after myself, never mind a child.

I gathered the tests, tucked them under the sink, and retreated to my bedroom. I left the lights off but opened the curtains to reveal the night sky. I never slept with the window covered. I couldn't stand feeling boxed in.

I braced my back against the headboard and wrapped my arms around my drawn-up legs. I rested my cheek on my bent knees and stared unseeing out the window. My future, up until that point, had looked blurry at best, but it was now a gaping, swirling maw of unknown.

Despite my best efforts to purge my heart of hope for a future with Vander, a sliver had remained, a tiny sliver that hung on even in the abyss of his silence. Now, the reality that I couldn't go to Vander pregnant, shredded it as well. Having another man's baby confirmed what I already knew to be true, but the confirmation still gutted me.

Tears burned at the back of my eyes. I tried to beat them back, but the erasure of his presence in my future sliced me sharply. I hugged my legs tighter and rocked myself back and forth as the tears rolled down my cheeks. I opened my mouth to pull in a steadying breath and quell the sob that gripped my throat. My saliva ran thick, and my nose ran thin, mixing with my tears. I needed a drink of water and a tissue but could not motivate myself to get either.

I turned my eyes from the window to rest my forehead on the unyielding bones of my knees, and I rocked myself through the shock of the loss.

I wished for a moment that the child inside me belonged to Vander, but I brushed it away before it became a solid thought. I got my period a week after our weekend together, which was a surprise because it was early. Historically, I missed my period when I was distraught, sometimes for months, which is why I didn't clue in for several weeks after being with Drew, that I might be pregnant. So, no. This wasn't Vander's child and wanting this child to be anyone other than he was, signified outright rejection. I'd never do that to my child.

I plodded into the bathroom, blew my nose, and washed my face. The mirror reflected the wreckage of the past hour. The sight drew me closer to the mirror where I promised my reflection, again, that these tears would be the last I shed over Vitalis.

I blew out a breath, my thoughts skipping like flat rocks over a glass sea.

Babies were so damn fragile. In a few months, my tummy would be round and distended like my sister's.

I smiled at that. We'd always hoped to have children at the same time.

There were going to be so many doctor's appointments, so many decisions to make.

Did I really want to bring a baby into the world? I could barely navigate it myself.

Would it be healthy? Oh, God, would it survive the pregnancy? The birth?

Shitfuckdamn!

I plodded back into my bedroom, changed into my sleepshirt, and settled back against the headboard. I looked out the window and stared down the darkness of the unknown.

The birth was the least of my worries. It, no, not it, he, would be outside of me in a few short months. He'd be exposed to all the elements, risking vaccinations, ear infections, the flu, riding around in cars and buses and going to school to be bullied and teased. What if the teacher didn't like him?

What if his father didn't want him? I hadn't seen Drew in the three months since the wedding.

I looked inwards. It didn't matter. I wanted him. I'd want him enough for both of us if need be.

I dipped my chin to look at my still flat tummy and drew in a shuddering breath. "Okay, big guy. It's you and me, now. And maybe Drew." I conceded, allowing for the possibility that the best man might want to be involved.

I barely remembered our night together. I remembered him as sweet and attentive. I remember he held me afterwards. I remember waking up for round two, in which we stupidly got carried away and didn't use a condom.

He texted me a couple of days later asking me out.

I groaned at the remembrance of turning him down. Despite my promise to move on, I still held out hope for Vander.

I pressed my forefinger into the divot bowing my lip. In retrospect, this would have been a lot easier if we'd at least had a first date.

I retrieved my cell and impulsively tapped out a text.

A few days later I sat shredding the napkin on the table in front of me. I should have chosen a more private location for this conversation.

He walked into the restaurant and looked around.

Shitfuckdamn, I forgot how good-looking he was. A spark of latent interest smoldered in my belly.

This could be a new beginning.

Or, I acknowledged to myself, it could go phenomenally badly.

His eyes lit up when they found me, and he smiled easily as he made his way over to my table. He leaned in, covered my shoulder with his big hand, and kissed me on the cheek.

Wow, he smelled good.

"Hey," he greeted me. "It's good to see you."

My mouth twisted to the side involuntarily, and his smile faltered. "It's not good?"

"Uh," I began. "Maybe you should sit down."

"Uh, oh. This sounds ominous." He placed his palms flat on the table and swung his long body into the seat opposite me. Lacing his hands together on the table in front of him, he met my eyes, his knowing. "Give it to me."

"I'm pregnant," I stated baldly.

He dropped his chin to his chest for a moment, then took a breath and looked back up at me. He offered a shaky grin. "I thought after so much time had passed that we'd dodged the bullet."

I smiled tentatively back. "No such luck."

He nodded, lost in his thoughts. Suddenly his eyebrows snapped together, and his brow furrowed. "Are you going to get rid of it?"

My eyebrows mirrored his. "No!" I snapped. "And it's not an it."

"Thank God," he said, sitting back with his big palm over his heart, looking out the window for several long moments. He turned back to me and reached a hand across the table.

I hesitated before putting mine in his. He shrugged and grinned. "What do you want to eat?"

I laughed and we ordered.

Over the next several months, we got to know each other. We dated and had sex, lots of it, starting from that first date. The fun we had at the wedding was not a one-off, which boded well for our future because we were preparing for a baby, and they tended to tie people together quite handily.

We were not in love, but the loneliness that had become such a deep-seated stain on my soul abated. Excitement over the baby, and Drew's easy-going manner and sweet attentiveness put me at ease.

61

Yiayia made her feelings about me dating an artist clear, but the news about the baby delighted her. Thoughts of Vander never disappeared entirely, but they receded to the realm of reminiscences, and they did not ever enter the zone where my future hopes lay.

In a different lifetime, Drew and I might have been best friends, or we just might have been everything to each other. Damn my stubborn heart. I supposed I could do worse than to shack up with my best friend, and I gave it serious consideration when we started talking about moving in together after the birth of our baby.

Drew accompanied me to all doctor appointments and ultrasounds. Astoundingly, he immediately joined the short list of people with whom I could comfortably go anywhere. I scheduled my appointments around his availability. Although he knew I got anxious going out, as well as in certain social situations, he did not understand the extent of the fear that dogged me, and I didn't fill him in.

My pregnancy progressed smoothly, so I continued working at Spuds as per usual. Any plans for franchising had been moved to the backburner, possibly permanently. I maintained my practice of sitting down with my planner morning and afternoon to ensure I mentally and emotionally prepared for appointments.

The weeks progressed smoothly until I was well into my sixth month and Amber was overdue.

The lunch rush at Spuds ended. I settled my growing bulk at my usual corner table and opened my planner to prepare for the week ahead.

My cell phone rang, the vibrations causing it to dance across the table in front of me. I scooped it up and glanced at the screen.

"Hi, Angus!" I greeted cheerfully.

"Ruby! Thank, God!" Every cell in my body stood at attention and the blood drained from my face at Angus's panicked tone. "I'm stuck in traffic downtown, Rubes. Amber's water just broke. You've gotta go pick her up and take her to Milltown General. The doctor will meet you there."

I breathed in deeply. It's okay, Ruby. Everyone is okay.

"Ruby? Rubes? I'm sorry, honey. I know this is hard for you, but it's you or a cab, and I don't want my wife giving birth in a taxicab."

"I.." I croaked, then cleared my throat. "I've got this. I'm fine, Gus. I'm on my way. I'll pick her up and meet you at Milltown General."

I ended the call, locked the front door, and exited through the back.

Amber sat on the couch reading a magazine when I charged into her place.

"Ruby?" she asked, startled. "What are you doing here?"

"Gus is stuck in traffic." I gasped for breath, leaning against the breakfast bar. "I'm here to take you to the hospital."

Amber eased off the couch and waddled toward me, smiling. "Deep breath, koukla, or I'll be driving you to the hospital. I'm just having a baby. Nothing could be more natural!" She rubbed my back then moved behind the counter to get me a glass of water. She passed it to me, and I tipped back my head and drained it. When I finished, Amber had disappeared.

"Amber?" I called confused.

"Down here," she gasped.

I looked over the counter to see her bent double, hands to her knees.

I awkwardly ran around the breakfast bar to get to her and hauled her up by her arm. She glared at me. "What's wrong?" I cried, panicked.

"Nothing is wrong," she gritted out through her teeth, her eyes burning twin holes through my soul. "I'm having a ...baaabyyyy..." She grimaced and squeezed her eyes shut. She tilted her chin up to look at the ceiling and took a deep breath. "Nothing could be more natural." She paused and rubbed her lower belly. "My bag is at the door, but we still have to pick up Yiayia. Do you think we could swing through the Dairy Queen drive-thru?"

I peered at her with narrowed eyes. She stared steadily back at me. "You, are a crazy woman," I said evenly.

She barked out a laugh. "I am. We'll see how crazy youuuuuu arrreee..." She reached for my hand and gripped it so hard my knees buckled. She was bending deep and dragging me with her.

"Amber, nooo! My hand!" Amber let out a deep, guttural groan that sounded like it came from a three-hundred-pound trucker with a bad case of food poisoning.

63

I laughed, hard, then gasped at the warm ribbon of fluid trickling down my leg.

"Shitfuckdamn! I think I peed!" I exclaimed, standing straight.

Amber, still bent in half, looked at my crotch. "Yep. You did. Go get changed and make it quick. We really gotta go."

"I'm going!" I ran awkwardly to her bedroom and pulled out a clean pair of underwear and leggings, tossing my pee-pee pants into her laundry hamper. I shrugged. I'd be back to do her laundry later while Yiayia cooked for them. Anyways, it wasn't the most disgusting of the body fluids we'd be dealing with today.

We swung by and picked up Yiayia, who waited on the front step with her purse at her side and her latest crochet project in a bag at her feet. By the time we got to the hospital, Yiayia shook her head at both of us. Amber and I were laughing too hard to care.

"If you say, one more time, that nothing is more natural than this, I swear I'm going to drop you off at the side of the road, and you can pull that baby out yourself!"

"It is natural," Amber argued. "It just hurts like a SONOFABITCH!" She bent in two again and a nurse came around the desk, pushing a wheelchair in front of her.

"Let's get you registered, shall we?" She took over, all business, and wheeled Amber over to the desk.

Amber twisted to look over her shoulder, her eyes wild and wide. "Ruby! Ruby, come with me!"

I barely got the paperwork filled out before they whisked Amber into a room to check her cervix.

I helped her undress and slip into a gown. I stood beside her, holding her hand as they propped her legs up into the stirrups and the nurse snapped a glove on. She placed one steadying hand on Amber's knee and held up two gloved fingers.

"Going to measure your cervix, okay, hun?" The nurse bent her elbow, and I felt my sister jolt slightly at the intrusion. The nurse pulled out and tossed the glove into the trash then announced excitedly, "You're having a

64

baby, love!" She turned to the other nurse in the room. "She's over nine centimeters. Page the doc."

The nurses worked briskly and efficiently, setting up equipment and wheeling in the bassinet, while I stood at Amber's head, holding her hand as she tried to breathe through brutal contractions that broke one on top of the other.

Both of us were sweating, and neither of us were laughing anymore. Amber's face was stark white from the pain.

"I'm done, Rubes. Can't do any more. I need an epidural or a c-section or both," she muttered then raised her voice. "This is crazy. This hurts, Rubes. It hurts so bad."

She opened her mouth to continue when a vicious contraction stole her breath. Watching on the monitor, my eyes widened along with hers as the line snaked inexorably upwards.

"Oh, God! It's too much! I can't!" Amber tossed her head back and forth, her eyes panicked, her heels digging into the thin mattress.

I pulled her chin round firmly to face me and stared fiercely into her pained eyes. "Oh, yes, you can. You're Amber fucking Vasilakis. Yiayia didn't raise no pussies!"

The incongruity of the words 'yiayia' and 'pussies' in the same sentence struck us both at the same time, and Amber groaned deeply and huffed out a sharp laugh along with the nurses.

A new nurse entered the room, announcing in a sing-song voice, "Dad's here! Come on in, Dad. You haven't missed anything yet."

I turned to see my brother-in-law angling his massive shoulders through the door before striding briskly into the room, his eyes trained on my sister.

"Gus!" Amber whispered, and her face reflected her relief.

He leaned over her in the bed, his craggy face tight with concern. He wrapped his big hand around the top of her fair head and leaned his forehead against hers. "Amber, baby, I'm sorry it took so long to get here."

"It's okay," she breathed, her eyes closed in relief. "You're here now."

The next contraction hit, but Gus's presence smoothed the edge off her panic. He held her eyes and breathed with her through the pain, and she laughed, actually laughed, when the pain receded.

Gus smiled into her eyes, then leaned closer and brushed his mouth over hers in the sweetest, softest kiss I'd ever witnessed in my life.

"I love you, Amber."

"I love you, too. We're going to be a family soon," she whispered.

He stroked her hair. "We were already a family, baby. We're just going to be a bigger family."

I shifted to move out of the room, but Gus caught my movement from the corner of his eye. "Hang on, Rubes." He turned back to Amber. "Is it okay if Ruby goes, or do you want her to stay?"

Amber peered at me. "You okay to stay, Ruby? I'd like you to stay, but you must be tired..." She petered off, then looked around. "Can someone get my sister a chair, so she can stay with me?"

I fidgeted, feeling out of place. "It's okay, Amber. Gus is here. I don't want to intrude."

Gus looked at me and smiled. "You could never, Rubes. If you'd like to stay, if it's not too much for you, please stay," Gus replied.

"If you two are done chatting," Amber groaned.

Gus immediately turned back to his wife. She gripped his hand, and he held her eyes while they breathed through the next contraction together.

An older nurse touched my elbow then smiled as she nudged me gently into a chair at my sister's other side.

Twenty minutes later, my nephew lay across my sister's chest, his body wet with amniotic fluid and streaked with blood, soft mewls coming from his tiny rosebud mouth.

Gus laughed at the sound, one large hand wrapped around the top of my sister's fair head, the other shielding his son's tiny rump. He leaned over them both, sheltering them with his body.

"Thank you, Amber," he choked out, his voice thick with emotion.

Amber smiled at him softly, tiredly, proudly. He dipped his head and brushed his lips over hers once again, then rested his forehead against hers momentarily before they both turned their attention to their son.

I covered my mouth with my fingers, stunned by the stark beauty of it all.

The purity of Angus's love for my sister acted as the defibrillator, jolting my loneliness to the forefront of my consciousness.

"Ruby," Gus began, "I can't thank you enough. I'm sorry I had to put that pressure- "

I cut him off with a slice of my hand. "She's my sister. It was my pleasure," I spoke quickly.

Amber's satisfied smile warmed me. "Come meet your nephew."

The beat of my loneliness settled back into its usual steady rhythm, pumping lazily through my veins, existing largely unnoticed in the background, and underlying all my other functions.

Chapter 9 - Validation

Ruby

Drew and I never did move in together.

When our son, Jace, was four months old, Drew cornered me at Spuds. By that time, he had Yiayia in his back pocket due to his inherent sweetness and loving attentiveness. He'd been pushing for Jace and me to move in with him, and I'd been putting him off for weeks. We hadn't made love since before Jace's birth, and I was more than okay with that.

We sat at my usual corner table and Yiayia retreated to the back to give us privacy.

He placed his palms face up on the table between us. I placed my hands in his and hesitantly met his steady gaze.

"It's not going to be enough for you, is it?" He asked sadly.

"You don't love me," I answered.

He smiled softly and squeezed my fingers. "I feel great affection for you. We have fun. We're good in the sack. We're friends. We have a child. I think we could be good together." He chuckled. "Even Yiayia finally likes me!"

I laughed and squeezed him back. He really was so very good-looking. He had the kindest eyes, the sweetest smile, and in bed he played me like a violin.

"And what happens when you find someone who makes your heart beat faster? Then what?" I asked softly.

He sat back in his chair but didn't relinquish my fingers. He sighed. "That ship has sailed for me, Ruby."

"There was someone once?"

He looked away. "A long time ago." He turned back to me. "Just as I suspect there was someone else for you as well."

I nodded. There was no point in hiding it.

He leaned forward again. "What we have is good. I think we can make it."

I huffed. "Make what? Make do? Don't you want more than that?"

His face lost all trace of its usual good-naturedness, and his eyes went hard. "Not anymore."

"See," I whispered, gently pulling my hands from his grasp. "I'd rather be nothing than be second best."

We remained close. Things got weird for awhile when Drew started dating a few weeks after our chat in Spuds, but we worked past it. The sharp spike of jealousy elicited by seeing him with someone else surprised me. He noticed, but by the time he confronted me about it, I'd already buried it. I often wondered if he and I missed an opportunity to be genuinely happy, if love wouldn't have come for us in time, if, in fact, it was already there, and we'd just failed to recognize it.

We saw Drew a couple of times a week, and he made it for Sunday dinner at Yiayia's when he could. He didn't have a high-paying job, so he didn't help overly much with the bills, but I didn't need financial help.

Amber hired a nanny shortly after Alex's birth, and shared her with me, which greatly alleviated my financial situation and ensured our boys spent their days together. I tried to pay her, but Amber shut me down, reminding me that I financed her education by running Spuds when Pappou passed.

The nanny wasn't the only thing the boys shared. Traditionally, Greeks name their firstborn sons after the husband's father. Angus, not being Greek, had no objection to Amber wanting to name their son after our father.

In fact, we both wanted to name our babies, if they were boys, after our father, as well as our grandfather. We decided early on that we would use both names. Amber named her son Alexander Jace, and I named mine Jace Alexander, in honor of both our father and our grandfather, Jason and Alexandros. They were growing up like brothers rather than cousins, and Amber and I loved it that way.

Although I maintained my bubble of Bayview Village, Milltown, and Bridgewater, I struggled even more with going anywhere last minute, safe zone or not, due to the perceived danger of bringing Jace with me. Unfortunately, Jace excelled at requiring me to make last minute changes to my schedule.

Ear infections were the worst, always cropping up in the middle of the night.

The first time it happened was a shock. His frantic screams jolted me out of a deep sleep. I rolled out of bed, landed on my feet, and stumbled halfway across the room before my eyes were fully open.

Yiayia opened her bedroom door as I slipped through Jace's doorway into his room. He thrashed in his crib, his little hand clawing at his ear.

"Hey, little man." I soothed, lifting him up against my chest. He curled into me for a moment, then arched his little back, throwing himself away from me. I caught the back of his head with my palm. I'd never seen him like this. "What's the matter, agapimeno mou?"

"He has ear infection, poulaki mou," Yiayia said, patting his little back. "See how he grab his ear? Take him to the doctor."

Panic mushroomed in my chest. "It's two o'clock in the morning."

Yiayia looked at me with impatience and pointed her arthritic finger at Jace. "He know that? No. We give him Tylenol, and you take him to the hospital. He gets the antibiotics faster and feel better sooner."

I turned my back and paced away, my screaming baby in my arms.

Shitfuckdamn. If Drew were here, I'd have no problem. He'd take us. I'd go with him anywhere, anytime. That thought niggled at my consciousness, but I took no time to explore it.

It was difficult to form a coherent thought with Jace's cries in my ears. I had no choice. He needed to see a doctor, but, oh, God!

70

I rolled my neck back and took as deep a breath as I could with my tightening chest.

You're ridiculous. This is so stupid! Your son needs medical attention, and you're going to stand here having a panic attack? Get over it!

Sweat pooled in my armpits and between my breasts.

I could smell myself.

Jace's cries sounded as if they were coming from farther away. I swiped the back of my wrist over my dewy upper lip, kissed Jace's downy head, and passed him to Yiayia.

"Here, Yiayia. Hold him while I get dressed."

In my bathroom, I splashed water on my face, then opened the cabinet above the sink and found my Lorazepam. It was the only medication I could tolerate, and it was only for emergency usage.

My trembling fingers fumbled to open the child safety cap. I shook several pills into my palm and tossed most of them back in. I slammed the two remaining pills resting on my palm into my mouth and sucked water straight from the tap.

I moved in a daze, my head slightly detached, dread pulling at my jelly legs with every step. All my instincts urged me to curl up in a ball on the floor, save the one that reached for Jace.

I peeled off my sweat-soaked pajamas. Grabbing Jace's wet wipes off the counter, I cleaned my armpits. A fresh one washed away the sweat pooled under and between my breasts. Another for my face and the back of my neck. I went to the bathroom quickly and wet wiped the sweat from my groin.

I smelled like a giant baby, minus the faint traces of urine.

Autopilot finally kicked in. I slathered my armpits with antiperspirant, brushed my teeth, and pulled on yesterday's clothes.

Yiayia met me in the hallway with a freshly diapered Jace wrapped in his blankie, the packed diaper bag over her shoulder. Thank, God, it wasn't cold outside.

"Thanks, Yiayia," I stooped to kiss her cheek and relieve her of the weight of my thrashing son. "You gave him the Tylenol?"

"Of course, poulaki mou." She paused, her sharp eyes scanning my face. "You want me to come with you?"

I froze. Every cell in my body screamed at me in self-preservation. I looked at her. She looked small and frail without her makeup and her flowery blouses. She even removed her jewelry at night. "No, Yiayia. We'll be okay."

She patted my cheek, relieved. She didn't understand my anxiety, and it stressed her out when I didn't have a handle on it.

I did a lot of faking.

"Good, poulaki mou. I go to Spuds tomorrow morning. You look after the moro and have rest."

"Thanks, Yiayia," I said.

Though my psyche shrieked in protest, I shook my head in disbelief that I had considered dragging her to the hospital in the middle of the night. Especially knowing one of us would have to look after Jace and the other would have to go to Spuds in just a few short hours.

As I buckled Jace into his car seat, the calming effects of the Lorazepam infiltrated my hijacked system.

I settled back into my body just as I settled in behind the wheel and closed my eyes. I went over the route to the hospital in my head, painstakingly tracing the familiar roads on my mental road map. I blocked out the sounds of Jace's screams as best I could.

Every minute you sit here stewing is another minute he's in pain. Move it!

Stop that. That's not helping. Deep breath, Ruby. Count it out. Four in, hold for five, seven out. That's it. Again. One, two, three, four, hold...

I breathe and live and move freely in my world.

I turned the key in the ignition and carefully backed out of the garage. I stopped again on the driveway. I checked my surroundings, bringing the night into sharp focus. I couldn't afford to panic. I pressed the button to close the garage door. Every action served to buy me a few more moments before I had to leave.

I forced my shoulders down from around my ears. The meds had kicked in as much as they were going to. Twisting around, I checked again to make sure I properly secured Jace in his car seat, then cautiously backed out of the driveway.

"Okay, agapimeno mou. Here we go."

In the hospital waiting room, a couple of small children screamed along with Jace while a few others had succumbed to sleep in their exhausted parents' arms. Older couples sat huddled together in various corners, and a large group of people took over one wall of chairs, some sitting, others standing, their faces pinched with distress.

After checking in, I paced along the windows. There were no chairs available near the exit, and I could not tolerate being closed in with a bunch of strangers. After an hour, Jace fell asleep against my shoulder. I heard murmuring behind me, then a gentle touch at my elbow. I swung around and had to tip my chin way back to look up into the face of the man who touched me.

He whispered, "My wife says you could probably sit now that he's asleep. You can sit beside her at the window."

I blushed to the roots of my hair. "That's okay," I stuttered. "I don't want to take your seat."

He smiled encouragingly. "My wife needs to be by a window. She thought maybe you do, too?" He gestured to the room behind us and the scattered empty seats. "I'll sit over there."

Jace's weight pulled at my arms. I looked to his wife. She indicated the seat beside her with a tip of her head and a smile. I smiled in relief. "Thank you," I murmured. "I appreciate it."

"No problem." He bent over his wife and kissed her cheek before turning to find a seat.

"Thank you," I whispered as I sat.

"It's okay," she whispered back. "I get it."

We did not speak after that.

I'd never felt so validated.

Chapter 10 - A Good Dad

"Jace, it's time to go to Thia Amber's!"

Jace loved visiting his Aunt Amber's place because he loved his cousin, his built-in best friend from birth. I watched in wonder as my little man loped into the room. He was not so little anymore. He'd grown a lot in the past year, and at almost eleven years old, he was beginning to leave the boy behind.

I never imagined I'd have a child if not with Vander. Fortunately for me, seeing Vander walk away from me the second time, with no hesitation, weakened the spell he had over me.

Thank, God. I wouldn't have Jace otherwise.

Jace slung his backpack over one skinny shoulder. He had dark eyes and dark, curly hair, like both Drew and me. He looked how I imagined a child of mine and Vander's would have looked. This was no surprise. Drew was tall and dark like Vander, which was the bulk of his initial appeal for me.

Drew moved away for a job opportunity when Jace was almost three. I didn't blame him. It was his chance to make his mark in an industry that was nearly nonexistent where we lived. By that time, Jace and I were only seeing him once or twice a month, and he was little more than a benevolent stranger who occasionally brought him treats.

I think I should have known what was coming when Jace asked him, in his baby-man English, 'What your name?' and Drew answered, "Drew." I gave him credit for keeping up with FaceTime for awhile, it's not easy to FaceTime with a toddler, and he visited Jace a couple of times during the first six months, but after that I got only excuses.

Eventually, after a year of near total silence, Drew told me he had married and was expecting a child with his wife.

She did not know about Jace and me.

I asked Drew to relinquish his parental rights, and he did, under the condition that should Jace ever need anything medical, that we contact him.

Occasionally, Jace asked questions about his father. He had no clear memory of him, and I answered as best as I could, but I could tell my time of reckoning was coming.

Angus filled in where he could, including Jace often with his and Alex's outings. Unfortunately, something happened between Gus and Amber and their relationship was currently in tatters, so Gus needed to spend time with Alex more than ever. While he always invited Jace to come with them, I managed to avoid it at least thirty percent of the time. Alex needed time with his father.

"Hey, Momma." Jace leaned into me, resting his forehead on my shoulder. I ran my fingers through his unruly curls, lightly scratching his scalp. Soon, it would be my head on his shoulder. I shuddered internally at the thought. Time passed so quickly.

"How are you, agapimeno mou?"

"Good, Momma." He stepped back and smiled, his eyes sweeping the kitchen, taking in everything at once, or so it seemed. "Where's Yiayia?"

"In the backyard, checking on her tomatoes."

Our backyard was tiny, as most backyards in the downtown were, but we never ran out of fresh vegetables in the summer.

"Shit! I locked the backdoor!"

I gaped at his use of the swear word. He laughed and clapped his hand over his mouth, then spoke. "Well, Momma, if ever there was a time to use it, locking Yiayia out of the house for the night would be it."

I laughed too, then heard her pounding on the back door.

"Better go let her in, or she'll boil you." I smiled. "Hurry before she gets scared."

"Coming, Yiayia," he yelled as he ran to the back door.

After a moment I heard her voice, still strong at eighty-five. "You trying to make Yiayia to sleep outside tonight?" I wandered into the hallway, giving myself a clear view to the back door. Jace closed the door and relocked it while Yiayia shuffled inside, one hand holding the edges of her apron up, her tomatoes nestled inside the makeshift bowl.

"Sorry, Yiayia," he said quietly. "That would have been bad."

"Bad? Bah!" She snorted. "Yiayia is strong! You think I can't break into my own house? Or go to my friend's house next door?"

"Mm-hmm." A smile pulled at the edges of his mouth. "But would you have been able to reach the latch to open the gate?" Jace teased.

She laughed. "Ach, I boil you!" She grabbed hold of his cheek in a pinch. Jace laughed through his 'ow'.

"Give these to Amber, koritzaki mou," Yiayia demanded as she unloaded her haul onto the counter. "She loves tomatoes."

I laughed out loud. "She doesn't love tomatoes, Yiayia. Amber hates tomatoes."

"Well, she gonna love these ones. Sweet!" She held one up in her hand. "Look at that skin. Is perfect!"

I smiled. This woman had carried me so often over the past three decades, it was a wonder to me that she wasn't bent in half.

"I'll take them, Yiayia," I agreed.

"Good girl."

Jace picked up his backpack again, and I grabbed my purse, my book bag, and the tomatoes.

"Look after Mommy, agoraki mou. Tell your cousin to do extra reading, or I boil him."

Jace and I both laughed at the idea of Alex reading. That would require him to sit for any length of time, and he rarely did that.

Driving in the car, side-by-side, was where Jace and I had some of our best talks.

"How was the first week back at school, agapi mou?" I asked.

"Good." He paused and fiddled with the radio. "There is a new club starting for adventurists."

My boy was quiet, introspective, and brave. So brave, he scared me on the regular. He had a thirst for life, and I feared he was a bit of an adrenalin junkie. Go-cart racing, skateboarding at the skateboard park, pounding up and down concrete stairs on his BMX bike, any opportunity he could find for his feet to leave the earth, he took it.

"Oh?" My heart thudded once, hard, in my chest, and I rebuked myself. How bad could it be? They were only in the sixth grade!

"Yeah, it looks good. I'd like to join. Is that okay?" He asked.

"Sure." I shrugged. "What does it involve?"

"Cool!" He breathed, then continued excitedly. "Weekly meetups after school, and monthly field trips."

"It's run through the school?"

"No. The university is running it. Some of the same people who ran the summer camps."

Jace and Alex went to summer camp at the university. They did an excellent job, rounding up physiotherapy, physical education, and sports medicine students to run and oversee the programming.

"That's good! Where are the meetings?"

"At the university, but don't worry. They have buses that pick kids up from their schools. You only have to worry about picking me up when it's over. Alex is going to join, too, so we can come home on the bus together, or I can get a ride home with him and Uncle Gus."

Jace and Alex attended the same school, played the same video games, and shared many of the same interests. They were on the cusp of their journey to manhood, and they'd both been deprived of a consistent man in their lives, though Angus showed up as much as he could since he and Amber separated.

They needed this.

"That sounds good, agapimeno. If Alex doesn't join, I'll figure it out. No problem." I assured him. I didn't want him to feel like he always needed to be thinking ahead, solving problems that weren't his to solve.

For some reason, the cars ahead of me slowed to a stop, unusual for this time of day. I ran my hands up and down the steering wheel.

"I wonder what's going on," I murmured.

"It'll clear in a minute, Momma."

I craned my neck, trying to see. I hated being stuck. I glanced at the rear-view mirror. Cars lined up steadily behind me. Soon I would be locked in.

"Maybe I should turn around?" I contemplated out loud.

"Just wait, Momma. It'll clear in a minute," Jace rested his hand on my shoulder, and I turned to meet his eyes. He smiled at me. Calm. Steady.

I sighed. "You're right. Always so impatient, aren't I."

"You're just excited to go talk to Thia and Minnie about your kissy books," he teased.

I laughed, even as my eyes darted between the stretch of cars in front and the line forming behind me, boxing me in. My armpits dampened. I rolled my neck. Traffic began to move, and I breathed a sigh of relief.

"What do you know about my kissy books?"

He smirked, his mouth lifted at one side. "I know more than you think I do."

"Really!" I drew the word out. "Maybe we should have a talk about all the things you think you know!"

"No, no, no!" He laughed. "Uncle Gus has me covered."

My eyebrows hit my hairline. "Since when?"

"Since last weekend when he told Alex and I we were becoming men," at this his skinny chest puffed out, "and that there were things we needed to know."

"So... what did he tell you?" I wondered why Gus didn't tell me. This definitely made the need-to-know category. I mean, if he was teaching my son about sex, shouldn't I know what he's teaching him?

I glanced at Jace. His eyebrows scrunched together. "Nothing yet. But he said when we have questions, to go to him."

I breathed a sigh of relief. Thank God for Gus.

"He's a good uncle," I said.

"A good dad, too." Jace murmured it softly under his breath, but I heard him just the same.

Chapter 11 – Aphrodite's Harem

Ruby

Amber's door swung open, and Jace ducked inside, kissing his aunt on the cheek on his way past. She smoothed his curls as he slipped past her.

"That kid's a shadow," Amber commented with a bemused smile on her pretty face.

If Jace was a shadow, Alex was the sun. Seeing them walking together was a study in opposites. My boy, his hands shoved deep into his pockets, loped along, quietly studying the world around him, his lips tipped up on one side in pleasure or amusement. Amber's boy was laughter and light in constant motion, bouncing on the balls of his feet, his hands sweeping in wide arcs as he spoke, his little face forever animated.

"Is Minty here yet?" I asked, dropping my purse on the hall table, and hugging my sister.

"Of course not!" Amber replied, laughing. "She's always late."

Just then, Amber's phone sounded a notification, and she picked it up. "That's her now. She wants to know if we want anything from Shop the Parthenon.

"Mm, yes, dolmadakia and halva."

"You're disgusting," Amber muttered as she texted my request.

We didn't share the same food preferences. Amber hated dolmadakia with a passion most would reserve for world hunger. She leaned toward meat and potatoes with a side of veggies, with everything on her plate keeping a respectable distance. I loved casseroles and stews. With our differing food preferences, Yiayia did a lot of extra cooking while we were growing up, determined that we ate until we choked every single night.

"What are you ordering?" I challenged.

"Olives," she smirked.

Olives were Amber's one tell of our father's Greek heritage. Where my eyes and hair were dark, hers were light. I spoke and loved the language, she struggled with it. I loved all Greek food, her preference was Canadian, with one exception. If there was an olive, any kind of olive within her reach, she'd eat it.

Tonight, we had our Bookstagram night. When Amber and Angus split, Minty got us hooked on Bookstagram. The three of us shared the one account and posted reviews weekly.

We named it Aphrodite's Harem. It was a drunken decision and we stuck by it. To the Bookstagram world, we were one woman. A fantasy woman. A woman who exuded sensuality. A woman at whose feet men fell. A woman unafraid and uncowed by her sexuality, unabashedly collecting book boyfriends and keeping them. A woman who was confident and self-assured.

None of us fit that picture, which made up half its entertainment value for us.

Minty was proper, with a capital P. She made Yiayia 'very proud', and Yiayia forever held Minty up to Amber and me as an example of perfect femininity. Minty dressed beautifully, and applied her makeup impeccably, anytime she left the house. She kept her home in pristine condition, hosted like a queen, and was unfailingly polite.

Amber was feminine and romantic. She loved vintage clothing and antiques, especially knickknacks and jewelry. We both understood that while Yiayia's ruby ring would go to me, the rest would go to Amber, who shared Yiayia's love for sparkly things. Amber thrived in her profession, which was helping people. She wore her dirty blond hair long and unencumbered. She favored loose, flowing dresses with flip-flops and eschewed makeup. More often than not, she could be found with her nose in a book. She was quiet, contained, gentle, and nurturing. In contrast, she boasted a bawdy sense of humor.

I wore jeans and a t-shirt, caps and running shoes, oversized hoodies and pyjama pants, mostly because I always seemed to be running to catch up and organize myself. When I did dress up, I gravitated towards boots and jeans. I liked to play with makeup, but usually kept it light. For special occasions, I tended toward simple dresses and pantsuits. Vander's cross, always, no matter the outfit. That had not changed.

Vander had reached out to me, several times over the past six years, but I never responded. I feared what I'd find out if I spoke to him, and how that might affect me. I had a son to raise, one that should have belonged to him, and I could no longer afford to be decapacitated by a broken heart. It took over a decade, his leaving me a second time, and a surprise pregnancy, but eventually I accepted that Vander and I were not to be. However firmly I believed in my heart that we were meant to be, we had missed our opportunity.

I touched the outline of his cross under my shirt. I should stop wearing it. Every time I touched it, I thought of him. At times, he even snuck into my dreams for the future, but I shook them off.

I wished I didn't have to shake them off so often. I sighed. Perhaps I should pack it away.

Amber came back from the games room, where she set the boys up for the night. She had a three-bedroom condo that she moved into after she separated from Angus. I thought it odd that she moved out of their family home with Alex, while Angus had stayed there by himself. Nevertheless, one of those bedrooms she made into a games room for Alex.

"They settled?" I asked.

She nodded, giving me her easy smile. "They're good. It always sounds like Alex is talking to himself in there because Jace is so quiet!"

We listened for a moment. I had to listen hard to hear Jace's low murmur. We burst out laughing and Amber threw an arm around me.

"You alright?" She asked, studying me as she sometimes did.

"I'm okay. I wanted to ask you the same thing. Have you seen Angus lately?"

Amber's eyes reflected her deep sadness. It used to be a mix of anger, confusion, and sadness that would flash in those light brown depths, then pain. Lately, sadness resided there alone.

"You ever going to tell me what happened?"

"Perhaps if it's ever over," she answered cryptically.

"It isn't over?" I asked.

She sighed and dropped her arm as she moved away. "I just don't know, Ruby."

Angus came around as much as Amber allowed. They'd gone through some heavy stuff, which ended in a separation that surprised the hell out of all of us. She would not share the reasons why, though I asked.

Repeatedly.

I didn't push anymore. I just vowed to be there for her whenever she was ready to talk. If ever. Amber protected those she loved, and she was protecting him, which meant she loved him still.

Minty's gentle rap at the door interrupted another one of our non-conversations about Angus. Whatever happened, I knew that it caused my sister anger, pain, and deep sadness. It made it hard for me to look at him sometimes, which explained why Amber refused to tell me what happened.

Minty rushed inside laden with bags as soon as Amber opened the door. "Sorry I'm late! There were tons of people at the craft fair today!"

Shitfuckdamn.

"I forgot about that!" I exclaimed. "I meant to drop by to visit you! Damn it! Today was the first of the season?"

"No worries, Ruby. You're a busy lady." She placed her bags on Amber's kitchen table. "I brought you three kinds of olives, lovely," she said to Amber, then turned back to me.

"Everybody and their dog came today. I got seventeen commissions! That's unheard of! I almost don't want to go back next week!" She laughed her tinkling laugh.

Even flustered, she still looked perfect. Wearing designer jeans and a soft, off-the-shoulder blouse, with her hair slicked back into a high

83

ponytail, and her makeup light, she could be the poster girl for any number of products.

"Are you going to be able to finish all of those?" Amber asked.

Minty looked at Amber serenely. "Of course! Next week I might get no commissions. My turnaround time is six to twelve weeks. I've got lots of time."

"Is Minnie here?" Alex bounded into the family room, Jace close on his heels.

Minty's face lit up. She turned and held her arms out. "Boys!"

They both hit her at the same time, nearly knocking her off her feet. When they were small, they couldn't pronounce her name properly and called her Minnie. She never once corrected them, and the nickname stuck, but only for them.

She pulled out a chair at the dining room table, and the boys did the same. "I've got something for you both."

Minty rarely showed up without something for the boys. I tried to dissuade her in the beginning, but Amber took me aside, and asked me to let it go. Minty didn't have children of her own. Amber told me that when she asked Minty to stop buying for Alex, the pain in Minty's eyes compelled her to retract the request immediately.

So, the boys gained a generous and benevolent aunt in Minty. Minty helped with driving when the boys needed it. Minty was the secondary emergency contact on their school and sports forms. Minty took them on overnights into the city, to the movies on New Year's Day while we helped Yiayia cook, and to their favourite restaurant for their birthdays. Just yesterday, Minty picked them both up after school to go out for Alex's birthday.

She handed an over-sized brown craft bag to each of them. "I hope you like them."

"Aw, Minnie, we always like what you bring us," Alex exclaimed, then hooted as he pulled his gift out of the bag.

Jace opened his own bag, and his jaw fell open. He pulled out a custom painted skateboard deck. He turned it over in his hands and ran his fingers over the design.

"Minnie," he whispered. "Did you paint this?"

"No," she smiled. "I told the artist all about you, and he came up with the design. She nodded toward Alex. "Same with Alex's."

"This is awesome!" Alex yelled. He jumped up and hugged Minty, nearly clocking Jace on the head with his board as he spun around.

"Alex!" Amber laughed. "Stop swinging that thing around!"

Undaunted, he headed to his mother to show her, then hollered at Jace to come back to the games room.

Jace placed his board gently back into the bag, stood, placed his arm over Minty's shoulders, and lay his cheek on top of her head. Minty closed her eyes. Her mouth tightened as her brow knit for just a moment. When Jace lifted his head, her smile was firmly back in place.

"You're welcome, sweetheart," she replied to his unspoken thanks, and he loped to the games room.

"Thank you, Minty. Thank you for giving them you," I said softly.

Minty raised startled eyes to meet mine, and she laughed her tinkling laugh. "Thank you for sharing your boy."

Amber stood and finished laying out the evening's treats on the coffee table. We settled on the couch. Soft music played in the background, serving to help drown out our conversation, which Alex usually had covered all on his own.

"I'm dying to know. Who's my book boyfriend this week?" I asked, pulling out my E-reader.

When it was my turn to pick, I always went for the Alpha take-charge type, the ones Kristen Ashley so perfectly depicted. Amber usually picked something paranormal, it didn't matter if they were vamps, werewolves, shifters, so long as there was a fated mate, she loved it. Seeing as it was Amber's pick, I expected something from Rebecca Zanetti.

"Ah, Minty will love him. He's dominant and..." Amber paused and wagged her eyebrows, "kinky."

"Mm, sounds good. What book is it?" I asked.

"The Naughty Pine. The author is Indie, Sibylla Matilde."

"Ooh, I've seen graphics for that one."

"Mm-hmm. I picked it special for you two. Dominant for you, kinky for Mint. I'm warning you, his name is Jace, but I've read the first few chapters, and we're just going to have to get past it."

I laughed. Minty smiled her enigmatic smile and opened her E-reader to download the latest book boyfriend, when Amber pulled three paperbacks out of her bag.

"Paperbacks for this one, ladies. It's a keeper."

We had certain criteria we covered in our reviews for @aphroditesharem, including steam and heat. We did not like closed doors. We assessed the likeability and believability of the characters, as well as the plot. We rated it overall for the feels factor, and we rated the Hero as a book boyfriend. AKA, whether we would want him in real life. We only posted books we rated a four or five. We considered ourselves to be book recommenders, rather than book reviewers.

"We should see if there are romance novels written by men. Straight men," I defined.

"Why? And why straight men?" Amber plucked another olive off the platter and popped it into her mouth.

"Your insides must be pickled after all these years," I teased.

"She does seem to have a bit of a fetish," Minty agreed.

Amber defiantly popped another olive into her mouth and smiled cheekily in response.

I continued, "Wouldn't you like to meet a man who understood what women wanted?"

"So, what? You're just going to find men that write romance novels and scope them out?" Amber asked.

"I mean, I've heard of worse plans," I laughed.

"Well, of course we all want a man who understands what we want," Minty said. "But wouldn't it be easier to first find a man you like, and then simply tell him what you want?"

Amber and I stared at Minty for a moment, looked at each other, and burst out laughing. I couldn't even find a man I liked enough to ask, and Amber couldn't even tell her own husband what she wanted from him. My crazy chortling set Amber off further, and it took a moment before she could speak coherently.

"I mean, said that way, it seems so simple, but it's so hard to explain," Amber began, her hands folded under her chin as she thought about it. "And some of the things I want are not things I should have to ask for. If I have to ask for it, it's probably not going to be genuine. I mean, I'm not a writer, it's difficult for me to express what I want, what I need. I think, for me, it's knowing he wants me and only me no matter what happens. That there can be no substitute."

I looked at Amber sharply, wondering if this was the key to her issue with Angus.

Minty nodded. "For me," she began, "it's the focus, in and out of bed. The attention the heroes lavish on the heroine, how they know them, can read them, how they are driven to give them what they want, what they need."

"Being his first choice and his number one priority," I added. The thought made me sad. I'd never been that to anyone. Certainly not Vander, and not Drew either.

"We should write our own romance novel," I grumbled.

"We could release it as a public service announcement." Minty laughed her tinkling laugh.

"I just told you, I'm not a writer!" Amber protested. "What would I write?" She deepened her voice and continued. "'He swung down off the castle wall, his broadsword in hand. The bitter winds whipped around us both, lifting the edge of his kilt and revealing the tip of his weenie.'"

My mouth dropped open, then I doubled over with laughter, clutching my stomach.

Minty covered her face with her hands. "Oh, my Lord, Amber! That was so bad!"

More laughter bubbled up from my stomach, and my chest filled with light to see Minty lose it. She had a good sense of humor, but she was usually so contained and proper. Seeing her lying on her side on the couch with her hands over her face tickled me.

I heard wild laughter coming from the boys, over and above Amber's snickering and Minty's tinkling laugh.

It was enough.
It had to be.

Chapter 12 – Not Enough

<u>Ruby</u>

It wasn't enough.

The vague sense of restlessness I'd been battling for weeks solidified into a physical yearning after our Bookstagram meeting. I needed something else, something more.

I stood hip to hip with Amber and Yiayia in the kitchen, peeling potatoes and chopping salad for our Sunday family dinner. Both boys were in the backyard, attaching trucks and wheels to their new skateboards.

Usually, on Sunday afternoons, conversation filled our little kitchen, but today I was lost in my own head. Amber was quiet, and even Yiayia had little to say.

"Okay," Yiayia dismissed us. "I finish. You go rest. Go!"

We didn't argue. Once we finished the prep work, Yiayia liked to do the actual cooking on her own.

Amber grabbed two sparkling waters, and we headed out to the front porch. We perched side by side on the concrete step, looking out over the street. Over the years, our neighbourhood became increasingly run-down until younger people started snapping up the older homes and remodelling. There were few of the original homes, like ours, left.

Everything changed.

Only I remained stagnant.

"What's the matter, Ruby?" Amber asked softly.

I sighed. "I just feel restless, stagnant."

Amber nodded slowly. "If you could snap your fingers and add something to your life, what would it be?"

I didn't need to think about it. I attended a conference that summer, I'd just been too afraid to move forward. "I would franchise Spuds and get out from behind the counter. Secure a brighter future for Jace, security for Yiayia."

"What do you mean, security for Yiayia?"

I sighed. "You know, just in case something happens to her health wise. Those homes, the good ones, they cost a lot of money. I'd want to give her the best care."

Amber leaned over and rested her head on my shoulder. "We will, Rubes. If it comes to that, we will do whatever it takes to get her what she needs."

I reached for her hand and linked my fingers with hers.

It seemed, no matter how we both had tried, that it was just us in the end.

"What do you want, Amber?" I asked softly.

She lifted her head and stared into the distance. "I just don't know, Ruby. I wish I did."

The boys burst through the front door with their new boards, Alex in the lead, Jace close on his heels. Yiayia's voice carried outside. "Agoria! Get your elbow pads or I spank you!"

Amber and I burst out laughing. The things that woman said.

"So, franchising?" Amber asked, and I nodded. "I think you should do it, Ruby."

"I think I will," I suddenly decided. "I've dreamed about it for a long time."

"Good," Amber declared.

"What about you? What are you going to do?" I asked.

Amber smoothed her long skirt over her legs. She took a deep breath. "I'm going to take a good long look at all my options and see if I can't make a decision about Angus and me."

"Would you go to counselling with him?" I ventured.

"He's offered. I don't know if I want to," she admitted. "He hurt me. A lot."

"Are you going to divorce him?" I murmured.

"He doesn't want that, but I don't know if I can get past it. It makes me a hypocrite because I hurt him first."

"What would you tell your client if they were in your situation?" I bent over my knees and rolled a small pebble back and forth with my index finger while I waited for her to answer.

Amber held her silence for several moments. "I'd tell her she needed to work out her personal issues that were contributing to the problem before deciding what to do about her marriage," she answered wryly.

I peeked up at her and bumped her lightly with my shoulder. She smiled and bumped me back.

Later that night, I went online and printed off a slew of information about franchising.

I took it to bed with me, but promptly fell asleep while trying to read through it.

Chapter 13 - Potato

<u>Vander</u>

Nerves attacked my gut.

Despite my prayers, it had been over ten years.

I pushed my fingers through my hair for the umpteenth time as I remembered standing in that damn parking lot praying it would not be another ten years before I held her again. I prayed again, standing outside her door, that the nightmare of separation would soon be over.

Would she accept me?

Would she believe?

Was she still my Ruby? It was a lot to expect, a lot to hope for.

The past eleven plus years had been difficult. The custody battle went on for well over two years, and my ex-wife pulled me into court regularly, for imaginary infractions, over the years since. The final agreement contained a codicil that we live within a few hours drive of each other. She insisted on it when I requested an agreement that would allow for longer visitations spaced out over the year, allowing me to move. She protested and continued to refuse me even after she remarried and had two more children.

Two years ago, her husband got a job transfer opportunity. She came to me with her tail between her legs, wanting the codicil lifted, claiming we could modify our custody agreement, and that she'd allow Georgie to fly back and forth for longer visits.

I smiled grimly at the recollection of that meeting. She tried to insist I remain in the same town, so Georgie could have that familiar environment, but her ability to manipulate my life had come to a screeching halt with her pending move. I started the process of moving my business almost immediately.

Letting Ruby go had been the right thing to do.

About a year after our weekend together, I found out she had a child and a man. I pondered, briefly, the tantalizing possibility that the child belonged to me, and would have followed up, if not for the very real presence of the man with his arm securely latched around her waist.

I understood the shock she felt seeing me with my arm around that girl on Facebook. It was not a good feeling, and I reacted much like she did, and refused to look her up anymore.

Over the years, I reached out to her, at least once a year, more often since we lifted the codicil. Half of me hoped she was free and would reply. The other half wanted her to be happy and settled with a family. When she didn't respond, I accepted with a grim sort of satisfaction that she had moved on. I hoped she'd built a beautiful family with a man who prioritized her in a way that I never had.

Interestingly, her lack of response didn't stop me from moving my business. Moving eliminated one of the obstacles between us. Going to her, something I should have done twenty years ago, felt right. If life ever granted us a third chance, I'd be ready.

Quite by accident, I found out she was single. I ran into a mutual friend of ours from university at a conference my company sponsored. We sat down and did the usual, running down the list of everyone we knew back in our university days.

"I saw Ruby, your old girlfriend, a few weeks ago. Are you guys still in touch?"

Every cell in my body came alert. "Not so much," I worked to sound casual. "Where did you see her?"

"At another conference. She lives in this area, and she's looking to franchise her restaurant. Apparently, she planned to do it years ago but put it on the backburner when she had a baby."

"I knew she had a child." I forced myself to keep my tone easy. "I never heard anything about a husband."

"No husband. She told me the only man she had room for in her life was her son." He shook his head and laughed ruefully. "She shot me down pretty quickly. If possible, she's even more attractive than she was back in the day."

I received that piece of welcome news yesterday.

I paced outside the door to Spuds, my hair practically standing on end from the mauling I'd given it. I smoothed it down, took a deep breath, and opened the door.

Ruby

With the lunch rush over, I spread my papers out on my customary table. The table in the back room sagged under the weight of the produce delivery that begged to be put away, but I planned to resist its demands for half an hour. I sat down to look at my options and consider my next steps.

I spread out the pamphlets I collected at the conference a few weeks ago and took notes on each by hand. The act of putting pen to paper helped the information to stick. The same information would make it onto my laptop later today. It had to. I would eventually misplace the paper, but it was much harder to misplace the laptop.

Not impossible, but harder.

The bell over the door jingled, but I kept my head down for an additional moment's reprieve before sighing internally. I stood and rounded the table, heading for the front of the restaurant.

Lost in my thoughts, I didn't lift my head until an electric frisson of awareness arced along my spine. I snapped my head up to assess the threat. Standing in front of me, long legs braced and face stern, stood my wildest dream and my favorite fantasy.

My breath whooshed out of me in a gasp. My heart galloped in my chest, and a shot of adrenalin set my legs in motion. I skittered backwards, slamming my hip into the corner of a table. I winced in pain, and rubbed my hip as he moved towards me, his face twisted with concern. My hand flew to the touchstone beneath my t-shirt, and I deliberately stepped back, carefully this time.

His eyes zeroed in on my hand, then lifted in question to my eyes.

I purposefully looked away. I needed a moment to compose myself, and I refused to play this game again. I had no idea what brought him here, and him coming without warning made me angry. What if Jace had been here and saw me react like this? He was a very observant kid. This would alarm him!

Oh, God! Did Vander know I had a son? Did he wonder at the timing of me falling into bed with someone else not two weeks after being with him? What did that matter? I lowered my brows. It's not like he had ever been celibate.

I turned my head to look at him. Standing not even four feet in front of me was everything I'd ever wanted, and every, single atom in my body pulled toward him. I forcefully restrained myself from moving and crossed my arms over my chest.

I tilted my chin up to look at him. "What are you doing here?"

"I came to see you." His voice was deep and steady.

Like him.

Unlike me.

I shook with emotion, and I could hear it in my voice.

"You should have warned me," I accused, even as my eyes ran up and down his body and scanned his face, greedily drinking him in. Would my feelings never fade? My stomach soured at the certainty of the pain to come when he would invariably walk away again.

"I would have, but you haven't responded to any of my previous attempts to contact you."

He hadn't moved. He held his arms stiffly at his sides, the only tell that his emotions were churning beneath the surface. His mouth was set, his eyes alert, his face stern, just as I remembered from when I'd last seen him. The lines on his face were deeper, the frown marks more pronounced.

95

I wished life hadn't caused those changes in him. I felt myself soften marginally. I sighed, decided to get this conversation over with, even as part of me, a rather substantial part, wanted it to go on forever.

I studied him, taking in the differences from the mental picture I carried of him in my heart. Far leaner than I remembered, streaks of silver now brushed his temples, and a closely clipped salt and pepper beard framed his perfectly formed lips. Deeper lines fanned out from the corners of his eyes. I hoped laughter placed them there.

I wished I'd been there to ensure it.

"You look well," I said softly, uncrossing my arms. I smoothed my hair, suddenly aware that if I noticed the passage of time, he surely did as well.

His mouth softened, and his eyes lost a hint of the hyper-focus. "You look beautiful."

I looked down at my jeans and t-shirt. "Oh, yes. I'm a regular fashion plate," I replied dryly.

"No," he laughed. "You're definitely not that, but you are beautiful."

To hear him laugh, after all these years, was a gift. I couldn't help but smile, but I tucked my hands into my back pockets and ignored his compliment.

"Would you like something to drink?"

He pushed his hands into his front pockets. "I wouldn't say no to a drink."

I nodded and gave him a wide berth as I walked around him. "Have a seat. I'll be right out."

I opened the door to the back and closed it gently behind me. Pressing both of my palms and my forehead against the closed door, I breathed deeply, forced my shoulders to relax, and worked to calm the trapped bird that had taken up residence in my chest. I pushed back the creeping black shadow of dread that threatened to engulf me, again, as it had every other time he left me.

Vander was here, in my store, in my space. I had no idea where his life had taken him in the last decade, and I was afraid to find out.

96

Take this as a gift, Ruby. You never thought you'd see him again. Just take the gift. You know how this story ends, and when it does, you can get back to your life as regularly programmed.

I grabbed a couple of bottles from the fridge and filled two cups with ice. I pulled the door open and held it open with my hip as I passed through.

I jerked to a stop momentarily when I saw Vander sitting at the table where all my notes and leaflets lay spread out. I continued toward him and set the tray at the edge of the table. I quickly gathered up my things and stacked them off to the side.

He accepted the drink I handed him and indicated my papers. "You looking to franchise, finally?"

I sat down across from him. "I have a son," I blurted out.

He dipped his chin once, easily rolling with the change in topic. "I know."

"You know? How do you know?"

"My custody battle lasted for over two years. I looked you up when it ended and saw that you'd settled down. I was sad for me but happy for you."

I nodded, suddenly weary of the twists and turns and near misses. "It didn't last. He relinquished his parental rights years ago."

"I'm sorry."

I sighed. "It's better this way. I prefer to rely on myself rather than a man who's here one day, gone the next." I winced even as the words spilled from my lips. I could not look at him. He might take those words personally. I shrugged mentally. If the shoe fits...

He cleared his throat. "My ex-wife and her husband moved. The custody agreement that didn't allow me to move without losing my visitation was revoked."

I felt my mouth twist with bitterness. "She trapped you quite neatly, didn't she?"

He looked away, something akin to shame mixed with not a small amount of anger on his face. "She did." He paused. "I take full responsibility. I should not have married her."

I sighed, then smiled at him. "Then you wouldn't have George, and what would your life be without George?"

He smiled back at me, and his face softened further. "Is having your son what waylaid your plans to franchise?"

I smiled. "Yes. But it was worth it. I never thought I'd have a child. He was a really good surprise."

"I'm happy for you."

"So." I picked up my pen and doodled flowers on the edge of my papers. "What are you doing here?"

I needed to know what his immediate plans were, if he had hopes of spending time with me, and if I wanted to consider going down that painful road again, knowing what would happen at the end of the weekend. I sighed internally. I knew I would take what I could get with him.

"I live here," he stated quietly, his eyes watchful.

I understood the words when I thought of them individually, but put together their meaning eluded me. The pen fell from my hand, and I slowly tore my eyes from my doodles to stare stupidly back at him. "What?"

One corner of his mouth curved slightly upwards. "I live here. I moved my business as soon as the ink on the new custody agreement dried. I wanted to be close to you. Yesterday, I found out you're single. Today, I'm here."

I pushed back my chair and stood abruptly, staring at him. Fear like I'd never known unfurled in my chest like a rose blooming on high speed time-lapse.

I pulled in a breath and lay my palm over my touchstone. I walked away from the table where he sat watching me and then paced back.

Anger that I didn't know I was carrying, suddenly boiled over. "You can't just show up here like this!" I wrapped my arms around my waist. "I have a son! I can't afford another broken heart!" He started to protest, but I cut him off with a slice of my hand through the air between us. "No. Just no. You need to leave. It shouldn't be too hard. You're good at that," I sneered.

I stomped off into the back room.

98

I paced back and forth in front of the produce table, shaking out my hands, filled with nervous energy. I needed to get away from him, from the hope that only he could awaken inside me. A foolish hope, one I should not begin to entertain considering our history.

Hope for what? We weren't even the same people anymore! He had a family. I had a family. He had responsibilities that never included me. I had responsibilities that had nothing to do with him.

I rubbed my hand over my chest. Just the idea of him living here had my stomach tied up in knots of anxiety. My heart skittered in my chest. I didn't know the ending to this story. What if we tried and failed? What if we ran into each other afterwards? What if I had to see him with someone else in person?

Bile rose in my throat at the thought. I needed stability. I needed peace. I needed certainty. I'd worked hard to attain that for myself and my son.

I circled the table loaded with produce, my arms wrapped in a tight hug around my waist. The broken heart that I painstakingly pieced back together, with nothing but determination, threatened to come unglued.

Fucking bullshit. That's what this was. He can't waltz in here and tell me he came to see me and that he moved and expect me to just roll over.

The thought that I hadn't actually given him a chance to tell me what he wanted niggled at my brain, but I dismissed it.

I eyed the table full of produce. My fingers itched with the desire to overturn the whole damn thing. I paused. That would make a big mess. One I'd have to clean up.

It would be expensive, too, I thought as I paced. I couldn't afford that.

I lifted a potato. I could afford one potato. I drew back my arm and heaved the potato at the heavy door. I jumped at the sound of the impact. It was much louder than I thought it would be, and infinitely more satisfying than I expected. I picked up another.

I heard running footsteps from the other side and Vander pushed through the doorway, his face alarmed, my name on his lips.

"Ruby!"

I stared at him in shock. I had momentarily forgotten he was out there. My anger quickly gave way to embarrassment.

"What happened?" He looked around the room, searching for the source of the loud bang. His eyes found the split potato lying at his feet. He looked up at me, his eyebrows arched in question.

"It fell," I explained, waving my free hand in a gesture that clearly said these things happen sometimes.

"It fell?" His face began to crease into a smile. He pointed to my other hand. I looked down at the potato I held in my fist. "Is that one going to fall, too?"

I stuttered for a moment before his smile penetrated the fog of my thoughts. I drew back my arm, and he chuckled as he quickly ducked out the door. "I'll see you tomorrow," he called over his shoulder.

The only answer he received was the reverberating hum of the second potato hitting the closed door.

Chapter 14 – No Takebacks

Ruby

I took extra care with my outfit the next morning. Little good it did. I'd hardly slept, and no amount of makeup could cover the bags under my eyes.

He probably wouldn't show. It was just an expression. *See you tomorrow.* People said that. Still, I put on my best jeans and chose one of my weekend t-shirts. I looked down at myself mockingly. A weekend t-shirt as opposed to a weekday t-shirt. My fashion sense was epic.

I tore them off and put my regular jeans and t-shirt back on. I didn't wipe off the makeup, though. I told myself I didn't have time.

I packed Jace off to school and headed to Spuds. Yiayia rarely came in anymore, thank God. I couldn't deal with seeing Vander in front of her until I understood what was happening.

For the first few hours in the morning, Spuds' doors remained locked while I prepared for the day. With my music pumping, I enjoyed those morning hours. By ten, orders started coming in for lunch, and by eleven I opened the doors. Minty and her girls, a few doors down, were among my best customers.

Minty worked with two crazy women she positively adored. One of them, Junie, was a total crackerjack. Willa was quieter and always smiling. They ordered from here at least twice a week.

Immediately next door to me was a tiny Greek grocery called Shop the Parthenon. The owners, Elisavet and Yanni, were Greek and well into their seventies. They were crazy nice, and just a little bit crazy. She ordered him around all day until he got tired, and then he retreated to his comfy chair in the corner with a Greek coffee and the daily newspaper, while she talked to her friends on the phone.

By quarter to eleven, I couldn't stand the anticipation any longer and needed to escape for just a few minutes. I slipped out the door and locked it behind me, then scooted over to Shop the Parthenon and ducked inside. The bouzouki music drifted softly from the speakers, barely discernible, and certainly undetectable once Yanni and Elisavet started talking.

"Yanni! Is Ruby! Ela, Ruby mou, sit down."

"Hi, Thia."

Elisavet wasn't really my aunt, but as a Greek woman, once you reached a certain age, you became 'Thia' to everybody.

"Yanni! Get Ruby something to drink. Ti theleis, koukla mou? What you want?"

Yanni came over to greet me, his hands empty, a smile on his weathered face. "Hi, Thio. How are you?"

"Good, koukla mou. How are you?"

"I'm good, Thio."

"What you want, koukla?" Elisavet asked. "Yanni, get the girl something!"

He held his hands out to his sides. "How I'm supposed to know what she want? She tell you, yet?"

"Huh," she grunted, then turned back to me. "What we can get you?"

"I need my dolmadakia fix, Thia."

Elisavet turned to order Yanni to go get it, but he was already on his way. Elisavet grasped my hand and pulled me none too gently towards Yanni's chair in the back corner. An old brown recliner, with a thick crocheted blanket thrown over the back, enveloped me like a hug. It sat ready for when the cold weather hit, when Elisavet would tuck Yanni under it, and make him a Greek coffee to warm him after being outside. Greek men like to be coddled by their women, and Yanni, as hard as he worked, was no exception.

"Sit, koukla."

I laughed. "I have to get back to work, Thia. I just wanted to say hi and grab a snack."

"Five minutes. You work too hard! You sit for five minutes."

There was no point saying no. It always surprised me that once she got me sitting, Elisavet ignored me entirely. I smiled inside, delighted with their antics. Yanni meandered back and forth while Elisavet ordered him to do what he had already set about doing. It made me miss my Pappou while simultaneously bringing his memory closer.

The door opened and drew my attention. I sucked in a breath, relieved Elisavet wasn't close enough to hear it. Vander stepped inside.

Being somewhat hidden in the corner, he didn't see me. I shrank back in the chair hoping he'd get in and out quickly, hoping he wouldn't ask Yanni and Elisavet if they knew where I was.

"Hello," Elisavet greeted him from behind the counter. "What I can get you?"

"Kalimera," Vander wished her a good morning in Greek, and Elisavet went all atwitter.

"You are Greek?" She asked excitedly.

He smiled. "I am."

"Where you from in Greece?"

"From the north. The province of Macedonia."

"What village you from?" Elisavet's excitement was palpable.

"Edessa."

"Edessa!" She smiled widely, then twisted and hollered to Yanni. "Yanni! Yanni! Ela, this boy is from Edessa!"

I smirked at the use of the term 'boy'. He was clearly all man. Over six feet tall, lean and muscular, with dark, wavy hair sprinkled with grey, for crying out loud. The grey hair made me sad. Well, it wasn't like I didn't hit the hairdresser every five weeks.

Yanni came from the back of the store balancing several cans of dolmadakia in his hands.

"Why you don't put it in the bag, Yanni?"

"You have the bags," he explained exasperatedly.

He turned to Vander, who watched them, a familiar hint of amusement on his face.

"So," Yanni began his inquisition as Elisavet bagged the dolmadakia. "Your people, they from Edessa?"

Vander nodded and shook Yanni's proffered hand. "You know Papadopoulos, Christos?"

"I'm sorry," Vander shook his head. "My parents brought me here as a small child. I don't know anyone there."

"What your last name is?" Elisavet cut in, leaning her forearms on the counter, her face animated.

"Vitalis."

"Vitalis, Vitalis..." Yanni murmured under his breath, staring into space and history, while Elisavet did the same.

Yanni's gaze snapped back to Vander, and he peered at him. "Your father, his name George?"

Vander's eyes crinkled. "Yes, George." This didn't mean much. Every third fellow in Greece boasted the name George.

"His mother, Voula?"

"Yes!" Vander answered, bemused.

I'd heard this same conversation, and variations of it, my entire life. Greece was a small country, and it was a small world. Everyone knew everybody, somehow. They connected through their villages, their churches, their marriages. Couples didn't get married in Greece, families did.

I looked at my watch. I had to get back and open the door to Spuds, and I didn't want to have to speak to Vander in front of Yanni and Elisavet. I squirmed in my seat.

Yanni went on to tell Vander more of what he remembered, and Elisavet seemed to remember my presence at the same time. She bustled over to me with the bag of dolmadakia cans in her hand.

"Here, koukla. Just take them. You going to be late!"

She passed me the bag and I bolted for the door. I saw Vander turn out of the corner of my eye, and saw his eyes widen. I laughed delightedly as I escaped out the door, leaving him to his fate.

Twenty minutes later, he walked into Spuds. As soon as he saw me standing behind the counter, he pointed at me and laughed, his teeth a flash of white framed by that beard that gave me ideas I'd sooner not have.

"You! You knew they would give me the Spanish Inquisition!"

I nodded and laughed. "They know about you. They're good friends with my grandmother."

He took off his glasses for a moment and scrubbed his hand over his face, smiling broadly. He moved to stand in front of me, one hand braced on the counter, the other on his hip. We'd bonded more than once over our shared Greek heritage and all the little idiosyncrasies that were inherently a part of it. Greek hospitality and nosiness went together.

"They wouldn't sell me any dolmadakia for you. Told me you didn't need my dolmadakia, and said, quite belligerently I might add, that they'd give you all the dolmadakia you want." He pretended to gripe.

I laughed, but I was touched, both by their protectiveness and his memory. I leaned my hip against the counter across from him and crossed my arms over my chest. His smile warmed me. "You were going to buy me dolmadakia?"

"You still like it?" He asked softly, turning to face me, both hands resting on the edge of the counter now.

"I do," I smiled, drawn to him as ever. "That's why I went over there. I've got four cans of it in the back."

"They warned me not to break your heart again. I promised them I wouldn't," he said softly.

The smile slid off my face. The funniness of the situation wore off, and I stepped back from the counter.

105

He sighed and dropped his chin to his chest for a moment. He looked up and peered at me from beneath his heavy brows. "You're going to make me work for it."

"For what?" I asked, crossing my arms protectively over my chest.

"Your love."

I guffawed. "No. That you have. It's my trust that is beyond your reach."

He studied my face for a moment. "I have your love, Ruby-mine?"

"Always. What? Did you think I'd be able to take it back?" I snarked. "But it doesn't mean anything." I shrugged and tried to rein in my swinging emotions.

He leaned his forearms on the counter and leaned over to meet my eyes. My gaze flickered up to his. He studied me intently. "How? How does it mean nothing? You don't believe that I love you, Ruby-mine?"

I shrugged again and edged further away from the counter, away from him.

"Not enough to stay."

He opened his mouth to protest, but I raised my hand to stop him. "I understand why you did it. I even agree. Mostly. But, watching you walk away from me has gotten old. I'm old enough now to know I deserve better." I shook my head when he tried again to speak. "Even if I don't deserve better, I'm old enough to know I don't want this anymore."

"Don't want what anymore? Me? Us?" He asked, his head cocked to the side, his dark eyes holding mine, a tiny thread of doubt weaving through the determination in his gaze.

I hated to be the one to put that there. The threat of tears stung my eyes. I rubbed Vander's cross under my shirt. Could I really turn him away?

"I just can't." I said softly, my plea for mercy welling in my eyes. Hurting him again was the last thing I wanted to do.

God knows, we'd hurt each other enough already.

"Can't? Or won't?" He murmured. "Would you wish me away? Would you take one night, or a single weekend, then wish me away, so you don't fall any deeper? Because I gotta tell you, Ruby. There's no further down I can go. I've loved you with my whole heart for more than half of my life, and I'm not going to walk away so easily."

I took a deep breath. I didn't want this uncertainty: torn in two, afraid, my world turned upside down. I needed to be straight with him, and end this before he got his hopes up.

"Every single person I've loved has left and taken a piece of my heart with them. There's simply not enough left to risk giving it to you again." I explained firmly.

"I'm giving you mine," he murmured softly.

My eyebrows pinched together with irritation. He wasn't listening. Pushing me, pulling at me, like everything else in my life.

"I don't want it!" I snapped.

He grinned now, the tender moment over. "Too late. No takebacks."

"You're not listening to reason!" I hissed, and watched, unwittingly fascinated, as his smile dropped, his jaw tightened, and his beautiful mouth flattened into a firm, unyielding line.

He leaned over the counter and pinned me with dark eyes, flashing with anger and years of hurt. "Look where listening to reason got us. I'm done listening."

My heart rate picked up, from anger or anticipation, I couldn't tell. What I could identify, and it made me angrier still, was hope.

We glared at each other across the counter for another moment, then he stood up straight, knocked on the counter briskly, and stepped back, his eyes trained on my face.

My stomach dropped, and I worked hard to ensure my dismay didn't show on my face.

He walked to the door and opened it, then turned to look at me.

His eyes softened.

"I'll see you tomorrow, Ruby-mine."

Chapter 15 – No Time for Logic

<u>Ruby</u>

Anxiety tied my stomach up in knots. Our conversation that morning played on a loop in my overworked brain. Knowing I had to tell Yiayia about Vander only made it worse. She probably already knew. God knows, Elisavet spent most of her day on the phone.

On the way home, I rehearsed how and when I would tell her, without Jace catching wind of it. I should have told Vander not to come to the shop when Jace might be there. I did not want those two crossing paths.

Vander belonged to my past, the most painful part. That said a lot because there was serious competition for that dubious distinction. I couldn't afford to allow him into my present. It had taken me forever to get a grip on my heartbreak and stabilize my mental health. I shuddered to think what it would be like to go through that again with Jace to witness it.

With his appearance yesterday, thoughts of what might have been, hounded me. No sooner did I push those thoughts away, than I thought about what could be.

If I had any hopes of avoiding the conversation with Yiayia, they were quashed as soon as I entered the house. Her bright, inquisitive eyes met me in the front hall.

I laughed at the look on her face, then teased. "Hi, Yiayia."

Her sparse eyebrows lowered in her dear wrinkled face. "Ela, none of that poulaki mou. Elisavet called. Vander is back."

"Shh, Yiayia! I don't want Jace to hear."

"Why not?" She exclaimed, ready to call the priest to set a wedding date.

"Vander is part of my past. There's no need to complicate things."

"Not according to Elisavet, he's not."

"Well, who are you going to believe?" I asked, exasperated. "Me or Elisavet?"

She eyed me for a moment before smiling at me fondly, and I relaxed. Then she said, "Elisavet, of course. You never had clear eyes where that boy is concerned."

"Boy," I snorted. "He's hardly a boy."

She laughed and winked. "Elisavet told me that, too!"

I heard Jace and Alex before I saw them, and I sliced my hand through the air, warning Yiayia not to say anything.

Alex came through the kitchen doorway ahead of Jace, walking backwards, his hands moving expressively as he described an 'epic fail' in basketball that day.

Jace walked with his hands stuffed deep in his pockets, his mouth quirked up in his signature half smile, his eyes reflecting his amusement. He caught sight of me over Alex's head.

His eyes lit up, and my heart expanded.

"Hey, Momma."

"Hi, agapimeno mou." I smiled.

Alex spun around and bounded toward me, throwing his arm around my waist, and giving me a squeeze. "Hi, Thia!"

"Hi, glykouli." I smiled down at him, knowing in a few short years I would be tilting my chin up to do the same.

He released me to Jace, who wrapped both arms around my waist and rested his cheek on my shoulder. "How was your day, Momma?"

I rubbed my hands over his back, noting the bony protrusions. He was growing again. He always got skinny before filling out again.

"I'm good, psychi mou. How about you?"

He released me and shrugged his skinny shoulders. "Good, momma. I was thinking, now don't get upset-"

"Oh, God!" I cut him off loudly with a groan, making him laugh. "What is it this time? Skydiving? Bungee jumping? Tree-trekking?"

His eyes lit up. "Tree-trekking?" I screeched.

Alex laughed. "Thia! It's safe! They have harnesses and everything!"

"Oh, my God!" I glared at them both, half-serious. They talked about this adventure group incessantly, and I wished they would pick up knitting instead. "I was joking when I guessed tree-trekking. If God meant for you to be up in trees, He would have given you wings!"

"They are boys, poulaki mou," Yiayia loudly interrupted my tirade in a well-rehearsed improv. She pinched their cheeks, one in each hand, and pulled. I winced in sympathy. Greek love hurt. "They going to be men, strong men." She released them, lightly smacking the same cheeks she had just pinched, and both boys rubbed their faces and laughed.

"So, can we go, Momma?" Jace asked, and they both looked at me hopefully. This boy would be the death of me. He had always pushed his limits. He loved the adrenalin rush.

I narrowed my eyes on my nephew. "Does my sister know about this?"

He smiled his most charming smile and put his arm back around me. "See, Thia, I figure if you're okay with it, she'll definitely be okay with it. We decided to work on you first."

I glanced at my boy to catch him rolling his eyes at his cousin. "You weren't supposed to say that part, Alex."

Alex grinned at me. "Naw, Thia's cool. She knows how we operate."

I chortled and hugged him. "I'll talk to your mom. If she's okay with it, I'm okay with it."

"Yiayia is okay with it!" Yiayia interrupted testily. "Why you no ask Yiayia?"

Both boys kissed her cheek, but only Alex answered. "Because you don't drive, Yiayia, and you'd snitch on us."

She barked out a laugh while reaching again for their cheeks. They successfully dodged her pinching fingers on their way to the front door.

"Don't go far. We gonna eat soon!" She bellowed after them.

They took their noise with them but left their happy vibe. I smiled.

"Good boys, poulaki. I'm proud," Yiayia said, returning to chopping the salad for dinner.

"You want help, Yiayia? What time is Amber coming?"

"She be here soon, koukla. You sit and have rest. You work too hard. You want coffee?"

"Maybe you should sit, Yiayia."

At eighty-five years old, Yiayia had slowed down. A lot. She still cooked every day. She claimed it gave her happiness to cook for us, and it kept her active.

"What else I'm going to do, poulaki? Go dancing? Dig ditches? Ech, I'm old lady but I can cook."

"I'll get a cranberry juice, Yiayia," I answered, moving to the fridge.

"Sit down, poulaki. I get it for you."

I took a seat and sighed, knowing the interrogation was coming.

Once she set the glass down in front of me, she sat down as well, pulling her chair to face me, so close that her knees bumped mine.

"Listen to Yiayia." I opened my mouth to protest, but she shut me down. "Ach! You listen to Yiayia, poulaki. Your lives took you apart, but your hearts are still one. Sometimes God is giving us second chances. Don't throw it away."

"We're different people, now. It doesn't make sense, Yiayia."

Yiayia sat back in her seat and her eyebrows hit her hairline. She pointed to me, then herself. "You telling me life don't make sense? You think I don't know?" She pointed back at me. "You need to learn this lesson. The world is yours, poulaki mou," she beseeched, then she leaned forward and grabbed my hand, closing it into a fist. "You must take what you want from it, or you gonna take what it gives you."

I looked down at her wrinkled and age-spotted hands, her fingers gnarled by arthritis. I smoothed the pad of my thumb over the smooth stones of her ring. She immigrated to Canada, newly married to my pappou, with no money, no English, no job, and pregnant with my father. She knew all about grabbing hold of life.

She lost her son, then her daughter-in-law, then her retirement, then her husband. She knew all about taking what life gave her just as well.

I wrapped my other hand around hers and looked into her bright eyes. "I'll think about it, Yiayia. I promise."

She grunted, using the table to push herself up. "Good. Now I feed you. You look skinny. How you work at Spuds and be so skinny?"

In fact, I was not skinny. At best, I was average. I could even stand to lose twenty pounds. Twenty pounds that snuck up on me bit-by-bit over the past decade. I didn't usually mind. I was fit and healthy, I just liked my food, so my muscles were well-padded. I wondered if Vander noticed the difference.

I shook myself mentally. What did I care? If I disappointed him, he didn't have to stick around. I got up to put my glass in the dishwasher. He excelled at leaving, I thought meanly. I pressed my lips together. I knew that wasn't fair, but I wasn't about to turn my life upside down for someone who wouldn't do the same for me.

A small voice in the back of my head whispered that he moved his entire life across the country just to be close to me, but I shut it down.

I wasn't ready to be logical.

Chapter 16 - Use Me

<u>Ruby</u>

Wednesday morning, I went to work with a plan.

Not knowing when Vander would show up was giving me ulcers and whiplash. Every time the door opened, my head whipped around. Scanning the front door, and the slice of sidewalk outside the front window, became my new hobby. The ringing of the phone startled me, and I couldn't stay in the back for any length of time in case I missed hearing him come in. Today, if he came, I would negotiate with him. If he wanted to see me, he could call me and let me know he'd be dropping by.

I nodded to myself as I parked my car. I could keep him away from Jace, and just plain keep him away, until I figured out what to do about him. After finishing my prep work, I settled at my regular table and opened my day timer.

A thought wriggled in through my subconscious. Would it be so bad to let him in? Yes, I thought emphatically. Yes, it would.

The strength of my desire to dive back in scared me. I'd barely survived the first time I lost him. The second time ruined me for anyone else. If he left me again, well, I couldn't even entertain the idea without breaking into a sweat. I could not risk falling apart when I had Jace and Yiayia to worry about.

The last time Vander walked away, I vowed to move on with my life. I had taken steps to do just that when I found out I was pregnant. After I had Jace, he became my focus and my purpose. I remembered the slimy mess of him as he broke from my body. I looked at him and saw nothing but potential loss and heartbreak, and I embraced him completely despite my fear.

That was more than a decade ago.

A decade.

In some ways, I found myself back where I started, looking at franchising Spuds. I always seemed to be ten years behind. It would be challenging, but I knew how to work hard, and the payoff would be worth it. Franchising would get me out from behind the counter and give me a little more freedom. More importantly, it would bring more income that would go a long way to securing Jace's future and could help with care for Yiayia if she needed it later.

That is where my future lay. That is where I needed to place my focus and my energy.

The door opened. I didn't need to look up to know it was Vander. Every fibre of my being went on alert, my very hair follicles tightened in anticipation. Goose pimples spread up my arms, down my legs, and the bottom dropped out of my stomach. I stubbornly kept my head down. I breathed in for three, held my breath for four, and slowly released it for a count of five.

Long legs stepped into my peripheral vision, and his strong hand pulled the chair out across from me. He sat down slowly and leaned his elbows on the table.

I dropped my chin to my chest. Caught in a battle between my heart and my brain, I could see no way forward that wasn't going to hurt.

"Ruby-mine," he whispered. "Do you really want me to go?" His voice was pained.

Tears welled in my eyes and dropped onto the table in front of me. He reached out a hand and touched his forefinger to cover one of my teardrops.

"I don't want to hurt you," he murmured, "but I don't know if I can avoid it at this point. If I stay, I'm hurting you. If I leave, I'm hurting you."

I nodded in agreement. I touched my forefinger to his, the first time I'd touched him in over a decade. Something akin to oxygen flooded my veins. I pulled in a shuddering breath.

"I had a plan this morning."

He turned his hand over, and slid it under my palm, the touch more steadying than intoxicating. Something about lining up matching body parts both soothed me and thrilled me on a visceral level. He closed his fingers gently around mine.

"Tell me about your plan," he coaxed softly.

I allowed my hand to rest in his, and took comfort from his touch and his deep, soothing voice.

"I was going to tell you that you have to call me before you come, so that I'm ready for you and not nervous. I was going to tell you that you can't come at a time when Jace might be here, because I don't want to involve him. I was going to tell you that we are different people now, and our time is over." More tears fell. The thought of pushing him away broke my heart, but allowing myself to hope for a future with him had the power to break all of me.

He squeezed my fingers gently. "How about this. You agree to go out with me on Friday or Saturday night, and I won't come into the store for the next couple of days."

I looked up to see the brackets around his mouth deeper than I'd ever seen them. His eyes held mine steadily. The resignation, regret, and sorrow that marked his gaze ten years ago was absent. I couldn't quite put my finger on what I saw in his eyes, but it wasn't resignation.

Go out with him on Friday or Saturday? Could I do that? "I don't know if I can do that, yet."

He smiled. "Yet. That might be the most beautiful word that I've ever heard pass your lips."

I smiled back at him, drawn in by his charm despite myself.

"Give me your cell phone, koukla mou," he quietly demanded.

I unlocked it and pushed it across the table to him, then, with my free hand, I swiped the tears from my cheeks.

He keyed in his number and called himself. "Let's keep in touch over the next couple of days. If I don't see you on the weekend, I'll come see you here at your store next week, and I'll let you know when I'm coming, so you're ready for me."

I nodded, unstopping the door that I'd dead bolted and wedged shut ten years ago. "Okay."

I felt the tension leave his body in a mighty whoosh that surprised me. I raised my startled eyes to his.

"Don't look so surprised, Ruby-mine. Nothing has ever been so important to me as what I stand to lose right now."

"I don't want to hurt you."

"Then don't!" He grinned, then pulled my hand across the table. Opening my fingers, he brought my palm up to his lips and pressed a tender kiss to its centre that worked its way directly into my heart. "I won't hurt you, Ruby-mine." He closed my fingers around his kiss.

With my fist tucked snugly inside his, he spread out my three remaining brochures. Touching my first choice, he said, "This guy is overpriced and he's a lazy fuck. I'm sure some of his consultants are okay but I wouldn't recommend them based on what I know about the owner." He tapped the remaining brochures with his finger. "These two companies are decent."

I crumpled the brochure he dismissed, so that I would remember to discard it. I would have ripped it in half, but that would have required me to free my hand from his, and my body refused to relinquish his hold on me.

He squeezed my fist. "Ruby, I'd like you to consider going with my company. This is what I do. I can help you."

I pulled my hand away, and his lips tightened in response.

"No. Absolutely not. What happens later when things fall apart? I just trot into your office and see you carrying on with your life without me?"

My eyes filled again, and I swiped my wrists across them impatiently. "Gah!" I stood up and walked away, needing to put some distance between us.

He sat back in his seat and raised his hands up in supplication. "No problem, Ruby. Let's do this, then. You choose whichever company you want to go with, and I'll guide you and advise you from the sidelines. Would that work for you?"

My thoughts were spinning. The truth was, I struggled to make even the smallest decision. I went over the same information repeatedly, but it wouldn't stick. My ADHD brain, while brilliant when I was highly interested in something, or when looking at the big ideas, did not do so well when it came down to the finer details.

If I chose one of these companies, Vander could help me to sift through the information and answer my questions. Something about the whole thing niggled at my conscience, and as soon as I identified the uncomfortable feeling, I sat back down in front of him, my eyes on the brochures on the table. I fiddled with the two remaining brochures, then picked up the third and ripped it in half while I gathered my thoughts.

"I don't want to use you," I murmured.

He leaned forward abruptly, and my head snapped up to face him. He held my eyes, fierce determination in his.

"Use me. Use me, Ruby. I've never wanted anything so badly as to be of use to you."

"I can't promise anything," I whispered.

"It's okay," he answered, a small half-smile on his lips. "I can."

Chapter 17 – The One Who Got Away

<u>Vander</u>

Back in my car, I rolled down all the windows and gripped the steering wheel. Bending forward, I rested my forehead on it momentarily. To be able to promise her something, anything, made me feel almost drunk.

I huffed out a dry laugh. For twenty years I'd bowed to circumstance and responsibility. Finally at a place in my life where I could put her first, I had every intention of doing just that. I was ready to promise her everything.

I smiled at the mental picture of the three brochures spread out on the table. She discarded the one I dismissed, and it warmed me that she trusted my judgement.

I told her the truth about that company. I knew for a fact that the other two companies were good. One was mine and the other belonged to my closest competitor, who, fortunately, owed me a favour.

Time for him to pay up. Pulling him up in my contacts, I left a detailed message for him.

I turned the key in the ignition, flipped on the air conditioning, and pulled out into traffic.

She would take some convincing, I knew that going in, but her apprehension exceeded what I'd imagined. I hoped like hell that she'd agree to go out with me this weekend, but I had serious doubts. That was okay. I had a backup plan.

Georgie spent the summer with me and would be flying out again for Thanksgiving. That gave me a month to set things straight with Ruby. She would have to meet George eventually. It would hurt her. God knew I wasn't chomping at the bit to meet Jace, but the sooner we ripped the bandage off the better.

It was just another obstacle we had to get past, a tough one, and unavoidable. Meeting each other's sons was only the beginning: I had no idea how the boys would react to us being together, or to each other. Georgie would have to share me for the first time ever, and it would likely be the same for Jace.

Regaining Ruby's trust was by far the largest obstacle. Her fear was stronger than her love at this point, and she was determined to deny us both all the good we would be together. If I wasn't sure of what I could give her, I'd feel bad for how hard I was willing to push her.

Arriving back at my office, I pulled into my designated parking spot. Located right on the border of Bayview Village, I didn't think she'd have a problem driving there.

My competitor was further out, which was another selling point in favour of my company. It should go smoothly, so long as she didn't realize that I was the alternative. If by some chance she chose to go with my competitor, I'd still walk her through every step.

Situated on the fifth floor of a glass office tower, my office overlooked parkland on one side and the city on the other, the parking lot spread out below, and a tiny sliver of the lake was barely visible in the distance.

Coming off the elevator, I stepped directly into the lobby. On the wall to the left lay a chaise lounge. Beyond that stretched a hallway with meeting rooms on one side, offices on the other.

My assistant sat at a curvy desk to the right of the elevator. A collection of comfortable chairs, angled and bracketing small side tables, lined the wall facing her desk. To her right lay the hallway leading to the conference room on the left and ending with a set of double doors that opened into my office.

I looked over the documents and memos spread across the surface of my desk and contemplated which of my consultants I wanted on Ruby's case. My cell rang. Glancing at the screen, I noted with satisfaction it was the call I'd been waiting for.

"Dolman. How are you, man?"

I heard Dolman chuckle into the phone. "Got an interesting voice mail today. Somebody's calling in a debt."

I relaxed back into my chair. "Yup. You remember the night we tied one on in Baltimore?"

"Ah, yes." He paused. "So, this is the one who got away."

"Ruby. Her name is Ruby."

Dolman sighed. "You lucky fuck. What do you need from me?"

I outlined my plan. It was simple. Show up, hear Ruby out, gently turn her down, or throw enough obstacles in her path that she would turn him down.

"You're paying, and I'm going to order the most expensive meal on the damn menu. It's only fair. You're taking my Saturday night and forcing me to turn down a business deal with a beautiful woman," he griped.

I laughed. "I'll even owe you one if she ends up going with my company. It shouldn't be too hard. She's whittled her choices down to you and me."

Dolman laughed, and then got serious. "You sure about this? Women tend to frown upon being manipulated."

A wrinkle of unease rippled across the surface of my thoughts, but I dismissed it. "I'm going to be there for her whether she wants me to or not."

At home several hours later, I grabbed a beer from the fridge, slid open the patio door, and stepped out onto the deck. The sun hung low in the sky, but it was still hotter than Hades. A lawn mower sounded in the distance. Who the fuck mowed their lawn in this heat? I should enjoy it while it lasts. The temperature would drop soon enough.

Leaning against the railing, I raised the bottle to my lips and drank deeply, eyes closed, savoring the sticky sweet malt coating my throat on the way down. The dew on the bottle reminded me of her tear on the tip of my finger, and my heart broke the tiniest bit at the recollection.

My brain told me to back off, give her a bit of space, and allow her to adjust, but my heart pushed to go harder. We'd lost so much time, and she'd been hurting for so long. The longer I drew this out, the longer she would stew in this no-man's-land of doubt and insecurity.

She would have to adjust on the fly because I could give her no quarter. The faster I closed this deal with her, the faster she'd get her happily ever after, and I'd get mine.

I gritted my teeth in irritation as I thought about my own life. I'd been alone for so long. Fuck, even when I was married, I was alone. At least in B.C., George lived with me fifty per cent of the time.

Since moving here, I rambled around this house by myself on the nights I didn't work out or work late. The loneliness I thought I'd grown accustomed to seemed to be growing exponentially by the day now that I knew Ruby was no longer tied to another man.

The pain of frustration would soon reach an intolerable level. I needed her here with me. Yanking a cheap plastic Adirondack chair closer to the railing, I sat down and propped my feet up on the lowest rail. The deck was nothing to write home about. I had ideas to improve the backyard but wanted her input.

The house itself was nice, if impersonal. It had been a model home a few years ago, but I had done nothing to personalize it, save for George's room. No woman had stepped foot into this house. I bought it in hopes of one day building a life with Ruby.

I briskly rubbed my hands over my face in a wasted effort to rid myself of some of my impatience. I took another swig of beer then unlocked my cell and pulled up her number.

Vander: How does Saturday sound?

Three dots showed up almost immediately. I waited while she composed her reply.

Ruby: I'm not sure if it's a good idea.

She was hesitant. At least she wasn't outright turning me down.

Vander: I've set up a meeting with one of the companies on your brochures.

Ruby: You did? When?

Vander: Today. I know the owner. He's willing to meet with you. He's free Saturday.

Ruby: Thank you! I suppose I could meet with him.

Vander: I'll pick you up at six-thirty.

Ruby: Wait. What? You're coming?

Vander: Yes. We're meeting him for dinner. That okay with you?

Ruby: Vander... I don't think I can do this. I don't have the strength. I'm being honest with you. You and I shouldn't happen. I don't want to hurt you.

Vander: Then don't. I'll see you at six-thirty on Saturday. You still live at the same address?

Ruby: You can't pick me up from my house! Unless Jace sleeps over at Amber's. You could maybe pick me up at Spuds?

Even in text, she blurted out all her thoughts unfiltered. It remained one of the many things I adored about her.

Vander: I'm not picking you up at Spuds. I'm picking you up from your home and I'm coming to the door like a fucking gentleman. I haven't had a chance to visit your Yiayia, yet. This will give me the opportunity to say hello to her.

Ruby: Why do you even need to visit her? You haven't seen her for over twenty years. Twenty years, Vander! And I'm not ready for you to meet Jace!

Vander: Well, you've got a few days to prepare yourself. Tell him it's a business meeting if it makes you feel better.

There was a long pause. I held my breath. Hoped.

Ruby: You're being kind of bossy.

I snorted. I wasn't the green boy she first fell in love with, and I definitely wasn't the shackled sad sack she'd hooked up with ten years ago. She would be the lucky recipient of the full force of my will and determination.

Vander: He's a busy man, Ruby-mine. He's in for Saturday. You want to do this or not?

Ruby: Quit calling me 'Ruby-mine'. I'm not yours, Vander. I don't know if I want to do this with you.

Vander: Who the fuck else would you do this with? Yiayia? Is she going to be able to drive you into Toronto?

I was a complete asshole, an utter bastard, for playing on her weakness. I hated myself for it.

Ruby: You swear a lot.

Ruby: It's irritating.

Ruby: Toronto? I'm sorry. No. I can't go. I can't. It's too far. Not enough notice. It's not in my safe zone. Can't he come here?

It killed me to hear her talk about safe zones. If only I had come to her in the beginning. I pushed the thought away. Going down that road of recriminations that led to guilt and doubt wasted time I could not afford if I wanted to convince Ruby to take a chance on me.

Vander: Ruby-mine, I'll take you. Happily. You don't have to commit to anything, just hear what the man has to say. He's an expert in the field and he'll give you his honest opinion.

Vander: And fuck is just a word.

Fifteen excruciating minutes passed. Her dots appeared and disappeared several times over the course of those interminable seconds.

Ruby: I feel like I'm using you.

Vander: You love me, Ruby-mine?

Ruby: That's not the point.

Vander: I'm at your disposal.

More excruciatingly long minutes passed. More of my hair turned grey waiting for her to respond.

Ruby: It's just a business meeting. Okay? It's not a date.

Vander: I'll pick you up at six-thirty.

Ruby: Okay. Thank you.

Vander: And Ruby?

Ruby: Yes?

Vander: You've always been mine. Just like I've always been yours.

Chapter 18 – A Different Road

Ruby

Six-thirty did not leave much time to get ready. Usually, I could get myself together in less than half an hour. Tonight, I reasoned to myself, I needed extra time because I needed to make a good impression, and present myself as a confident, professional woman.

Yes indeed. A confident, professional woman who needed her unboyfriend to drive her because going anywhere new by herself could send her into a catatonic state.

The possible catatonia merely worked to distract me from the real problem, which was that this was a date. With Vander. Which he so sneakily, and bossily, arranged. Something about that appealed to me.

I'd gone shopping for tonight, and my outfit told the real story. When faced with the choice of a pretty sundress, or a professional summer suit, I opted for the sundress, even as I wondered at my apparent self-destructive tendencies.

I dried my hair quickly, then rubbed a bit of curl cream through the waves to tame the frizz. I yanked my dress off the back of my bedroom door, and pulled it over my head, smoothing it over my hips. I quickly lined my eyes, added a dab of eyeshadow, and several layers of mascara. I had a weakness for mascara. I glossed my lips and stepped into my sandals, just as the doorbell rang.

I hung back in my room, like a coward, and waited. There was no point in going downstairs to save Vander from whatever Yiayia had on her mind. She'd have her say whether I stood there or not, and I didn't want to hear it. I gave them a few minutes, then made my way downstairs.

Yiayia's eyes sparkled, and she held one of Vander's big hands in both of hers. I rolled my eyes, the turncoat. She was Team Vander all the way. She turned to face him, and he tipped his chin down to look at her, one side of his mouth tipped up in a smile.

"You show my girl a good time tonight. Stay over. Enjoy. I don't want to see you until tomorrow!"

I scoffed. "We're not staying over, Yiayia. It's a business meeting."

"That not what Vander say."

"Who are you going to believe?" I snapped. "Vander? Or me?"

She smiled and her dark eyes twinkled with mirth. "Vander!"

He laughed. "If we decide to stay, I'll text you."

My yiayia could text like nobody's business. She would not allow the tech world to leave her behind. She even had an Instagram account, although it had more pictures of tomatoes on it than anything else.

Evidently, Vander somehow knew about her texting capacity and already had her cell number.

My skin prickled with heat and indignation. I never even agreed to a date, and they were shacking me up in a hotel room.

"I'll see you later tonight, Yiayia," I said pointedly on my way out the door.

Vander opened my car door, and I slipped inside. I swallowed my ire and decided to make light of the situation.

He swung into the driver's seat. "You look beautiful, Ruby. I like your dress."

I flushed at his compliment then ignored it. "I think my yiayia is shipping us."

"Shipping?" His eyebrows arched in question.

"Yeah, shipping. It's what the kids say these days. Short for relationship. She 'ships' us."

He chuckled, his eyes alight. "At least she's not trying to cockblock me."

I smirked. "No, definitely not that."

I'd forgotten how easy I could talk to him, be with him. My brain flashed a warning to resist his gravitational pull. I reminded myself of the pain that was an inherent part of loving him. It should have been easier to remember, the stabbing pain of losing him was my constant companion.

"Don't think too much, Ruby-mine," he murmured, and I realised I'd stopped talking.

"Vander, I- "

"We're not going to talk about this tonight, Ruby-mine."

He glanced sideways at me before returning his eyes to the road. He reached for my hand. I snorted even as I slid my palm against his. The sharp current of attraction warred with my apprehension.

"Tonight, we're going to see about this business of yours. Tonight, we're going to focus on possibilities for the future."

I wrapped my fingers around his hand tightly, despite my next words. "You're not going to be part of that," I whispered.

He squeezed me back. "I'm not going anywhere."

"It doesn't-"

He pulled my hand over to his thigh and held it there. "Not tonight, Ruby."

I attempted to tug my hand from his, but he held tight. He slanted a hard look at me that flipped my stomach and made my panties wet.

I sat back in my seat, shocked at the strength of my response to him, surprised at the change in his usually good-natured, easy-going demeanour. I did not know this Vander. I felt my arm go slack.

He gave me a gentle squeeze in response and turned the conversation back to Spuds.

Before long, he pulled into a parking space and turned to me.

"This meeting is only a starting point. I'm going to introduce you to Gary Dolman, you'll tell him about Spuds, your hopes and goals for franchising, and we'll see what he has to say. You don't need to commit to anything tonight. In fact, it's probably better that you don't. Not until you also meet with the other company."

"You know them, too?"

"I do. They're equally good. You can meet with both, and then decide. Alright?"

I took a deep breath, and a short nod.

"Are you nervous?" He asked.

I glanced at him and pulled my shoulders up to my ears. I couldn't help my smile. "Excited!"

His smile was wide and warm, his eyes warmer still as he scanned my face. "I love to see you like this. This is how I remember you."

I felt sudden sadness at the girl I used to be. The girl who jumped in with both feet. The girl with a ready laugh and a thirst for adventure.

"Stay with me, Ruby. Focus forward," he murmured.

My eyes flew back to find his cool and determined. Ah, here was the sharp businessman. I'd never seen this side to him, it reminded me that he was a different person now.

I nodded sharply. This was a good opportunity. I needed to stay focussed. I opened my door and twisted to get out.

He met me at my side in time to close my door, and we walked across the lot, his warm hand light on my back. Lord, that felt good. I leaned back slightly into his touch.

It had been so long since I'd been touched.

Last fall I'd gone out on a date with a nice man who had touched me just like this, eliciting a gentle buzz of warmth and possibility. That date lasted approximately five minutes before he admitted he was in love with someone else. I wondered if things worked out for him and his lady love.

Vander's hand elicited an altogether different response. His touch was the only one I'd ever craved. Heat spread outwards from the warmth of his palm on my back, edging across the expanse of my skin.

128

My breasts tingled and my chest expanded. I longed to turn to him and press my body against his. I yearned for more of his touch, more of his warmth. I trembled. It was mine for the taking. But for how long?

I leaned away from him and heard him sigh. I glanced at his face and was immediately arrested by the tenderness in his gaze.

He brushed the backs of his fingers down my cheek. "There's no point in fighting it, Ruby. It's always been us. It's always going to be us."

The sting of tears prickled behind my eyelids. I blinked them back and looked at my feet and my polished toes in my new sandals. "I can't think about this right now."

"Fair enough." He relented immediately and I composed myself. He placed his hand back on my lower back, gently propelling me forward. "Let's go in and see if our table is ready."

The restaurant boasted a large seating area, and the hostess led us to a table against the wall of windows where a middle-aged man, a few years older than us, rose to his feet with a smile on his face.

He held out his hand to Vander, a warm twinkle in his eyes. Vander shook his hand and gave him a wry smile. I hadn't realized until that moment, how weird it might be for Vander to introduce a potential client to his main competitor.

A frisson of regret spooled in my tummy.

Vander turned toward me and placed his hand on my lower back. One side of his mouth curled into a smile at catching me in the act of studying him.

"Ruby, this is Gary Dolman. He's a good friend and a fierce competitor. Gary, this is Ruby. She owns Spuds and we think it would make a great candidate for franchising."

Gary grasped my hand with a firm handshake and greeted me with a smile that reached his eyes. I liked him immediately. Over the course of the evening, as he spoke about what his company could offer, he revealed a few obstacles.

First, his offices were a good half hour outside of my safe zone. I wouldn't have to go too often, but this was not necessarily a point in his favor. Not going regularly, and often, meant I wouldn't attain any level of comfort.

Each time I had to drive to his office would be a battle, and being so far outside my zone, I could not be certain of victory.

The fact that he did not currently have an available consultant to assign to my case created a second obstacle. There would be a three to six month wait.

Third, while his company recommended locations, they leant heavily in favor of extensive travel to meet with franchisees.

The fourth obstacle was cost. Of course, I knew franchising would be expensive, but I did not know the possible range could be so vast.

After he left, I relaxed back into my seat. Vander had asked questions I hadn't thought about, to which he most certainly knew the answers. He'd championed Spuds, he'd been respectful and encouraging towards me throughout the dinner, and he'd smiled proudly when I spoke about Spuds' history.

I loved having him in my corner.

"Well? What do you think?" I asked.

He nodded thoughtfully. "Altogether positive. He thinks you've got a viable business model. That's the most important part."

"It's more expensive than I thought it would be."

"Your expenses will run at the lower end of the scale."

"You think?"

His mouth curled up at one side and his dark eyes twinkled. "I know."

I laughed. "Of course. I forgot for a minute that this is what you do."

His gaze sharpened. "Let me do it for you."

"It's tempting. It's tempting to let you because, in this, I do trust you."

"In this."

"I didn't mean to say that, but yes." I met his eyes defiantly. "In this."

He sat back in his chair, curling his hands into loose fists on his powerful thighs.

I tried not to look but I loved his legs, I'd always loved his legs. My eyes drifted along the curve of his thigh. I remembered the last time we were together, how he spread my thighs with his and slid his hard cock against all my wet, giving me exactly what I needed. I closed my eyes, remembering it took only a matter of moments from that point for him to drive inside me.

I pulled myself from my reverie and forced my eyes back to his face and gasped.

Gone was the affable half smile.

The determined businessman? History.

Here sat Adonis, and Adonis could read my mind just as easily as I could read his. A dark flush stained his high cheekbones and his eyes glittered dangerously. He pressed his lips together in a firm line and the muscle at the side of his jaw ticked, clearly visible through his short beard.

I remembered the tickle of his beard against my palm and slammed my thighs together tightly, then cursed myself for giving so much away.

"Ruby," he growled quietly.

Retreat! My brain screamed at me.

Retreat! I shook my head sharply.

"No. No, no, no, no, no. We are not doing this."

The tension slowly left his body, and I watched as he took a deep breath, forced his fists open, and rubbed his palms down the long length of his thighs.

My eyelids drifted to half mast.

"Ruby," he laughed this time. "You're saying no but you're not making it easy to switch tracks."

"Put your thighs under the table," I whispered without thinking. My mouth fell open. "Shitfuckdamn! Can we forget I just said that?"

"No," he said, smiling warmly at me. "That I cannot do. What do you say we get out of here? There's somewhere I want to take you."

I stood, shifting my weight from one foot to the other. "Um. I'm not sure. Maybe we should just head home."

"Yeah?" He asked, his eyebrows arched in question. "You ready to face your yiayia? Or would you rather time your arrival home for when she's asleep?"

I thought for a moment. I didn't want to hear any lectures tonight. My yiayia excelled at a lot of things. Unfortunately, respecting personal boundaries wasn't one of them. "Where are we going?"

He laughed and held out his hand to me. I stared at it. Leaned toward it. Then turned, picked up my purse, and grasped it in front of me with both hands. His proffered hand hovered in mid air between us. Waiting.

I shifted on my feet, undecided. I watched his face, not wanting to hurt him but unwilling to act as a couple.

He stepped forward and gently disengaged one of my hands from my purse, then drew it through the crook of his arm.

I raised my eyes to his face to find his gaze soft and warm on mine. I smiled tentatively and curled my fingers lightly around his bicep, and he smiled back at me. His bicep was hard beneath my fingers. I inadvertently squeezed and he huffed out a laugh.

I rolled my eyes at myself but left my hand where it was.

Outside, the sun was almost a memory. I could smell the first hint of autumn in the air as Vander walked me to my side of the car. I released his arm and turned to get in, but he left his hand on the handle without opening it. I looked over my shoulder to find his face bent close to mine over my shoulder.

"Ruby-mine," he murmured.

I dipped my chin to my chest, avoiding his gaze. Resisting him, this close to him, was an exercise in futility. Could I really cut him out of my life? Knowing he lived only fifteen minutes away? Inside my freaking safe zone?

I leaned back, ever so slightly, against him. I felt his chest expand against my back with his indrawn breath. "I don't want to go down this road again, Vander," I admitted.

His other hand came around and he flattened his palm against my stomach. My head fell back involuntarily to his shoulder.

132

His big hand splayed over my womb, pressing me back tighter against his warm, solid frame. I imagined him over me just like this. I nearly moaned but I bit it back at the last second.

His lips brushed along the side of my face, his short beard a delicious tickle. He kissed the shell of my ear, his warm breath sending tingly warmth across my chest and tightening my nipples, his deep, mellow voice a caress.

"We're going down a different road this time, Ruby-mine."

I found my voice, and it came out strong. "I don't trust you," I stated.

"You will."

He released me and opened my door, waited until I swung my legs into the car, then shut the door and strode around to his own side.

Chapter 19 – Let the Chips Fall

<u>Vander</u>

Taking Ruby here was a calculated risk, one I hoped would pay off. Already in Toronto for the meeting, I had two choices.

Twenty years ago, I took her to the Danforth where she drank too much, then danced on the table in the Bouzoukia. It remained one of my most treasured memories, one I'd taken out repeatedly over the years.

The second option was the Distillery District where we had escaped to just over a decade ago, on the one weekend rescued from the hell of our separation, before I fucked things up yet a-fuckin-gain.

I chose The Danforth, a memory from when we still had hope, something I needed to instill in her again.

"Where are we going?"

Pulling out of the parking lot, I flicked on the indicator to turn. "Nowhere we haven't been before," I smiled at her reassuringly, then paused for a moment. "Do you need to know where we're going, Ruby? Do you feel secure coming out of your safe zone with me?"

I'd done some reading, picked up a bit of information, and wanted to understand the parameters that Ruby operated within. I reached for her hand and held it on the seat between us.

"Um... I wouldn't say safe, exactly, but I'm not sure if the anxiety is coming from not being in my safe zone, or just being with you period."

"Is there anyone you can go anywhere with? Has there ever been anyone you could go anywhere with?"

"Drew," she answered immediately then sucked in a breath before she hurriedly continued, "for a little while. With Minty or Amber, I can go anywhere, anytime. Gus, Amber's husband, is a safe person for me."

"Would you still be able to go anywhere with Drew?" I forced my voice to remain neutral.

"No. I don't think so. No. The answer is no." She looked out the window as the night flew by them and then sighed. "We were never in love. It was a drunken hookup at my sister's wedding, two weeks after the conference."

She tried to pull her hand from my grasp, but I held on.

She whispered, "You didn't call. Or text. I was heartbroken, he was sweet."

She relaxed her hand in my grip and continued. "We were friends. Friends with a child. He wanted to see if we could make it work, but I never wanted to be someone's consolation prize."

I winced. I'd done exactly that to my ex-wife, not that she didn't put me in that position in the first place. Although I wasn't thrilled hearing about her relationship with Jace's father, for me, it definitely belonged in the need-to-know category.

"Are you still in touch with him?"

"Not at all."

"Do you have questions for me?" I ventured carefully.

"No." Her answer came firm and fast. "I don't want to hear anything about anybody you've been with."

Her hand trembled in mine. I stroked the inside of her wrist with my thumb. "There's only one thing I need you to know. I've only ever loved you."

"Fat lot of good it's done me," she muttered.

"You're right. It's going to be different from here on out," I promised.

135

She took a deep breath and I waited to see where she'd take the conversation next. "How often do you see your son?"

She went from calling him 'Georgie' to calling him 'your son', reminding herself of the history between us, the fact that I had a life separate from hers, just as she had a life separate from mine.

"I get him for eight weeks every summer, as well as March Break and Thanksgiving. We share Christmas," her hand jerked in mine, and I stroked her wrist again, "which means he spends all of Christmas break with me one year and comes to me on Boxing Day on alternate years."

"That's it?" She whispered. "That's not very much."

I risked a glance at her face to find it stricken. She gave me her big brown eyes. "I'd hate that."

"I had to fight, and fight hard, to get that. It's practically all the time he's not committed to school," I explained. "I also get weekends here and there. As per my visitation agreement, I have the option to fly in, rent a hotel suite, and spend time with him in his hometown a few times a year, provided I give ample notice."

"Do you do that?"

"I do."

"Does she co-operate?"

Despite not wanting to know anything about her, she cared about how she affected me because Ruby had a big heart.

"She does not, but her husband is a good guy, and he ensures that George gets his time with me."

"I remember you said she remarried." Her hand slackened further. She felt threatened by my ex-wife. My ex-wife felt threatened by her. What a fucking mess I'd created.

"She married a really good guy. Hopefully, she doesn't fuck it up, because he loves Georgie and Georgie loves him. I'd hate for Georgie to lose his other dad."

I was pinning my hopes on George being just as okay with having a stepmom, too. Laidback and easygoing, most things rolled off George's back. He liked fun and adventure like both of his dads. Usually, he took change in stride.

"You're okay with George calling him 'dad'?"

"He is his dad. He's been in his life since George was a baby. He's given him two younger sisters. He takes him to all his lessons, talks to him about girls, looks over his homework, makes him take out the trash. In some ways, he's more his dad than I am."

"That must be very painful," she murmured.

I squeezed her hand. "It's not as bad as it used to be. Georgie's happy, well-adjusted, and we are close. That's all that matters."

"You talk to him a lot in between visits?"

"Yes. We text every day, he calls me whenever he wants to, and we FaceTime at least once a week. You'll meet him in a few weeks."

Her hand jerked in mine. Fuck, had I realized all those years ago that holding her hand gave me a direct barometer to her thoughts, I might not have fucked up so colossally.

She started to protest, but I cut her off. "He's a good kid, Ruby-mine. You'll like him. I promise." I waited a beat and when she didn't respond I continued. "I know how you feel. I'm not entirely looking forward to meeting Jace, either."

Her hand spasmed again, and I quelled a smile. "But Jace is yours, and you are mine, so he's automatically important to me. I'll meet him, I'll get over the fact that another man planted him inside you, and I'll love him for who he is."

"It hurts," she whispered.

"I know that, too," I murmured back.

I squeezed her hand and released it to navigate the narrow side streets of the Danforth in Greek Town. When I pulled into a narrow space and put the car in park, she perked up.

"Do you remember that Bouzouki place we went to? Do you think it's still here?" She asked, her eyes alight. The sheen of tears lingered, but she plowed through.

I leaned over and quickly kissed her cheek. "C'mon. Let's go find out."

137

We walked, her hand tucked into the crook of my arm. She absentmindedly stroked my bicep, intermittently squeezing the muscle as she looked around. Always so tactile.

I had a flash of memory of going with her to a fabric store when she went through her sewing phase. Not a single swath of material escaped her questing fingers. That phase only lasted a couple of months. She didn't have the patience for measuring, cutting, and the painstaking process of piecing it all together.

After that she took up painting. That lasted even less time.

"Remember when you decided you wanted to paint?"

She laughed. "Yes. I was terrible!"

I chuckled. "You were. What was it after that? Knitting?"

She twisted her lips to the side. "Crochet."

That time I laughed out loud. "You made me that enormous hat."

She chortled. "Remember the needle felting?"

"You stabbed yourself so many times trying to go faster!" I chuckled and lifted her fingers to my lips, kissing the imaginary wounds.

She brushed the tips of her fingers across my lips, her eyes pained. She tucked her hand back in the crook of my arm and looked away. "I've never been very patient."

"No," I agreed. "Patience has never been one of your gifts. What else have you tried over the years?"

She looked up to the sky, thinking. "Um... not much. I read. I have a book review account on Instagram with Amber and Minty. That's it really."

"I find that hard to believe. You had the most insatiable curiosity, and you got bored so easily. You're telling me you haven't tried other things?"

"I haven't!" She exclaimed, as if she only just realized it herself. "I think I was depressed for a while. Coping with my anxiety and my grief, working, going to therapy, and then Jace, took up all my energy. There wasn't, and isn't, room in my head for anything else." She turned to look at me. "Which is why this is such a bad idea. I don't have the mental capacity to deal with the fallout of us. Not again."

I pulled her out of the way of the people traffic and turned towards her. Cupping my hands around the sides of her neck, I tipped her chin up with my thumbs.

"For tonight, just for tonight, let's enjoy each other. Can you do that?" I grinned and dipped my face closer to hers. "You're stuck with me until Yiayia goes to bed, you may as well have some fun."

She huffed out a soft laugh and relaxed into my hands. I stroked my thumbs down her throat, careful to keep eye contact and to keep my gaze soft. Her face softened and she acquiesced. She was on edge, taking on too much with the franchising, and my presence in her life right now was not helping.

That would change.

I intertwined my long fingers with hers and continued walking. The bouzouki music drifted out into the street long before we got to the café. She squeezed my fingers delightedly.

"You hear that?"

"I do," I chuckled. "You going to dance on the table again?"

She chortled. "You never know!" I laughed out loud at her answer and threw my arm around her shoulders, tugging her close to my side.

She wrapped her arm around my back and looked up into my face. She was so little. And so strong.

I dipped my head, and she immediately stiffened. Switching tracks quickly, I dropped a kiss onto the top of her head.

Her body relaxed even as her face fell in disappointment. She didn't want to want me, but her reactions made it clear that she did.

I watched the storm of thoughts pass over her eyes and sought to intervene quickly before she pulled further away.

"Ready?"

Her big eyes got bigger. "Ready?" She squeaked.

I fought the smile threatening the corner of my mouth and pointed toward the door. "To go in. We're here."

She collected herself and pulled away. I released her, placed my hand to the small of her back, and opened the door.

139

Inside, the song was just winding down. The players finished with a flourish, and the café erupted into cheers.

These were not tourists or visitors, these were locals. The smell of ouzo and olive oil permeated the walls. When a plate broke in the kitchen, the entire floor bellowed, "Opa!" and tipped their glasses.

Ruby laughed out loud. We arrived at the perfect time when the balance was slowly tipping from civilized to celebratory. The middle-aged hostess greeted us in English, and I answered in Greek. Her eyes lit up.

"You are Greek?"

Ruby rolled her eyes and smiled. We were about to play the six degrees of separation game that she found so humorous. "We are," I smiled, hugging Ruby close.

"You live around here?" She switched from English to Greek.

"I just moved to Bayview Village, but Ruby has lived in Milltown all her life."

The hostess turned to Ruby. "I have friends in Milltown. You know Elisavet? She owns Shop the Parthenon."

"I do," Ruby smiled, answering in Greek. "Her store is next to mine."

"Bravo! What is your store?"

"Spuds."

"Ah, yes. Sorry about your grandfather, koritzi mou. A good man. How is your grandmother?"

And so it went, the way it always did. Both comforting and exasperating, there was no anonymity in the Greek community. Everyone was family. Or mortal enemies. I wondered if our shared heritage would help me this time as it had in our beginning.

Finally, the hostess led us to a table then brought shot glasses of ouzo. "To Pappou," she said seriously and knocked back a shot of ouzo.

We lifted our glasses. "To Pappou."

Ruby choked, and the hostess smacked her back sharply. Ruby's eyes watered as she sputtered and choked and laughed.

The hostess went on smacking Ruby's back as if nothing was amiss. "What you want? Meze? More Ouzo?"

"Can you give us a minute with the menu? Ruby will take a water for now and then we'll order."

"Kala." She nodded and left.

Ruby swiped two fingers under her eyes to sweep away the tears. "Oh my gosh, Vander! Freaking Greek people!" She chortled.

My smile stretched my cheeks. I hadn't felt this happy in years. "It never gets old, Ruby-mine."

"I love our people, I do, but I need a chiropractor now!"

I laughed out loud and grabbed the menu. "Meze? Or dessert?"

Her dark eyes twinkled. "Both!"

We ordered, and the music picked up again. I nursed an ouzo with ice and ordered Ruby the same. The bouzouki band enthusiastically played all the old favourites. By the time Ruby was halfway through her third ouzo, it was obvious it was time to cut her off.

"Oh, Vander! I haven't had fun like this in years! Remember karaoke?" She leaned towards me and popped an olive into my mouth. "Eat, poulaki mou." Her inner Greek woman was emerging. I couldn't say I minded her feeding me.

"How could I forget, Ruby-mine?"

Her eyes twinkled. "You really are a terrible singer."

I grinned. She picked up the last dolmadakia and bit it in half. She chewed slowly. "Mmm, this is so good."

She looked at the remaining half in her fingers and then looked at my mouth. A fire lit in my gut, but I grinned. I couldn't help it. She never could hide her feelings.

She leaned forward, her face mere inches from mine. "Let this be a testament to the depth of my love for you." She popped the remaining half into my mouth but didn't back away.

I chewed slowly, my eyes on hers as she watched my mouth. I licked the juice from my bottom lip. Her eyes went half mast and her sweet lips parted.

"Ruby," I growled.

"Yes," she breathed, still not retreating.

I leaned in, pressed my mouth to the outside corner of hers, and held it there. She inhaled deeply, pressing her face closer to mine as she exhaled. "I love you too much, Vander."

My heart picked up its pace. The jolt of desire made me want to claim her. I dragged my lips to her cheek, grasped her around the back of her neck and pressed her forehead to my shoulder. I nuzzled the side of her face and softly, reverently, kissed the shell of her ear. "I love you, too, Ruby-mine."

I felt the exact moment she got scared. Her body stiffened and she pulled away, laughing nervously. "Wow. Maybe we should get going."

I looked pointedly, for a brief moment, at my groin. "I'm going to need a moment, Ruby."

Her eyes widened and then heated. "Really?" she breathed. She leaned over and looked at my groin.

I snorted. "Of course. My God, I haven't touched a woman in years, and you are not just any woman."

"How many years, Vander?" She suddenly appeared completely sober.

"I don't know, Ruby. Many. Do you really want to have this conversation? Is it really relevant?"

"I think I'd just like to know all the ways you continued living your life when you left me behind, that's all," she spat out.

I knew this conversation was overdue, but this was not the place for it. I don't even know why I said anything about other women, other than the aching drive inside me to drag all our shit out into the open and push her to communicate. Some small part of me thought my abstinence might convince her that I only wanted her.

"Let's continue this conversation in the car, Ruby-mine," I spoke firmly. It was more than safe for me to get up, there was no longer anything to hide.

On the way to the car, I kept her hand firmly tucked into the crook of my arm. Her body vibrated with emotion. I bought that a decade ago, I knew I did, but I wasn't looking forward to it. More than anything, I didn't want to say the wrong thing. All I could do was be honest and let the chips fall.

Lack of communication had always been our downfall.

Chapter 20 – Nameless, Faceless, Forgotten

<u>Ruby</u>

I ground my teeth together as we walked back to the car. I tried to pull my hand away from him, but he held firm. Rage, grief, fear, despair, distress, rejection, heartbreak, all the feelings I locked in that tiny box, and pushed deep into the pit of my stomach so many years before, broke out, and the force of them physically rocked me.

Emotions vibrated through me as he unlocked the passenger side door. I slid inside without looking at him. He reached out and ran his hand over my curls, and I shuddered at his touch, wondering how many others his hands had touched since they'd last touched me.

My hands trembled violently. I fumbled with my seatbelt, securing it just as he opened his door. I clenched my hands into fists to steady them, pushed my heels into the floor, and pressed my back against the seatback to ground myself.

You're okay Ruby. You'll be home soon.

When he slid into the driver's seat, I swiveled my head to look out the window, in part because I didn't want to look at him, in part because I did not want to break down in front of him.

He reached for my hand, but I yanked my arm away from him.

"Just take me home," I gritted out.

I heard him sigh as he started the car.

Vander navigated in and out of the narrow streets until we reached the highway, and the hum of the engine filled the space between us.

I watched the world spin by, the lights of the oncoming cars blurring as my eyes filled over and over. Every ounce of pain he ever caused me leached out of the box, and I feared I would never get the lid back on.

I relived watching him leave me at the train station, and my heart broke for the girl sitting and screaming in her car afterwards, too distraught to drive.

Tears ran unheeded down my cheeks.

I retasted the bile that rose in my throat when I saw the evidence of his moving on with other girls before I slammed the monitor off.

I struggled to take a deep breath, but my lungs were frozen.

I stood in the cold watching him walk away from me yet again without looking back, without a text or a phone call, shredding my already broken heart.

A sob broke from my throat. I wheezed in a breath and tried to fill my lungs. I tipped my chin up and dug the heels of my hands into the seat as I choked back the distressed noises coming from my throat.

I heard his pained whisper of my name in real time.

Again, I sat in Spuds and let go of Drew, and all we shared, the love and family we might have made, if I'd been able to let Vander go.

My face flamed with the shame of what I denied my son.

For someone who walked away *without looking back.*

For someone who showed up out of the deep blue expecting to pick up where we left off, no matter the agony he inflicted on me.

I clenched my hands into fists on my lap and stared straight ahead. I needed to end this.

"You. Left. Me." I bit out, my voice thick with saliva and tears.

"Ruby..."

"No!" I spoke harshly, slashing my hand through the space between us. "You don't get to talk. You went on with your life. You finished school, hooked up with other women, got married, and had a child. Only when I happened to stumble into your space at the conference, did I even register for you."

"That's not true, Ruby," he stated firmly.

I glanced at him incredulously, then turned back to the darkness outside. "You looked me up after your divorce?" I asked bitterly. "You thought, 'Hey! I wonder whatever happened to that girl I promised to love forever?' That never crossed your mind?" I shook my head. "Bet I was an easy lay, a trip down memory fucking lane-"

"Ruby! It wasn't like that-"

I turned to him then, a scream locked and loaded in my throat, when a sliver of cognizance urged caution while he was driving. I took a breath.

"Just take me home. I'm not doing this with you again."

"Can I talk? Can I explain?" His tone had taken on a hint of the desperation I lived with daily.

"I don't want to hear about her," I scoffed. "I don't want to hear about any of them. Tell me, did you hook up with Miss Soft Voice? Was she next on your hit list after me?"

"Who is Miss Soft Voice?" He asked exasperated.

"She was at the conference. I saw the way she looked at you, saw you think about it, before you found me in the lobby."

"Ah."

"Ah," I mimicked, then gagged, bending over my bent knees. "Oh, God!"

"Ruby! Ruby, no, baby. I never slept with her. She's one of my consultants. There's nothing personal between us. Never has been."

"I'm not your baby," I cried, turning to really look at him for the first time.

His eyes were wide, the lines around his mouth burrowed deeply behind the shadow of his beard, and his lips were compressed into a straight line.

"You'll always be mine, Ruby," he stated softly but firmly.

"You left me!" I screeched, the raw pain of more than three decades of abandonment that began with my mother, and ended with him, echoed within the close confines of the car. I clasped my hands over my ears and bent low over my lap.

It's okay, Ruby. You're okay. I live and uh, move, in my ... I'm free...

My breath came in shuddering gasps.

Home. I need to go home.

I heard the ticking of the indicator and felt the car slow.

No, no, no, no, no! I want to go home. I need to get home.

I took time to breathe, to steady myself, then readied myself to sit up and calmly insist that he take me home.

By the time the car stopped, I was somewhat steadier. I sat up and looked around. He had parked in the empty lot of an industrial building that had closed for the night. I scanned the dark, empty space surrounding us.

"Oh, no," I gasped.

I didn't know where we were, nobody else was there, and anybody I imagined might be there was no one I wanted to meet. The sickening prickle of my blood draining from my face met the congealed dread in my stomach.

I yanked my seatbelt and stabbed at the button to release it. Without taking my eyes off the windows, I scrambled across the seat away from the door. I pressed my back against Vander's side, keeping my eyes on the window.

"Get me out of here," I panted. I swiveled my head, scanning everything I could see through the darkness outside, so afraid to look, more afraid not to.

"Ruby," he whispered. "What is happening?"

147

I twisted my neck to meet his eyes. His widened when they met mine.

"Get me out of here, Vander! This is not a safe place!" I beseeched him.

He nodded once, acquiescing. "Okay, Ruby. I've got you, baby." He leaned across me, grasped the middle seatbelt, and secured it around my waist.

I leaned forward with my face in my hands and whimpered.

He was taking too long. I could hear my breath rapidly rasping in and out.

He started the car.

Headlights entered the deserted street.

I dug my fingers into his thigh. "Oh, God!"

He stretched his arm across my chest, pressing me back into the seat, and wrapped his hand around my outer thigh. I grasped his arm crossed over my breasts with my other hand, curling my fingers into his bicep. I squeezed my eyes shut. My chest cavity emptied of everything but the pounding of my heart.

"You're okay, Ruby-mine. I've got you, koukla mou."

"Don't let go," I gasped, clinging to his limbs and closing my eyes against the outside world. I shuddered as the oncoming headlights registered across my closed lids.

"Never," he affirmed, his voice gruff. "Never, Ruby-mine."

I pulled in half a breath, then another, and another, until I filled my lungs.

Vander pulled back onto the main road, then the highway.

The smooth rumble of the familiar highway, bringing me closer to home with every passing second, slowly eased the panic inside me. When it abated to a tolerable level, a familiar, bone deep weariness took hold.

I leaned my head on his wide shoulder and slightly loosened my death grip on his limbs. His solid presence steadied me.

Twenty minutes later, we crossed the city border into Milltown.

"I'd like to stop somewhere and talk. Is there somewhere that you would consider safe for us to do that?"

148

My heart skipped in my chest. "If you take me home, I promise, I won't get out of the car until you've had your say. Please take me home."

He rubbed his hand up and down my thigh. "Okay, Ruby mou. Okay."

In the driveway, he rolled the windows down a bit and turned off the ignition. I stayed where I was. Still feeling exposed, I did not want to sit close to the car door, but my breath came easy.

Still stroking my thigh, he asked softly, "What happened there?"

I leaned my head back on the seat. "I don't want to talk about it."

"What do you want to know, Ruby? I'll tell you anything or everything. Whatever you need to know to move forward. There is only one truth I want you to know right now if you'll let me give you that."

"Okay," I murmured tiredly. "Tell me."

"Twenty years ago, I honestly believed you didn't love me enough to make a life with me, and that was why you weren't coming for the summer. Nothing else made sense to me."

I stayed quiet. I promised I would hear him, and I would, but that didn't mean I would be willing to open myself up again to the soul-destroying pain only he was capable of inflicting on me.

"I failed three courses that first semester back," he stated.

I flinched and he continued.

"I nearly flunked out of my program entirely. In hindsight, I wish I had transferred here, but I truly believed you didn't want me. I moved on because I didn't know a different choice existed for me."

I closed my eyes, swallowed down the tears struggling to rise in my throat, and nodded. I could understand that.

"After the conference, I didn't look back because I knew if I didn't leave right that second that I would abandon my son. I thought of nothing else that whole weekend and came perilously close to doing just that. I couldn't live with that."

I understood that as well. I nodded.

"I didn't contact you because I was stuck there, you were stuck here, and I wanted you to have a chance to build a life with a man who could put you first. I felt I owed it to you."

149

That.

That I would not accept, and I shook my head to make sure he knew it.

I looked at him, expecting to see sorrow, regret, and resignation, but found only determination.

It scared me.

He would not make this easy for either of us.

I took a deep breath to try to clear my head of the leaden heaviness, but fatigue rendered my voice dull and monotone.

"You broke me. You broke my faith in what I believed we were. The only thing you didn't break was my love for you. But my love for you annihilated my chance at happiness and having a family of my own." I paused. "I don't think we can get past the pain of our history. I don't trust you, Vander. I don't trust you with me, and I definitely don't trust you with Jace."

He nodded and squeezed my thigh. "That's fair, Ruby."

His arm still banded across my chest like a seatbelt, and I still clung to him like a life raft. "Do you think you bear any responsibility for what happened between us? If you had told me you were sick, if you had messaged me after the conference, things would have been different."

"I know that, too."

He continued softly. "You've lost faith in us. I understand that. I lost faith, too. That's what happened twenty years ago. I could blame you for that and refuse to open myself up again. At the conference, I thought the exact same thing, but one look at the pain on your face told me I'd fucked up and misread the situation."

I nodded. I owned part of the blame, but it didn't change the cesspool of pain between us.

He continued. "Isn't it possible you are misreading this situation and you're going to regret it if you don't allow us to have our shot?"

I pulled in a shuddering breath. He dangled the proverbial carrot within my reach, the one I'd longed to taste my entire adult life. I feared its aftereffects more than I desired it.

"There's one significant difference between us, moro mou." The endearment slipped out involuntarily. "You went on with your life. I didn't."

He snorted and his dark eyes flashed. "Really, Ruby?"

I'd poked the bear. This Vander, I knew: a little short-tempered, sarcastic at times, unwilling to accept anything he considered bullshit. Well, I had a temper, too.

"How many?" I demanded. "How many women, Vander?"

"Too fucking many, Ruby," he bit out harshly.

I flinched, but he continued on undaunted.

"All nameless, faceless, and forgotten because they weren't fucking you. I've been lonely my entire adult life, except for Georgie, because I didn't have you."

A light shudder traveled through me.

He sighed and bent his neck to press his temple to the top of my head. "I haven't touched a woman in more than six years because the substitutes could no longer take the edge off my loneliness. I bought a house for us in Bayview Village that I haven't done anything to because I'm waiting for you to tell me how you want it. I don't have friends here. I work, I work out, I go home. Alone. When George is here, I live. Other than that, I focus on my work, and I exist. That's how well I've moved on."

My heart ached. "I don't want that for you," I admitted.

He nuzzled my hair. "I didn't want it for you, either."

It dawned on me, then, what he'd sought to spare me by walking away the second time. I still disagreed with his decision, but I understood it better. My heart ached for his loneliness. At least I shared my life with Jace, Yiayia, Amber, Alex, Angus, and Minty.

I unlatched my seat belt and twisted around to face him. Putting my back to the window caused another spike of anxiety, but I needed to hug him. Winding my arms around his neck, I tucked my head under his chin and hugged him close. His hands came around my back and cradled me closer. A tremor rippled through his long body and he blew out a long, slow, breath. His heart pounded beneath my cheek. He lay his cheek atop my head, and I felt safe, cocooned away from the outside.

I didn't want him to hurt.

After awhile, I gently disengaged and moved away from him. His hands followed me lightly, until I was out of his reach. I opened the car door and stepped out, scanning my environment.

The nights were getting cooler. I wrapped my arms around my waist.

"Ruby?" He questioned.

I bent down and looked at him. His dark eyes held light and hope, while mine were dark and dull. "I can't answer that question right now, Vander."

He took a steadying breath but held my gaze. "That's okay, Ruby-mine. We've got all the time in the world."

I froze, staring at him.

That was patently untrue.

Things happened unexpectedly all the time.

"Are you tired? Are you okay to drive?"

His eyes skittered between mine. "Of course, I'm okay to drive."

"How far away is your house?"

I looked at my watch, then looked out at the street.

What if I never saw him again?

How could I leave it like this?

"What's going on right now, Ruby?"

I bent back down to look at his handsome face. "I'm scared something is going to happen to you." I placed my palm over his cross. Suddenly I wanted him to wear it. I started to tug it over my head.

"What are you doing?" Exasperation, confusion, alarm, I could hear all of it in his voice.

"I want you to wear this and text me when you get home."

He laughed. "I'm not taking it. We've covered this subject before."

I stopped fumbling and narrowed my eyes at him. "Don't laugh at me," I snapped.

His face grew serious and stern. "I'm not laughing at you, Ruby. I'm just trying to keep up with your thoughts and emotions."

"Maybe I'll prove to be too much for you," I sniped at him.

He leaned towards me slightly. "Try me," he retorted. "And I'll show you just how well I can handle you."

He gave me a heated look, and I huffed in disbelief.

"Give me a kiss, then go into the house and lock up," he demanded. "I will text you when I'm home."

My eyes bugged out of my head, and the corner of his mouth curled up. I stood up straight and drummed my fingers on the roof of the car. That bitch, 'What if', spun her stories in my head. I couldn't leave him like this.

I bent down and crawled across the seat until we were face-to-face, a handful of inches between us. He remained still, watching me, his gaze steady.

Even as I watched, his mouth softened, and the deeply etched lines around his mouth eased.

I did that. I did that for him.

I inhaled, filling my lungs with the heady scent of ouzo and his aftershave.

"I do love you, Vander," I said with a soft sigh.

"I love you, too, Ruby-mine," he murmured.

I grasped his wrists, so he couldn't prolong the kiss, and gently pressed my mouth to his, unmoving. One breath, two, sharing air, coming home. I inhaled deeply, the oxygen seeming to go straight to my head. I could stay linked to him like this forever.

His wrists flexed in my hands with his desire to be free. I squeezed them tighter and slowly pulled away before he could touch me.

Eyes that moments ago were warm and steady, now burned with heat, and it lit the fuse of desire low in my belly. My nipples tightened; my panties dampened.

I instinctively leaned towards him, licking my bottom lip, and his full, soft lips parted, inviting me home. Suddenly realizing I was succumbing to his charm, I released his wrists abruptly, and drew back.

He moved fast. With one hand behind my head, the other at my back, he yanked me forward and covered my mouth firmly with his.

I cried out against his mouth in surprise, but he swallowed it. I pushed against his chest even as I opened my mouth under his and hungrily stroked his velvet tongue with mine. Curling my fingers into his shirt, I hung on.

His hands gripped me tightly as his mouth moved expertly over mine, and I gave into the piercingly bittersweet pleasure of being in his arms.

I'd forgotten how right it felt to be near him. Mouth to mouth, chest to chest, I desperately wanted to line up the rest of our body parts, cradle his pelvis with mine, twine my legs around his.

The faint taste of ouzo, the contrast between his sweet mouth and the soft rasp of his beard, his tongue tangling with mine, all worked together to silence the cautionary voice inside. I wound my arms around his shoulders and pressed my aching breasts against his hard chest. I squirmed in his arms and clamped my thighs together in an attempt to appease the demand at their apex.

His big hand, at my head, held me steady while he nipped and sipped at my lips, drawing my tongue into his mouth, licking his way past every barrier my brain attempted to erect. Oh, to give myself over to him, to not think, to let him take control! His other hand ran smoothly up and down my spine, from the nape of my neck to the top of my ass. I arched under his hand and pulled him closer.

He groaned deep in his throat and gripped my hair. Pulling my head back gently, he bent to trail his lips along my jaw, drag his tongue along my throat, press his lips to the juncture between my throat and my shoulder, his beard abrading my sensitive skin.

My head fell back into his palm.

I was ready.

Ready to take off my clothes and straddle him in the front seat of his car, parked in the driveway of the house, in which my son and my yiayia were (hopefully) sleeping.

Reality hit me like a blast of icy water, and I pulled back, my eyes wide. This was too much, he was too much, irresistible even. I scanned his face, looking for clues to I don't know what, but he only looked back at me steadily, the fire temporarily banked.

"Goodnight, Ruby-mine," he muttered gruffly. "I'll text you when I get home."

Twenty minutes later I got a single word text.

Home.

I realized I'd been so wrapped up in reliving his kiss that I'd forgotten to worry. I sent back an equally short reply, *Thank you.*

I climbed wearily into my bed, knowing that kiss had unlocked the door, and fell asleep within minutes.

Chapter 21 - Emoji Man

Ruby

Sunday morning, I woke bleary-eyed and exhausted with an emotional hangover. A soft knock sounded at my door.

"Come in," I called.

Jace stuck his head in the door. "Hey, Momma. How did the meeting go?"

I lifted my arm in invitation, and he jumped into the bed beside me, tucking his head onto my shoulder.

"Good, pouli mou." I stroked his unruly curls back from his face.

"You going to do it?" He asked curiously.

"Maybe not with that company. I'm going to call the other one and see what they say."

"Yiayia said you were out with a friend last night."

I stiffened, then cleared my throat. "The man who took me to the meeting is someone I used to know in university a long time ago."

"Yiayia said he used to be important to you a long time ago."

Frigging Yiayia.

"He was."

I always strived to be honest with Jace. I never wanted to break his faith in me. I scratched his scalp lightly.

"Is he still?"

Jace sounded curious, not worried, but I wanted to be sure. I blew out a breath. "Would it bother you if he was?"

"I don't know," he answered honestly. "Is he a good man?"

I nodded firmly. "He is. He is the best kind of man. Kind, sweet, hard-working, an excellent father..."

At this I felt Jace go rigid. "He has kids?"

I continued to stroke his hair and kissed the top of his forehead. "One. A boy a couple of years older than you."

Jace sat up and looked at me. "So... if you guys got married, I'd have a brother?"

I laughed out loud. "Jace, we haven't even been on a proper date, and you're marrying me off? You want a brother that badly?"

"No, I have Alex," he answered seriously. "But I'm growing up and I don't want you to be alone." He paused. "Can I meet him?"

I chuckled nervously. "You want to check him out? See if he's good enough?"

"Yup," he agreed.

I thought about it. "Let's just see what happens over the next little while, and if I think it's necessary, I'll introduce you."

"Okay, momma. Are we still going out for breakfast?"

Sundays were my only guaranteed day off, so Jace and I usually went out for breakfast before heading to the pet store to stock up on whatever he needed for his fish tank. It was our 'catching up on Jace's life and making plans for the week ahead' time.

"Yeah, moro mou. Give me twenty minutes."

Half an hour later, I pulled into a lucky empty spot at the West End Diner. We'd been coming here since Jace was a baby. Stepping through the door, the familiar chaos welcomed us inside.

"Ela, moro mou!" Maria, the owner, barrelled down on Jace. "So big! So strong!" She pinched his bicep and Jace grinned. "Ela, agori-mou. Come to the kitchen while Mommy has some rest." Maria turned to me, her eyes kind as always. "Have some rest, koritzaki mou. I'll put our boy to work."

She walked off with him, and I heard her giving him the rundown. "I have made four desserts for today. You must try them all and tell Thia which one-"

The slamming of the kitchen door cut off the rest of her sentence, but it was the same routine every week. Maria and her family had watched Jace grow up, and they'd been dragging him into the kitchen for extra treats since he was three years old.

Maria's daughter, Voula, who was my age, directed me to sit at the booth they reserved for staff and family while she brought me a coffee. She slid into the booth across from me and leaned her elbows on the table. "I have four minutes. Tell me about tall, dark, and handsome. Elisavet told me he came into her store to buy you dolmadakia," she demanded in her deep, raspy voice.

I rolled my eyes, and Voula laughed. Her laugh was just as loud and obnoxious as mine. Many were the occasions we caught hell for laughing in church. It was with Voula, I got caught climbing out the window of the church during Greek school. It was with Voula, I smoked my first cigarette, and it was with Voula, that I committed my first and only act of vandalism, by covering her first boyfriend's front yard in toilet paper when he decided to move on with another girl without breaking up with her first.

When you share that kind of history with someone, they feel entitled to the details of your life. Even apart from that, our shared Greekness was enough for her to demand answers.

"He's my university boyfriend. He moved here and we're catching up."

"He's hot, hmm? Has Jace met him yet?"

I frowned at her, unusually irritated by this line of questioning. "No, Voula, of course not. I haven't seen him in years and I'm going to introduce him to my son?"

"Right, right, of course." She looked around; people were lining up at the counter. "Shit! I gotta go. We'll talk soon."

I was rethinking the wisdom of going there when I got a notification on my cell phone. I opened the message without thinking.

Vander: Good morning, Ruby-mine.

I moved my thumb and hit the text box to reply, then thought better of it.

Vander: I know you've seen my message, and I've seen your dots. Don't overthink it.

Ruby: I'm not!

Vander: Good. How's your morning been?

Ruby: Fine.

Vander: What are you doing?

Ruby: I'm out for breakfast with Jace.

Vander: He's there with you right now?

Ruby: Well, he's in the kitchen with the owner. They're Greek.

Vander: Ah. Is that typical?

Ruby: We've been coming here since he was a baby. It was one of the first outings I was able to do on my own with him.

Vander: Do they know about your agoraphobia?

Ruby: Is there anything that happens that the Greek community doesn't know?

Vander: True.

Ruby: They know about you, too.

Vander: What do they know about me, koukla mou?

I could almost hear his deep voice, laced with humour.

Ruby: Elisavet told them you tried to buy me dolmadakia. Lol. She says you're very handsome.

Vander: I am very handsome.

Ruby: You have a big head.

Vander: That, too.

I thought he was making a reference to his other head, and I didn't know how to respond. If I called him on it, he'd tease me mercilessly. Did I want to head into sexual innuendo territory with him? I mean, obviously I wanted to, but should I?

Vander: Stop thinking.

Ruby: Don't tell me what to do.

Vander: Can I see you today?

Ruby: Are you crazy? Were you not there last night?

Vander: Were you?

Ruby: Yes, I was the one having a panic attack.

Vander: Oh. I thought you were referring to afterwards.

Ruby: You're very pushy. You've grown into your Greekness.

Vander: You better believe it. Better for you to just give in. You're only going to exhaust yourself fighting me. Can I see you today?

I thought about him sitting in his house by himself and my heart broke a little bit, but if I met up with him, I'd get immediately sucked into his vortex. I wasn't ready. Though, I admitted to myself that it was inevitable.

Ruby: Sunday is family dinner day. Amber and Alex are coming over.

Vander: Tomorrow?

Ruby: I don't know.

Vander: Make a plan with me, Ruby-mine, or I'll show up every day.

Ruby: Hang on! Let me think! I don't have my planner with me. See? See what you do to me? I never forget my planner. Ever. I once had to take a phone call during a pap smear. You're making me crazy. I can't think straight when you're around.

Vander: You think too much. Today or tomorrow? What's it going to be?

Ruby: Let me text you later.

Vander: You'll text me?

I heard the anxiety in his voice in my head.

Ruby: Yes. I promise. After dinner.

Vander: Love you, Ruby-mine. Talk later.

My thumb hovered over the keyboard. I didn't know what to write.

Vander: Stop thinking.

Ruby: Fuck off!

Vander: I look forward to the time when I can punish you for your insolence.

Ruby: You did not just say that.

Vander: I did, and I will. Be warned.

Ruby: You're threatening me with battery?

Vander: You'll love every second of it.

I squirmed in my seat, noticing the dampness in my panties.

Ruby: I'm buying a vibrator.

Vander: I'll go with you. We'll buy lots of toys.

"Hey, momma."

I tossed my phone straight up in the air. Jace reached out and caught it before handing it back to me. "You okay, momma? Your face is kind of red."

"I'm good, agapimeno mou," I gasped. *Shitfuckdamn!* "You just startled me." Quick, change the subject. "What are you going to order? How much did you eat back there?"

One side of his mouth tipped up in a mischievous smile. "I told Maria I wouldn't order breakfast if she made me eat all four desserts, so she said I had to take one bite of each and take the rest home." He poked the Styrofoam container on the table between us and smiled.

My cell phone buzzed in my hand and Jace looked at it quizzically. "One minute, agori mou."

Vander: Ruby?

Ruby: Jace is here. Talk later.

161

He sent a heart and I barely held in my laugh. I never would have pegged Vander for an emoji man.

I rested my elbows on the table and tuned in to my son. "Give me all your news, agapimeno."

His dark eyes skittered across my face. "I have some forms for the Adventure Club."

I fought to hide my trepidation. "Oh, yeah? Permission forms?"

"Yup!" He smiled, relieved. "There are two options. You can sign a separate permission form for each field trip, or a blanket permission form for all of them."

My eyes bugged out of my head. "A blanket permission form? Are you crazy?"

Jace's dark eyes sparkled with humor, and he laughed. "I knew you'd react like that! I got the individual forms."

I nodded emphatically and huffed. "A blanket form!" I exclaimed, shaking my head in disbelief. I threw out my arm in a sweeping invitation. "Here, take my son anywhere you want. Helicopter tour? Sure! Tree-trekking? Why not! Bungee-jumping? Sounds good! Cliff-diving? Make sure you take one last picture of him before he jumps!"

Jace wrapped his arms around his skinny belly and leaned towards me over the table, his face split wide with his laughter. He enjoyed making me squirm.

"I love you, Momma."

I smiled back at him and reached for his hand across the table. Even his hands were starting to feel different. My little boy was growing up and grabbing life by the horns. Though the anxiety crippled me, I needed to ensure I stayed out of his way.

Chapter 22 –Empty Chairs

<u>Ruby</u>

Once home, Jace and I released his new fish into the tank. I adored that tiny, perfectly balanced world. I was almost envious. We added plants and took plants away, got a bigger tank when warranted, balanced the chemicals, periodically changed up their environment, and provided everything they needed. I spent hours in front of that tank, watching them swim back and forth, and soaked up the peace.

I tore myself away from the tank and directed Jace to finish his homework. Amber and Alex would be there soon, and once Alex arrived, all homework bets were off.

I contemplated confronting Yiayia about talking to Jace, but she hadn't said anything wrong. Her talking to Jace mostly irritated me because it was necessary. Somebody had to say something, it should have been me, but I resented the pressure to conform to someone else's timeframe. Vander was pushing me faster than I wanted to go.

I snorted out a laugh. Twenty years in the making could not under any circumstances be considered fast, but a lot of rubble lay on the road between then and now, with precious little high or even solid ground to balance it out.

Had we been together all these years, there would certainly have been rough patches, but I had to believe there would have been long stretches of good times, too. Our history, laid out the way it was right now, resembled a broken road, and I wasn't eager to travel it again.

Yiayia came in from the backyard, our large colander tucked under her arm. She walked slowly, almost shuffling, her back stooped. Her appetite decreased a little more every year, and she had become quite thin. My irritation with her melted away.

"What have you got, Yiayia?" I asked.

Her head snapped up. "Koritzaki mou! I didn't know you was back!" She picked up her pace. "I got eggplants, lots of beans, and the last of the beets."

I took the colander from her and peeked inside. "You got a good haul, today." I carried it into the kitchen, her shuffling steps sounding behind me. I set it down on the counter and turned to see her bright eyes fixed on my face. Hopeful.

"How was last night, koritzaki?" She asked brightly.

I fought to hide my smile. "Interesting, Yiayia. But I don't think he's the man for me."

Her face fell, and I could hear the disappointment in her voice. "Why not, koukla?"

I shrugged. "He just isn't able to give me what I need right now."

She grunted. "What you need?"

"Well," I went on, carefully choosing my words. "I really wanted to get things moving right away, but he says it'll be three to six months before he can start and that even then it might be slow-moving."

Yiayia stood straighter. "Is that right?" She asked indignantly.

"Yup! It's not unexpected, Yiayia. He's a busy man."

"Huh! Too busy, maybe!" She threw the beans into the sink, slid her ruby ring off her finger and placed it carefully into the little dish beside the sink, then began scrubbing the life out of the beans.

I needed to let her off the hook before she destroyed our dinner. She would be less than pleased with me if my little joke ruined her beans. I leaned my hip against the counter beside her.

"Why are you so upset, Yiayia?"

She threw the beans down and turned to look at me. "A man shows up after twenty years for his girl he better be ready!"

"What are you talking about, Yiayia? I just met the man."

Yiayia side-eyed me for a moment, then caught on. "Ela, koritzi mou, I spank you for that!"

She held up her hand and waved her palm at me. A palm that had never once touched me with anything less than love. I'd been on the receiving end of a thrown slipper a time or two, but never her hand.

I laughed and hugged her. "That's what you get for being nosy."

"Ach," she shrugged me off and went back to her beans. "I'll chop you like the onions."

I laughed and hugged her from behind until she patted my arms crossed over her chest. This woman.

"Okay, Yiayia. I liked him and I think I could work with him. He thinks we have a viable business model, but he doesn't have a consultant free for three to six months."

"Why you don't go with Vander's company?"

My mouth fell open in surprise. "How do you know what Vander does?" I passed her the dishtowel to dry her hands.

She smiled sneakily and folded the dishtowel over the sink. "Elisavet. She has the internet. We look him up on the lap pad."

"Elisavet uses the internet?" I raised my eyebrows. "Good for her!"

"Ach, she talk too much, work too little."

I snorted out a laugh. "You jealous, Yiayia? You want an iPad for yourself? I have one you can have."

She turned and patted my cheek. The top of her head only came to my nose. We used to be the same height.

"I don't know, poulaki mou. I'm happy with my cell phone. Tell me about Vander."

I sighed. "I don't know what to tell you, Yiayia. He wants to be together, and I just don't know if I can, at least," I held up my hand to stop the torrent of words poised on her lips, "not right now."

"You still love him, poulaki mou," she stated. She pulled out the cutting boards and placed one in front of each of us.

I sighed again, deeper, then admitted, "I will always love him, Yiayia. I will never love another, but I can't handle seeing his back again."

"You think he walk away again?" She asked incredulously.

I held my hands out to my sides. "What, in the past twenty years, has he done to prove otherwise?"

"He move his business all the way across the country, psychi mou," she peered at me seriously, her eyes concerned.

"How do you know that?" I asked, exasperated.

She grinned. "Elisavet."

I groaned and pulled out the knife to slice the eggplant. "What are we making, moussaka or melitzanosalata?"

"I make Amber moussaka, poulaki mou."

I threw my arm around her shoulders, suddenly feeling sorry for my sister. She didn't seem right lately.

"How about we make roast beef as well? We'll have a regular feast today."

Her eyes lit up. "Good idea. Jace, he look skinny lately."

Amber and Alex arrived shortly afterwards. Amber's face went a little green when she caught sight of the piles of fried eggplant, making me happy I suggested roast beef.

Yiayia sent us out of the kitchen to 'have rest', and I settled with Amber on the front step.

I bumped her lightly with my shoulder. "How are you?"

She gazed off into the distance, her arms wrapped around her bent legs. "I don't really know, Ruby." She turned her head and studied me. "How about you? How is it with Vander back on the scene?"

Other than a brief phone call to bring her up to date, we hadn't spoken about Vander.

I shrugged. "I don't know. He wants to be together."

"Yeah?" Her pretty mouth twisted. "He going to stay this time?"

I flinched. "I guess that's the million-dollar question, isn't it?"

She blew out a breath. "I'm sorry. That was uncalled for. The man moved his entire life across the country. I'm thinking he's committed."

My eyebrows rose in surprise. Amber didn't trust, or forgive, easily. "You think I should give him a shot?"

She rolled her lips together, then turned to face me again. "Maybe. Maybe you should consider it."

The sadness in Amber's eyes brought tears to my own. "Honestly," I whispered. "If you and Angus can't make it, what hope is there for any of us?"

She dropped her eyes to look at the ground. "Don't count us out just yet, Ruby."

I felt my eyebrows go up again and wondered at this point if I shouldn't just have them pinned up there permanently. "Are you getting back together?"

She smiled faintly and bumped me lightly with her shoulder. "I guess that's the million-dollar question, isn't it?"

Yiayia called us inside for dinner. Amber and I carried the casserole dishes of moussaka, roast beef, lemon potatoes, and beans to the table, while Yiayia brought in the huge bowl of Greek salad. I don't know how many times I told her the boys wouldn't eat the salad, but she still made enough to feed an army.

Yiayia made the sign of the cross over her chest, the rest of us followed suit, and she immediately began hounding the boys.

"You got your homework done, levendis mou?" Yiayia asked Alex.

Alex grinned at her. "Of course, Yiayia!"

Yiayia narrowed her eyes at him. "You are too charming." She turned to Amber. "He did it?"

"Don't worry, Yiayia," Amber replied, closing her eyes around a bite of lemon potato. "Mm, I love these."

"Ah, bravo!" Yiayia praised her for eating.

Alex grinned at Jace, and the corner of Jace's mouth quirked up.

Yiayia turned back to Alex. "Tell me what you have done for homework today."

167

Jace lifted his plate towards Yiayia. "Yiayia, would you put me a little salad?"

"Of course!" She exclaimed happily. She side-eyed me smugly and piled his plate with Greek salad. I caught Amber's eye across the table and saw humor reflected in their whiskey-colored depths.

The boys talked about the Adventure Club, which Yiayia championed. Amber mentioned her hope to book a short vacation getaway, and we discussed Spuds' prospects of becoming a franchise. Amber and I watched the boys dodge Yiayia's questions about school, homework, and girls, with compliments about the food, or requests for more.

They had to be bursting.

Finally, Amber took pity on them. "You boys can be excused."

They pushed back from the table in unison, and kissed Yiayia on her cheek as they passed to head up to Jace's room.

"They ate well today," Yiayia commented. "I'll ask about homework more often."

Amber and I laughed at the satisfied look on Yiayia's face.

She turned to me and demanded, "Tell me about your date with Vander."

Amber lifted her plate. "More moussaka?"

Yiayia looked at Amber incredulously. "Is not going to work for you!"

I chortled, Amber laughed and Yiayia snorted.

We had love. We had fun. We had companionship. At that moment, all I saw were two empty chairs where Gus and Vander should have been.

Vander

I pushed her too hard.

Seven o'clock was closing in, and she still hadn't texted. Sitting here on the edge of my fucking seat, waiting to hear from her, had me feeling like a teenager.

It was not a comfortable feeling, and this wasn't some teenage crush that would be replaced with another six months down the road. This was Ruby, my Ruby, and I could not afford to fuck things up. I grabbed a beer from the fridge and slipped out onto the deck.

Flopping down heavily into my chair, I propped my bare feet up on the railing. I hated sitting inside by myself. With Georgie around, the impersonal house was tolerable. Without him, the silence bouncing off the walls nearly deafened me. I'd been alone for too damn long, just like Ruby.

What was the difference between us? Why was I willing to jump in and take the chance while she was not?

I struggled to see our situation from her point of view. She said she understood why I didn't follow her when we were in university. She got it that I was operating under a lack of intelligence.

"Ha," I snorted. Excellent choice of words.

Ruby understood, and even agreed, that I had to live where George lived. It was the fact that I didn't contact her. I explained the sacrifice I made for her, but she didn't know that at the time.

For more than a decade, she believed I had abandoned her. Then, after all that time, I marched into her work and expected her to leap into my arms. No wonder she reacted by pushing me away. What a fucking mess. A mess of my own making. If only I listened to my heart and not my head.

For the first time, I realized there was a very real chance she could walk away and take her heart, and mine, with her. The thought alone caused an ache in my chest.

I'd fight.

This time I'd leave no stone unturned, no word unsaid.

My cell buzzed in my hand, and I looked hopefully at the screen, but it was work. I responded then jotted off a quick email directing reception, my personal assistant, and top consultant to a meeting in the morning to address the subject of the email. They also needed to be briefed on the situation with Ruby.

What a fucking joke. I huffed out a laugh. Telling them to fast track her, and not disclose my name. Cloak and dagger, pre-pubescent, neurotic bullshit.

Ah, well, for Ruby, I'd do anything. I wanted her to have her franchising opportunity and knowing her issues, I was the best person to help her navigate the maze.

The phone buzzed again, and I sighed as I checked to see who had responded. Did my people not take a fucking day off? Seeing Ruby's name on the notifications, I sat forward and dropped my feet to the deck.

Ruby: Hi.

I took a deep breath. Just being able to talk to her was a balm.

Vander: Hi, beautiful.

Ruby: Did you forget my name?

She was feeling feisty. Was she teasing or lashing out?

Vander: Is it tattooed on my heart?

Ruby: Maybe it should be.

I snorted. Looked like I would be getting a tattoo. My yiayia would be rolling in her grave.

Vander: You want to get a matching one over your heart?

Ruby: Might be a tad egotistical to have my own name tattooed on my chest.

Vander: Ha-ha. I don't want you to do it anyways. I don't want some man touching your breast.

Ruby: Why would it have to be a man?

Vander: Fine. If you find a female tattoo artist, you can tattoo my name over your heart.

Ruby: Funny guy.

Vander: How was your day with Jace? How was family dinner?

Ruby: It was good.

Vander: Details.

Ruby: You want to know?

I snorted. For fuck's sake.

Vander: Yeah, Ruby. I want to know everything.

Ruby: I can hear your snark.

That made me laugh. God, I loved her.

Vander: I'll dial it back. I want to know. I want to know about your life, your family, your son. I want to know everything.

Ruby: We had dinner with Amber and my nephew, Alex. Alex doesn't like to do homework and Yiayia hounds him about it. Jace and Alex discovered that they could distract her by asking for more food or complimenting her cooking. Jace ate a mountainous pile of salad for his perfidy.

Vander: He asked for salad?

Ruby: Yup. With all the offerings on the table, he panic-asked for salad. Poor kid.

Vander: And did it work?

Ruby: For them, yes. Amber and I tried it when she started questioning me about you, but it didn't work for us. Yiayia was onto them the whole time, but she took the loss in exchange for the food win.

Vander: I miss my yiayia.

Ruby: She passed?

Vander: Long time ago.

Ruby: Your parents are okay?

My parents loved Ruby, and they were almost as devastated as I was when she dropped out of school. They gave me the money to fly out to see her and had encouraged me to go to her for the summer. My mother told me, more than once, there was more going on.

Fuck me. Forget listening to my heart, I should have just listened to my mom.

Vander: They're good. Retired now and spending half the year at their home in Greece. I'll take you. You and Jace and Georgie.

Ruby: You're getting ahead of yourself.

Vander: I'm two decades behind.

Her dots appeared and disappeared a few times. I hoped she didn't start with all the reasons she couldn't be with me.

Ruby: Tell me about Georgie.

171

I blew out a breath, surprised and relieved at the turn in the conversation.

Vander: Tell you what: we'll take turns asking questions and we'll both answer them so I can get to know Jace, too.

Ruby: Why?

Vander: Because he's yours. And you're mine, I thought. *But first, you were telling me what Yiayia was saying about me.*

Ruby: Was I?

Vander: You were. Just tell me one thing: Is she for me or against me?

Ruby's dots appeared and disappeared once again while she decided how to respond.

Ruby: For you. How old is George?

I grinned. I'd add a visit to Yiayia to tomorrow's agenda.

Vander: George turned 13 on March 9th. How old is Jace?

Ruby: He'll be 11 on December 16th.

I was gratified that she finally showed an interest in Georgie. The boys had a love of skateboarding and video games in common. I brainstormed ideas for things to do with the boys together. I wondered if Jace would like to try rock climbing at the indoor facility where I trained.

Vander: When should I meet Jace?

Ruby: Vander, I don't know if I can do this. You tie me up in knots. This relationship is unbalanced, and I don't want to be the one who is more invested.

Vander: Our relationship is a knot. It's a fucking mess. I realize this and I'm going to sort it out. You're not more invested. If anything, I'm more invested. I moved my entire life here based on nothing more than a dream. I didn't even know you were single when I picked up and moved, just on the off chance that there might be an opportunity for us sometime in the future. I'm not going anywhere.

Fifteen agonizing minutes passed while I waited for her reply.

Ruby: I'll see you tomorrow?

My cheeks filled up with air and I blew it out forcefully. Longest fifteen minutes of my life.

Vander: Yeah, koukla. You'll see me tomorrow.

Ruby: Goodnight, Vander.

Vander: Goodnight, Ruby-mine. I love you.

Dots, no dots, dots, no dots, dots...

Ruby: *I love you, too.*

Fuck, that felt good. Feet back up on the railing, I leaned back in my chair and took a long pull of my beer. Two nights in a row. We were making progress. I thought back to the taste and feel of her lips, and re-read our texts from the evening, committing all I learned about Jace to memory.

It was a good night.

Chapter 23 – Be Here

<u>Ruby</u>

I cleaned up, then settled at the corner table with my notes and brochures, determined to move ahead. The door opened, bringing the sounds of the busy street and a wedge of afternoon sun inside. My head snapped up in anxious anticipation, but it was just Minty and her girls.

I blew out a disgruntled breath, half relieved, half disappointed. They looked disgruntled. I waved them over to my table. "Join my pity party. Sit your butts down and tell me your troubles."

"Are you like a bartender? People spill their troubles to you?" Junie joked.

I shrugged. "It's a potato bar, for some people it's close enough."

Minty sat down beside me, and her presence, as always, comforted me. Junie and Willa took the chairs opposite.

"What's wrong, Ruby?" Minty asked, rubbing a slow circle over my back.

I sighed. There were too many to mention, and none I wanted to talk about, yet. I chose the least of my problems. "Franchise trouble."

Junie's eyebrows shot up. "You're looking to franchise this place?"

I snorted. "Trying to. It's not going all that well."

"For what it's worth, I think you've got an excellent concept with this place," Willa offered. Willa was one of those people who always made you feel good. She just had that sunny way about her.

"Thanks," I replied gratefully. "I think so, too. I've run this place since I was twenty years old. I'm ready to take it to the next level and get out from behind the counter."

"Can we help?" Junie offered. "With marketing or design?" Junie was full of energy, and she would be awesome to have on my team, if I ever actually needed one.

"Thanks, Junie. I'll definitely let you know," I smiled anxiously. There were so many decisions to make, it was easy to feel overwhelmed by it all. I needed to take the attention off myself.

"Now. Tell Ruby what's brought you three stomping in here like you're ready to bite some poor, unsuspecting potato in half?"

Minty scowled. "Asshole client!"

All three of us looked at her in astonishment, and then laughed.

She sat primly, her small, enigmatic smile on her face. She continued, "You cannot deny that today he was particularly obnoxious?"

"No, he was!" Junie assured her. "I'm just not used to hearing you swear."

Minty shrugged. "It's what you both call him in the office. In my head, he's 'asshole'. I'm not even sure what his real name is anymore."

I laughed. Minty had surprised me again. It appeared she was a bit of a mama bear with Junie and Willa. "I love you, Minty. I do." I hugged her sideways and stood. "What can I get you guys to eat?"

They left me much more relaxed than they found me. I didn't know Minty's girls well, but what I knew, I liked. Junie was a riot, and Willa, I just wanted to wrap my arms around her.

I sat back down at my table and studied my notes. I really didn't want to wait any longer to get started. I picked up the last brochure and turned it over in my hands.

I had nothing to lose. Vander recommended them and he would not lead me astray. Ten minutes, and one phone call later, I had an appointment with one of their consultants for the following day. Lucky for me they had an opening.

I gathered up my notes into a pile, then heard the door open. I knew without turning that Vander was there. Seeing him was like opening the door a crack to let the sunshine in. I turned to him with a smile.

He stopped dead and stared at me for a moment before his face lost the serious, stern look I'd come to expect. His shoulders dropped and he pushed his hands deep into his pockets, the lines around his mouth softened, and his lips tipped up on one side.

"Hi," I greeted him softly.

"Hi, yourself," he teased me.

"Drink?"

He nodded, and I headed behind the counter to open the door to the back room. My stomach fluttered with excitement. I placed my palm over it to calm it to no avail. I took a deep breath. My brain screamed a warning that I was treading into dangerous territory, but my heart and body charged forward.

God, I felt alive in a way I hadn't in a long, long time.

He sat at the table drumming his fingers on my pile of notes, his dark eyebrows drawn together. He smiled at me when I sat down across from him, and I pushed his drink across the table towards him.

He glanced at the pile and frowned. "I wish you'd let me help you with this."

"I will," I nodded. His face lit up, but I raised my palms and shook my head, realizing he thought I had decided to go with his company. "I don't want to depend on you entirely. I've made an appointment, but I'd like to be able to bounce things off you."

His eyes flickered with something akin to unease, and I rushed to reassure him. "If it's awkward for you, I understand. I don't want to put you in a position where you feel uncomfortable."

He took my hands across the table and looked at me, his dark eyes intense, his face serious. "Ruby, I'd do anything for you. I will do anything for you. I'm all yours."

I moved to pull my hands away, but he held fast. A memory struck me. It was at this very table where I pulled my hands away from Drew's in much the same way. Some latent instinct warned me not to make the same mistake again.

I relaxed my hands in Vander's grip and his expression softened.

I affected him.

My stomach dipped and my heart fluttered in my chest like a bird in a cage. I wrapped my fingers around his and his entire countenance warmed.

The flush of pleasure that washed over me warmed my chest and creeped up my neck to my face. I dipped my chin but couldn't stop my smile.

He stroked my palm with his long fingers and brushed his thumb gently over the back of my hand. His touch felt both new and familiar.

I wondered how we would be together after so many years. I imagined his fingertips trailing across my throat, down between my breasts, over my tummy...my lips parted, and I drew in a quick breath.

He chuckled. "Oh, Ruby. You never could hide what you were thinking. I cannot wait to get you under me."

My head snapped up, and I scanned his face nervously. His smile warmed me. He gave my hands a reassuring squeeze.

"Stay with me, here, baby. Don't get scared," he coached.

I nodded. "I'm trying."

His lips split into a huge grin, his bearded cheeks creasing. "Ah, Ruby-mine, thank you." He leaned in and pinned me beneath his dark gaze. "You'll be okay. You'll be more than okay. I promise you, koukla."

I nodded hesitantly. Was I ready to take a chance? Was it as great a risk as I was making it out to be?

Yes. Yes, it was. Something might happen to George, and Vander would be off like a shot. His business might fail, and he could decide to move back to B.C. His parents might become ill, and he could leave to care for them.

There were so many reasons, good ones, for him to leave, and only one reason for him to stay. Me. I'd never been enough before, had anything really changed?

Protecting myself by walking away seemed like the more prudent choice, but there was risk in that as well. I would not survive seeing him with someone else. I knew he wouldn't continue to live like a monk if I shut this down.

Trapped between Scylla's rock and Charybdis, the beast and the storm, no way out but through, and no sure way to protect my heart... or my mental health.

He broke into my thoughts. "Will you go out with me tomorrow?"

Go out with him? I reined in my catastrophic thoughts and remembered the meeting tomorrow. I briefly considered telling him about it, but decided I wanted to do it on my own this time. Going to the meeting would be enough excitement for me for one day.

"I can't tomorrow," I said slowly, "but I could swing Wednesday or Thursday if you're available."

"I'm available, Ruby, anytime, any place, for anything, for you."

I flushed with pleasure. A warning flashed in the background of my thoughts, but I tuned it out. Maybe, just maybe, this was our time. It wasn't like I could avoid him forever. I'm sure I could send him away, but then I'd be risking running into him in town with someone else. If there's one thing that would send me back into the house for good, it might be that.

Vander

One more stop to make before heading back to the office to work late.

After ringing the doorbell, I took a few steps back and pushed my hands into my pockets to wait.

She opened the door, then skewered me with her eyes. "What took you so long to come see me?"

I chuckled and stepped forward. "You going to invite me in, Thia?"

"Thia? Huh. Since when you call me Thia?" She stood with her hands on her hips.

So feisty. I grinned. I could easily see where Ruby got her fire. I acknowledged the rebuke. "Yiayia. You going to invite me in, Yiayia?"

"Ela, agori mou!" She reached up and smartly patted my cheek, perhaps a little harder than necessary, but at least she smiled into my eyes when she did it. I bent to accept her kiss. "Is good to see you. Come in, poulaki mou. You ate?"

"I'm good, Yiayia."

The other night picking up Ruby, I'd barely taken in the little house. It had not changed in the twenty plus years since I'd stayed there. It even smelled the same.

Regret hit me solidly in the solar plexus, the blow almost physical. This house reflected Ruby and me, like a time capsule from the past, neither of us moving forward despite the steady shifting of the sands of time.

Being immersed in the home where I'd lost my heart and my future, threw me back into the mindset of the twenty-something kid I used to be, the one who barreled in to reclaim his girl. How much hope I had that weekend! More than hope, I came with a mission I was certain I would conquer.

I had not felt that kind of hope and certainty since.

Was anything different this time? Determined not to make the same mistakes, I pondered the differences between then and now.

"Sit down," Yiayia ordered. "You want coffee?"

"I'll take a coffee, Yiayia." I pulled out a chair at the small table where I could easily see her as she moved around the tiny kitchen.

"Ah, bravo, agori mou. Tell me. Why you here now?"

"I moved here."

She paused to peer at him. "Why you move here? Why you leave B.C.? Why you no move to Toronto? Or Montreal?" She drilled me with questions as she kept watch over the small pot of coffee on the stove.

I smiled into her bright eyes and gave it to her straight. "Ruby's not in Toronto or Montreal. I need to be close to Ruby, to be ready for her when she's ready for me."

179

Yiayia quietly attended to the stove for several moments, then placed a Greek coffee and a plate piled high with cookies in front of me. Sitting down, she folded her hands together on the small table.

I took a bite. "So good, Yiayia. No one makes koulouraki like you."

She smiled. "Ah, bravo. Eat. You come to dinner Sunday, then you taste real food. How long since you had real Greek food?"

I suppressed a grin. "It's been a while."

"What you like? Pastitsio? Moussaka? Stuffed peppers? Meatballs? What you want me to make for you?"

"I'll gladly eat anything you make, Yiayia, but Ruby is not ready for this. She doesn't want me around Jace yet."

Yiayia leaned forward. "You see her the first time you left her?"

I shook my head. "I didn't leave her."

Her eyebrows shot up. "You was here?"

"No."

"No. You left her," she reaffirmed.

I winced and acquiesced. "I should have been here."

"Yes, but you wasn't. I was. Amber was. We watch her fall apart and we pick up all the pieces."

"If I had known, I would have come."

She nodded and pain flashed across her wrinkled face. "I should have found a way to call you."

Ah, fuck. That's not what I meant. I patted her little hand. "No, Yiayia, this was not your fault."

She shook my hand off and carried on, undaunted. "What about the second time? You were here the second time?"

"I couldn't."

She jammed her finger down on the table to make her point. "You could. You made a choice." She shrugged her shoulders and sat back. "The right choice, but still was your choice. Did you see her that time when you walk away? No. Who see her fall apart? I see her. I pick up the pieces. She don't

180

know what she need. I do. You know, too. You listen to her, you won't even be here."

That was the difference.

It was so simple, really, I had to, at the very least, be here. Had I transferred when we were in university, I would have learned what held her back. Had I traveled to visit her after the conference, had I been here, Jace would have been mine.

I nodded to Yiayia. "I'll be here on Sunday."

She nodded in approval. "Good boy. You ate the donkey, only the tail is left. Is not the time to lose your appetite." She stood and turned to the fridge. "Now. I make you a roast beef sandwich, then you get out of here before Jace come home and see you." She shuddered dramatically and twinkled at me conspiratorially. "Ruby will make me like the onions."

Chapter 24 – Mental Road Maps

<u>Ruby</u>

I lay in bed, mentally traveling all possible routes to the meeting I had with the consultant that morning. The location was good, well within my safe zone. There were many different routes to getting there. Lots of choices.

I could take the highway.

My heart thudded once, hard, in my chest, stealing a single breath. What if I blew out a tire at high speed? I pictured my little car skidding into the next lane, a transport truck barreling down on me, ticking the corner of my cute little bumper, sending me rolling and spinning across the highway. I could hear the sound of tires screeching as a second transport truck swings sideways, rolling over my little car. I could hear the crunch of the steel frame as it folds around me.

Bye, bye, Ruby.

No highway.

My eyes were wide open but unseeing. I released my grip on the bedsheets. Easy there, Ruby. You're okay. I closed my eyes and took a deep breath.

Plenty of backroads, some more back than others. I could take Snake Road up through Bridgewater, such a sweet small town.

Was that too isolated? What if I hit a deer on Snake Road? I would have to be constantly vigilant. I huffed. Of course, I was always vigilant when driving. When was I not vigilant?

A scene from a movie I'd seen years ago unspooled on the canvas of my mind. A murdering rapist waited in secluded areas and shot the tires out of cars to secure his victims. He walked up to the car with a friendly smile. I saw the back of his hand coming fast towards my face. My breath rate picked up.

That was far-fetched even to my mind, though not outside the realm of possibility.

No Snake Road.

I needed a route that was not too busy, but not isolated either. I'd take York Boulevard to Plains Road then head up to Dundas Street which would take me almost to the door of the office. Just one more small turn. Dundas could be busy.

No. Enough. I took Dundas all the time. My nerves had nothing to do with the route, and everything to do with the fact that I was nervous for the meeting.

I hoped there was easy parking.

I got up and made sure my Emergency Auto Service card was tucked securely into my wallet and plugged my phone in to ensure a full charge, before getting into the shower.

A little over ninety minutes later, I turned off the ignition, peeled my fingers off the steering wheel, and flexed the stiffness from my joints. It turned out to be an easy drive and I made it with several minutes to spare.

I opened the window to breathe in the warm September air. Why was it September always smelled like back-to-school even decades since I'd been there?

I scanned the building. It was new, modern, lots of glass. I liked that. I hated feeling closed in. I stepped out of the car, briefcase in hand, and slung my purse over my shoulder.

Once inside, I checked for the company name on the board to verify that it was indeed on the fifth floor, then punched the button for the elevator. I gave my appearance a cursory glance in the elevator's mirror.

My new suit fit me perfectly and filled me with confidence. My makeup, light and professional, highlighted my features just enough. I couldn't do much with my hair. It waved and curled where it wanted, but I had at least somewhat tamed the frizz. The look in my eyes nearly stopped me in my tracks. They looked bright and alive, full of hope and excitement. I grinned at myself in the elevator mirror and then chortled.

The elevator door opened directly into the lobby. I checked in with the receptionist on my right, then took a seat on a chair across from her desk. A chaise lounge lay along on the wall of windows to my right, a hallway stretched out behind me, and a shorter hallway lay to my left.

I should have chosen the chaise lounge. I could have seen everything from that vantage point.

I heard a door open and close in the hallway behind me, followed by a series of rapid footsteps. A man with an open, friendly face came around the corner and smiled at me.

He stuck out his hand. "Hello, I'm Dylan."

"Ruby." I stood, shook his hand, and smiled.

He waved his arm to the side in invitation. "This way, please. Let's grab a room and see what we've got."

"Thank you for fitting me in so quickly."

"My pleasure. How are you feeling about your new venture?"

"Excited, nervous, apprehensive..."

He chuckled. "Lots of emotions go along with a project of this magnitude." He invited me to take a seat, then sat in a chair kitty-corner to me at the table. "My job is to take as much of the apprehension and nerves out of the equation as possible."

Dylan pored over my reports, took notes, looked at pictures, and listened to my vision, nodding and asking clarifying questions as I spoke.

"Okay, Ruby. I've got what I need for now. Are you available to come back Friday morning?"

I needed to check with my part-timer to see if she would be able to make it in, but I thought there was a fair chance. If I had to, I could close Spuds for a few hours. I'd had to do that a lot over the years.

"Is it okay if we book it, I'll double check that I can make it, and call this afternoon if Friday won't work?"

"Absolutely."

Dylan walked me out to the elevator, shook my hand once again, and I made my way to my car.

Vander

I watched Ruby walk briskly to her car. Her head swiveled left and right as she scanned the parking lot. I rubbed at the tightness in my chest. It hurt to see her so nervous and apprehensive when I remembered her lightheartedly bumbling and barreling through life. What must it be like to have a spirit like that trapped under a glass? She closed her car door and backed out of her spot.

The knock I'd been expecting sounded at my door.

"Come in."

Dylan opened the door and stepped in, a ready smile on his face. "Hey, boss."

"What have you got for me, Dylan?"

Dylan came around and sat on the chair across from my desk, throwing a file on top of the pile already on it.

"Photocopies of everything and I'll set up the digital copy this afternoon and give you access."

"How does it look to you?"

"I think it's good," Dylan spoke slowly. "She seems averse to any kind of travel which is obviously a concern. The financials are solid. It'll take some doing to choose a new location without her doing the legwork, but I think I can at least narrow it down to two or three that are relatively close to make it more palatable for her."

"Don't force it. Apply the same parameters. There's no point marketing to an area unlikely to see success."

Dylan stood. "Absolutely." He rounded the chair and headed to the door. Opening it, he turned back and smiled. "She's beautiful, boss. Good luck."

I smirked at him. "I'm going to need it."

Dylan laughed. "Especially when she finds out it's you behind the big door."

I rolled a pen back and forth across the top of my desk and stared out the window. When Ruby found out, there would be hell to pay. Apprehension gave way to humour.

It wouldn't be the first time I'd triggered her temper.

The text I'd been hoping for, finally came at quarter to eight that evening.

Ruby: Hi, Vander. How was your day today?

I wanted to say it was better for having seen her. It didn't sit well to hide all the facts from her.

Vander: Busy, Ruby-mine. How was yours?

I could hardly believe I was sitting on my deck having a beer and texting with her. I stared off into the night, dreaming of the day I'd come home to her in this house, our house, with our kids in it. I hoped it came soon. The weather was changing fast, and I was loathe to spend the evenings inside alone.

My phone buzzed and I smiled at her return message. Instead of answering she asked another question.

Ruby: *Do you like your work?*

Vander: I do. It's not the most important thing in my life, but it's one of the only things, so it's become all-encompassing to a certain extent. I'm looking for ways to pull back now. I won't be keeping this pace now that you're back in my life.

Her dots appeared and disappeared several times. I was about to tell her to stop thinking when her single word response came through.

Ruby: Yeah?

Maybe, just maybe she was starting to believe.

Vander: Yeah, koukla. You are my first priority.

Ruby: How can you even say that? What if George needs you? Or your parents become ill? Or your business fails?

I snorted but had to acknowledge that in walking away ten years ago, I earned her doubt.

186

Vander: I will never leave you behind. If I go somewhere, and you can't come with me, I'll go and come back as quickly as possible. I will never leave you.

Ruby: What if George gets sick or hurt?

Vander: We'll go and check on him, with Jace, and then we'll come back. If Jace can't go, you and I will go. If you can't go, I'll go. But I'll always come back.

Her dots appeared, but I anticipated her next words and continued.

Vander: Same goes for my parents. And if my business fails, which it won't, I'll do something else. Here. Close to you.

Ruby: How can I be sure?

Vander: Because I'm giving you my word.

Ruby: And what happens if I can't be what you want me to be?

Vander: You're already what I want.

Ruby: I mean, what if this never happens between us?

Vander: Then I'll continue as I have been until you marry someone else. If that happens, I'll leave you in peace. As far as I'm concerned, you are already my wife, and I will treat you as such. A man doesn't leave his wife for his kids, or his parents, or his job, and I won't leave you.

There was a long wait. No dots. I was about to change the subject when her message appeared.

Ruby: I had a meeting with the other company today.

Okay. Hopefully, that would sink in.

Vander: How did that go?

Ruby: I'm going to go with them. The consultant was friendly and confident. If he feels that I should go forward, I'm going to do it. I have a follow-up appointment on Friday.

Vander: Good, koukla. That's really good. Are you excited?

Ruby: Nervous.

Vander: I'll walk you through everything.

Ruby: Dinner Thursday?

Holy shit. She just confirmed without me having to push.

Vander: I look forward to it. Will I meet Jace when I pick you up?

Ruby: No. Not yet. He'll be at Amber's.

Vander: Soon, okay, Ruby? I want to meet him soon. This weekend.

Ruby: What time on Thursday?

Vander: Seven, okay?

Ruby: Yes.

Vander: Goodnight, Ruby-mine. I love you.

Ruby: Goodnight, moro mou. I love you, too.

Chapter 25 – Stalker Territory

<u>Ruby</u>

Thursday morning, I woke up with a smile on my face, which sent me into full-fledged damage control mode. While Vander claimed he wouldn't leave me, his situation hadn't changed all that much. If anything, his responsibilities were scattered further apart with his parents living in one province, his son in another, and him here with me. I feared getting caught between his responsibilities and torn apart.

In ten short days, Vander had moved from being a memory to 'there was no way on God's green earth that I would let him go'. I closed my eyes in resignation. I was going to do this. I huffed. Did I really have a choice? Being with him was almost instinctual.

The workday dragged on interminably, but eventually I stood waiting for Vander on the front step of my house. Irritated to find myself standing on this precipice, I was not in the mood for Yiayia's less than subtle hints. Vander hadn't told me where we were going, so I dressed in my usual jeans but with a light off-the-shoulder sweater instead of my trusty t-shirt.

He smiled easily as he stepped out of the car. He lifted a hand to wave to my yiayia in the front window, and I rolled my eyes. I turned and blew her a kiss, forcing a smile to my face, then clomped down the steps to the car. He met me at the passenger side and opened my door.

I glanced up at him to see amusement on his handsome face.

"What?" I snapped.

He grinned. "Cranky today. Let's see if I can do anything about that."

I huffed and swung into the car. He laughed as he slammed the door. I refused to look up at my yiayia. No doubt she stood at the window, threatening me. I turned towards the window when he swung into his side to hide my smile.

"I think I need to remind you of how it is between us." He met my doubtful look. "I'm serious. Underneath the pain and separation of the past twenty years, you're still Ruby, I'm still Vander, and we still belong together. Circumstances tore us apart, neither of us wanted to be apart."

"We're still inundated with 'circumstances'," I agreed testily. "Wouldn't you say?"

He looked a bit worried. "We are. But there is a difference now."

"Yeah? What is it? Enlighten me because I'm not so sure I see it."

He sighed. "I'm here, Ruby, and I'm not going anywhere. Not for any reason. There is nothing that will keep me from you. I will do anything and everything within my power to ease your way and keep you with me whether you want me to or not."

"You're treading dangerously close to stalker territory," I smirked.

His mouth curled up on the one side as he slid a sneaky glance my way. "Don't say I didn't warn you."

He held his hand out to me, palm up, and wiggled his fingers impatiently.

I slapped my hand down on his and he curled his fingers around mine with a smirk. "That's better. If you're within touching distance, I want my hands on you."

The feel of his palm against mine soothed me and I felt my ire slowly melt away. Palm to palm, mouth to mouth, chest to chest, feet tucked together under the blankets, knees pressed together under the table, I wanted it all. I craved that physical connection to another human being.

I'd dated occasionally after Drew moved away, but casual sex, while occasionally scratching the itch, really wasn't anything worth writing home about, not without the right partner. If I wanted to get off, I used my vibrator. God knows it was hit and miss, miss, miss, with the men I had dated. Even Drew, who hit all my hot spots, did not ease the craving I had for touch.

It was Vander's touch I missed all these years, and now I had it.

Vander stroked the inside of my wrist with his thumb. My lungs expanded with air. He filled me in ways I'd forgotten.

"Where are we going?" I asked.

"Are you comfortable with me in the driver's seat?" He asked in response.

I didn't need to think about it. "Yes."

He squeezed my fingers lightly. "Then let me surprise you."

I laughed when I saw the sign for the beach cut-off.

He looked at me sideways and grinned. A short while later we pulled into the parking lot across from the Go-Karts.

"I know you're probably hungry, but I thought we'd do this first."

I smiled at him as I opened my door and stepped out of the car. "You're taking your life in your hands delaying my dinner!" I teased.

He locked the doors and jogged around to my side, his handsome face creased into a wide smile. He held up his hands to show me what he had. "I bought you a giant cookie and a chocolate milk to tide you over. You can eat it while we wait for our turn."

"Ah," I nodded approvingly. "You're a good man, Charlie Brown."

I reached for the paper bag, and he pulled it up out of my reach, his eyes twinkling. "You didn't think I'd give it to you for nothing, did you?"

I crossed my arms and frowned, taking in his smug expression. Somebody needed taken down a peg or two.

I took a tiny step back, then dragged my eyes slowly up his body, lingering on his muscular thighs, giving a little sigh at his groin, parting my lips when I reached his chest, I licked my bottom lip as my eyes followed the lines of his wide shoulders. Tipping my head back, I allowed my eyes to go half mast as I stared up into his gorgeous face.

He wasn't laughing anymore. He held the bag limply in his lowered hand, his cheekbones a dusky pink, jaw clenched, dark eyes glittering with anticipation.

Taking a tiny step towards him, I slowly lifted my right hand and placed it over his heart. I felt his chest expand under my palm and I spread my fingers over his pectoral and squeezed the hard muscle.

He stood unmoving, as if afraid to break the spell.

Tilting my head to the side, I held his gaze before tilting my chin up and offering him my mouth.

He dipped his dark head towards me slowly, his gaze skittering between my eyes and my mouth.

When he was an inch away from my mouth, I spun away and snatched the bag out of his hand. Lifting it above my head I danced away from him. "I got it, I got it!" I yelled, howling with laughter.

For a moment he looked shocked, then he smiled.

It wasn't a comforting smile, and my breath caught in my throat. He dipped his chin and looked at me from beneath his dark brow.

Still, I could not resist taunting him. I waggled the bag in front of my body, giving him my most evil smile. "I got it, I got it..."

He stood back on his heels and nodded affably.

I tipped my chin down and dropped my eyes, smiling smugly. Ruby for the win. I uncurled the top of the bag to peek in, and he made his move.

Two long strides brought us chest to chest. He wrapped one arm around my waist, and his other hand tangled in the back of my hair, my hands holding my cookie bag trapped between us.

"My cookie!" I exclaimed.

He grinned down at me, his eyes hot, his hold unrelenting, and quickly backed me up against the car, pressing the length of his long, heavy body against mine. He dipped his head and rubbed his beard against the side of my face. His scent, his warmth, his touch, my need. He drew back slightly and met my eyes, his mouth firm.

I stared into his eyes, caught in a bubble outside of time where nothing existed save the invisible thread that linked his heart to mine.

"My cookie," I whispered.

He pressed his hips closer, and I felt him harden against my stomach. My eyelids fluttered shut. I fought the almost irresistible urge to spread my thighs around his slim hips. He tightened his grip on my hair and my head fell back in his hand. Desire pooled in my womb, and I barely held back my moan.

"What are you going to give me for it?"

"What do you want?" I asked, my voice raspy.

"Everything," he muttered, then dragged me up, bringing my mouth within a breath of his.

He held me still for a long moment, my lips just barely touching his. I'd never wanted anything as desperately as I wanted his mouth on mine. His hand in my hair held me immobile, and my helplessness fed my need. A low, needy moan broke from my throat.

"Yes, baby," he whispered harshly, his fingers clenching harder in my hair. "Moan for me. Want me the way I want you. Need me the way I need you. Open for me the way I've opened for you." He licked my mouth.

I opened.

With his mouth barely touching mine, he ran his tongue along the inside of my bottom lip. He drew back and nipped it sharply with his teeth, before pulling it gently into his mouth to soothe the sting.

My eyelids drifted shut. My entire universe centred around his fist in my hair, his determined mouth, and the hard length of his body against mine.

Please, please, kiss me.

As if he heard my unspoken request, he slanted his mouth over mine and delved inside, stroking my tongue, coaxing it out to play with his. I moaned into his mouth, wanting more. He pulled back and brushed gentle kisses over my gaping, gasping mouth. Too soon, he stopped, and, tucking my face into his shoulder, his bearded cheek pressed to my forehead, he hugged me.

"Vander..." I begged.

He chuckled roughly. "Gotta keep it PG, Ruby-mine."

Awareness of where we stood slowly washed over me, and I blinked with embarrassment.

He untangled his fingers from my hair and smoothed his hand over my curls, then slid his arm from around my back, and stepped back, his hands light on my hips.

I swallowed hard and tamped down the desire coursing through my veins.

He cupped my jaw lightly and smiled down at me. "Did your cookie make it?"

I glanced around, noting with relief the lack of an audience, and pushed myself off the car. He took another step back to give me some room. I opened the paper bag with shaky fingers and peeked in.

"Well. It'll be easier to share now." I muttered wryly.

He slung his arm around my shoulders and pulled me tight into his side as he led me across the parking lot. "You're going to share?" He grinned, looking down at me.

"I always share," I stated primly.

"Not always..."

I laughed, knowing immediately the incident he referred to. "That was one time! Anyways, if you wanted a cookie, why didn't you get yourself one?"

"Because I don't want my own cookie. I want your cookie." He squeezed me. "Give me a piece."

"What are you going to give me for it?"

He slanted me a hard, warning look. "More than you're ready for if you're not careful."

I quickly handed him a piece of cookie, and he laughed.

The sound filled me with light.

We didn't have long to wait for our turn. The first few spins around the track he beat me by miles. I determined I would not let him win the last lap. I took off before he finished counting down and weaved my way back and forth, cackling like a maniac, doing my best to keep him from passing me.

194

I clearly heard him cuss me out, his laughter reaching me over the growl of the tiny engines, and I laughed so hard my stomach hurt. Nearing the finish line, I stopped weaving and pressed the gas down as far as it would go, leaving him in my dust.

I jumped out of my kart, rubbing in my win.

"You, Ruby-mine, are a sore loser and a sore winner," he pointed at me with a grin as he removed his helmet. "And you're a cheater!"

"Cheater!" I scoffed. "Now, who's a sore loser?"

He slung his arm around my shoulders as we crossed the lot to his car. Once buckled in, we headed towards Bayview Village. "Where are we going?"

"Do you trust me, Ruby-mine?" He asked again.

"Yes," I replied, with no hesitation.

"Then let it be a surprise."

He pulled in the parking lot of a popular Greek restaurant.

"Oh, Vander, I'm a mess! I can't go in there." My hair, between the wind and the helmet, looked like a cross between a bird's nest and a beehive.

"We're not going in. I ordered ahead. Sit tight," he said. He jogged to the door of the restaurant and returned within a few minutes, our food packed up to go.

I got an inkling of where he wanted this night to go, and despite my body's Ra-Ra-Ready-to-go, my mind was not yet on board.

"Um, Vander, I-"

"No expectations, koukla. Just going to give you the ten-cent tour of my place. I need to snag you to myself for a little while, and at my house we'll have no interruptions."

I swallowed hard and nodded.

He held his hand out between us, and I placed my palm over his. "No worries, koukla. You're good."

Chapter 26 - Uh Oh

<u>Vander</u>

The Ruby who raced me around the track was the Ruby I fell in love with: a fun-loving free spirit, brimming with ideas, and barreling into new experiences with little forethought. I caught glimpses of her, like when the air vent disturbs the window blinds, causing slivers of sunlight to race across the shadowed floor, then disappear.

With Ruby, the shadows overtook her light just as quickly.

Our past was painful, I could not deny that. Even so, I looked to our past to sustain me, she used it to build her walls. Each time I broached the subject of us belonging together, she focused solely on the pain of our separation, and seemed to have forgotten the joy we shared, the fun we had. I intended to remind her of how we used to be together, and how we would be again.

If I pushed her, by the way she'd lit up when I kissed her, I could easily get her back into my bed. Once there, she'd be locked in, but I wanted her faith, or at the very least, her hope, first.

Saying that, if I had to wait much longer, all my good intentions would crumble to dust. Keeping my hands off her was becoming increasingly difficult. Twenty years ago, we'd only begun to discover sex. At the conference, desperation and grief tainted our lovemaking.

A whole new world would open for us once we came together this time. I couldn't wait to make love to her slowly, tease her, play with her, explore with her, make her forget, make her fly.

I watched her as she took in the house. She looked around but seemed nervous. She wouldn't even step over the threshold of the master bedroom.

I told her about my visit to see her yiayia, and my invitation to Sunday dinner while we ate our souvlaki, sitting on the couch in front of the coffee table in my family room. She nodded slowly, the wheels turning behind her dark eyes, but she didn't protest.

After dinner I pulled out the box that triggered the end of my marriage, and watched her as she sat on the floor, and pored over the photographs. With every memory recounted, delight flitted across her pretty face. She smiled and laughed, her face going pink with her pleasure, occasionally asking for updates on friends we had back then.

Ever so slowly, sadness rolled in, flattening her delight.

"Why are you sad, Ruby-mine?"

She trailed her fingers across a few of the photos, separating a few out of the pack. I hoped she asked for them.

A fat tear rolled down her flushed cheek. She swallowed hard. Indicating the pile, she whispered, "We were happy."

I nodded firmly. "Yes."

She shook her head. "I'm not that girl anymore, Vander."

"I'm not that boy, anymore," I retorted.

"I think... I'm worried... I think we're setting each other up for a world of pain."

I acknowledged her fear with a nod. "We might hurt one another. We probably will; couples do. But we are going to happen, Ruby. I'm willing to be patient, to a point, but you and I both know you're fighting a losing battle. We belong together. We've always belonged together."

She sat quietly for a pregnant moment.

"I'm scared, Vander. I can't take another loss. What if we try and it doesn't work out?"

I struggled for patience. "If we called it off right this second, could you walk away? Unscathed? Because I can't. I fucking promise you, Ruby, if we don't work out, it won't be because I leave."

"I don't want you to come on Sunday."

"Why?" I demanded.

"Jace has never had a father. He wants one, badly. What if he gets attached to you and things don't work out?"

My promises simply bounced off her walls. Pushing my irritation aside, I reassured her. "I'm here, Ruby, and I'm not going anywhere. If Jace lets me into his life, I won't leave him, either."

"How can you be so sure?"

"You're thinking of this all wrong. What you should be asking is, how can I not be?"

She huffed out an unladylike snort, and I stifled a laugh. Slicing me an irritated look, she pulled the few photos she separated from the pack towards her.

"I'm taking these," she challenged.

I laughed and lunged for her over the photos, wrapping my arms around her and taking her down to the floor. "My little Spartan, always fighting."

I grinned down into her wide eyes. Rolling, I pulled her on top of me and dropped my hand to her jean-clad ass. I yanked her flush against my hard groin and stared hungrily into her suddenly flushed face.

She immediately parted her thighs around my hips, her gaze locked onto my mouth. She rolled her hips, then tipped her chin back and closed her eyes at the delicious contact.

I loved to see her like this, needed to see her like this, head thrown back, eyes closed, lips parted, want and need carved in harsh lines onto her pretty face. Wrapping my other hand around the back of her neck, I pulled her mouth close to mine.

Her winged eyebrows furrowed, and a tiny whimper broke from her lips as she writhed against me again. I dug my fingers into her round ass and ground up against her heat, hard.

She gasped and I lifted my head, locking my mouth to hers. I fucked her mouth with my tongue, encouraged by the mewls and whimpers coming from her throat.

She gripped my shoulders and rubbed frantically against me, the muscles of her butt undulating under my hand.

"Vander," she groaned.

I remembered she couldn't come like this.

Grasping her round hips between my palms, I lifted her off me.

Her eyes flew open. "No!"

I rolled her quickly onto her back. Pressed against the length of her side, I slammed my mouth back down on hers and she greedily sucked my tongue into her mouth. I held her tightly against my chest with one hand, while I released the button and zipper of her jeans with the other.

She started to quake. I trailed my fingers along the edge of her lace panties, waiting for her go-ahead.

Tunneling her fingers through my hair, she kissed me deeply, lifting her hips off the ground, chasing my fingers.

Satisfaction rolled through me in waves at her response, but I wanted her 'yes'. I dipped just inside the front of her panties, and her breath hitched in anticipation. Withdrawing my fingers, I caressed the triangle of skin exposed by her open zipper.

She moaned in dismay.

I smiled against her lips.

Her eyes flew open, and she gripped my hair sharply. "Don't play with me, Vander."

"Oh, I'm going to play with you, Ruby-mine. I'm going to play with you a lot," I assured her, my voice gruff.

I watched, fascinated, as the colour rose in her face.

She stared back at me hungrily.

Holding her eyes, I smoothed my palm firmly up the inside of her thigh over her jeans. When I reached the apex of her thighs, she closed her eyes and squeezed her thighs closed, trapping my hand against her heat. I pressed up against her.

"Vander, please..." She breathed, looking up at me from beneath her half-closed lids.

Immediately I pulled my hand free, dove into her panties, and cupped her core. Her neck arched back, and her eyes closed. "Ah, yes!" She hissed.

Her juices coated my fingers, her heat enflamed me. The urge to free myself from my jeans, and replace the fingers I curled into her, was only slightly weaker than the drive to do right by her.

Dragging her wet up to her clit, I circled the swollen bud, pushing her higher, denying her the quick release she sought.

"Vander, Vander, Vander," she chanted against my mouth, her hips flexing against my hand, her thighs starting to shake.

"Yes, Ruby. Yes, baby," I breathed into her mouth.

I licked across her parted lips and her little tongue peeked out. I sucked it into my mouth then withdrew. Locked onto her face, I tapped her clit, once, twice, circled, pressed, and she cried out, arching back, pressing her head back into the carpet.

I stroked her folds lightly, bringing her through to the end, watching the pleasure suffuse her face, noting with satisfaction the tension draining from her body.

It didn't last.

Awareness flooded and she met my eyes, tears in hers.

I yanked my hand out of her pants and covered her with my body. Bracing my elbows on either side of her head, I stared down into her eyes.

"No, Ruby, don't," I said firmly. "Stay in the present."

She nodded and swallowed.

"That's it, baby. Just enjoy."

Her hands rounded my back and gently stroked up and down. I buried my face in her neck.

"What about you?" She murmured.

I kissed her neck, feeling her shiver at the contact with my beard. I raised my head and read the trepidation in her eyes.

"My pleasure is your pleasure, Ruby-mine."

Disappointment flashed across her face, and I quickly tucked my face back into her neck to hide my smile.

She smacked my back. "I know what you're doing, Vander."

"What am I doing, koukla?" I couldn't entirely keep the laughter from my voice. The fact that my cock was strangling in my jeans helped.

"You're trying to make me desperate for you," she snapped.

"Is it working?"

She snorted out a laugh, pushed at my shoulders then changed her mind and pulled me into a hug. "Yeah, baby. It's working," she admitted.

Jumping to my feet, I pulled her up.

Gently, I cupped her jaw. "I'm trying so hard to go slow. Do you think you could pick up your pace just a tiny bit?"

She dropped her gaze and pressed her forefinger into the divot of her top lip for a moment. "I can do that."

My lungs expanded with relief, and I pulled her into a tight hug. I kissed the crown of her curly head. "C'mon. I'll take you home."

I went to my lonely bed dreaming of the time when she'd be slipping in beside me, and when I woke the next morning, it was with that same thought.

Later that day, I watched from my office window as Ruby walked briskly across the parking lot towards my office. She had her second consult meeting today. I needed to tell her it was my company. Sunday, after dinner.

I took off my glasses and scrubbed a hand roughly over my face. In hindsight, perhaps this was not my brightest idea.

An hour later, caught up in phone calls, I missed seeing Ruby leave. Dylan popped in and briefed me on their meeting. It was a good opportunity to gather the rest of the senior staff for our daily touch base. I paged my assistant to come in, as well as my other two senior consultants, one of which was Despina, 'Miss Soft Voice'. I cringed, hoping that wasn't going to be a problem for Ruby.

It was a quick, ten-minute meeting. By this time, they were a well-oiled machine and I trusted them to do their jobs and do them well. Despina hung back to go over an idea she had while everyone else gathered their things.

We were laughing together at a rare joke cracked by my profoundly serious assistant, as Dylan opened the door, and they began to file out. Despina leaned against my desk, and I stood relaxed across from her, my jacket open, hands tucked into my pants pockets.

Someone else said something and my assistant laughed. I watched, satisfied by the work environment I created, as my consultants bantered back and forth.

I looked further down the hall to see a small figure seated on the edge of the chaise lounge, and immediately locked onto a pair of large, brown, shocked eyes. Her shock quickly morphed into anger even as I watched.

I heard Dylan's, "Uh oh," at the same time as Despina quietly exclaimed, "Oh, no!"

I excused myself and barreled past my staff down the hall towards Ruby. She stood up right before I reached her and opened her mouth to speak, her eyes snapping.

I took her firmly by the elbow.

"Hold on, Ruby. This way, please."

I took advantage of her shock and fury and ushered her quickly into the closest conference room. I'd have preferred the relative privacy of my office to have this conversation but didn't relish dragging her through my staff to get there.

As soon as I closed the door and turned to her, she unleashed, her face red, hands fisted at her sides.

"What the fuck is going on here?"

Chapter 27 - Bookstagram

<u>Ruby</u>

Jace and I plodded up to the door of Amber's condo. I swear, I was still shaking from yesterday. Even though Vander and I had gone out for coffee last night and talked things through, I still desperately needed to talk to Amber and Minty.

The deception bothered me, and my pasted-on smile wasn't working if Jace's sidelong glances were anything to go by.

"You okay, momma?" Jace ventured in the car on the way over.

"Yes, agapimeno mou. It's just this whole franchising venture that has me all twisted up." That was true.

"Well, you don't have to do it if you don't want to," Jace answered matter-of-factly.

I raised my eyebrows. "That's true."

I started to wonder if franchising would give me the satisfaction and fulfilment I hoped for.

The mental and physical stagnation leeched all my energy. I needed something new, something fresh. I'd thought about selling Spuds in the past, but I didn't want to let go of that very physical link with my past, with my family.

What would I do if I didn't have Spuds? I could look for something else, but a new job would be unpredictable. What if it required business trips? What if I had to go into Toronto for training?

My brow furrowed. Franchising was my best option to shake things up a bit without toppling my carefully balanced world.

"Just have fun tonight, Momma. Don't worry about things."

"Smart advice."

I reached across the seat and caressed his soft cheek. Soon there would be downy fuzz on his face, and then he'd be shaving. I stopped that line of thought before I started blubbering about his wedding.

At Amber's, he and Alex immediately retreated to the games room. Minty and Amber stood staring at me.

"What?" I snapped, irritably.

"What happened?" Amber's eyes scanned my face worriedly.

Minty grabbed the mini tubs of ice cream. "Will we need these?"

I sighed and flopped down on Amber's couch. "Bring them. No need for a bowl, just grab me a spoon."

We curled up on the couch together. "So, you know how I had my second meeting with the franchising consultant yesterday?"

"Yes," they answered.

"Well, it turns out it's Vander's company."

Two mouths dropped open. I saw Minty's brain working furiously behind her astonishment. "Didn't he recommend that company to you?"

"Yes, sort of, I already had chosen them as one of my options."

Minty moved over beside me and placed a comforting hand on my knee. "Start from the beginning."

"I met with my consultant, Dylan, and everything went smoothly..."

Leaving the office, I felt much more confident, secure in the belief that Dylan knew what he was doing, and that I would have Vander's guidance on top of that. I got all the way to my car when I realized I forgot my day timer in the meeting room. By the time I made my way back upstairs, the receptionist was no longer at her desk, so I sat down on the chaise lounge to wait.

I heard voices and laughter coming from the office down the hall. The door opened and I smiled as Dylan walked out, a huge smile on his face. Curious, I scanned the other faces in the group, then finally looked into the office through the open door.

Vander stood framed by the doorway, his suit jacket open over his wide chest, his hands tucked deep into his pockets, an easy smile on his handsome face.

What the hell?

Framed beside him, a woman leaned against his desk, smiling at him, and not just any woman, but Miss Soft Voice.

I turned my gaze back to Vander and met his eyes. I sucked in a deep breath.

The smile dropped from his face immediately. He twisted his wide shoulders and knifed through the group, barreling towards me, holding my furious gaze. He reminded me of someone in that moment, but I was too enraged to dwell on it.

I rose to my feet. I'd buy another day timer. I was leaving.

Next thing I knew, I found myself in a conference room with Vander, and not the same one I was in with Dylan, so I still couldn't get my damn book back.

I slammed my purse down on the table. "What is going on? Is this your company?"

He stood looking down with his hands deep in his pockets. He pressed his lips together, then took off his glasses and scrubbed his hand over his face. He sighed, then met my eyes.

"Yes."

"Unbelievable!" I paced back and forth then stopped and glared at him. "I told you I didn't want to go with you!" I hissed.

He pressed his lips together, his eyes following me as I paced. "I know."

"What the fuck, Vander? This is crazy!"

205

He relaxed back into his heels and settled in. "I told you. I'm going to be there for you even if you don't want me to."

"You can't just," I sputtered, "steamroll over me!"

He held up his hand. "Hang on, Ruby. That's not what happened. You narrowed it down to three companies, including mine. You could have gone with the other company."

"Really? Really, Vander?" I took a step towards him. "Isn't it a bit convenient that you set up the meeting with them?"

He flushed.

My mouth fell open. "Oh, my God! You sabotaged it!"

He winced. "Just a bit. Not totally. He didn't tell you anything that was untrue, except for the fact that he probably had a consultant that would have been able to start sooner than six months from now."

"He lied to me?"

"He owed me a favor... this is not going well," he muttered looking down at his shoes. His eyes beseeched me. "I am trying to be there for you. I am trying to give you all of me. I am trying to give us a chance, ease your way in life, look after you, love you!" Vander's voice rose steadily as his anger sparked. "You're not letting me in! You're going to throw away our chance, our only fuckin' chance, at happiness! Do you expect me to stand by and let that happen?"

"Maybe you should! Maybe if it's this difficult, it's not meant to be. Maybe we're fooling ourselves!" I retorted.

He stepped back and turned away with his hands on his hips, his chin tipped down. I watched as his back heaved with his deep inhale.

My head lifted off my body, as if I'd slipped off a curb, leaving my head suspended above me. A cold, sick feeling crawled up my throat. Alarms rang in my brain, and fear ricocheted down my limbs.

Turn around.

He turned to face me, calmer now.

"I know you're pissed, but don't take it too far, Ruby-mine."

Relief flooded my system, making me feel almost faint. Instead of calming me, it angered me further.

I pointed at my chest, incredulous. "I'm taking it too far? Me?"

"Okay," he soothed. "This might have been an error in judgement. I concede that. But can you at least admit that no one would be more invested than me in guiding you through this process?"

I exploded. "You're not hearing me. At all. I tell you how I feel and all you do is bulldoze right over me! You're not giving me any space, a chance to think! I'm afraid, Vander!"

"You think I'm not?" He retorted, throwing out his hands to his sides. "With you throwing your hand up to keep me at arms' length? Fuck, Ruby! I'm not telling you not to be afraid. I'm telling you to be fucking brave!"

"Brave?" I yelled. "I'm trying not to be stupid! You put me aside! Twice!" My voice went higher with the incredulity of our situation. "What has changed? Why should I believe you have staying power now?"

The walls began to close in. There wasn't enough air in this entire building for me to adequately fill my lungs. "I can't do this." I grabbed my purse off the table and took two steps towards the door.

"I should have transferred schools." His deep voice broke through the silence between us, and his quiet words ground me to a halt. I turned my head slightly to the side, listening despite myself. I wanted answers. God help me, I wanted to let him in, but he needed to give me a reason.

I twisted towards him. "Why didn't you?" I asked, my voice thin and reedy.

He stood still, his hands deep in his pockets, and held my eyes. "I told you before. I wanted you to meet me halfway. Fifty-fifty. I wanted to be sure I wasn't in deeper than you were."

I felt my shoulders drop. "I was in deep."

"I know that now. I made a mistake. Both times. After the conference, I should have held on. I thought I did the right thing, the loving thing, by letting you go. But even before that," he continued evenly, "I should have transferred. I should have been all in, one hundred percent, even if you weren't."

I turned away and dropped my chin to my chest, defeated. I was in 100%. How could he not see that?

"I was." If he couldn't understand all that he took away from me, how could he understand how difficult it was for me to trust him?

I heard his footsteps as he walked up behind me and placed his hands gently on my shoulders. He sent a shiver through me with a firm kiss to the nape of my neck.

"You weren't. If you were, you'd have trusted me with your secret." His voice was gruff when he continued. "You asked what has changed. It's this. I'm one hundred percent in, Ruby-mine. I'll take your five, your twenty, your eighty, whatever percent you want to give me. I'll take it. But I'm in, one hundred percent."

I brought myself back to the present and looked at my girls. Amber pulled her lips between her teeth and looked down at nothing.

Minty squeezed my knee. "I'm not sure if I'm impressed or appalled," she mused, a small smile on her face. "He's a bit of an alpha, isn't he?"

Amber looked up and refocused. "You'd never think that if you met him," she defended. "He's really very sweet and polite."

"No, no," I interjected, waving my hands in front of me as if to erase what Amber thought she knew. "He's changed. He's not the soft, sweet boy he used to be."

Minty laughed her tinkling laugh. "Well, thank heaven for small mercies! The last thing you need is a soft man, honey. Looks like you might be getting your ideal book boyfriend after all!" Minty wagged her perfectly arched brows.

Amber laughed.

I flopped backwards onto the couch. Done.

Vander

I sat on the deck in my fleece hoodie with a cup of coffee.

The past two days were harrowing. We cleared things up Friday night. She even kissed me, lightly, when I dropped her home after our talk, but things between us were still shaky. She asked me again not to come tomorrow, to give her another week. I refused.

On the upside, I was now solely in charge of her file.

When I suggested I take over from Dylan, she narrowed her eyes. "You may as well. I'm sure Dylan had to report every last detail to you anyways."

I laughed. Ruby smiled despite her ire.

"You know," I teased, "it's not everybody who gets the CEO treatment. There aren't too many files I handle directly anymore. What are you going to give me in compensation?"

Her mouth fell open comically and my heart lifted. Snapping her jaw shut, she snorted, "A black eye if you pull any more stunts." She looked at me suspiciously.

I raised my hands in surrender, chuckling. "That's it, there are no more surprises, Ruby-mine. I promise."

Chapter 28 – Greek Mythology

<u>Ruby</u>

"What's his name again, Momma?" Jace asked, lining his cutlery up evenly beside his plate.

We were sitting across from each other at the West End Diner early Sunday morning. I'd just finished telling him about Vander, how important he was to me, why we separated, and that there were still strong feelings between us.

"Vander."

Jace nodded thoughtfully. "He's Greek?"

"He is." I watched the emotions flit across his face. A bit of apprehension, mostly curiosity.

He raised his head and met my eyes steadily. "Are you guys getting married?"

I shook my head. "It's too early for that, but we do care about each other very much."

Worry creased his forehead. "Does he know about me?"

I felt my eyebrows hit my hairline. "Of course! You think anyone who knows me, doesn't know about you?"

He smiled, but my heart hurt. I did not ever want him to feel as though he was in the way or a burden.

"He wants to meet you. That's why he's coming today."

"Yeah?" His little face broadcast hope, and I mentally berated myself for all that I denied him.

"Absolutely."

I steered the conversation onto safer categories, like wilderness survival and tree trekking, while we finished our breakfast. We walked out waving our goodbyes to Voula.

We stocked up at the pet store, then made our way home. In the car, he looked quietly out the window. I pulled into the driveway, and he looked down into his lap.

"Do you think he'll like me?"

I reached over and scratched his head lightly. He needed a haircut. His waves had grown long enough to loop up into curls.

"If he doesn't, he's getting kicked to the curb."

Jace raised laughing eyes to mine. "Momma, nobody says that anymore."

"Oh, yeah? What do they say? What's the lingo nowadays?"

"Nowadays? Really, Momma?" He laughed.

I opened the car door and stepped out. He met me by the front of the car and threw his arm around my waist, and I squeezed him tightly for a long moment. When we got inside, I sent him off to do his homework, then slipped into my bedroom for a minute to breathe.

A few hours later, I waited on the front step as Vander pulled in and parked his car across the street. I watched him lope across the street with his easy stride and remembered how overjoyed I was to see him on my front step that day more than twenty years ago.

A smile tugged at my lips. It had been a long time coming, but maybe it was finally our time.

He stopped and smiled down at me, flowers in one hand, a gift bag with a bottle of wine in the other.

I stood up and dusted off the seat of my jeans. "You brought me flowers?"

He leaned in close but didn't try to kiss me. He smiled wickedly. "The flowers are for Yiayia, the wine is for you."

I laughed, and he pressed his forehead against mine. I took a deep breath. This would be okay.

Amber and Alex arrived a couple of hours before and the boys were ensconced in video games in Jace's room. This meant I had time to get Vander in, let Yiayia gush over him, and re-introduce him to Amber. After my story at our bookstagram meeting last night, Amber had joined Yiayia on Team Vander.

With Yiayia and Amber out of the way, I'd face introducing him to Jace.

I knew Vander. He was kind. He would put his own feelings aside and do everything in his power to put Jace at ease.

He gifted me with tiny touches while we moved around the kitchen and dining room with Yiayia and Amber. He linked his pinky with mine for a few seconds, brushed the backs of his fingers over my cheek, slid his hand to the small of my back, but didn't linger. I was glad. I didn't want to bombard Jace at this first meeting.

Dinner was finally ready. Yiayia and Amber were already in the dining room arranging the platters on the table, and Yiayia called the boys down to eat. I grabbed the last one and Vander preceded me through the doorway with the bowl Yiayia had asked him to carry to the table.

I heard the boys making their way downstairs as we placed the food on the table, Alex's feet pounding down the stairs while Jace followed more sedately behind him. They were not in our line of sight yet.

My stomach fluttered with nerves and Vander twisted his neck to look back at me as if he knew and gave me an encouraging nod and a smile.

Alex came sliding into the room on his socks and Vander chuckled for a moment before going positively still. Jace loped over with his hands tucked deep in his pockets and his chin angled down.

I moved in front of Vander, my eyes on Jace, and opened my arms. Jace gave me a hug before turning to Vander who stood staring at him openly. I laughed nervously.

Maybe Vander wasn't as ready for this as he thought he was.

I looked to Yiayia to see her standing with her mouth open in shock. Amber called Alex over to her. They were making this so weird.

I stepped forward, drawing Jace with me, and sent Vander a warning look.

"Vander, this is my son, Jace."

Jace stuck out his hand as I continued. "Jace, this is Vander."

Vander shook himself out of his stupor and reached for Jace's hand. "It's a pleasure-" He cleared his throat. "It's a pleasure to meet you, Jace. Your mom has told me lots of good things about you."

Vander didn't let go of his hand immediately as he studied Jace's face. Jace studied him right back, like two alpha males having a stand-off? I could not fathom what was going on in Vander's head.

I touched Vander's back lightly and he startled then released Jace's hand. I turned and introduced him to Alex.

In the bustle to wash hands and get seated, I caught Vander's eye and murmured, "Are you alright?"

His expression hardened and his lips pressed together thinly. "I'm fine."

It was obvious he was not okay. I didn't want to force him to stay if he didn't want to. I knew I shouldn't have allowed him and Yiayia to bully me into this so soon.

"If you don't want to stay, I can make an excuse for you," I offered stiffly.

"Oh, no, Ruby," he snorted. "You're not getting rid of me that easily."

What the hell?

Yiayia bustled in telling everybody where to sit. I hated the strain evident on her face and endeavoured to put everyone at ease. I'd have it out with Vander later. Conversation stuttered along at first but picked up when the boys began telling Vander about their Adventure Club.

Vander smiled easily at Jace and Alex and peppered them with questions they were only too happy to answer.

I relaxed back in my seat only to see Yiayia and Amber looking at each other worriedly. I raised my eyebrows in question, but Amber just shook her head and offered me a hesitant smile. Was Amber having second thoughts about being on Team Vander?

I can't say I was impressed with his reaction to Jace at first, but he seemed to be pulling it together. It's not like our situation was easy. She needed to give him a break.

After dinner, I stood up and put my hand on Vander's shoulder to ask if he wanted coffee. He went rigid beneath me, and I drew back my hand. No matter what he promised, it was evident to me that he was not okay with this, not at all.

Nerves assaulted my tummy, and I knew I, for one, would not be partaking of any extra caffeine. Amber and I excused the boys and Vander watched Jace until he left the room before meeting my eyes, a mix of anger and hurt swirling in his.

I tried to offer him a comforting smile, but I knew well what he was dealing with, and knowing it would be my turn soon, his reaction did not instill me with confidence.

"Do you want coffee, moro mou?" I asked him softly.

He looked down and rubbed his palms down his thighs. "I, uh, I think I'll pass, Ruby. I need to get back and finish up some work for tomorrow."

He stood and gathered the heavy platters from the centre of the table. Yiayia and Amber stood watching him warily.

I sent them both what I hoped was an encouraging smile and followed Vander into the kitchen. He turned and put his hands on my shoulders and set me aside, without speaking to me or meeting my eyes, to go back into the dining room.

My mouth fell open in shock.

This had gone phenomenally badly. I heard him thanking Yiayia for dinner and promising her he'd be back in a few days to see her again. That, at least, sounded promising.

I slipped on my shoes to walk Vander out and waited for him outside on the porch.

He came outside in a daze and jolted when he saw me. Anger flashed in his eyes.

"It was too early," I whispered.

I knew it. We didn't have the foundation for trouble. We never did, maybe we never would.

He stood in front of me, staring down at me with a mixture of grief, anger, and hurt. "I need to think."

My blood ran cold. "You need to think," I repeated flatly.

He raised his hand to brush my cheek but stopped short of touching me. He swallowed hard and looked away but not before I caught a glimpse of what suspiciously looked like tears.

"I'll call you."

Jogging down the steps, he loped across the yard to the street.

Turn around.

Crossing the road, he opened his car door and paused.

Please, turn around.

He shook his head, slipped into his car, and drove away.

I sat down hard on the top step.

What kind of fool was I? There was a saying, how did it go? Fool me once, shame on you. Fool me twice, shame on me. What kind of fool came back for a third round?

He'll 'call me'? Oh, no. Nuh-uh.

This ends now.

I opened the front door, grabbed my purse and my keys, and yelled to Amber and Yiayia that I was going out. I heard Amber call my name, but I didn't have it in me to have a long, drawn-out conversation.

So wrapped up in my head, I barely noticed the drive to Vander's house, I parked behind his car and bounded up the steps to his front door.

His front door. Not mine. Not ever going to be mine.

I let go of Drew out of some misguided notion that Vander and I had something special, and I didn't want to settle for less.

I scoffed.

I didn't date because no one came close to making me feel what Vander did.

I made myself physically sick, both times, when he turned his back on me.

I would have laughed at my foolishness if I wasn't so disgusted with myself.

Raising my fist, I rapped my knuckles sharply on the door. My cell phone buzzed in my pocket. I ignored it.

He opened the door, his feet bare, a beer dangling loosely from between his long fingers. His hair stuck straight up, and his face was the very picture of abject misery. I almost felt sorry for him, until I thought about Jace.

I stepped up into his space and he stepped back allowing me in. He turned and walked through the kitchen, and I slammed the door behind me.

Shaking with rage, I opened and closed my mouth unable to say anything other than, "You!"

He held up a hand, with his back to me still, and rasped, "I can't do this right now."

"You can't do this," I mocked. "You can't do this right now? Well, I'm sorry, but you don't get to call the shots this time." I seethed.

He turned his head to the side, looking at me over his shoulder. "I don't get to call the shots? What are you talking about?" He sneered.

I paced back and forth in the entranceway, my arms folded tightly across my chest, keeping my eyes on the side of his face I could see.

"After the conference, you decided we were done. You show up two weeks ago, and you decided it's our time, you decided you're going to manage my franchising, you decided it's time to meet Jace, and then you decide it's too much and think you're going to decide when we're going to talk about it?" I laughed bitterly.

"I knew you didn't have it in you to stay," I hissed. "I knew it! And I trusted you anyway! I trusted you because," I stopped pacing and stared at him, jabbing my finger in the air with every one of my next words. "I. Have. Loved. You. Always!"

I held my hands up in the air. "I am all kinds of fool to do so, and I can forgive myself that weakness but allowing you to meet my son? That I will have a hard time getting past."

He turned to face me, silently, his eyes assessing.

I put my hands on my hips. There was no putting a lid on this now. My phone buzzed again in my pocket.

"Do you know I turned down marriage with his father under the misguided idea that you and I had something special? I denied *my* son his *father* because I wanted to feel about Drew the way I feel about you."

He dropped his chin and set his beer down carefully. He braced his hands on the counter and leaned back against it, watching me rant from under his brow.

My arms had taken on a life of their own, waving and slashing at the air as I unloaded every ounce of my anger and frustration on him.

"I made myself sick, physically sick, both times you left me. I didn't date. I still don't! I wasted twenty fucking years of my life pining after a love that only ever existed in my imagination!"

Tears of frustration leaked from my eyes, and I viciously wiped them away.

Vander leaned across the counter and reached for his cell phone.

I wanted to fly at him and knock it out of his hand.

He clicked through for I don't know what, but for fuck's sake, was this really the time?

My own phone buzzed again. I was going to have to pick that up.

"Until the conference, I actually believed that you loved me wholly and completely, exactly the way I wanted to be loved, the way I have been longing to be loved my entire life!" I laughed and threw my hands up into the air. "And it doesn't fucking exist! You're a fucking myth!"

Seeming to find what he was looking for, Vander eyed me and pushed off the counter. He held out his cell phone to me and I glanced at the screen briefly. I dismissed it until I realized what I'd seen and then swung my eyes back to his screen, confused.

"Jace?" I asked quizzically, reaching for his phone.

He moved closer to me.

"Look closer," Vander murmured gruffly, holding his phone out to me.

I cupped my hand under Vander's to hold his phone steady. The boy on the screen looked astonishingly similar to Jace, but there were enough differences that on closer inspection I could see that it wasn't him.

My cell phone buzzed in my pocket.

I felt odd.

A little detached.

I dropped my hand and took a step back from Vander. My saliva stuck in my throat, and I tried to clear it. The world moved in slow motion and my vision tunneled.

My voice came out in a whisper as I slowly raised my eyes to his. "Who is that?"

Tears streamed down his tortured face.

"George."

Chapter 29 - Roller Coaster

Vander

She didn't know.

If there was one thing I knew for certain, it was that she didn't know. My anger at her melted away, and I leaned back against the counter to wait her out.

I needed to put aside my own feelings of anger, grief, and despair. I'd planned to work through some of those tonight, on my own, so I could be clearheaded when confronting Ruby with the truth tomorrow.

I spun the mental rolodex of pictures in my head. There were hundreds of pictures of George on my phone, I definitely had pictures from two and a half years ago when George was the same age as Jace was now.

Jace.

My son.

With Ruby.

The son I unwittingly abandoned.

I reached for my phone and opened the photo app, worried about how hard this would hit Ruby when she realized the truth, how angry she would be that I never reached out to her after the conference, how guilty she was going to feel about Jace, about me, about Drew.

I found the picture I was looking for. The resemblance was uncanny.

Showing it to her, I watched as she struggled to come to terms with what she was seeing. My heart ached for her, for myself, for our son, for the family we could have been all these years.

She raised pain-filled eyes to mine. "Jace?"

It took another moment, and I welcomed her touch as she held my shaking hand steady to study the picture on the screen.

I heard her cell phone buzz again, and guessed it was her sister. Both Amber and Yiayia looked back and forth between me and Jace all through dinner.

I watched the emotions skitter across her face and my heart ached for the shock and pain I was about to deliver.

She whispered, "Who is that?"

"George."

She stumbled back and wobbled a little before reaching out to brace her hand on the wall beside her. She pulled her phone out of her pocket and stared at the screen before accepting the call.

"Amber?" She sounded young and lost as she listened to Amber.

"I know. He just told me." She sniffed. "Of course, I didn't know! I would have told him." Tears ran down her face unheeded. "I'll, um, call you later... Wait! Can you, can you take Jace home with you tonight?" She whispered. "I don't want him to see me like this."

She raised a shaking hand to cover her eyes. "Mm-hmm. Okay. I love you, too. Mm-hmm. Text me when you leave, and please tell Yiayia I'm going to be late." She listened while Amber spoke, nodding and adding the occasional mm-hmm, and then disconnected the call.

Always, where Ruby was concerned, I was hopelessly inept. I stood with my hands stiff at my sides, like a gunslinger ready to draw, as she tucked her phone back into her pocket, her chin angled towards the floor, her eyes staring at nothing.

Without looking at me, she spun slowly on her heel, her body strung tight like a bow. "I better go..."

220

Two steps plastered my chest to her back, and I wrapped my arms tightly around her waist, curving my body protectively around hers.

She curled into herself for just a moment, choking back a sob. Then her back arched, her head pressed back against my shoulder, and the most godawful sound erupted from the depths of her ruptured heart.

I hung onto her, tried to turn her in my arms, but she twisted away, gasping for breath.

"Ruby," I whispered, pained.

She grasped my forearms, holding onto me just like she had in the car the other night. She tried to speak, but her words were incoherent.

"Ruby, Ruby, baby..." I murmured in her ear.

I heard the hitch in my own voice.

She sucked in a whistling breath. "You would have come back," she sobbed. "For him, you would have come back. I wasn't enough, but he would have been. We could have been a family!" She cried, her soft, curvy, body convulsing with the force of her grief.

Her words broke me.

God help me, what I'd done to her in my weakness.

The sword I'd fallen on a decade before twisted in my chest and I pulled it free.

I wrapped around her tightly, and tucked my chin against her neck, my mouth to her ear. "You were enough, Ruby. You've always been enough. It was me who wasn't enough. But I swear to God, baby, I'm strong enough now to be everything you need. Both of you."

Her knees buckled, the last of her resistance worn away, and she turned and buried her face in my chest, the sounds of her cries muffled in the folds of my shirt.

I wrapped her up tight.

I didn't deserve her.

But I'd go balls to the wall until I did.

Ruby

"I'm so sorry, Vander," I murmured.

221

"So am I, Ruby-mine." He pressed a kiss to the top of my head.

I lay curled up on his lap in the corner of his couch, my head nestled under his chin.

I cried, he cried, and we talked everything through.

We'd lost so much time.

Jace lost so much time with his father. Another tear trickled down my face.

"Enough, Ruby. That's enough, now. We go forward. You'll talk to Jace tomorrow. We'll do the DNA test so long as he's okay with it, but no matter the results, we're going to be a family."

"Maybe we should just hold off making any plans until we know for sure."

"Why?"

"Because if you're wrong, and he's not your son, we're back to where we were."

"First of all, I'm not wrong. Secondly, I've no interest in going back to where we were. Whether Jace is mine or not, and he is, we need to be a family."

He stroked my back, soothing me with his big hands, then continued. "I'm going to tie you to me so tightly that you'll be begging for space."

I huffed out a laugh then pulled out my cell phone to call Yiayia and Amber. I needed to let them know I was okay. I pressed my lips together, unsure about this new definition of 'okay'.

"Are you checking on Jace?"

"Calling Yiayia first to tell her I'll be home soon and then I'm going to check on Jace."

He dragged his hands up and down my back. "You're not going home. Tell Yiayia you're staying here."

"I can't," I protested.

"Why not?" He kept up his slow, easy pace, his strokes putting me at ease, making me want to stay.

My head spun. Why not indeed. It was foolishness, at this point, to hold off.

I loved him. I always had. I wanted to have a family with him, and it looked like we had one. I was almost certain that Jace was his and I did not want to stand in the way of Jace having his father.

Now that my life was most certainly tied to Vander's forever, letting him go was not an option. It never was.

So much change in so short a time. I couldn't believe he'd only been back in my life for a couple of weeks. So much change knocked off my equilibrium. Tonight's revelations knocked my entire world clean off its axis.

"Take the leap, Ruby," he urged. "I promise I'll catch you."

"What were you going to do if I didn't come tonight?"

"I planned to drink myself stupid, wake up with a hangover, and then have the same conversation that we just had, only I'd have done it tomorrow night."

"Were you mad at me?"

He sighed. "I considered the possibility that you withheld him from me. I'm sorry for that. Mostly I was shocked that he was mine, sickened that you'd had to raise him without me, then so fucking sad that I'd lost so much time with him, and you. I'm angry with myself. None of this would have happened if I hadn't let you go a-fuckin-gain. I don't want to lose another second with either of you."

"You didn't even touch me," I whispered. "You went to touch my cheek, but you didn't."

"I didn't deserve to touch you."

"You're touching me now."

He squeezed me tighter. "Yes, and I thank God for that fact."

I shifted off his lap to sit beside him, called Amber first, then Yiayia.

Yiayia was inconsolable, crying that she should have called Vander and told him about the agoraphobia. I spent fifteen minutes on the phone with her, reassuring her that there was no way she could have found his contact information even if she had decided to tell him.

Finally, I told her if she couldn't settle down, I would have to come home. She threatened to boil me if I came home and promised she'd be okay.

Tomorrow I'd ask Gus to contact Drew.

After ending the call, I lay my head back on the couch. It was only nine o'clock but felt like the early hours of the morning.

Vander stood up and pulled me up beside him. "Let's go to sleep, agapi mou."

I glanced at his face, once again set in harsh lines from the day's events.

"Just sleep, Ruby-mine. I'm just going to hold you in our bed while you sleep."

I looked down, overcome by the fact that we now had a bed and were going to share it for the first time. Finally, I nodded, and he led me to his bedroom.

He gave me a t-shirt and stripped down to his boxer briefs. He got in on his side, opened the covers to invite me in, and I slipped in beside him. Pushing his arm beneath me, he rolled me until my back was pressed flush against his chest.

With his knees tucked behind mine, his chest lined up along my back, one arm stretched out underneath my head holding onto my wrist, the other looped over my waist, his fingers linked through mine, he kissed me behind my ear, and we slept.

Sometime later I stirred and felt him awake behind me.

What seemed like a reasonable choice, the only choice, a few short hours ago, now felt rushed and foolhardy. All the old doubts and fears returned to plague me.

"You're okay, koukla," he murmured in my ear.

Oh, God, his voice in my ear, husky from sleep, buzzed straight to my clit. I pressed back against him, arching my back involuntarily, my heart at war with my brain.

He ran his hand down my stomach, over my hip, and down my thigh, then back up to brush his thumb across my nipple.

I turned my head toward him and he feathered kisses along the side of my face while his hand repeated its downward journey to my thigh, then back up to cup my breast, pinching and rolling my nipple between his long fingers.

I dropped my head back to my pillow and his mouth hit my neck.

I moaned.

The bristles of his beard, the softness of his lips, the slickness of his tongue, and the scrape of his teeth sent waves of pleasure to my toes.

I pushed my hips back into his groin, but his knee blocked me from nestling in. I wiggled in frustration. He ran his hand down my side to wrap firmly around my hip, shifted his knee, and rolled his pelvis against my ass, rocking that delicious hardness against me.

I hummed in anticipation, forgetting every single other thing in that moment, my attention laser focused on that heat. I reached behind me, grasping for his hip, pulling him closer. I mewled in protest when he pulled away, but he only rolled me onto my back and deliberately settled himself between my thighs.

My breath caught and I lay still, looking up into his shadowed face.

He pushed himself up to his knees, grasped the hem of my t-shirt, and swept it off over my head. He dropped his mouth to my chest and kissed my chest above my beating heart before rearing back and hooking his fingers into the sides of my panties.

His lips followed the path his fingers forged as he slowly worked my panties down my legs. Standing at the foot of the bed, he pushed his boxers down over his hips to the floor.

My stomach dipped and I grasped the sheets in my fists. This was happening too fast and not fast enough. I watched as he bent and pressed a soft kiss to the inside of my ankle and the sweetness of it released my breath.

This Vander was my Vander.

Pressing kisses along the length of my legs to my thighs, he brushed over my mons with a muttered curse, and moved up my body until he stretched out over me, bracing his weight on his arms and knees, his thick, muscled thighs spreading mine wide, the hair on his legs tantalizing the inside of my thighs.

Bending his neck, he brushed his mouth across mine, softly, reverently.

225

I pushed my thoughts away and rolled my hips impatiently, running my hands down his sides as he hovered over me. Slanting his mouth across mine, he kissed me gently as he slid deep inside.

We both stilled at the sweet relief of his homecoming.

He stroked the hair at my temples with his thumbs, his dark eyes locked on mine, and touched the tip of my nose with his. Moments like these only happened in my dreams and dreams dissipate like smoke in the morning.

I trembled.

He kissed me softly.

I struggled to maintain my grasp on reality. Reality taught me that this wouldn't last, people don't stay.

He countered every thought with a kiss, peeled back the layers of protection I'd built to house the fear and anxiety inside. The door that he'd cracked open only a week before swung wide on rusty hinges flooding my doubt with his faith, my despair with his hope, my dark with his light.

Utterly exposed and completely defenseless against him, I knew the only way out now was through, and I doubted my heart would survive another loss.

Oh, God!

I closed my eyes.

Emotion welled up in my chest, the pain from the bumps along our broken road hitching my breath and escaping in rivulets from beneath my closed lids.

He kissed each tear away.

Then he moved, his long, hard body sliding over mine. Cradling my head between his palms, he watched as I battled my demons.

Bit by bit, the pleasure he doled out, so exquisitely, eclipsed the fear, anaesthetized the pain, and focussed my attention to the perfection of his body inside mine.

I ran my hands down our sides, reveling in the feel of our bodies' alignment. I reached around to grasp the tightened muscles of his ass, felt them flex as he slowly pumped in and out of me.

I dragged my palms up to flatten them against his back.

I pulled him closer, crushing my breasts against his hard chest.

Lined up our heartbeats.

Prayed I was as deeply entrenched in his heart as he was in mine as my heart set its rhythm to his.

I whimpered with the need to be closer. I wrapped my hand around the back of his neck and yanked his mouth to mine.

Tasted what I'd hungered for all these years.

He pulled my thigh higher around his hip, opening me further, and leaned into the kiss even as he snapped his hips, hitting that sweet spot before pulling back and doing it again.

Sweet relief hovered.

I arched beneath him, clutching his back, my leg curled tightly around his hip, battling through the fear, working through the pain of the past.

I touched him and kissed him everywhere I could reach, striving to reassure myself of his solid presence.

My pussy spasmed around him, urging me onwards, my body completely onboard while my heart tentatively reached towards belief.

My mind struggled to reconcile all that had happened in the past few days along with what I falsely believed to be his abandonment over a decade before.

I drew back and took in his face, serious and intense as he stared down at me. I lifted my hips to meet his thrust. He kissed me.

Perhaps, he wasn't a myth.

I pressed my lips to his and he groaned into my mouth.

Perhaps, now was our time.

I twisted my neck to the side, silently asking him to kiss my neck.

He dragged his lips down my throat, his breath ragged.

Perhaps, I could keep him.

I scraped my teeth along his collarbone, and his hands plunged into my hair.

Perhaps, he would stay.

I was on a rollercoaster, experiencing that split second of awareness, at the peak of the precipice, that there was no going back and nothing on earth that could slow the momentum or stop my plunging descent. A brief nanosecond in which to decide whether or not to peel my fingers off the bar, let go, and enjoy the ride, or hang on for dear life, white knuckled, eyes squeezed shut until it was over, and I could get off.

On this ride, I didn't fully trust the seatbelt to hold me.

With both fists, I grasped his hair tightly at the sides, and pulled his face away from my neck. He stilled inside me with a soft grunt, his arms trembling around me.

Staring into his dark eyes, mine flashed out a warning, my voice strained and loud in the quiet of the night.

"Don't you ever fucking let go."

He nodded shortly, his eyes steady on mine. "I promise."

I let go of the bar.

Come what may, I was in.

All of me for all of him.

I gentled my hands in his hair, scraping my nails lightly across his scalp. I cupped the back of his neck, flexed my fingers into his back. I kissed his jaw, ran my nose alongside his, brushed my mouth across his sweet lips.

My name a pained whisper on his lips, he began to move again inside me.

Lifting my chin, I accepted his kiss.

Parting my lips, I accepted his tongue.

Tilting my hips, I accepted his body.

Opening my heart, I accepted his promise.

Chapter 30 - Reflections

<u>Ruby</u>

Awkward doesn't begin to describe it." I cringed. "How would you feel if you had to tell Alex you were wrong about who his father is because you'd fucked two different men two weeks apart?"

Amber and I sat hip-to-hip on the front step, waiting for Vander to come home with Jace. After talking to Jace about the paternity test, I told him Vander wanted to pick him up after school and take him out. Jace was a ball of nervous excitement. His dreams of having a father were taking shape right in front of him. Amber sat quietly, listening, as I rehashed the awkward conversation with Jace.

She looked down and sighed, then nodded. She bumped me lightly with her shoulder. "You dirty slut."

I chortled.

She smiled. "You're so far from that, Ruby. You were entitled to fuck whomever you wanted. You weren't committed to him or anyone. It's just ludicrous that the first time you have sex in ten years it was with two men two weeks apart." She laughed incredulously. "So ridiculously far-fetched."

Sharing with Amber lightened the weight that had settled over me since Sunday night with Vander's revelation.

"I wish you'd let me share your burdens, Amber," I murmured.

Amber wrapped her arms around her drawn up knees. "Just because I don't give you the details doesn't mean you don't help me carry it."

A tear spilled over and slowly rolled down her face.

I put my arm around her shoulders, and she put her head on my shoulder. She drew in a ragged breath, then relaxed against my side.

Vander

Caffeine at night had never been a problem for me, and I often enjoyed a cup of coffee in the evenings. I sat out on my deck and sipped the bitter brew, turning the collar of my fleece up around my neck. It would be too cold to sit outside soon. A fire bowl for the patio would be perfect. Picturing Ruby and I cozied up in a blanket drinking coffee by the fire at night, while Jace slept in his bedroom inside, made it a done deal.

I'd swing by the Home Store tomorrow, and pick one up, in between my appointment and picking Jace up after school.

Jace.

What an unbelievable development.

I'd gone to dinner at Ruby's, fully prepared to put on a good front when I first met Jace, and ready to swallow the pain of meeting a child I wished was mine.

Fuck.

Alex came in first, sliding over the wood floors on his sock feet. I laughed, and thought, 'there's Ruby in boy form'. My fears dissipated and I loved him immediately.

Then Jace loped in.

Hands in his pockets.

Unruly mop of curly hair.

Dark, luminous eyes.

Half smile exactly like his older brother's.

A current like an electric shock ran through my body at the sight of him.

230

Yiayia's eyes darted back and forth between him and I, and Amber lost what little colour she had. Ruby, her focus wholly on Jace, was oblivious.

My emotions swung between anger, guilt, and despair. Anger with myself for having missed so much, despair over the fact that Ruby was a single mom all these years, guilt that all of it was due to my misguided attempt at self-sacrifice. I pushed away the worm of a thought that was so disturbing I could not acknowledge it, even to myself.

I barely made it through the dinner.

Yet, at the same time, nothing could tear me away. Sitting at the table with Jace, I was enthralled. Soaking up his answers to all my questions, listening to him converse with his cousin, witnessing his easy love and affection for his family, I couldn't get enough.

After he left the table, I couldn't get out of there fast enough.

Thank God, Ruby's temper sent her barreling over Sunday night. If not, I would be breaking the news to her tonight, and not out spending this precious time with my son.

I picked him up after school and met Amber's husband Gus at the same time. I invited Gus and Alex to come with us, but I was grateful that he declined. He'd be picking up Alex again tomorrow, paving the way for me to spend more time with Jace.

Jace was quiet at first but loosened up when I suggested we grab a bite to eat at the drive-thru and go hit some balls. We spent two hours batting. He was tireless.

Walking out of the batting cages, I caught sight of us walking side-by-side. We both had our hands jammed deep in our pockets, and Jace scanned his environment with a quiet curiosity that reminded me so acutely of George, it hurt my heart.

I swallowed the lump in my throat, then cleared it.

"Your mom told you that I think I'm your dad?" I froze at my use of the word 'dad', wondering if he'd deny me.

He glanced at me sideways and answered with a question of his own. "Do you love my mom?"

I answered immediately, my voice firm. "I do."

"You going to leave her again?" He pushed softly.

I winced. I'd failed so astronomically with them both. "Never."

Jace nodded and looked to his feet as we made our way to the car. "And if the test comes back and you're not my dad, then what?"

Taking a chance, I wrapped my hand around the tender nape of his neck. I felt him tense. "If your mom will have me, I'll still be your dad."

Turning the corner, I caught one last glimpse of us in the window. To any casual observer, there was nothing earth-shattering about the reflection: a large, stern, bearded man with his hand set affectionately on the back of his child's neck. The child, young and slight of build, loping along easily beside him. The resemblance between us such that no one would question whether he was my son.

My world, however, had been picked up and shaken. What I knew, was that I'd lay my life down for him in an instant. The dusty glass of the storefront mirrored our first father-son chat, a picture and a promise I would carry with me all the days of my life.

Getting in the car I turned to him and asked, "If we pick up KFC, would Yiayia boil me?"

Jace huffed out a laugh. "Even if you picked up Greek food and brought it home, I think Yiayia would give you a pass." Suddenly he looked down into his lap, then murmured, "I've never seen Yiayia cry before."

Yesterday, Jace walked in on Ruby comforting Yiayia when she got home from work. The poor lady felt guilty for not doing more, not questioning more.

Squeezing his shoulder, I reassured him, "It's a difficult and painful situation for everyone, including you and I, but we'll get through it." Grasping my wallet out of my pocket, I pulled out a business card. "This is my cell. You call me if you need to talk. Fuck. Call me anytime, for any reason, whatsoever."

Jace laughed. "I'm not sure Yiayia would excuse an F-bomb!"

I chuckled, relieved to see the smile back on his face. "I'll keep that in mind. Now, tell me what's your favourite fast food, and we'll see how much we can get away with before Yiayia puts a stop to our fun."

He laughed out loud. My heart clutched at the sound and buried it, striving to stockpile memories for a painfully barren mental photo album that should have been nearly eleven years full.

All the way home, he chattered about the Adventure Club. Another link in the chain proving my paternity. I put a rush on the test results. I prayed I wasn't wrong.

Jace jumped out of the car as soon as I cut the ignition in the driveway.

Ruby anxiously assessed Jace as he approached her.

I retrieved the chicken from the backseat and loped up to where she and Amber perched on the front step.

I smiled down at Ruby, and her eyes skittered back and forth between Jace and me before allowing me a small smile.

"What did you do?" Amber teased Jace. "Yiayia is going to make you like the onions."

"No way, Da-Va-" Pink dusted Jace's cheeks as he caught himself, then he jerked a thumb in my direction with an easy grin. "He's got a free pass for at least a month."

Amber laughed and caught hold of Jace's hand. She kissed it and sent him inside to find Alex. Standing, she offered her cheek for my kiss, took the bucket of chicken from my hands, and opened the front door, smiling. "I'll see you guys inside."

I sat down next to Ruby with my legs stretched out in front of me, my ankles crossed, my hands linked together on my lap. I wasn't sure how much touching this Ruby would be comfortable with. When we were together twenty years ago, she was effusive with her affection.

Dipping my head to the side, I touched my forehead to hers. "Hello, Ruby-mine."

She smiled and leaned in closer, sliding her hand along the inside of my arm to link her fingers with mine. I closed my eyes and basked in her light.

"How'd it go?" She asked softly.

"Good, Ruby. Really good." I squeezed her hand reassuringly.

"So." She cleared her throat. "What's next?"

233

"I'd like to pick him up tomorrow as well. The test results should be here Thursday. If it's okay, I'd like to be here when we tell him."

She tensed beside me. "What if it's negative?"

I snorted. "Ruby. It's not going to be negative. He walks like me, looks like me, could be George's twin for fuck's sake. He talks like me, likes all the same things I like, it's not going to be negative."

"But what if it is?" She whispered.

I kissed the top of her head and murmured, "I'm going to tell you the same thing I told him. If it's negative, and you'll let me, I'll still be his dad."

Ruby froze, then clapped a hand over her mouth. She bent over her knees while her body heaved.

Immediately, I scooped my arms under her and pulled her onto my lap. "Easy, baby." I dropped kisses along her hairline. "Easy, agapi mou. It'll all be alright in just a little while."

She nodded but stayed curled against my chest for several minutes while she pulled herself together. I ran my hands up and down her side, dropped kisses onto her head, and felt her tension melt away.

With a deep inhale, she pushed herself off my lap. I stood and dusted off the back of my pants. Turning towards the door, I caught a glimpse of Jace watching us, his eyes large, a small smile on his sweet face.

Dinner went smoothly, much more so than on Sunday, and I laughed at Alex and Jace's antics as they verbally danced around Yiayia, and she allowed it.

More than once, I caught Jace studying his mom.

Alex focussed more on me. Like his aunt, he wore his emotions on his sleeve, and he did not appear to be at all sure about the changes that were afoot.

I took another sip of my coffee.

Leaving them at the end of the night rubbed me the wrong way.

I wanted them here with me.

Chapter 31 – Thank you

<u>Ruby</u>

First thing Thursday morning, I checked my email for the test results. Of course, they weren't there. It was still early, and Thursday was an estimate at best.

While I showered, I negotiated with myself over how often I would check my email. I decided once after the lunch rush, once after Jace got let out of school, and again before closing for the day. There was no point checking any more than that.

I pulled on my clothes and stuffed my cell phone into my pocket, then immediately pulled it back out. There was no harm checking before going downstairs. Jace didn't know the test results were coming today. I'd better not check before seeing him for breakfast. I tucked my phone back into my pocket, made it halfway down the hall before stopping and pulling it out again.

No email.

Okay. Deep breath, Ruby.

This was going to be a long day.

Thankfully, a steady stream of customers kept me busy, which wasn't unusual for a Thursday. Minty and the girls came in for lunch. Yanni picked up an order for himself and Elisavet after the initial rush, standing and chatting with me at the counter, until Elisavet stuck her head in my door and berated him for taking too long.

I cleaned the front counter and had just reached for my phone to check for the email when the front door swung open. Resigning myself to waiting another few minutes, I lifted my head.

Vander stood just inside the door, watching me. "Are you okay?"

"Uhh..." Why was he here? Did the results come in? Why wouldn't I be okay? Okay that he is Jace's father? Okay that he's not?

"Are they in?" I whispered.

He nodded and moved closer, I spun around and paced away.

"Ruby." He said firmly.

"Give me a moment."

Now that the time had come, I wasn't sure I was ready for the disappointment if Jace wasn't Vander's. I never wanted to reject any part of my son, and surely, wishing away his paternity fell under that category?

"Ruby."

I waved him off while I stumbled through my mental gymnastics. Whatever the results, Jace was my son and that was enough. If Vander stayed true to his word, Jace would have a stepdad the same way George did, and that was good, right?

"Ruby." Vander's hands landed firmly on my shoulders and turned me around. I slowly lifted my eyes to his, wondering if I'd find the answer there.

Vander cupped my face in his hands and rested his forehead on mine. "We have a son, Ruby-mine," he murmured.

I froze, momentarily awestruck, and then my knees buckled beneath me.

Vander wrapped his arms around my waist, pulled me close, and tucked his face into my neck, bending me backwards. Emotion rolled off him in waves and threatened to suck me under. I clung to his broad shoulders, tense with his overwhelming emotions.

I ran my hands over him gently, soothing him, coming to terms with the beautiful reality that the wish that secretly haunted my dreams all these years came true.

I tunneled my fingers through Vander's thick hair, and he pulled me up to my toes, wrapped up tight in his love. He felt solid beneath my hands, solid and present and real.

A half sob, half laugh broke from my throat. "He was made by love, Vander. He was made by our love."

"Yes, baby," he muttered brokenly, his hands running up and down my back as he set me on my feet and tucked my head against his chest while I embraced him.

He sniffed and pulled in a shuddering breath, then tipped his head down to rest his forehead on mine.

"Thank you, Ruby."

The memory of Gus bending over Amber, his forehead pressed to hers, the fragile proof of their love lying between them, popped into my mind. I smiled at the fact that I, too, got my tender moment.

After he finally released me, he rolled up his sleeves and helped me close the shop. We worked naturally alongside each other, and every time our eyes met, we grinned, or I teared up, or laughed, overjoyed by our news like any couple who just discovered they were pregnant.

We decided to pick Jace up together and give him the news.

Dropping off my car at home, I slid in beside Vander, and he reached for my hand. Nerves assailed me once again and Vander gave my hand a reassuring squeeze.

"Let's just be happy with our news for the moment," he said. "However Jace reacts, we'll deal with it. Together."

"Maybe I should tell him by myself," I fretted. "I know you're his father, but he barely knows you."

"Ruby, he wants this. If he felt in any way ambivalent about it, I'd agree with you, but he wants this. If I don't show up now, how's he going to trust me to show up later?"

"This is true." I pressed the tip of my forefinger into the divot at the bow of my lip. I would have to get used to sharing Jace with Vander.

We saw Jace roll out of school on Alex's heels, and Vander got out of the car. The boys saw Gus first and headed his way. I had a clear view of Jace and Alex as Gus pointed out Vander and then lifted a hand in greeting.

237

Jace's face lit up, making me glad that Vander pushed to come. I watched him lope over with my heart in my throat. He always wanted a dad and now he would have his own.

I glanced at Gus and Alex, waving though I knew the chances of them seeing me in the car were slim.

Alex's brow furrowed.

Like me, he didn't like change unless he instigated it. Like me, it took him awhile to adjust. Like me, the events in his life had shaken, not stirred, his world, and he struggled to reacclimate himself. And like me, he wore his emotions on his sleeve.

I needed to give Amber a heads up, and make sure to include him in the life we were building.

Jace made it to the car, and Vander drew him in for a man hug. Jace's arms went right around Vander's back for a moment before he slid into the backseat and leaned over to kiss my cheek. "Hey, momma. I didn't know you were coming today."

"I didn't have any supper orders, so I closed up early."

"That's good. So, what are we doing? You seem weird."

I glanced at Vander. He twisted so that we were both facing Jace over the seat backs. "The test results came back today," I said and Jace's eyes locked onto mine. "Vander is your dad."

Jace stared at me, his face expressionless. Finally, he spoke, "Is."

"Yes. Vander is your father. He is your real dad," I reiterated to make sure he understood.

He dropped his gaze for a minute and then started nodding his head. He snuck a quick, assessing peek at Vander's face then met my eyes again.

"Cool," he said.

Vander chuckled beside me, and I stared back and forth between them.

"Can we go get something to eat? Can we go to the West End Diner?" Jace asked.

Oh, God. Baptism by fire.

"Don't you think we should tell Yiayia and Thia and Thio and Alex first?"

"Can we just call them?" He pushed.

Jace never pushed, and we only went to West Side Diner on Sunday mornings, and then I got it. He wanted something familiar.

"Sure, yes. We can do that. Is that okay with you, Van?"

Vander sat looking at Jace with that familiar half smile and Jace mirrored the same smile back at him.

"Sure, buddy." He turned to start the car. "I've heard good things about this place."

By the time we got to the restaurant, I had finished with my phone calls.

Voula greeted Jace and me as soon as we walked through the door. "Hey, koukla! You can take your usual table..." She petered off when she caught sight of Vander. Her eyes lit up with appreciation and she wagged her eyebrows at me. "You're going to need a bigger table today. Who's this?" She asked Jace.

Jace grinned easily. "This is my dad."

Voula's eyes flew to mine, and I nodded. The reassuring pressure of Vander's hand met my back, and I cleared my throat. "This is Vander. He was my university boyfriend, and he is Jace's father."

"Aw," Voula grinned. "You're Mr. Dolmadakia."

I laughed out loud. Leave it to Voula to break the tension. Vander grinned at me, bemused. "Mr. Dolmadakia?"

I shrugged. "Elisavet talks too much."

Vander

"Well, that was anticlimactic," Ruby said drily.

We dropped Jace off at Yiayia's to have a sleepover with Alex, while Ruby and I stole a few hours to ourselves. I tucked her hand under mine on my thigh, then pulled out of the driveway and headed for my place, hopefully soon to be our place.

"He took it well."

"He didn't waste any time claiming you," she murmured.

I glanced at her. "That's a good thing, no?"

239

"It is…" She petered off then continued firmly, "It is. I just need a moment to catch up. I'm going to be bombarded with questions."

"Ruby," I hesitated. "You know you don't owe anyone any explanation."

"They're all going to wonder," she muttered grumpily.

"So? Let them speculate. As soon as they see him and I together, their doubts will be laid to rest."

"They're going to think I lied about Drew, that you were a deadbeat dad, they're going to think a whole lot of things."

"Again, so? What does it matter to you? To us? To Jace? I think most people will take it like Voula did. And those that don't, don't matter. Those that do matter, know the truth. No one else is entitled to your life story."

She was quiet for a moment, then nodded. "Okay."

"Yeah?" I wanted to make sure.

"Yeah." She smiled. "It's been a while since I shook things up in the Greek community."

I laughed and squeezed her hand.

Inside the house, Ruby wandered into the kitchen and started opening cupboards and drawers.

"What are you looking for?"

"Hmm?" She answered distractedly. "Nothing, really. Just looking."

"Just being nosy?" I teased.

She arched her brow at me. "Did you not say this is my house? Am I not entitled to open the cupboards in my own house?"

I dipped my head to give her that point.

She smirked and turned her back to me.

I took the opportunity to step in close behind her and cage her in between my chest and the counter. I dipped my chin and gently took her earlobe between my teeth.

She tensed and then melted back against me.

"You want something to drink, or should I take you straight to bed?"

"You should definitely take me to bed." She turned to face me and looped her arms around my neck. "In fact," she smiled cheekily, "you've been terribly remiss."

I raised my eyebrows. "Really?" I pulled her away from the counter and started walking her backwards towards our bedroom.

She nodded. "Mm-hmm. I'd go so far as to say you've been stingy."

"Stingy?" I barked, incredulous. "Stingy with what precisely?"

She shrugged her shoulders and tried to look innocent. "Orgasms."

I laughed and dipped down, wrapping her up against my chest so that her feet dangled above the floor. "You're going to pay for that."

She smiled. "I hope so."

I grinned at her. "Let's see if you still think so in half an hour."

I put her down at the side of our bed and turned her to face away from me. Dragging my hands down her arms, I grasped her hands and stretched her arms up over her head.

"Hold them there," I murmured in her ear as I grasped the hem of her t-shirt, letting the tips of my fingers lightly caress her sides as I slowly tugged her t-shirt up over her head.

She moved to lower her arms, but I stopped her with a palm to each bicep. "Hold, Ruby."

She stiffened momentarily and I thought for a moment that she would refuse. I grinned. I knew she would fight me eventually. She didn't have the patience to wait, or the desire to take direction.

I wanted to see if I could change her mind. It didn't escape my notice that this would be the first time we'd made love for fun in over twenty years, and I wanted it to be memorable for us both.

Trailing my fingers lightly down her arms, over her shoulders, and across her back, I flicked open her bra so that it hung open at the back but still clung to her breasts. My fingers whispered against her ribs. Careful not to touch her, I pulled the lacy fabric up and over to join her t-shirt on the floor.

I had a moment of regret that I didn't savour the sight of her in the lacy bra before taking it off. She'd always loved lingerie.

I dropped a kiss on her shoulder, and a tiny pant escaped her lips. Moving closer so that my chest brushed against her back, I licked the juncture between her shoulder and her neck, and her head dropped to the side to give me access.

The view from my angle enabled me to see straight down her body, the fullness of her breasts, the soft roundness of her tummy, her stockinged toes curling into the carpet. Scraping my beard along her neck and shoulder, dropping soft, wet kisses in my wake, I instructed her, "Put your arms around my neck."

She made to turn, but I grasped her hips and held her in position. She nodded then dropped her hands to grasp the back of my neck, causing her back to arch, making her breasts an offering.

Stepping closer, I ground my pelvis against her ass, so she could feel how she affected me. She moaned, allowing her head to drop back on my shoulder. Stepping away from her, she protested and arched back into my groin.

I grasped her hips once again, and held her firmly in position, lifting my mouth from her neck, I warned her, "Behave or I'll stop."

That iron hit her backbone once again and she looked at me sideways, her brows furrowed. "Maybe I'll stop," she snapped.

I traced the waistband of her jeans and flicked open the button, palmed her ribs and swept up to cup her breasts in my hands, pinching the rosy nipples between my thumbs and the side of my forefingers. She groaned and rested her head back on my shoulder.

"Will you though?" I teased.

"Vander," she warned, tightening her grip on the back of my neck.

I chuckled against her neck, and she shivered.

She was a dream.

Rolling her nipples, kneading her breasts, kissing her neck, I stepped forward and rolled my pelvis against her ass.

"Vander..." This time, my name fell like a plea from her lips.

I pulled down the zipper of her jeans and worked them down over her round hips. Ruby's body had matured. She was strong, and firm, but rounded and my hands ached to hold onto her as I drove up inside her.

Taking her hands from the back of my neck, my erection trapped behind my fly, I rubbed against her bare backside, and she arched back into me. Curling my body around hers, I placed her hands flat on the bed, grabbed hold of her hips, and kissed a line down her spine as she arched beneath me.

I dropped to my knees, she stiffened, and started to push herself upright.

"I'll stop, Ruby."

"Vander," her voice quavered with nerves, "I feel too exposed..."

I stroked her bare hips and the roundness of her ass. "I disagree. You're not exposed nearly enough. Hands to the bed."

She hesitated, so I threaded my hand between her thighs and gently massaged her core.

"Okay," she breathed, and relaxed into her position.

I pulled her jeans down to her ankles and helped her step out of them, then removed her socks, placing her feet back down on the floor before edging them apart.

"Um..."

"Shh, Ruby," I soothed, firmly stroking up the inside of her leg to the top of her thigh.

I gathered some of her wet and painted the tops of her thighs. I could feel her struggling with the vulnerability of the position.

Desperate for her trust, I stood to give her a break. I flicked open the button of my jeans to give my strangled cock more room.

Hearing the button, she arched to offer herself to me and I placed my palm firmly on her back. "Just like this, Ruby-mine. I want you just like this, arched, ready, offering."

She moaned and rocked back, searching for me to fill her.

Pressing against her back, I instructed, "Rest your head down on the bed. Get comfortable. You're going to be here for awhile."

She complied and I nudged her feet a little further apart before dropping back to my knees.

"Vander! What are you doing?"

I couldn't answer. All her bounty lay spread out before me. I kneaded the flesh of her buttocks. Kissed the line where her ass met her thigh. Breathed in the scent of her arousal. Stroked her wet folds until she started to push back against me, then mashed my face against her pussy, licking and sucking and stroking her with my tongue.

She went rigid for half a second before sensation overwhelmed her and she stilled, then arched back, and gave herself over to me.

I spread her open with my hands, nipping and teasing her swollen flesh. No longer hesitant, Ruby mewled every time I broke contact and pushed back, chasing my tongue. When her thighs began to shake, I gave her one last lick then pulled myself away.

"Vander," she gasped, then nodded her approval when I stood up behind her.

I pulled down my zipper a little more. She wiggled her round ass, ready for me to fill her. I pulled in a deep breath, refocussed, and pulled her up and around to face me.

Her pretty face flushed pink, eyes heated, she threw herself against my chest and pulled my head down to hers. She stopped a breath before her mouth met mine and I thought for a moment she would deny me, not wanting to taste herself. She angled her head and licked my mouth slowly from corner to corner and I groaned.

This woman.

Everything.

I grasped her hair and pulled her head back, then gave in to the lust striving to take over for just a moment as I kissed her, hard.

Her hands ran up and down my back, yanking my shirt out of my jeans. She drew back and her trembling fingers feverishly worked the buttons loose. She pushed it over my shoulders.

I pulled it off the rest of the way, then pulled her against me, her beautiful breasts mashed against my chest. I ground against her belly and her whole body shook with need.

We were getting there.

Her hands went to the opening of my jeans, and she froze.

"What's this?"

She trailed trembling fingers gently over my fresh ink.

"I told you I was going to tattoo your name over my heart."

"It's your ribs."

"Still over my heart," I admonished, raising my eyebrow at her. "I didn't want it to get lost in my chest hair."

She chuckled. "And this?"

She traced the Roman numerals on the inside of my bicep.

"My sons' birthdates."

She traced Jace's. "Is this Jace?"

"Of course," I snorted. At least this gave my poor dick a break.

"You got the year wrong."

"What?" I barked in shock.

"The year. You got the year wrong."

I looked at my bicep. "Are you fucking kidding me? I know I told them the right year. What did they put?"

She shook in my arms. Startled I turned to look at her face screwed up trying to hold in her laughter.

"Ruby!" I yelled, then laughed. "That was mean, Ruby-mine."

She chortled away, grasping onto my arms in her mirth, wiggling with delight. I couldn't help but laugh with her. Standing with her naked and laughing in my arms was not part of tonight's plan but it far from sucked.

Holding her close, I dipped my head to look at her. "Do you like it?"

She wrinkled her nose. "They're crusty."

"Well, they're not healed yet!" I said, exasperated.

She twinkled at me. Getting under my skin was all part of her game.

It was time to take over and bring my woman to her knees. My dick perked up at the thought. That thought helped me refocus.

"I like it," she whispered, then stretched up to press a kiss to my lips. "I love it." She licked my throat. "I love you."

She ran her hands down my sides and traced the edge of my jeans.

I allowed her to lower the zipper the rest of the way before capturing her wrists and pushing her gently backwards onto the bed.

She pushed herself further in, spread her legs, and opened her arms to me.

This was the stuff of my dreams. I took her in, all her womanly softness, pink, swollen, mouth parted, fingers beckoning, and crawled onto the bed beside her.

"Pants. Off." She ordered and I moved up the bed, taking her hands with me, and trapping her wrists together above her head.

"Uh, oh," she muttered, realizing this wasn't going where she wanted it to go. "Vander, no, please Vander," she tried negotiating, and I silenced her with my mouth before I laughed.

She wriggled to get closer to me.

I slung my thigh over both of hers, trapping her legs together, and holding her still.

She moaned and squeezed her thighs together looking for relief.

Keeping my mouth on hers, I gentled the kiss, opening my eyes to watch her face as I trailed my fingers over her collarbone, across her chest and down between her breasts. Cupping one breast gently, I pinched her nipple, hard, and her eyes flew open as she gasped into my mouth.

Holding her gaze, I stroked firmly down her torso to the juncture of her thighs.

Her eyelids drifted shut. She nodded and breathed, "Yes, baby," as she tilted her hips up for my questing fingers.

Ah, Ruby-mine. How long I've wanted you like this.

I slowly dipped a finger into the cleft between her clenched thighs.

She struggled to open but I locked her down with my thigh. Her brow furrowed and she tilted her hips allowing me enough space to stroke her swollen bud, pulling a gasp from her lips.

I feathered kisses along the side of her face and rolled my finger against her clit. Her thighs began to quake, her breath came in shallow pants.

I removed my finger, and she let out a low moan of protest.

Her wrists lay lax in my fist. I released them and she didn't move.

"Leave them there," I ordered.

Shifting my weight, I moved down the bed, spread her legs and knelt between them. Dipping my head, I licked her slowly from bottom to top, flicked my tongue against her clit, then plunged my tongue inside her.

She bucked up against my face, and I retreated back to her breasts, toying with first one, then the other. I praised her for leaving her hands where they were and dropped kisses over her upturned face. Once she resettled, I went through it again. This time she stayed motionless, her tummy quivering beneath my palm as I licked her.

I brought her to the brink, again and again.

When every breath became a moan, when her body writhed on the bed beneath me, when her hips tilted up in entreaty, I got up on my knees and hovered over her.

"Ruby-mine, give me your eyes."

Her heavy lids flickered open, dazed with passion. She was ready.

I kissed her lightly on her mouth then kissed and tongued my way back down her abdomen, not stopping until I covered her once again with my mouth.

"Oh, oh, oh..." she chanted, her heels pressed into the mattress, pelvis tilted up.

I licked her, flicked her clit, then pulled it firmly into my hot mouth. She cried out and reared off the bed, grasped the back of my head, and mashed her pussy into my face as she came violently against my mouth.

When she stopped shaking, she melted back onto the bed, languid, sated. I crawled up beside her, stroking her tummy lightly.

"How are you, Ruby-mine?"

"Mm... as soon as I recover, I'm going to kill you," she murmured.

I laughed then yanked my jeans down over my ass, spread her legs around my hips, and thrust inside.

Immediately wrapping her legs around my back, she grasped my hair and plundered my mouth. I lasted all of thirty seconds before succumbing and came on a grunt, my face tucked into her sweet throat.

Chapter 32 - Rip off the Damn Band-Aid

Vander

By the time I took Ruby home, it was early morning in Greece. I waited a couple of hours, then FaceTimed my parents. Equal parts shocked, dismayed, and excited, it would take them a few days to adjust to the news, but promising them a FaceTime meeting with Jace helped.

I needed to tell George. This was not news I wanted to text, so I waited until after school and asked him to FaceTime from a private location. Unfortunately, this was not an odd request. If we tried to talk around his mother, she often interfered. A few minutes later my phone buzzed.

"Yassou, Georgie mou," I greeted him, smiling. He looked relaxed and ready for the weekend. His newest baseball cap spun backwards, his eyes alight with curiosity and pleasure.

"Hi, Dad. What's up?"

I wished I could do this in person. I took a breath, meeting his eyes through the screen. I hated this distance. It was better than a text or a phone call, but I wished he was sitting in front of me where I could lay my hand along the back of his neck and touch his forehead to mine, where I could gauge his reaction more closely, where I could follow up throughout the day, checking in to make sure he was okay.

"I'd uh, prefer to do this in person, but this kind of news can't wait-"

"Are you sick?" George cut me off and sat up straight.

"No! No, Georgie. It's good news, really good news, just surprising and unexpected."

"Okay..."

"Do you remember why I told you I picked this place when I moved?"

"Yeah, your high school girlfriend or something?"

"University. But yes. What I didn't tell you was that I met up with her quite by accident about 11 years ago. She had never moved on from what we had. She didn't even date. We had a weekend together and I had the brilliant idea to let her go afterwards so she could find happiness and build a life without me. She thought I abandoned her. Two weeks later-"

"She didn't date for, like, years?"

"Yeah, Georgie. Let me finish. This is difficult and I don't want you getting the wrong idea about her, okay?"

"Sure, dad. Go ahead."

"So, two weeks later, she slept with someone else. A few months later she found out she was pregnant. She thought the baby was his, turns out he's mine."

George's face paled. "How do you know?"

"I went to her house to have dinner with her family and meet her son. I knew right away he was mine. He looks just like you."

"Are you sure?"

I nodded firmly. "We did a paternity test to confirm. There is no possibility that he's not my son."

"Huh," George grunted. He stared off into space, processing the information, then met my eyes. "You missed his whole life so far."

I winced. "Yeah."

"I'm sorry, Dad."

Grief and pride filled my chest and threatened to overflow. Grief at the stark truth of his statement, and pride that he could think of my feelings in the face of the bomb I just dropped on him. I could do nothing but nod in that moment.

He continued. "So, I guess I have a brother?"

I smiled. "He could be your twin."

I answered the rest of George's questions about Jace and Ruby, told him about Yiayia, and his cousin, Alex. George had two sisters, and one much younger, little girl cousin. Having a brother and a cousin not that much younger than him was quite a shift.

"Do you still want me to come out for Thanksgiving?"

"What? Fuck, yes. Why would you even ask? In fact, I need to talk to your stepdad privately. I want you to come out one day earlier and stay an extra day. Would that be alright with you?"

"Mom's not going to like it. I'll ask Dad to call you."

"Yeah, I know. She doesn't like for you to miss school," I defended her. Although she didn't deserve it, George did. "I'll talk to your dad. And, Georgie, let's just keep this between us for the moment, okay agori mou?"

He nodded, but still looked a little unsure when he signed off. I texted him right away telling him how much I loved him and not to worry about Thanksgiving, that we'd work it out. I confirmed our call time for the next day and told him I'd text him with a few different options for when I'd be by myself, and the rest when he could meet Jace and Ruby.

I didn't expect it to be difficult, but I was still relieved to have it over with.

On Saturday, Ruby worked at Spuds, and Jace spent the day with me. Amber agreed to let Alex come along as Gus was out of town. The boys chatted in the backseat, having decided to both sit in the back rather than take turns up front.

My initial assessment of Alex was correct. Like Ruby in boy form, his brain churned a mile a minute, and he broadcast his emotions far and wide for all to see. It was wildly apparent that he was not at all sure about me, or more specifically, how the changes I brought might affect him.

I pulled into the parking lot and opened my door while they spilled out the back and looked up at the sign on the building.

"Cool," Jace breathed.

Alex looked sidelong at me, then slowly followed Jace inside as I held the door open to Mountains, the indoor climbing gym I frequented.

251

Alex hopped from foot to foot while the instructor explained the safety rules and harness system to the boys. Jace took it all in, asking questions, and nodding quietly, as he listened to the answers.

When the instructor quizzed them back, focussing mainly on Alex who did not appear to be listening, Alex got every answer correct. The instructor cleared both boys to climb with me belaying.

"Won't we get bored waiting? Can't we both climb at the same time?" Alex asked.

"You won't get bored. You'll need the rest in between climbs. It will also give you time to study the wall before you go up, get familiar with the location of the footholds and handholds."

"You can go first, Alex," Jace offered.

"You sure?" Alex shifted his focus to Jace, shifting back and forth.

"Yup. Go ahead."

I checked Alex's harness and got him started on the wall. He made it up a third of the way before getting stuck.

"I'm done!" He yelled down to me.

"Want me to guide you higher?" I asked.

"No. I want to come down."

"Okay. Remember what the instructor said. Lay back in the harness and bounce down lightly on your toes."

Alex descended perfectly, and traded places with Jace. Jace got a little further up the wall before he, too, got stuck.

Alex, standing still and quiet beside me, said, "I can see where he needs to go."

"Yeah? Where do you think?"

"If he brings his right foot up at a forty-five-degree angle, there's a big yellow rock he could step on."

"That's what I would say."

"Should we ask him?" Alex looked up at me, and I noted again how much like his aunt he was, though they looked little alike.

"Go ahead and ask him if he wants help."

Alex cupped his hands around his mouth. "Want me to tell you how to get up, Jace?"

Jace shook his head no.

"Looks like he wants to take a minute to figure it out himself."

Jace bent his neck to check for footholds and Alex saw the moment he noticed the yellow foothold. "Yes!" he hissed.

Jace managed another ten feet before signalling his readiness to come back down. He sat back in his harness and walked down the wall, bouncing lightly onto his feet when he hit the floor.

"That was awesome!!!" He grinned at both of us. "My arms are shaking!"

I chuckled. "Yeah, buddy, it's tiring."

"Can you do it, um, Uncle Vander?"

I loved hearing that. As an only child, I had no nieces or nephews. I swallowed my grin and answered. "Yeah, buddy, I can do it."

"Can you show us?"

"I don't have a belayer right now, but I'll tell you what. There's boulder climbing at the other end of the gym. I'll climb whichever one you want me to. That'll give you a bit more time to rest and then you can do another climb if you want."

Alex, the little shit, immediately went to the most advanced climb. "Can you do this one?"

"I can, but I'll need to warm up first." I hopped on the wall on an intermediate climb and pulled myself along the rockface to the top.

"Wow, that was fast!" Jace stood with his hands in his pockets, his eyes trained on me like beacons.

"Can you do the other one, now?" Alex asked.

The advanced climb Alex chose, required the climber to move horizontally to the floor at two different points, and although I had experience, it was still a difficult climb.

"Let's give it a try."

At the top, I looked down to see both boys grinning and cheering. I laughed out loud. They were great kids.

And one of them was mine.

They climbed a total of three more times each before their arms and legs gave out. Jace reached the top before Alex, but on the last climb they both reached the top.

I grabbed bottles of water for both. They slumped on the bench and sucked them back.

"Hungry?"

"Just thirsty," Jace replied.

Alex didn't speak. Alex didn't move. Climbing might be good for him, help him to expel all that extra energy.

It expended a lot of calories, too. As soon as they replenished their fluids, the hunger would hit.

Back in the car, they compared notes on their climbs, and I turned the car towards Spuds to feed them and see Ruby.

"Uh, actually, I am starting to get hungry now," Jace said from the backseat.

I realized either he didn't know what to call me or wasn't ready to call me dad. I swallowed my disappointment. It was too much to expect him to call me dad right away.

"Yeah, agori mou, I thought you might be. You want to go eat at Spuds? See your mom and pick up treats at Shop the Parthenon?"

"That sounds good. What do you think, Alex?"

"Yeah. Does Minnie work today?" Alex responded.

"We'll ask my mom when we get there."

"Alright, my son? We'll go to Spuds?" I confirmed.

Jace's hopeful eyes flew to mine in the rear-view mirror at the endearment, and I realized uncertainty about me plagued him.

"Yeah, uh, yeah. That's really good..." He petered off. He'd get there in his own time.

Much to their disappointment, Minnie, who I found out was their honorary aunt, and was named Minty, was not working, but Ruby called her cell and she said she'd head over.

"She's going to come here just like that?" I asked.

"Well," Ruby blushed, "she wants to meet you and she lives upstairs."

I grinned. "Oh, I see. Hmm. What does she know about me?"

Ruby chortled, her eyes twinkling. "Probably more than you want her to."

I groaned and turned away and she laughed harder. I stalked towards her, pulled her into my arms and kissed her while she laughed, momentarily forgetting about the boys.

When I finally pulled back, Ruby dipped her head to hide her face, but she couldn't hide her blush. I chuckled, wanted to see more of that.

Releasing her, I turned to the boys. Jace looked slightly bemused, but the sadness on Alex's face gutted me.

Alex looked exactly like I felt the better part of twenty years.

I sat down in the seat across from them and sought to distract Alex. "Tell me about Minty, and why you call her Minnie."

Alex perked up while Jace kept an assessing eye on me.

The door opened, and I turned to see a pretty woman about my age.

She looked the very definition of high maintenance. Her blond hair was pulled back in a sleek ponytail, showcasing her jewelry and her perfectly made-up face. Designer jeans encased her long legs, and it was my guess that the blouse she wore was of equal quality. She was the polar opposite of Ruby.

Ruby was in the back, but as soon as Minty saw the boys, her face broke into a broad grin, and she held out her arms.

"Boys!"

I turned around, wanting to see the boys' reaction to her, but they were already out of their seats, all bright eyes and broad smiles. They near bowled her over, crashing into her the way they did.

They broke into excited chatter about rock-climbing, and she stood patiently, taking in every detail, her hands resting on their shoulders as they explained how they got to the top.

"Jace made it to the top two times, but next time I'm going to make it up every time."

"I can take you after school one day?" She offered.

Alex laughed. "No, Minnie. You have to be a trained belayer."

She nodded. "Alright, then. I'll look into that."

Jace took half a step back and looked over her outfit. "You might need to wear real jeans and a t-shirt... Do you have track pants, Minnie?"

Alex cut in. "Do you have running shoes, Minnie?"

She chuckled softly. "I'll buy some just for you."

Alex released her but Jace took hold of her hand and led her over to me. With every step she took closer, a mask of cool composure settled over her face.

She held out her hand to shake mine. I opened my mouth to speak, but somehow with her eyes, she cut me off.

Dipping her head to Jace, she murmured, "Would you like to introduce me?"

Jace's chest puffed out and he looked at me.

"This," he indicated Minty, "is my Aunt Minnie. But only Alex and I call her Minnie, you can call her Minty." He took a deep breath, and if possible, his chest puffed out further. "Minnie, this is my dad, but you can call him Vander."

A smile teased the corners of her lips, and humor flashed behind her cool, brown eyes. Turning to me, she smiled politely. "It's lovely to meet you, Vander." She released my hand.

"Likewise."

"I understand you've settled in the area?" Her eyes held a challenge.

I looked at her, slightly startled to discover a bit of a mama-bear. I found myself charmed. "Yes. I'm here for good. Unless, of course, Ruby moves, in which case I'll be following her."

Her face lost a bit of its coolness, and she gave me a more genuine smile. "That's good to hear."

Ruby bustled out from the back and Minty's face warmed completely. What an interesting woman. Her man must have his hands full.

I took the boys next door, where Jace introduced me as his dad to Yanni and Elisavet.

"You're his father?" Elisavet's eyes darted back and forth between the two of us.

"I am," I answered firmly.

"But-" She began, but Yanni interrupted.

"Of course, he is. Look at the boy. He look just like his father."

Yanni extended his hand, and I shook it. "Welcome home, agori mou."

It appeared Voula was not prone to gossip. Now that Elisavet knew, the entire Greek community would be caught up by lunchtime tomorrow.

Good.

Rip off the damn band-aid.

One more to go.

Chapter 33 – Dad Bod

<u>Ruby</u>

The boys had a wonderful day, and Minty approves." I grinned and threw my arms around Vander. It felt so good to be able to do that whenever I wanted to.

"How did Jace react when you kissed me today? I was afraid to look." I cringed.

Vander's face was thoughtful. "Jace looked bemused but not upset." He winced. "Alex on the other hand, was positively gutted."

"Levendis mou," I whispered. Alex reminded me so much of myself, I couldn't help but empathize. "His parents' separation has been hard on him."

"Why did they separate?" Vander maneuvered us to the couch and sat down, pulling me onto his lap.

"I honestly don't know." I shrugged worriedly. "Amber would never say. Gus had a horrific health scare, something with his heart. He was incredibly ill for a while. She took care of him, but she became really subdued. I thought it was just because of what happened to him, but as soon as he got better, she left him."

He nodded. "Relationships are complicated. We know that well enough. They haven't started divorce proceedings?"

"No." I shook my head. "She's not sure what she wants." I shook the dark thoughts away. "Tell me about your day."

"I introduced Jace and Alex to George."

I jumped. "Oh, man. How did that go?"

Vander laughed. "It's not complicated for them. They all exchanged contact information, they're planning to play Minecraft online together tonight, and they're looking forward to meeting each other in person next week."

"Wow. That's so soon." I swallowed.

I had so many feelings, the most predominant one being jealousy. I moved to get off his lap, but he held me fast.

"Ruby," he spoke firmly, and I chanced a glance at his face. He wore that stern, stressed look, and I hated that I put it there. "You have absolutely nothing to worry about."

"I hate it that you were with her." I threw up my hands and tried again to get up. "I know it's crazy, and I know she's far from the only one," I rolled my neck in discomfort, "but you actually married her and started a family with her."

"We've never talked about this, Ruby, because you haven't wanted to, but George came first, then the wedding. I only married her because of George, and it was a grave mistake."

"Okay." I forced myself to settle on his lap, but I could not force the stiffness out of my spine. He ran his hands up and down my spine, over my thighs, his chin tipped down.

"I'm sorry, Ruby. I hate that I did this to you."

I released the breath I didn't know I held and melted against his wide chest. "I'm sorry, too."

His arms tightened around me. "I'm never, not ever, going to let you go. Which brings me to my next point. I want you and Jace to move in with me here."

I sat straight up again, and he huffed out an exasperated laugh.

"I can't. We can't. I can't leave Yiayia to live on her own, take Jace out of his school, take him away from Alex and everything he knows."

"So, what do you suggest? We date? Forever? I drop you home every night? Visit with Jace and not live with him?"

"No. Of course not. When you put it that way, it sounds ridiculous."

"In what way doesn't it sound ridiculous?" He retorted.

"Okay, Vander," I snapped. "I already agreed with you. Why don't you move in with us? I'm already in the master bedroom, it's not a big deal if you move in. Jace can stay in his school, Yiayia won't be alone, it's perfect!"

"There aren't enough bedrooms."

"What are you talking about? Jace has his own room, so does Yiayia, and so will we."

"What about George? And don't say the boys can share. That would be a disaster."

"Fuck."

He laughed and hugged me. "I love it when you're feisty instead of fearful."

"Humph."

"Would this be a suitable time to tell you George wants to meet you?"

I fell back and let my body flop back in his arms. "Oh, God! Fine! I'm not ready but I suppose I better break the ice seeing as how he's going to be here in a little over a week."

"We'll FaceTime him now?"

"Okay." I looked at him sideways. "Is there anything else you'd like to spring on me?"

He held up a finger. "One more thing."

"Ugh... go ahead."

"Jace introduced me as his dad to Elisavet and Yanni."

I stiffened. "What did they say?" This was awkward. They knew Drew well back in the day.

"Elisavet seemed unsure, but Yanni stepped in and smoothed everything over. He shook my hand and welcomed me home."

"Please tell me there's nothing else."

"There's nothing else. Let's call George and then I'll take you to bed."

"Maybe I'll take you to bed."

He nodded and smiled affably. "I'm amenable to that change in plans."

I guffawed, and Vander pulled out his cell phone.

"Vander, what if he doesn't like me? What if he blames me for you and his mom splitting up?"

"He and I worked through all that a long time ago. You don't have anything to worry about."

"How do you know?" I challenged.

"I just do, and you will, too, if you stop delaying the inevitable. Stop being a wuss."

"Oh. My. God." I glared at him. "You think you're going to get laid after this?"

"Yup, I do. Now stop talking about jumping me when I'm calling my son."

I pressed my lips together and went to move off his lap. He held me tight. "Vander, it's not appropriate," I hissed.

"Yassou, Georgie mou," he laughed.

I swung around to look at the phone to see a face that looked far too familiar. Vander angled the phone away from me to keep me out of the picture which was the only thing that saved his worthless ass.

"Hey, Dad. Why are you laughing?"

"Ruby is trying to get off my lap and I'm not letting her. She thinks it's inappropriate to meet you sitting on my lap."

George laughed out loud. "Fuck, dad. Don't embarrass her!"

"He swears?" I blurted out involuntarily.

"They're just words, koukla mou," Vander teased.

"Let me see her, Dad," George demanded.

Vander shifted the phone, and I came face-to-face with my nightmare. He assessed me quietly while I did the same. Vander's eyes, Vander's lips, Vander's dark curly hair, Vander's olive skin, Vander's narrow face, pointed chin, strong brow, looking at George I could hardly believe I didn't know Jace was Vander's.

Finally, I broke the silence between us. "Hello, Georgie. You look just like your dad."

He smiled and my stomach dipped. A few years from now, he'd be the spitting image of the Vander I first fell in love with.

"Hi, Ruby. It's fucking awesome to meet you," he twinkled, and I threw up my hands. Both he and Vander laughed.

"Oh. My. God. There's two of you now to torture me!"

"You don't ever swear, Ruby?" George asked.

"I only ever say one, and it's rare," I stated primly.

Vander laughed beneath me. "Tell him what it is."

I glared at Vander then turned back to George. "Shitfuckdamn."

George laughed, and I realized all my fear was for naught. This was Vander's child. I looked at him and saw only the man I loved. That might change once I met his ex-wife, but for now, I felt okay.

"Well, if you're only going to swear once in a while, better make it a good one."

"Exactly," I agreed, smiling.

After the initial joking, George got a bit more serious and asked us questions about the plans for Thanksgiving.

We decided to take the boys away to Blue Mountain for a couple of nights and come back in time to eat Thanksgiving dinner with Yiayia, Amber, Gus, and Alex. Vander relayed the plan to George.

I drifted away from the conversation for a bit, lost in my own thoughts, when I heard 'mountain biking'.

"What?" I asked Vander.

"We're going to rent mountain bikes and do the mountain trails."

I couldn't remember the last time I got on a bike. I didn't have one as a kid, and I wasn't sure I even knew how to ride one. Certainly, I wouldn't be able to ride one down a mountain.

"When you say 'we', you mean..."

Vander grinned. "George, Jace, and me. You can stay at the lodge and read your kissy books-"

"Vander! Shame on you!" I swung around to George. "Don't listen to him!"

"I won't, don't worry, Ruby."

Shortly after getting off the call, and feeling much lighter, Vander shuffled me into the bedroom.

I pulled his t-shirt out of his jeans, and he yanked it off over his head, dropping it to the floor. I ran my fingers lightly over his abs, remembered how he said all he did for years was work and work out.

I wanted to lick him.

Run my tongue over those ridges.

Follow them down, trace those veins with my teeth, take him in my mouth.

I looked back up into his eyes that looked pitch black in the dim light. His messy hair, his beautiful lips slightly parted as he stared down at me, while his hands ran up and down my back.

I looked down at my full breasts, softly rounded tummy, and thought about the cellulite on my thighs.

"Are you very disappointed with me?"

"What do you mean?" He asked gruffly as he whipped my t-shirt over my head. I wore a red lace set that was more lace than fabric. He traced the edge of my bra with his finger, his eyes following the curvy path.

"You know... hmm... that feels good... um..." I stilled his hand for a moment to get my thought out. "You are a wonderful man, and you're so beautiful. You could be with a much younger, much more beautiful woman." I ran my fingers over his abs. "We don't match."

He grabbed me and kissed me impatiently on my mouth, then maintaining eye contact, he proceeded to run his palms roughly over my

263

Devin Sloane

hips, grabbed hold of my ass and massaged it in his big hands before gently cupping my breasts, as if weighing them in his hands.

One corner of his lips tipped up and he placed my palm over his erection. "Does this seem at all disappointed?"

"No..."

He pushed me gently back onto the bed and then grinned as he climbed on top of me and caged me in, straddling my thighs and leaning over me on his forearms.

"Anyways, now that I have you and one of my boys in my life full time, I'm going to be rockin' a dad bod in no time."

I chortled and his face broke into a broad grin before he pressed his lips to mine and chased all thoughts from my head.

Chapter 34 – Pile it On

Ruby

I stretched myself awake. Mm, I could get used to waking up with this pleasant ache between my thighs.

The West End Diner waited for Jace and me, and I'd already slept in. In the shower, I wondered if Maria knew about Vander being Jace's dad. I cringed, hoping nobody questioned me about it.

I needn't have worried. Maria flew out of the kitchen in fierce mama bear mode and told Jace and me how happy she was for us that we reunited with Vander.

Loudly.

I don't know why that surprised me. Greeks barely have volume control on a good day. When they got emotional, they held nothing back.

On the way back out to the car, Jace wrapped his skinny arm around my waist. "Well, Momma, if they didn't know about... uh... dad before, they know now!"

I laughed and hugged him.

"You can call him 'dad', you know. He is your dad."

Jace quietly contemplated before he replied, "I just want it to be for real, you know? Like, I don't want to call him dad, and then he takes off. Uncle Gus, he's a dad, a real dad. I don't know yet if Vander is a real dad."

I bled internally hearing his words, bearing witness to the legacy I'd given him. "I understand why you might feel that way, and you take your time, but I believe he's a real dad. When he found out about you, he cried for all the time lost. Even if things between him and I fell apart, which they won't, he would never abandon you."

"You're okay with me calling him dad?" He asked softly.

My mouth fell open in surprise. "Why wouldn't I be, agapimeno mou?"

"Well, it's just that you've been mom and dad for so long, it's like he's trying to take your place."

We stood at the passenger side of the car. I turned and placed both of my hands on his shoulders. "Look at me, agapi mou. I'm always going to be exactly what I am, but we'd be fooling ourselves to say you haven't been missing a father in your life. The fact that you haven't had him since day one is a freak accident, a mistake. If he had known, he would have been here. Don't punish him for something that was out of his control." I paused to gauge his reaction. The longing on his face pierced my soul. "He's a good dad, and he's yours. You can claim him if you want to, he's already claimed you."

Shortly after we got home, Amber and Alex arrived. Alex came inside with a face like a thundercloud.

"Ela, levendis mou," I called him to me.

He came without hesitation and leaned his forehead against my chest.

"What's wrong, agapi mou?" I murmured, stroking his fair hair. I could feel his body vibrating with his emotions. He was so much like me, this boy.

"I asked my dad to come for dinner today, seeing as dads are allowed now, and he said no."

Amber stood frozen in front of me, her hand braced against the air, her face stricken.

I raised my eyebrows in question, and she pressed her lips together and shook her head no, then pointed to herself. Gus was available, it was Amber who wouldn't let him come.

I lay my cheek on top of his bent head. "Honey, I bet he wanted to come really badly. Your dad loves you. So much."

Alex wrapped his arms around my waist and pressed in close. "I miss him," he said tightly.

I swallowed hard, met Amber's eyes, the plea plain in mine.

She stood with her hands over her mouth, her eyes glossy. She nodded resignedly. She needed to figure this out. She slipped away into the dining room.

"You want one of my famous super tight burrito hugs?" I asked him.

He laughed. "You're not big enough to do that anymore."

"What?" I yelled in mock outrage. "I so am!"

I wrapped my arms around his back and tucked my head over top of his, then threw one leg around his knees, nearly toppling us both to the floor.

"See, Thia!" He yelled, laughing. "You're too small now!"

I hugged him lightly, my forehead pressed to his.

"You might be right," I murmured. "I nearly killed us both. Tell you what, though. I'm always going to big enough for you to bring me your troubles. All or any of them, all or any of the time. Okay?"

"Okay, Thia." He pressed closer for a second, then murmured, "I love you, Thia."

"I love you, too, levendis mou. I love you, too."

After Alex left to play with Jace, I found Amber sitting on the front step. I grabbed her sweater off the staircase railing, dropped it over her shoulders, and sat down beside her.

She stiffened beside me. "Please don't say anything."

"Can I sit with you?"

"Yeah. I'd like that."

The weather began to change. Some of the trees were starting to reflect the colours of fall, and the air had a nip to it, especially in the evenings.

I snuck a peek at Amber's face, devoid of hope.

"Koukla mou," I whispered, bumping her lightly with my shoulder.

She stared off into space. "Do you think people should stay together for their kids?"

I looked down. We both knew the answer to that. "No, Amber. I don't think so."

She sat still and quiet for a moment, then gently bumped me back, before getting up and going back into the house without another word.

I said a prayer for my beautiful sister, then followed her into the house.

Vander

Although he introduced me as his dad, Jace still hadn't called me 'dad'. I wanted that. Badly. I wondered if he held resentment or distrust. I didn't blame him. Trust had to be earned and I'd done a shit job so far with him and his mom.

Sitting at the table with the family, my family, felt fucking incredible.

Yiayia asked to meet George and we managed a quick FaceTime where he charmed Yiayia and Amber without dropping any f-bombs.

He read the relief in my face when I turned him back towards me. His mouth tipped up on one side, just like Jace's did when something amused him, and his eyes sparkled with humour.

"Okay, buddy. I love you. Talk to you soon."

I ended the call to find Jace studying me carefully. I smiled at him, and he smiled back. We'd get there.

"Uncle Vander, can we go rock climbing again?" Alex asked.

"Yeah, absolutely. We can go this Saturday if you want. What do you think, Jace?"

"Yeah, uh... yeah, I'd like to go."

"Is that okay, Ruby? Amber?"

"Yup," Ruby replied, nodding. "I have to work again because I traded a day with my part-timer."

"Gus usually spends Saturday with Alex," Amber answered.

"If he's available..." Alex grumbled, and Amber's cheeks heated.

"He had a business trip last weekend, agapi mou. That's all. Your dad loves you and wants to spend time with you."

"What about you?"

Amber sat back in her chair in shock. "Of course, I love you!"

"No," Alex replied, waving away Amber's words. "I meant does he love you? Does he still love you?"

Amber's face fell. "Yes, agapi mou. He does."

"Do you love him?" Alex whispered with his heart in his eyes.

A tear slid down Amber's face. I ached for them both. "Yes, agapi mou. I do."

"Then, why?" He asked, exasperated.

"It's complicated." She held up her hands to hold off the words about to leave his lips. "I'll spend some time with your dad and figure it out. I promise I'll talk to him, and we'll make some changes. I'll ask him to come to dinner next Sunday, and I'll make sure he can be here for Thanksgiving the following week. Okay?"

Alex opened his mouth to reply but I cut in. "How about we ask your dad to bring you to meet Jace and me for rock climbing? You can show him what you can do, and we can go out for lunch afterwards. What do you think?"

Alex's face lit up. "Can I, Mom?"

"That's between you and your dad, agapi mou. Whatever Daddy decides is fine with me."

"Okay, agoria!" Yiayia announced, her eyes suspiciously bright. "Unless you want to do the dishes, you go play."

Both boys bounced up. "We'll clear, Yiayia," Alex offered as he and Jace grabbed the serving dishes and moved them to the kitchen.

"Be careful, agoria. Those are for your mommas when I am dead. I don't want them broken."

"You're going to live forever, Yiayia," Alex shouted back.

"Good boys. I am very proud," Yiayia said. She turned to me. "They ate well. You, not so much. You don't like Yiayia's cooking?"

I lifted my plate and passed it to her. "Pile it on, Yiayia. I'm working on my dad bod."

Amber snorted, Ruby elbowed me in the ribs, and the tension broke.

The following week was filled with outings and visits with Ruby and Jace, both together and separately, and at times with Alex.

Ruby and I spoke further on the topic of moving in together, but we had yet to come to a decision. She had many excuses but no solutions. I wasn't sure what exactly held her back.

Jace still hadn't called me dad, but with the way things were going, it was only a matter of time. I never failed to wrap my palm around the nape of his neck when he came close, and he came close increasingly often.

He even FaceTimed me one day at work, right in the middle of a staff meeting. I answered his call and made a point of telling my staff I needed a few minutes to talk to my son, then went to my office to chat with him.

I began seriously looking at the possibility of selling my business. Being tied to the office lost all its appeal. I could sell it tomorrow to Gary Dolman, knowing he'd keep my staff on, but I wanted to offer it first to my senior consultants.

They'd made a shit ton of money working for me, and between the three of them, I had no doubt they'd be able to take over if they wished.

I needed to get moving on Ruby's file as well.

My life felt full for the first time in a long, long while.

Chapter 35 – Mountains to Climb

<u>Ruby</u>

As much as I loved Vander, as much as I loved the changes he wrought in my life and Jace's, those same changes stressed me out. Certain things, like my home, my Yiayia, and my routines, steadied me in my world.

Vander stormed in three weeks ago and blew up my routines, wanted me to move out of my home to live with him, and I wasn't sure where Yiayia fit in with all of that.

When Minty and Amber confirmed Bookstagram night, I jumped at the opportunity for a bit of familiarity.

Earlier, Gus and Alex met up with Vander and Jace for breakfast, then went rock-climbing, go-karting, and I don't know what else. When I got home after work, they were all at my house, tired but happy, with Yiayia in her element cooking for 'all my boys'.

We ate together, sans Amber, then Jace went home with Vander, and Alex went home with Gus.

"Are you going to be okay on your own, Yiayia?" I asked for the tenth time while we washed the dishes.

"Yes, poulaki mou. Go to your book night. You are staying at Amber's tonight?"

"I think so." Without the boys, we planned to let the wine flow a little more freely. "But I can take a taxi home, it's no problem."

"No, poulaki. You need this." She patted my cheek with her tiny, wrinkled hand, her ruby ring glinting in the light. "Is good for you, these changes. Don't fight him, poulaki. God made him for you."

I rubbed the pad of my thumb over the smooth stones, taking comfort in the link between us. Yiayia was born in July, same as me, and my father named me Ruby in honor of her. "I'm afraid, Yiayia."

"Bravo. If you wasn't, is not real, and you need real, koukla. Too long you live in fish tank world. That is not a life!"

"It wasn't a bad life, Yiayia," I protested softly.

Yiayia pinned me with her dark eyes. "Was half life, koukla."

"So, I need a man to live a full life?" I snorted.

"No. You need to be brave to live a full life. You have to face your fears to be brave."

I huffed in exasperation. "Yiayia! All I've done for twenty years is face my fears."

"Bah," she dismissed twenty years of therapy with a wave of her hand. "Those fears is nothing compared to the big fear inside you. You beat that one, and then you be free, poulaki."

"Okay, Yiayia." I didn't know what she was talking about. I didn't want to know what she was thinking about, but I hugged her so she would think I agreed and stop worrying.

"Bravo, koritzaki mou. Bravo."

She felt frail in my arms, and I teased her. "You need to eat, Yiayia."

"No appetite, koukla. Old people, bah, we don't need to eat too much. We live off our dreams for our children. Go have a fun with your sister." Yiayia got a faraway look in her eyes. "She needs to face some devils, too. Poulaki mou."

She raised her finger as if just remembering. "I have something for you to take tonight." She made her way over to the fridge and pulled out a platter beautifully covered in cheese, olives, crackers, dips, raw veggies, and pita bread.

"Oh, Yiayia! That's wonderful, thank you!" I rescued the heavy platter from her hands. "I always loved this platter."

"Is whole set, will be yours when I die." She swept her arms out to encompass the whole house. "All is yours. Yours and Amber's."

I laughed. "Well, don't die anytime soon, Yiayia. I'm not living here without you."

"Meh, is life, poulaki mou."

Death and dying were her favourite topics. Next, she'd be telling me-

"Guess who die," she challenged.

Yup. I knew it. "How can I possibly guess, Yiayia?"

"You remember your Greek school teacher in grade one?"

I tried but couldn't recall. "No."

"Hm, maybe was Amber's teacher. Georgia Pappadopolous. I'm sure you remember. She move to Greece after only one year here. She die last week."

"She was a friend of yours, Yiayia?"

"No, but she younger than me. Makes me happy."

I raised my eyebrows. "Happy?"

"Of course," she replied. "I live good life, long life. A good life with a good man, a good life with my good girls. I gonna go call Amber, see if she remember Georgia."

At Amber's, I admitted I had not yet started The Naughty Pine. Minty and Amber wrote the review while I listened in. The more they talked, the more I wanted to read it. I decided I'd read it when Vander and I took the boys to Blue Mountain.

"So," Minty sat back with a full glass of wine. "Tell me about hunkalicious."

I laughed. "What do you want to know?"

Amber snickered. "She wants to know everything."

Minty took a sip of her wine and smiled. "She's not wrong."

"You want the good or the bad first?"

273

"Mm, the bad," Minty said.

"He's pushy. He kind of just steamrolls over me at times, like how he did with the franchising. He's pushing for Jace and me to move in with him, he pushed me to meet his son, George, as well. When he wants something, he pushes. He can be sarcastic and snarky. Sometimes he's impatient."

"Has he pushed for anything you didn't want?" Amber asked.

"No. No, he hasn't."

"And the good?" Minty asked.

"He's fun, makes me laugh, holds me when I get scared, sat through a panic attack and carried on like nothing unusual happened. He's affectionate and attentive. Tells me how much he loves me. Took the heat when I let him have it about our past. Apologized for leaving. Both times. Was honest about his past." I shuddered.

"Let that shit go, Ruby," Minty admonished firmly. "Everybody has a past. Everybody makes mistakes. If he committed himself to you and then took other women, okay, you have the right to hold it against him."

"It makes me feel sick. He moved on, I didn't."

"Whose choice was that?" Minty asked softly. "You could have gone to him as well."

I felt betrayed. "You were there, Minty," I snapped. "You saw how I was."

"I did." She nodded slowly. "I also saw the decisions you made. Not all of them were forced."

I took in a deep breath, ready to argue, but she continued.

"I'm not trying to challenge you." She stopped then laughed her tinkling laugh. "Well, I guess I am trying to challenge you a bit. You're not the victim. You made just as many mistakes, just as many bad decisions back then, and this is good."

I snorted. Amber remained silent but looked like she'd been punched. Finally, she asked, "How is that good?"

Minty answered, "Because you can make different decisions this time around."

I turned my attention back to Amber. "You okay, Amber?"

274

"No?" She hesitated. "I've been pushing Gus away for the past year in hopes that I'll fall out of love with him, and leave him for real, but it's not working." She looked at me. "You saw Alex the other night. This is hurting him. I need to make a decision either way."

Minty lay a cool hand on Amber's knee. "I don't know all the details but let me ask you one question. You don't have to answer it out loud. Are there decisions you made that make you less of a victim, too?"

"The short answer is yes. I just don't know what to do about it."

I grabbed a plate and filled it, going heavy on the olives, and passed it to Amber. "In a perfect world, what would you want? I mean, if you weren't worried about what people might think, if you could make yourself forgive the past, if you could change decisions you made, decisions he made, but couldn't change anything about who he is, what would you want?"

"Him," she answered immediately. "But I don't know if I can get past what he did, even if I understand it."

Minty slapped her hand down on Amber's leg. "That, my friend, is a question for another day. Today's answer is a start. Admitting what you want is one step closer to getting what you need." She paused. "Now drink up. I brought movies that we'd never be able to watch with Jace and Alex in the house."

Only Amber made it into a bed, stumbling into her room at two o'clock in the morning. Minty and I passed out on the couches, and I froze half the night with only a lap blanket. In the morning, Minty woke me up and pushed me to get into the shower. She was already showered, dressed, and ready to go.

"Ugh, how are you functioning?"

"Here." She handed me a glass of water and a pain killer. "This and a hot shower will help. I'm going to get Amber moving. Getting her out of bed in the morning is like trying to wake the dead."

I could hear Amber complaining from my perch on the edge of the couch. I remembered that both Vander and Gus were coming to Yiayia's for dinner.

I ran into Amber's room and jumped on her bed. "Get up, lazybones. Today is the start of a new era. An era where we are not victims, where we

275

captain our own ships, lay down our own road, charter our own voyage, and plough our own row!"

Amber held out her palm. "You're too much this early in the morning."

Minty smiled. "I, for one, am not in favour of a lifetime of ploughing my own row."

Amber lay back with a groan and covered her eyes with her forearm, and I chortled which made Amber laugh.

"Who's ploughing your row? Do I know about this?" I demanded.

Amber peeked out at Minty from under her arm, waiting for her answer.

"No one. But that doesn't mean I'm content to leave it that way. All our talk yesterday about being victims and owning our decisions made me realize I've got some bad decisions of my own to claim, and maybe some decisions to unmake."

"Well! Alrighty, then! Let's go ladies! We've got mountains to climb!"

"Oh, god! Enough with the metaphors!" Amber grumbled, and Minty laughed her tinkling laugh, then dropped a pillow on Amber's grumpy face.

Chapter 36 - Tattoos

Ruby

For all my talk about wanting space, I couldn't wait to see him.

Jace slept over at Vander's for the first time, and I realized, belatedly, that I didn't worry about him at all. They'd been together for almost twenty-four hours. They spent yesterday morning and part of the afternoon with Gus and Alex, and then Vander took Jace shopping.

Jace hated shopping.

After breakfast, Amber and I left Minty and headed straight for Yiayia's. We invited Minty to join us, but as usual, she declined. We got there long before we expected any of the boys.

Yiayia was already busy in the kitchen when Amber and I rolled in. We took our places at the counter and grabbed our cutting boards.

"What are we making today, Yiayia?" Amber asked softly.

"We gonna make pastitsio for Gus," she answered. Then she turned and lightly pinched Amber's cheek. "I gonna make roast beef and lemon potatoes, too, koritzaki mou. Yes?"

Amber nodded and I detected the sheen of tears in her eyes. She cleared her throat. "Yes, Yiayia. That sounds good."

Yiayia looked up at Amber and patted her face before turning away to get something from the fridge. "Is good he is coming home, poulaki. Is no good to leave a man out in the cold like a dog."

Amber flushed bright red, then all colour drained from her face. I reached down between us and grasped her hand. She interlaced her fingers with mine and breathed slowly through her nose.

I needed to change the subject, fast, to get Yiayia off this topic. I wracked my brain, and before I could think it through, I threw Vander under the bus.

"Vander got tattoos."

Amber turned to look at me, incredulous, and I gave her big eyes. She shook with laughter, and it was worth it to bring her out of whatever place she'd sunk into.

"What you mean, 'Vander got tattoos'?"

I shrugged, regretting my bucket mouth.

"He got tattoos."

"How many?"

"Does it matter?" Amber asked.

"Oxi, no. It don't matter. Is against God to get tattoos." She muttered something under her breath then spoke again. "What he get?"

"My name over his heart, his sons' birthdates on the inside of his bicep."

"Humph, maybe he need to add a cross at least."

"And the evil eye?" Amber suggested.

Yiayia stopped in her tracks, glared at Amber, and made the sign of the cross over her chest. "Stop yourself! Evil eye! Cross is all he need."

I laughed. Amber elbowed me in warning. Yiayia did not find it quite so humorous yet. She looked at us sideways and I chortled. I couldn't help it.

She raised her hand in a motion to spank. "I make you like the onions, Ruby!"

She shuffled over and laid a tender hand on each of our faces. "You are good girls. Yiayia is very proud."

An hour later, Amber and I were outside sitting on the step when Vander and Jace pulled up and parked across the street. Our driveway had barely enough room for one car when mine was in the garage, and right now Amber's car filled that space.

I stood up when they got close and held my arms out for Jace. He leaned in and gave me a quick hug then pulled back, his face animated.

"You had fun, agapimeno mou?" I murmured.

"So much fun. I even liked shopping!"

I pretended to faint, and he grabbed me and laughed. I looked up to see Vander smiling tenderly at us. The pleasure of that look hit my gut and I looked down, unable to bear the full force of the sweetness.

"What did you shop for?"

"Bedding and posters for my room at... uh... the other house."

Suddenly light-headed, I sank back down to the step. "That's great!" I said with false enthusiasm.

Vander frowned.

"What kind of bedding did you get? What kind of posters?"

"Blue, all blue, and the posters are Minecraft and Star Wars," he answered, then went on to detail the posters he got and where he planned on hanging them in his room.

I nodded. "Sounds good, agapi mou. You have homework?"

"A bit, yeah. I'll go get it done before Alex gets here." He turned to Amber and gave her a kiss on her cheek. "Hi, Thia. When is Alex going to be here?"

"In an hour, glykouli mou."

Jace went into the house, and I looked pointedly away from Vander.

"Ruby?" He ventured.

I held up a hand. "Give me a minute. I'm trying to process."

"Can I help you?" He ventured.

I turned and gave the steamroller a scathing look. "How exactly are you going to help me?"

Amber stood, kissed Vander's cheek, lightly scratched the top of my head, and went inside without a word.

He sat down beside me and sighed. "I've made no secret of the fact that I want to be a family, that I want you and Jace to move in with me, but this was not about that."

"Then what was it?" I bit out.

"Have you seen George's room? It's the only room in the house with any personality, the only room I put any effort into. Jace needs a room at my place, hopefully it'll be our place, but either way, he needs his own space. I needed to show him he has a place with me."

I deflated completely. "Oh."

"Oh, as in, okay?"

I side-eyed him and twisted my lips. "Yeah. Oh, as in okay."

He put his arm around me. "Can I have a kiss and hug hello?"

I leaned into him, and he chuckled. "That's better. You scared me."

I raised my eyebrows. "I scared you?"

He snorted. "Fuck, yeah. You think I want to do anything to piss you off or scare you away?"

It hit me in that moment that he felt as insecure as I did with our new but old relationship.

I melted against him. "I'm not going anywhere, Vander. I promise you."

He drew in a deep breath then released it. "Yeah?"

I raised my chin for his kiss. "Yeah."

We were still sitting there when Gus pulled up with Alex.

Gus hadn't changed much in all the years I'd known him. Like Vander, he wore glasses now, and the lines around his mouth had deepened in the past few years. His hair was a little thinner on top, but he was still a handsome man, with a killer smile, complete with a deep dimple on one side.

He walked up the driveway with a hand on Alex's shoulder and I flashed back to the delivery room, and the relief I felt upon seeing him angling his massive shoulders through the delivery room door. I remembered the moment Alex was laid on Amber's chest, how Gus hovered over them both, one large hand covering Amber's head, the other laid protectively over Alex's little bum.

A gentle giant, really, he'd always doted on my sister, until a few years ago. Thinking back, their troubles began before his accident. I remembered he was sad, then irritable, then increasingly distant.

Polite, but distant.

That was not the Gus that plowed up the driveway. This Gus appeared focussed and intense.

"You been working out, Gussie?"

He winced. "Rubes, please. I'm not a grandmother."

I laughed at our old joke.

Alex came barreling through raising his hand for a high five on his way into the house. I stood and kissed Gus's cheek. "How are you, Gus?"

Pain flashed in his eyes before he pulled the shutters back down. "I'm good, Ruby. How are you doing? Lots of changes for you. Good ones?"

"I'm right here," Vander interrupted drily.

Gus grinned and stuck out his hand. "Hey, man. Good to see you. Alex had a blast yesterday."

"He made it to the top a few times," Vander added. "I was proud of him."

"Yeah, he's a good kid. Lots of energy, he just needs to channel it. Reminds me of his Aunt Ruby. He said he wants me to try rock climbing with him."

"We can go one night, and I'll belay you, if you want to give it a try."

"I might take you up on that. The gym is boring as all hell."

"What gym do you go to?"

Gus mentioned a popular gym close by, then added, "It's nothing more than a meat market."

"I found a great place. It's actually a boxing club, but they take on a limited number of monthly memberships. I'll ask if you can come and check it out. It's not as readily available all hours of the day like your gym, but there's never a wait for machines and it is decidedly not a meat market."

"That sounds good, actually."

"I know the guy who runs it, Dean. He's a great guy. He used to be a boxer years ago and his heart is still very much in it."

"Just let me know when and I'll be there." He smiled at me. "I'm going to go see Yiayia, take the heat for not being here for a while."

"You going to be coming regularly now?" I asked softly.

Gus turned his head and looked across the street for a minute. "You know what, Ruby? I think I am." He turned back, offered me a tight-lipped smile and a nod, then went inside.

We could hear Yiayia's exuberant greeting from outside.

"She misses him," I said softly.

"She misses Amber," he replied. "She wants to see her happy, again. I'm assuming they were happy at some point?"

"So happy," I murmured. "Turned me green with jealousy on more than one occasion."

"I'm sorry, Ruby."

His apology startled me this time. "You can't keep saying sorry, Vander."

"I can when it's warranted, Ruby-mine." He paused. "Are you happy now?"

"I'm happier than I ever dreamed possible."

His handsome face broke into a grin. "We'll see if we can't get you dreaming bigger then."

I stood to go in, and then remembered. "Vander..." I opened the front door. "I told Yiayia you got tattoos."

He made a grab for me, but I escaped, cackling, into the house.

Inside, Yiayia fussed with the table settings. She placed herself at the head as usual. After that she mixed things up a bit. Where Amber and I usually sat beside her followed by Alex and Jace, and then Gus on the other side of Alex, Yiayia arranged it so that the boys were at the end of the table, with Vander and Gus sitting immediately next to Amber and me.

I smelled meddling.

I thought Vander's tattoos would have been enough to throw her off course, but it looked like there was no such luck. What other topics could I toss into the mix? Blue Mountain, meeting George, Thanksgiving, bringing up Elisavet was always good for a five-minute rant.

Armed with my topics, we brought in the serving dishes and sat down around the table.

Gus was so big he couldn't help but regularly brush up against Amber. The first few times it happened, she visibly flinched, and Gus shrank back to give her more space.

He looked miserable, and Amber looked brittle, as if she was about to break.

Gus pushed his chair back from the table and Amber's gaze swung up to his face. He didn't meet her eyes.

Grasping the back of Alex's chair, he said, "Buddy, let's move you down a bit. Mom has barely enough room to get her fork into her mouth without elbowing me."

Alex laughed and lifted his bottom while Gus moved his chair a good half a foot, then shifted his own and retook his seat.

Turning to Amber, he murmured, "Is that a bit better, beautiful?"

Amber's throat worked as she swallowed, and she gave him a tiny nod.

Everyone was quiet, making their sweetly painful exchange easily overheard. Amber shifted in her seat and rolled her lips between her teeth.

"So!" I broke the silence. "About Vander's tattoos, anything to say, Yiayia?"

Gus shook his head and smiled down at his plate.

Yiayia took the bait and Amber relaxed. I slowly turned my head to look at Vander who stared at me bemusedly.

"Why you tattoo your body, agori mou? Is no good!"

"She said if you get a cross, she'll forgive you," I added.

Vander slid a half-smile my way and muttered, "Maybe you should stop talking?"

283

Amber laughed out loud, and Gus chuckled, his big shoulders shaking.

"You got a tattoo?" Jace asked.

"Yeah, buddy. I got three actually," Vander answered him calmly.

"Can I see?"

Vander nodded. "Absolutely. After dinner I'll show you."

"No. You won't," Yiayia scolded. "He don't need to see that."

Vander leveled a look at Yiayia, calm but uncompromising. "He'll see it after dinner because it would be inappropriate for me to take my shirt off at the dining room table." Yiayia opened her mouth to speak but Vander continued in a tone I had not heard from him before. "This is not a discussion, Yiayia mou, but your concern is noted."

Yiayia's mouth snapped closed, and she sat quietly smiling for a moment before answering. "Well, then. I want to see, too."

Amber snickered. "You just want to see the abs Ruby told us about, Yiayia."

Vander groaned, took off his glasses, and rubbed his hand roughly over his face.

I chortled.

Gus chuckled.

Amber snickered.

And the boys looked on in fascination.

Alex turned to Jace. "It's much more exciting when the dads are invited." He turned to his dad. "Do you have any tattoos, dad?"

Gus blushed. "Yeah, son. I do."

"You do?" Amber asked, her mouth gaping.

Gus slid a sideways glance at her and nodded.

"Can I see?" Alex asked.

"Of course, son."

"Amber, Ruby, if you guys have tattoos you better just tell me now!" Yiayia interrupted.

"Not me, Yiayia," I said.

Amber quietly admitted, "I don't. But I'm not opposed."

"Humph." Yiayia sat back in her chair. "Maybe Yiayia gonna get one. I gonna get a tomato on my golo."

Amber and I looked at each other and howled.

"What?" Alex yelled. "What did she say?"

Amber shook her head, and I just laughed.

Vander turned to Alex with a grin. "She said she's going to get a tomato tattooed on her ass."

Alex's mouth dropped open. He looked at Jace who wore a matching expression, and they fell into each other, laughing.

After dinner, Vander called Jace to go upstairs with him to my bedroom.

When they came back downstairs, Jace easily measured two inches taller.

Chapter 37 – Brother From Another Mother

Vander

I barely saw Ruby over the next three days as she fretted over our plans for the weekend. Every evening I stopped by to see her and Jace but couldn't get her to leave with me for even a couple of hours. She said she had too much to do to get ready, but from where I stood, she worried a whole hell of a lot, but accomplished little.

Wednesday night, I finally clued in. Going to a new place outside of her safety zone, in combination with meeting George and being forced into proximity with him for three days, had triggered her anxiety.

I didn't realize, until that night, that I'd harboured a thread of residual resentment that she didn't try harder to get to me that summer. Knowing that what I was presently witnessing represented a massive improvement, pushed that resentment out and replaced it with compassion.

Her agoraphobia trapped her; her anxiety controlled her.

I wondered what she would do, who she would be, without it.

Later that night, long after Jace and Yiayia headed for bed, Ruby sat on the couch beside me writing out multiple versions of the same list over and over.

"Are you worried you'll forget something?"

"No. I'm worried I won't have what I need."

"You know," I palmed the back of her neck like I did with my boys, "whatever you need, I'll get it for you. No questions asked."

She stopped and tipped her head back, resting her head against my hand. "I'm being crazy, aren't I."

I pulled her gently towards me, so she fell into my lap. "Well, you're definitely not relaxed. I can help you with that." I ran my fingers through her hair until she began to breathe easy.

This loving, fragile, fiercely determined woman was mine to care for, mine to love. I shifted our positions and turned her in my lap, bringing her chest to mine, and kissed her softly.

A soft sigh escaped her sweet lips, and I inhaled it. My arm around her back cradled her tenderly leaving my other hand free to stroke her hip, her thighs, her tummy, and finally to cup her breast.

I rubbed my thumb across her nipple through her t-shirt, and her chest expanded with air as she arched into my hand.

Then her brain must have caught up with my intentions because she stiffened. "Vander, I don't know if this is a good idea..."

"Shh, baby. I'm just going to touch you, help you relax. All clothes are staying on. It's all about you."

Her outfit, yoga pants and an oversized tee, couldn't have been more perfect if I planned it. I drew the shirt up, then slipped my hand down the front of her pants, barely brushing the top of her mons.

I brushed my lips across hers just as softly, and she melted into my lap.

"Much better," I murmured against her lips. "I don't want you getting upset. Whatever you need I'll get it. Don't you know I'll do anything for you?"

287

I kissed her closed eyes and pushed my hand in further to gently cup her sex. She closed her thighs around my hand. I stopped moving and simply kissed her.

Tears burned at the back of my eyes, and I closed them tight to beat them back. In my wildest dreams I never imagined caring for her like this.

I wiggled my hand gently. I whispered against her lips, "Open, sweetheart."

Ruby let one of her thighs fall open, allowing my fingers to reach that part of her that I wanted to taste.

Hot and wet, she coated the pads of my fingers as I drew her wet up to circle her clit. She tensed, tilting her hips for more.

"Don't tense your muscles, don't worry about orgasming, just let me give you pleasure. There's no rush."

She nodded and sighed, brought her arm up to rest loosely around my neck and dropped her head back onto my shoulder. "That's it, sweetheart."

I stroked gently through her slit, collected the wet from her core, spread it over her folds, soaked her little bud. Slowly, it hardened. I maintained my gentle pace. I kissed her forehead, feathered my lips over her closed eyes, touched the tip of my nose to hers, lay my bearded cheek against her smooth one. I dipped my fingers in her wet, drew it up to her clit, circled tightly, then tapped. Again.

She opened her eyes in surprise, her pupils blown wide, her mouth parted softly.

"Don't tense up, let it happen if it's going to happen. Don't force it, don't chase it," I ordered her gruffly.

Her face full of wonder, she trained her luminous brown eyes on mine.

I felt the first spasm and her thighs shook.

Dip, circle, tap. Dip, circle, tap.

Dip, she clenched around my finger, her hands grasped my shirt, circle, tap, tap, tap.

Her neck arched back, her body quaked, and she soaked my hand.

Dip, circle, tap, tap, tap, until the last tremor passed, and I covered her sex gently with the palm of my hand.

Then the tears came. Overtired and strung too tight.

"Shh, baby." I stroked through her folds. "You're okay. Everything is okay."

I kissed her forehead.

Taking a deep breath, she cuddled into my chest. When her breathing evened out completely, I withdrew my hand from her pants, hugged her tightly, and pulled her gently to her feet.

I led her, stumbling with fatigue, to the door. "Lock up, Ruby-mine, and go to bed."

"You want to wash your hands before you go?" She mumbled.

I grinned at her wickedly. "I may never wash this hand again."

She huffed out a laugh and I dropped a kiss on her soft mouth. "Go to bed. Sleep now that you're relaxed. I'll see you around lunchtime after I pick up George from the airport."

"Text me when you get home," she mumbled and locked the door.

As I pulled out of the driveway, I could still see her hand pressed against the glass of the door.

Ruby

Vander: We're on our way.

Ruby: Okay.

I sat staring at the phone, and was still staring at it, when Jace came in from outside.

"I love being off school when no one else is. The whole world is quiet." He paused. We did, after all, live in the city. "Well, quieter."

I smiled and informed him. "They're on their way, agapimeno mou."

"Can you believe I have a brother? I mean, Alex is just as good as a brother, but George is actually my brother." He laughed. "He's my brother from another mother."

I cringed, and Jace caught it. "Oh, man. That was dumb. I'm sorry, Momma."

Forcing out a laugh, I said, "Let's just agree that you won't ever say that again, okay?"

"Yeah, Momma. Sorry." He hung his head.

I pulled him in close. "You understand why it's hard for me? I've loved Vander since first year university, I never stopped. He moved on because he thought I didn't love him. It hurts that I allowed my illness to steal him away from me."

"Is George a bad thing for you?"

"God, no! George is Vander's, and yours, so I already love him and want every good thing for him. And I'm happy that you have a brother. Both things can be true. I can wish nothing ever separated Vander and me, and I can be happy that you have a brother. Okay?"

This was the most difficult conversation I'd ever had with Jace. I thought we'd reached the pinnacle of difficulty with the conversation preceding the paternity test, but this one was worse. It was the first time I'd ever lied to him.

Looking at him, I realized that him being Vander's son shaved off some of the pain of George's existence. Hopefully, by the end of the weekend, what I said to Jace would have at least some truth to it.

Jace set our bags at the end of the hallway, ready to go into the car. I had the same rolling suitcase that I'd had on that conference, the conference where we made Jace. Two things could be true at the same time. I could be devastated at the outcome of the conference, and still feel grateful that Jace came out of it.

Yiayia came up behind me and placed her hand on my shoulder. "Yiayia is so proud," she whispered, her voice breaking.

I nodded. A single tear escaped. I sniffed and dried my face. "It's okay, Yiayia. It is what it is."

"It is whatever you make it, poulaki mou."

Ah, Yiayia's wisdom. I'd take that nugget with me.

The front door opened, and I heard Yiayia effusively greet George, then heard Vander's smooth, deep voice as he introduced his sons to one another. I could delay no longer.

I put on my best rendition of a smile and walked into the kitchen, my eyes on the boys.

"Hello, George." I smiled at him and held out my hand. "I'm Ruby. I'm really happy to meet you, finally."

George looked both smaller and younger than I envisaged.

George extended his hand and shook mine, his eyes skittering over my face. "Are you sick?" He blurted out.

My eyes bugged out. "I'm sorry?"

"Are you not feeling good? You're very white."

"Oh," I waved a hand dismissively, "I didn't sleep very much last night. I'll get lots of rest this weekend."

I couldn't look at Vander. Furious with myself for being so emotional, furious with him for not believing me when I said I loved him, furious with him for not choosing me after the conference, though I knew it was unfair.

"How was your flight?"

"It was okay." He pushed his hands deep into his pockets and looked at the floor.

The tension in the kitchen was almost palpable. Could no one else think of something to say? My God, help me. I was the adult here. I needed to pull it together.

"Let's get some lunch. Yiayia is the best cook." He looked up at me cautiously. I winked. "She'll tell you that herself!"

"Okay, agoria." Yiayia clapped her hands. "Come eat. I don't want you to starve when you head out to the wilderness."

George's mouth fell open, and I laughed. I closed the distance between us and put my arm over his shoulders, hoping he wouldn't reject me.

"Does she remind you of your Yiayia?"

He glanced up at me quickly, looked to his dad, and then looked back at me, "I think she's worse!"

I laughed and gave him a quick squeeze and released him. "Don't let her hear you. You'll only encourage her."

He laughed and looked, again, to his dad.

"You can go on into the dining room with Jace and Yiayia," Vander instructed.

As soon as George left the room, Vander stepped forward and put his hands on my shoulders to turn me around.

I flinched then shuddered at his touch. I looked down at the floor, both sickened and ashamed.

He lifted his hands quickly, then seemed to change his mind and put them back more firmly than before. Stepping up close behind me, he dipped his head and spoke quietly in my ear.

"I'm sorry I failed you. I'm sorry I'm causing you pain. I love you. I've only ever loved you. I'll never love another. I'll never touch another."

I turned to face him and looked at his face for the first time since I'd seen him the night before. Lines of worry bracketed his mouth and tightened his lips. His dark eyes shimmered with both pain and regret. I placed my palms over his bearded cheeks, held his beautiful eyes, and breathed through the pain.

He looked into my eyes, tightened his lips, and swallowed hard. Dropping his hands to my waist, he pulled me closer and tipped his forehead down to rest on mine.

"Your pleasure is my pleasure, your pain is my pain," he whispered, his voice raw. "Please don't leave me. Please, God, I'm sorry, but please accept my boy."

I shook my head and then nodded. "Never. Of course," I promised immediately.

He grasped my wrists and pulled my arms around his neck, held me tight, and tucked his face into my neck. His chest expanded against mine with his deep inhale.

Anxiety.

Anxiety that I caused.

I smoothed my hands over his back, stroked his hair.

I needed to figure out how to forgive him and move on.

Chapter 38 - Unfathomable

Ruby

George was not what I expected.

The few times we FaceTimed, he smiled easily and spoke with confidence, giving the impression that he was older than thirteen. Seeing him in person, I realized how young he truly was. The growth spurt common to teenage boys was still a couple of years away, and in an unfamiliar environment, he seemed unsure of himself.

Both boys were quiet in the back of the car as we started our journey to Blue Mountain.

Vander held my hand on his thigh the way he always did. Within a few minutes, the stress and fatigue of the past few days caught up with me and I fell asleep.

Laughter, Vander's deep chuckle layered with boyish giggles and guffaws, woke me. I kept my eyes closed. This was the stuff of my wildest dreams: kids in the backseat, mom and dad in the front, chatting and laughter and togetherness.

I listened to the boys talking about their most embarrassing moments. George's voice sounded incredibly similar to Jace's. I wondered if they'd both have Vander's deep, melodic voice when they were grown.

I sighed. Vander squeezed my hand.

"Good sleep, Ruby-mine?"

"Mm-hmm. Excellent."

George finished his tale, and I chortled while Vander chuckled.

"Dad, you're so right! Ruby's laugh is crazy!"

I twisted in my seat to smile at him, genuinely this time, and he smiled back.

Vander's hand tightened on mine like a vice.

"Uh... are we staying in a hotel?" Jace asked.

"Condo. More space to spread out and everyone can have their own rooms," Vander answered.

"There are four bedrooms?" Jace asked, and I froze in my seat.

Vander looked like he'd swallowed a fly. "Uh, three bedrooms, buddy. Your mom and I will be sharing a room."

I twisted to check on Jace, but he only looked thoughtful, then asked, "Are we going to live together?"

Vander answered, "As soon as your mom is ready. We're going to get married soon, too."

I tried to pull my hand away, but Vander held it fast and grinned at me. "What? Are you not going to marry me and live with me?"

"You might want to ask first and not just assume!" I snapped.

He stroked my wrist with his thumb. "I just did."

"Did what? Ask?" I responded incredulously.

"Yeah. I asked if you're not going to marry me and live with me."

"What kind of proposal is that?"

"Probably the only one you're going to get. I'm not going to take the chance of asking. Just going to book the church and tell Yiayia to make sure you get there."

I laughed. "Steamroller!"

He grinned. "I told you. I'm not the boy you remember."

I turned around to see George's eyes skittering back and forth between us, and Jace smiling happily.

"You guys okay?" I asked softly. "Your dad is springing this on all of us at the same time."

"I'm good, Momma. Will I have to leave Alex?"

"I don't want you to have to leave Alex. That would not make me happy," I answered. "George? You okay, honey? You must be used to his steamroller behaviour."

"You're not mad anymore?"

I raised my eyebrows in surprise. "Mad? When was I mad?"

Jace interrupted. "My mom is *super* emotional. She's usually happy." He paused. "I only ever saw her mad one time. That was scary."

"When was that?" I asked, curiously.

"When that man at the grocery store pushed past Yiayia and she nearly fell."

I winced. "Yes, well, that wasn't my best moment... but he had it coming to him."

Jace laughed. "There was that other time when my teacher kept Alex and I after school and forgot to call you."

"Well, I was worried out of my mind. That was a stupid reason for a detention in any case," I grumbled.

"I remember when that kid punched Alex and you went and knocked on his door and talked to his parents."

"It was the right thing to do. He shouldn't have punched Alex."

"There was that other time-"

"Oh my gosh!" I yelled and saw George flinch. "Stop telling George all my sins or I'll take you to Yiayia and she can boil you!"

Jace laughed. "She'd just pinch my cheeks." He turned to George. "I think that's worse than boiling."

George laughed and I was relieved. I took note of his reaction to tell Vander later.

Vander

As long as I live, I will never forget the pain on Ruby's face, and the uncertainty on George's, when they came face-to-face for the first time.

I told George our story when I first told him about Ruby, and he immediately worried that she would be angry with him. I assured him she would not, and I prayed I hadn't lied to him.

When she refused to look at me, the bottom dropped out of my world. In that moment, I knew fear, and I knew I'd do anything to keep her. Even if I had to resort to steamrolling. I'd steamroll her right into bed, then I'd steamroll her to the nearest church, even a courthouse. I would not lose her again.

Once she fell asleep in the car, the boys loosened up and started talking. I listened, not for what they were saying, but for the sheer pleasure of hearing their voices. George had always brought light to my life. Jace was beyond my wildest dreams. Having them together, with me, with Ruby?

Unfathomable.

Walking into the condo with them fed my craving to have Ruby and Jace move in with me. When George came home, life would be just like this for the four of us.

The boys dumped their bags at the front door, then immediately unpacked Jace's PlayStation and hooked it up to the television.

I watched Ruby as she puttered about, searched out the bedrooms, poked around the kitchen, opening the cupboards and the drawers, checking out the fridge, and peeking into the oven. I grinned to myself. I wonder what she thought she'd find in there.

She headed to the family room, checked out the books on the shelf, turned the lamp on then off again, checked the thermostat, then turned to the sliding doors and stepped out onto the balcony.

I followed her out.

She stood with her hands resting lightly on the railing, taking in the view of the mountain, the forest, and a pie-shaped slice of the village.

I stepped up beside her and leaned against the railing, afraid to touch her, hoping she would reach out to me.

I didn't have to wait long.

"Vander, what the hell are you doing?" She grabbed my arm and pulled. "You don't *lean* on a railing! It's not for *leaning*!"

I stepped back from the railing.

"What's it for, then?" I asked bemused, chuckling.

"It's a safety measure. You don't ... *test* it!" She looked at me, exasperated.

I reached over and gave the railing a good shake, then reassured her. "It's solid, Ruby-mine. We're good."

"Humph. You didn't know that when you leaned against it," she grumbled.

"This is true." I crossed my arms over my chest. "But I don't question if my steering wheel is going to work before I drive my car. I don't wonder if the chair legs are securely attached before I sit down. I don't concern myself over things like that. If something happens that's not supposed to, I'll deal with it."

She looked over the railing and pointed. "You'd have a tough time dealing with it from down there," she countered.

I reached for her and pulled her into my arms, grinning. "Tell me you're not coming biking with us tomorrow."

She narrowed her eyes at me. "Why?"

"I don't want you embarrassing the boys."

"What?" She yelled. "I wouldn't embarrass the boys!"

I pitched my voice higher. "Could you tell me Mr. Bike Rental Man, do you have training wheels for these bikes? Do any of these bikes come equipped with an armoured trailer? Are there speed limits on the mountain? Do you have butt pads in case they fall on their little tushies?"

She glared at me, but I could see her fighting her smile. "You know what? Maybe I will go with you tomorrow! God knows you've got about as much safety sense as a gnat!"

I heard a groan coming from the family room.

It came from Jace. George watched us, a worried look on his face. I wondered what that was about.

"Mom. You can't come. You'll ruin everything," Jace laughed.

George looked at Jace with big eyes, then swung his gaze back to Ruby. He wasn't used to this level of banter. He didn't grow up in a big, loud, Greek family.

She laughed. "You're wrong. I'm just going to make sure you wear a helmet. And pads. And if there's a butt pad, you can wear that, too."

I grabbed her and spun her around into a hug.

"Let go, you big oaf!"

"I'll make sure they're safe, Ruby-mine." She assessed me, her hands trapped between our chests. I wanted to check how Jace was handling this, but I needed to reassure Ruby. "I'm not ever going to be careless with you or the boys."

"Or you, either," she grumbled.

I nodded and couldn't help the corner of my mouth from tipping up. "I'll be careful, too."

"Fine. You can go. Without me."

I looked over at the boys to see Jace looking relieved and happy, and George studying Ruby. He didn't seem to know what to make of her. I understood. His mother could be a bit shrewish.

Ruby clapped her hands. "Okay! Let's get the bedrooms sorted."

At the first bedroom, Ruby stopped and opened the door to show the boys. "This one has one double bed. One of you can have this room. I don't care who." At the next door she stopped again. "This one has two singles. You guys work it out between yourselves where you're going to sleep."

"Momma, where will you be?"

"I'll show you." She turned and walked down the long hall to the bedroom at the end. "This is the master. Dad and I will sleep here." She turned to look at Jace. "Okay?"

He nodded. "What do I do if I need you?"

Vander answered, "If you need mom or me, you come knock the door. Don't hesitate, just come knock the door."

Jace seemed to accept that readily enough.

299

George stood outside the door to the second bedroom with a funny look on his face.

Ruby lifted her chin. "Okay, Georgie? Same goes for you."

His face cleared and he gave her a thumbs-up.

"Okay, muscles. Put the bags in the rooms and we can go explore."

We hit the village first.

Laid out in the shape of a giant teardrop, the centre held a life-size checkers board, a small park for younger children, a fountain, and a bandstand that currently hosted a live band, all of which were separated and surrounded by wide walkways. Stores and restaurants bordered the perimeter of the teardrop, and the lodges reared up behind them.

We were not the only ones who wanted to get away for the long weekend. More people than I expected milled around, sweaters and light jackets knotted around waists, the sun shining warmly overhead.

Within the first five minutes, Ruby bought the boys bear paws. When they finished those, she got all of us hot chocolate. It was unseasonably warm for hot chocolate, but the smell of chocolate coming through the door made it impossible to resist.

At the bakery, she gave Jace her credit card and ordered them to pick out treats for later, with the warning that if they didn't get her something good, she got to pick the movie. A few doors down sold old fashioned kettle corn, as well as popcorn in every flavour you could imagine, and a few you didn't want to. Ruby declared popcorn necessary for movie watching. She picked her own flavour, telling the boys she couldn't take the risk of letting them choose for her flavour because she loved popcorn too much.

At the toy store, she noticed George looking at the collector cards and bought him two packages. Jace got a book of puzzles which triggered a memory of Ruby carrying a puzzle book around in her backpack for times when she didn't have anything else to do.

With everything she bought him, George checked with me to see if it was okay.

Finally, when I got him by himself for a moment, I asked, "You okay, buddy?"

He looked surprised. "Yeah, dad. I'm good. She's nice."

"She is." I smiled at him. "You don't have to check with me if she wants to buy you something. If you want to accept it, say thank you. If you don't, just say, no, thanks. Okay?"

He nodded.

"Does she make you nervous?"

He shrugged. "She's kind of loud and... enthusiastic. It seems like she's mad, but then she's not."

"Ah," I said. "Ruby likes to play. She also has lots of emotions and she doesn't do a great job hiding them." I shrugged. "I think it's good. You always know what's going on with Ruby if you pay attention."

"She's not like mom, is she."

I jolted. I should have been expecting it, but I wasn't. "How do you mean?"

He shrugged again. "I'm not sure. Just, she's different. It's like, she actually likes you."

I laughed. "Why are you so surprised that she likes me? Am I not likeable?" I scrubbed the top of his head. "Do I smell?" I pulled him into a light headlock and tickled him. "Do I have bad breath?"

He poked me hard in the ribs and I released him. "Ha! Got your weak spot!" He exclaimed.

Just then, Ruby and Jace returned from picking something out for Alex.

"You beating up your dad, George?"

George looked to me quickly then answered, "Just a bit."

"Good, good." She nodded. "Get some cracks in for me."

The look of yearning on Jace's face chopped me in the throat. I threw my arm around him. "You'll stick up for me, won't you agori mou?"

He smiled quickly and nodded.

I released him and he opened the bag to show George what they chose for Alex. Ruby and I walked on ahead.

I slung my arm across her shoulders, and she leaned into me.

"You're going to suffer for the next two nights," she snickered.

"I am?" I asked, surprised. "Why?"

She gave me a funny look. "The boys are right down the hall."

"So?"

"We can't let them hear us," she hissed.

I laughed. "Remember last night? Consider that to be practice for this weekend."

"Hmm," she teased. "So, I'm the only one getting any action this weekend?"

I laughed and shook my head. "Nope. I'll be taking mine, too."

"Are you sure?" She teased. "You didn't have a practice session. Maybe you should just abstain and focus on me."

I grinned at her wickedly. "Oh, I think I'll be okay. I'm not the one moaning, and begging, and 'oh, oh, oh'-ing."

Her mouth fell open and she pulled away from me. "Vander!" She snapped. "I do not *beg*."

I slid a sideways glance at her and took her hand. "Would you like me to put that to the test?"

She snapped her mouth shut and turned away, but not before I saw her smile.

"Is that a no? You would not like me to put that to the test?" I teased.

"Maybe I will say no."

I pulled her closer. "You threatened me with that before. If I remember correctly," I dipped my head down to hers, "and I do, that was the same occasion that you begged."

She laughed and threw herself into my arms.

I grinned down at her, so petite, so fiery.

Her eyes smiled up at me. "I love you. Do you know that?"

A hint of my underlying anxiety revealed itself. "Are you doing okay with everything?"

Instead of answering, she asked, "You love me?"

I nodded seriously. This was not a joke or a game of any kind. "With my whole heart, for my whole life."

She lifted her chin for a kiss. "Then I'll be okay."

Chapter 39 – Tell Me About Her

<u>Ruby</u>

I walked down the hall towards the bedrooms. I realized I didn't know which room Jace picked, and both doors were closed.

I knocked gently on the first door but heard no answer. I pressed my finger into the divot of my top lip. If Jace was in there, he would've answered. I moved to the second door and knocked gently.

"Come in," Jace called.

I opened the door with a smile on my face. "Oh!" I stopped in surprise. Jace was in one bed, George was across from him tucked into the other. "You guys are sharing?"

"Yeah," Jace answered. "We promise we won't stay up too late."

I moved into the room and sat on the edge of Jace's bed. "That's fine." I swept his hair off his forehead. He was losing his baby look. In fact, I'd only to look across the room to see what was coming.

I turned and smiled at George who pretended not to watch. "You guys look alike; do you know that?"

George nodded hesitantly.

Where was the boy from the FaceTime chats? This child was unsure of himself, or more accurately, unsure of me.

I turned back to Jace. "You're getting up early tomorrow to go mountain biking. Don't stay up too late, agapimeno mou."

He nodded and I bent over to kiss him on his forehead. "I love you, s'agapo, with all of my heart."

"I love you, too, Momma."

I stood. I felt awkward walking out without visiting George. I took a few steps towards his bed, and he followed me with big eyes. At the bottom, I leaned over and placed a hand on his foot over the covers.

"Goodnight, Georgie," I said softly. "Sweet dreams, honey."

"Goodnight, Ruby."

Vander waited for me in the master with more than a hint of anxiety on his face.

It was not unfounded. My feelings were all over the place.

While I mentally berated myself for holding the sins of the mother against the child, I still struggled to not think of her, when I looked at George. I especially tried not to think of her standing with Vander in front of the altar joined by God, and worse, not to think of her keeping Vander away from me for a decade while she carried on with her life.

I was furious with myself for allowing Vander's past decisions, decisions that I not only understood but even contributed to, to bother me.

Sending a vague smile in his direction, I escaped to the bathroom to get ready for bed.

As soon as I closed the door, I sagged back against it. The effort required to smile, and laugh, to make George comfortable, to tamp down my jealousy, to hide my pain from Vander, was exhausting.

Now that I was alone, the thoughts and feelings I'd run from all day caught up to me and pounded on the closed doors of my mind. With every door I slammed shut, another swung open.

She kept Vander away from me, she used George to do it, and Vander allowed it.

Slam.

Vander would always be involved with her because she was the mother of his son.

305

Slam.

I'd have to meet her eventually.

Slam.

I pushed the heels of my hands against my eyes.

Our wedding, if we got married in the church, would be a different ceremony than Amber's, a different ceremony than Vander's first marriage. Our wedding would kick off with prayers of repentance for Vander's divorce, and the church would not recognize our marriage in the same vein as it considered his first marriage.

Slam.

He didn't put me first. He walked away from me. Twice.

Slam.

Slam.

Slam.

Tears of sorrow, tears of frustration, tears of rage, tears of despair, tears of grief, and I swallowed them all.

I turned on the shower and stepped in. The shock of the icy spray slammed all the doors shut. I forced myself to stand under it until it warmed. Tipping my face up, my tears got lost in the spray.

I would have to love him, too.

I would have to accept her into my life.

Our marriage would not be considered holy in the same way his first was.

My breath left me in soft hiccoughs at that final admission. I arched my neck back, feeling the sting of the spray on my face.

I had to face all that I'd lost, all Jace had lost.

A soft sob escaped my lips.

Wrapping my arms around my waist, I pushed back the knowledge that I brought this pain upon myself through my own decisions.

My dream waited for me on the other side of the bathroom door.

George came with the deal. George's mother came with the deal. Our wedding of repentance came with the deal.

No matter what I thought I deserved, Jace deserved his father.

No matter how I screwed up, no matter that Vander chose to leave, George deserved to feel at home in his dad's house.

I took a deep, steadying, breath. I needed to suck it up and put on my big girl panties.

Slam.

Slam.

Slam.

I turned off the water.

Dwelling in the past served no one.

Except her.

Vander

I turned off the television and listened to the muffled sounds of grief that came from the bathroom.

I sat down on the edge of the bed and stared at the floor. I wondered if she would ever conceive of how much I loved her. I wondered if she'd ever be able to forgive me, or herself. I wondered if we could be a family with George in the mix, and I wondered how to make it better, or at least tolerable, for her.

I wondered how I'd survive if she walked away.

Fuck.

This.

This is what she went through when I did exactly that to her.

In that moment, I finally understood.

At the conference, she held nothing back, she even accepted George.

And I walked away.

You dumb fuck, Vander.

The water stopped, I turned off the overhead light, and turned the bedside lamp on. I placed my glasses on the table, pulled the covers back, and got into my side.

She padded softly into the bedroom, then paused three feet from the bed. "Vander, I..."

"Shh, baby. Just come to bed. I know you're sad. I'm sad, too."

Her face crumpled for a moment, then she pulled in a deep breath and crossed the rest of the way to the bed. She climbed in and I lay on my side facing her.

She lay quietly for a moment, then turned to me. A silent tear leaked out from the corner of her eye, slid over the bridge of her nose, and dropped onto the pillow.

"I don't know why this is so hard," she whispered. "I understand why you did what you did. I understand why I did what I did. I don't know why I can't just get past it."

"It's only been a few weeks, Ruby. Don't be hard on yourself," I murmured.

She nodded, her mouth drawn down at the corners, making her look older than she was.

I continued. "I understand, you know, why you're struggling. What I did was wrong. I thought I was being noble, but I was being an ass."

She chortled, and the extra years sloughed off her face.

"I'd take it all back, if I could."

"All of it, Vander?" Her mouth twisted with disbelief.

I smiled a half smile at her. "I wouldn't wish George and Jace away. We wouldn't have either of them if I had transferred in university, so even though it was painful for both of us, I wouldn't go back to that time and lose George and Jace." I took a breath. "If I could go back, I'd go back twelve years, and I would have called you as soon as I got off the plane in B.C."

Tears welled in her eyes.

"Yeah?"

My own eyes welled over. "Yeah, koukla. I would give anything to go back and do it differently."

It was true. While custody would have been horrendous, I would take that risk if I had to do it all again. She was my woman. She would be my wife. She had to come first.

"Anything?" She looked doubtful.

I nodded. "Anything."

She lay her hand over my cheek and closed her eyes.

Within moments, she drifted into sleep.

I pulled her into my arms and followed her under.

The next morning, when I woke, she was wound around me like a kudzu vine. Even in sleep, she was tense. I didn't have time to do anything about it with the boys up and moving around, but I held her snugly in my arms and rubbed her back until she woke, boneless and relaxed.

All day yesterday, she seemed perfectly happy, but I now recognized her manic energy for what it was, a mask to hide her pain.

What would it take to heal her?

I hoped a few hours to herself would help. She didn't often get time alone. We ate breakfast together, then the boys and I left her in the square and headed off to get our bikes.

By late afternoon, both boys were covered in mud that disguised more than a few scrapes. They were sweaty, happy, and exhausted when we walked into the condo twenty minutes after dropping off the rentals.

Ruby came in from the balcony when we arrived, and her mouth fell open at the sight of us. I chuckled, Jace laughed, and George smiled at her surprise.

She came closer and noted the bear paws in the boys' hands. "You guys ate with those dirty hands? That's disgusting!" She screwed up her face.

"Does that mean you don't want yours?" I held the bag up over her head.

She reached for it, and I pulled it out of her reach. In a flash, George poked me in the ribs, and I dropped my hand.

Ruby grabbed the bag and danced away, laughing. "George! You're the man!" She yelled.

I grinned at George, then looked at Ruby and smiled at her evilly.

She took one look at my face and backed up. "Oh no," she warned, holding her hand up. "You stay back!"

"Jace," I asked. "Doesn't your mom look like she wants a hug?"

Jace's mouth tipped up on one side while Ruby gave him her mom eyes.

I continued. "She just looks so huggable to me. What do you think, George?"

George's eyes skittered back and forth between us.

Ruby smiled a triumphant smile. "George would never do that." She held up the bear paw as proof. "George is my hero."

George laughed, then held up one finger. "In medieval times, the lady would grant the hero a kiss." He paused. "We'll take a hug instead."

"George!" She yelled. "Traitor!"

We laughed as she ran through the kitchen towards the front door. If I hadn't tripped over one of the boys, I would have caught her.

Once we cleaned up, we headed down to the village for dinner.

I held her hand while we walked, pulled out her chair at the restaurant, pressed my knee to hers under the table, and listened attentively when she spoke. The boys and I entertained her by telling her the mishaps and mayhem of our mountain biking adventure, well, some of them. I watched while George warmed up to her, and she relaxed around him.

After dinner, we walked hand-in-hand while George and Jace went off in search of snacks for the movie, and she got quiet.

We found an empty bench at the edge of the square. I pulled her down beside me and cuddled her close. We could see the boys from where we sat as they walked in and out of stores, in search of a treat that would guarantee them the right to pick the movie. The stakes were high. Ruby showed them the trailer for her choice at dinner, and they were not on board.

Jace looked up at George often as they loped along, both with their hands tucked deep into their pockets.

"Tell me about his mother."

"Now?" I practically squeaked.

She nodded, her face serious and intent, as if she was bracing herself for bad news.

I carefully slid my palm across hers, taking hold of the barometer to the inner workings of her mind.

"What do you want to know?"

"What did she mean to you before she became your ex-wife?"

I blew out a breath. Here was my chance to explain.

"We dated. We were not exclusive. She got pregnant and told me it was mine. I waited until George was born, then requested a paternity test. When it came back, I proposed."

Ruby listened but didn't move or respond in any way, so I added quietly, "It was not some great love story; it wasn't a love story at all."

I hurried on, hoping I'd find the right words to impress upon her how little she had to worry about. "I'd always wanted a family, but I'd only ever loved you. When George was born, he became my family."

I took a breath. "Ruby, there was never anyone special after you. One woman was as good as any other, and she had George, so I committed myself to her. Just not in the way she wanted."

Ruby's hand lay still, almost lifeless, in mine. I couldn't tell if giving her my story was helping my cause or hurting it, but in the end, all I could give her was the truth. I continued.

"When she found the box with our photos, she confronted me and demanded I throw them out. I wouldn't do it. She was angry and I was shocked."

Finally, her hand jerked in mine, and she flicked her eyes at me briefly.

"Why were you shocked?"

I raised my eyebrows, it still astounded me. "Because I thought we had an understanding. We were never in love. We were not even exclusive before we got married. When I expressed the reasons for my surprise, she told me she hadn't dated anyone else for months before she got pregnant with George."

Ruby's hand spasmed, and I squeezed it gently.

"Do you want me to continue?"

She nodded, her gaze aimed towards the middle distance, staring at nothing.

"Overnight she went from playing the part of a happy, stay-at-home mom, to a victim suffering the ill effects of her husband's emotional affair. She moved out of our bedroom that night."

Ruby froze beside me, and I immediately regretted my choice of words. I should have just said she moved into the guest room. I clutched her hand tightly in mine and hurried on.

"She took all her clothes and toiletries to the guest bed and bath. For two weeks she raked me over the coals, calling me at work to berate me, every night accusing me of using her. One of those nights she let it slip about how wrong she was to think I'd be a good dad and that if she could go back, she never would have... she didn't finish the sentence, but I believe she was about to say she never would have gotten pregnant."

Ruby gasped and wrapped her fingers around mine tightly, dropping her gaze to the ground in front of her.

"The next day when I got back from work, she had moved all her clothes and toiletries back into the master bedroom and told me she forgave me. I couldn't pretend anymore. I slept in the guest room, and the next day I moved to a hotel until I found an apartment."

"That's terrible," Ruby whispered.

"It wasn't good," I agreed.

I studied her profile.

Her eyes scanned the empty space in front of her. Finally, she looked at me.

"That is not how I pictured it," she admitted.

I held her eyes, relieved to note the absence of the usual jealousy and insecurity. "I doubt any of it was how you picture it," I asserted.

She nodded. "What does George know?"

"Only the basics. That it wasn't a love match, but that he is loved." I paused thinking back to that painful conversation that happened only a year ago. "He doesn't need to know anything more. Not yet."

Ruby's hand tightened around mine, and she asked softly, "Is she good to him?"

I squeezed her back and felt my heart rate begin to return to normal. "She loves him, but she expects a lot from him, and lets him know when he doesn't deliver. His stepdad balances her out."

Ruby's hand stiffened in mine. "He seems nervous to me, Vander," she murmured hesitantly, "as if he's waiting for me to explode."

I noticed the same thing but put it down to worrying about Ruby's feelings for him. I squeezed her hand reassuringly. "I'll check into that."

Slowly, I became aware of our surroundings once again, the people walking and talking, eating and shopping, cuddled up in their jackets and hoodies in the cool October evening. The temperature had dropped since the day before.

"Okay." Her body softened against my side.

I breathed a sigh of relief that I was finally able to explain how it was, for me, without her. I kissed the top of her head, and she chuckled.

"What are you laughing at?" I asked, looking down at her, bemused.

She lifted her chin to indicate the boys coming towards us from across the square. "They're on a mission."

They loped along, two messy, curly heads, hands in pockets, lips tipped up on one side. Jace scanned his surroundings, taking everything in. George's gaze remained on Ruby, not Ruby and me together, just Ruby. Her face. Assessing. A ribbon of unease uncurled in my gut.

I looked at Ruby to see her smiling softly. "Well, Georgie? Do you think your snack earned you the right to pick the movie?"

He grinned easily and opened the bag to show her his selections.

She peeked in. "Damn," she whispered, and George laughed.

313

Chapter 40 - Uh...

<u>Vander</u>

I stood outside the bedroom door, listening as Ruby said goodnight to the boys.

She murmured softly to Jace. His voice reached me easily.

"It's just weird to call someone dad for the first time."

"Mm-hmm. The good news is that you'll only have to do it once. There will be no other occasion where you'll have to call someone 'dad' for the first time."

"You think he wants me to?"

Ruby snorted. "I know he does. He loves you."

George interrupted. "Just do it, man. You can't just keep calling him 'uh' every time you want to get his attention."

Ruby chortled. She must have turned towards George because her voice came through clearly. "He does respond to 'uh', doesn't he?"

George chuckled. "He does." Then, in a more serious tone, he said to Jace, "He's a good dad, Jace. He won't let you down."

I swallowed hard. The truth is, I had let Jace down. Astronomically.

For a moment, there was complete silence, then Ruby spoke. "Tomorrow, I'm going to call him 'uh' and see if he responds."

"I'm going to do it, too," George laughed.

Ruby's voice came closer as she crossed the room. "Would you like to collect that hug now, my knight in shining armor?"

"Okay," George hesitated.

I heard the rustle of covers as George sat up.

"Oh, you're a good hugger, just like your dad," Ruby murmured. "You'll make a good dad one day. A good husband, too."

"Thanks," George whispered.

"Goodnight, agoria mou," Ruby said.

Goodnight, my boys.

I walked into the room, straight to Ruby, and pulled her against me, curling my body around hers for just a moment.

Releasing her, I went to George and went through our nightly, manly, fist-bump routine before I kissed him goodnight. "S'agapo, Georgie mou."

"I love you, Dad."

Crossing to Jace's bed, I sat on the edge and brushed his hair off his forehead. "The moment George was born I fell in love with him. There will never come a time I don't love him. The moment I saw you, I knew you were mine, and I fell in love with you. There will never come a time I don't love you."

Jace looked back at me with big eyes, so I continued. "You call me Dad whenever you're ready. I'll answer to 'uh' until that time."

Jace chuckled, and I grinned at him.

I decided to take a chance. "Do you need a manly fist-bump before I kiss you goodnight?"

"I grew up with Yiayia. If I resisted kisses, I'd be dead."

Ruby chortled behind me, but it sounded a little choked.

I leaned over and kissed my son goodnight for the first time. "Goodnight, agori mou. S'agapo."

315

Taking Ruby's hand, I led her to the door, my eyes stinging.

"Uh..."

I stopped at the door and turned back to Jace. "Yes, agori mou?"

"Goodnight, Dad."

I swallowed over the lump in my throat. "Goodnight, son."

Ruby tugged me out the door.

George's voice sounded clearly from the bedroom. "There. Was that so fucking hard?"

Ruby yelled in exasperation, "George!"

Laughter rang from their bedroom, and I shuffled Ruby towards our room.

Overcome with emotion, I needed her. Carefully closing and locking the door, I spun her around and slammed my mouth over hers. With my fist in her hair, I tugged her head back, opening her to me fully, and plundered her mouth.

"Vander!" She gasped when I came up for air.

I couldn't speak.

She hugged my boy.

My boy called me 'dad' for the first time.

She was laughter, she was light, she was sunshine.

She was mine.

I pulled her sweater off over her head, unsnapped her bra and pulled it down her arms. Dropping to my knees, I took her nipple into my mouth and swallowed it.

She groaned and I bit her sharply. "Quiet, Ruby."

Her body trembled and I felt her nod.

I soothed the bite with my lips and tongue, then lavished the same attention on the other one. Her fingers tunneled through my hair, and I dug my fingers into her ass, holding her pelvis tight against my chest.

Without releasing her breast, I snapped open the button of her jeans and tugged down the zipper. Working them over her rounded hips, taking her panties down with them, I palmed her bare ass. I smoothed my hands up her back and down over her rounded backside, squeezing and kneading the plump flesh.

I sat back on my heels. "Hold onto my shoulders, Ruby-mine."

Lifting one foot, then the other, I removed her pants and tossed them aside, then took her hands off my shoulders so she stood straight in front of me.

Ruby

Kneeling before me, his eyes took me in slowly until finally he met my eyes. "I will worship you with my body until I die."

My eyes stung and I drew in a shuddering breath.

Grasping my hips gently, he pulled me towards him and brushed his lips across my stomach. First with the tips of his fingers, then with his tongue, he traced the roadmap of stretchmarks Jace left across my stomach. "Thank you for Jace."

Emotion rippled over his face and through his body. He pressed his face against my mons and wrapped his arms around the backs of my thighs, forcing me to grab onto him for balance.

I soothed him, smoothing my hands over his hair, laying my palms on his broad shoulders.

Standing, he pulled me flush against his chest and kissed me. His lips were gentle, but his body trembled with the effort to hold back.

I wrapped my arms around his neck, pressed my lips to his, and he let go, tasting, sucking, nibbling, filling, kissing me breathless.

He backed me up and lay me across the bed. Quickly undressing, his gaze never left my face until he climbed in beside me.

Hovering over me, balanced on one forearm, he reached out and smoothed his hand over my breast, across my abdomen, around my hip and down my thigh. He watched his hand make the journey, then met my eyes again.

"You belong to me, and I desire only you."

His sweet words opened my legs like a key in a lock, and he lay his long body over mine, his cock nestled against my clit. He flexed his hips, and I tipped my head back at the pleasure.

"Vander," I whispered.

He kissed my throat, licked my pulse, ran his teeth along the edge of my jaw.

"Everything I have, is yours," he whispered back.

I hooked my ankles around his thighs and rubbed against him, wanting everything he had to give me, including his pain, including his past.

Pushing up on his hands, he glided back and forth across my slit, spreading my wet, nudging my clit, watching my face.

Pressing my palms to his chest, I flexed my fingers in the crisp hair. With my fingertips I traced my name on his ribs. With my thumb, I stroked the birthdates of first Jace, then George. His eyes darkened.

"In me," I ordered, and he smiled.

Lowering his chest to mine, he rolled so that I straddled his hips. He grasped my ribs, pushing me up off his pelvis, then locked eyes with mine.

"Ruby-mine," he said, his voice gruff with emotion. "I belong to you and you alone. Take what's yours."

He took hold of his cock and I lowered myself onto him, taking my time, taking all of him. Once fully seated, I brought my eyes back to his.

His jaw tight, lips pressed in a firm line, he rolled his hips.

A moan escaped from my lips, and he grasped my neck, pulling me down, swallowing the sound with his kiss.

"Shh, Ruby-mine."

I nodded and pushed off his chest to sit back up. He linked his fingers through mine then pushed my arms up. "Over your head, baby. I want to watch you take me."

Stretched out before him, I rose off his pelvis, tilting my hips to hit that magic spot inside, before sheathing him with my body.

Over and over, rising and falling, pleasure building, fear falling away. A sense of belonging, the thrill of homecoming, and the sweetness of surrender, broke over me like a tidal wave, sweeping away the debris of our painful past.

Hard hands on my ribs, pulled under, Vander over me, face set, shoulders bulging, slamming into me again and again until shaking, trembling, with his face tucked into my neck, he filled me with his love.

Walking up the path to the house, we were a different group of people than those who left only two days before.

Yiayia's eyes swept over us as we walked in.

"Ah, bravo, koritzaki mou."

She came to me immediately and patted my cheek then did the same to Vander as he bent to kiss her.

She opened her arms to the boys. "Agoria mou! Ela styn Yiayia sas. Come to your Yiayia."

Jace glanced at George. "Watch your cheeks. She pinches."

Yiayia laughed and enclosed them both in her arms. "Good boys. Yiayia is very proud. Now, get out of my kitchen. Go find Alex."

She turned to Vander and me, her eyes shining. "You made beautiful family, poulakia mou."

It sounded funny but it was also true.

Vander tugged me into his arms. "Ruby made us a beautiful family."

We found Amber sitting by herself in the living room, staring out the window into the backyard. She startled when we walked in, then assessed us in much the same way Yiayia did. She smiled at me.

"All good, Rubes?"

I bent and kissed her cheek. "All good, Ames."

Vander bent to receive her kiss on his cheek, snagged the converter off the coffee table, and sat back on the couch.

"When's Gus getting here?" he asked.

Amber's brows pinched. "He should have been here already."

Vander's attention swung to her immediately. "He'll be here. There's nowhere else he'd rather be."

319

"How do you know that?" She challenged.

Vander's lips tipped up on one side. "I have eyes. He loves his wife. He'll be here."

"Anyways!" Amber glared at him. "How was your weekend?"

Vander turned back to the television, and I twisted towards Amber.

"So. Jace called Vander 'dad' for the first time..."

Half an hour later, Yiayia called us to bring the platters to the table.

Gus still hadn't shown up, and he hadn't called.

Amber paced across the length of the living room, chewing on the side of her thumb.

"Have you messaged him?" Vander asked.

"I'm not his keeper!" Amber snapped. Immediately she closed her eyes. "I apologize, Vander."

The front door opened, and we heard Gus greet Yiayia. I looked at Amber, expecting to see relief or even anger, she appeared to be perfectly composed.

Yiayia set us up at the table in a different formation than last time. She put Vander at one end of the table, and Gus at the other. Amber and Alex were on either side of Gus, Jace and I sat on either side of Vander. George sat between Alex and Jace, and Yiayia took the seat between Amber and me, directly across from George.

She wagged her arthritic finger at the boys. "I be watching you three, make sure you eat," she warned them, and they laughed.

We were nearing time for dessert when Vander dropped his bomb.

"Where's your church, Yiayia?"

"Why? You want to go?"

"I need to talk to the priest about a wedding date. I'm thinking to do it before Christmas when George will be here."

My fork slipped out of my hand.

"What?" I asked stupidly.

Vander's eyes shone with mischief. "I told you. We're getting married. I thought we should do it sooner rather than later. What do you think?"

"I think," I bit out. "You should have asked me first."

"He did ask you," Jace volunteered.

"Well, he steamrolled you," George clarified.

I glared at both boys. "Do you want to wear powder blue tuxedos for the wedding? Take care when picking whose side you're on. Wedding pictures last forever!"

Jace laughed, but George had the grace to look at least a little concerned. I wanted to reassure him, but I also couldn't let Vander get away with his constant steamrolling.

Vander put his arm around my shoulders.

I shrugged him off.

He chuckled.

"Ruby-mine, you know I'm not a patient man. The whole family is here, it's a good opportunity to talk about the changes that are coming. Do you agree?"

"Yes," I grumbled. Truthfully, it thrilled me to hear him talking about getting married so soon.

I turned to Yiayia. "Vander wants us to move in together."

"Of course!" Yiayia exclaimed.

I looked at Vander, incredulous. "Well, that was a whole lot easier than expected!"

Turning back to face Yiayia, I continued. "Vander's house has a nanny suite on the main floor and the kitchen is huge. I think you'll be very comfortable, Yiayia, and you're going to love cooking in that kitchen. I can't wait to show it to you!"

Yiayia laughed. "Oh, no, koritzi mou. I not moving. I stay here."

My mouth gaped open.

Amber's eyes flitted back and forth between us.

"I don't think it's safe for you to live alone, Yiayia. What if you fall?" I hedged.

"If I fall, I fall. You get me the necklace button. If I fall, I push it. There you go."

"Will I have to change schools?" Jace asked, his face pinched.

"No, agori mou. You'll come in with me everyday and go to school from Spuds. At the end of the year, we'll decide on a more permanent solution."

"Yiayia," Amber ventured. "How about you move into the condo with Alex and I?"

"No, poulaki mou. I stay here in my neighbourhood with my friends. Here, I know where everything is. I go to Bayview Village, how I'm going to see everyone? No. I stay here."

"Why don't you move in with me?" Gus's deep, gravelly voice interrupted. "We have the nanny suite on the main floor and we're in your neighbourhood."

Amber gaped at him, her fair skin turning red with anger. "How is that a good idea?"

"How is it not?" He challenged her, levelling her with his cool, grey, gaze.

I'd never once seen this side of Gus. For most of their marriage, he doted on her endlessly. After their separation, he acted more like a wet cat than a man. This hard-faced, steely-eyed man was a stranger to me.

"You're a – a – a single man..."

Gus deliberately placed his fork and knife on the side of his plate before looking at Amber. "I am not, in fact, a single man. I am a married man, living in our family home without my family, and there is no reason Yiayia cannot live there with me."

"Won't you be, going out a lot?" Amber sputtered.

"No, Amber. I do not 'go out'. Nor will I 'go out'. Get that, at least, through your head."

Amber's eyes flashed and I got ready to clear the room. Amber rarely lost her temper, but when she did, she did it up right.

Yiayia clapped her hands. "Okay, is settled. I move into Gus and Amber's house with Gus. After I move, Ruby gonna sell this house. Gus will help,

322

and you and Vander get what you want where you want so Jace and George gonna be comfortable."

Amber's brows lowered and Vander cleared his throat loudly. I looked to him and saw Alex watching his parents with a pained look on his little face.

I leaned behind Yiayia and tugged Amber's blouse sharply. She spun towards me angrily. I mouthed, 'Alex' at her and she composed herself immediately. It was disconcerting how quickly she could pull up that mask.

"Is our house on the same bus route as Yiayia's house?" She asked Gus, knowing the answer full well.

Gus played along. "Yes. I think it'll be an easy transition for Yiayia. And, with my business, I'm in and out all day so she won't be alone for hours and hours at a time."

Amber nodded and smiled tightly. Turning to Alex, in a bid to distract him, she asked, "How great will it be having Yiayia living with us?" As soon as the words left her lips, her mouth dropped open as she realized her mistake.

Even Gus's head snapped up at her words, hope so raw and pained in his eyes it hurt to look at him.

"We're going home?" Alex whispered.

"Um..." Amber sat at a loss for words.

Gus quickly interjected, his hand coming up to cover Amber's on the table.

This was the first time I'd seen them touch in months. Amber stared down at his big hand on top of hers.

Gus spoke softly to Alex. "Not yet, buddy. No decisions have been made. Your mom and I have a lot of things, private things, to work out before that happens."

"You won't let her come home, yet?"

Gus caressed Amber's hand with his thumb, then moved his hand off hers as he leaned towards Alex to get his full attention. "No digging for information, Alex. This is private between mom and me."

Finally, I noticed George. His eyes were huge in his sweet face.

"Well, George!" I joked. "There's never a dull moment around here. What you need to know is that we all love each other. Being a family is not always easy, agori mou."

"Isn't that the fucking truth," George grumbled.

"George!" I yelled.

Vander started laughing first, then Gus joined in, followed by Amber, and the boys. I managed to keep a straight face.

Then Yiayia asked, "What he said?"

Jace and Alex lost it, and Amber dismissed them all from the table, choking with laughter.

George's flight left early the next morning, and he wouldn't see us all until the Christmas break. He said his goodbyes, received hugs, kisses, and a hearty cheek pinch, and we headed out to the porch so I could see them off.

Vander suddenly excused himself to run back inside to talk to Jace for a minute.

George looked pensive.

"You okay, Georgie?" I asked softly.

"I always thought my dad was a happy guy until now."

My heart dropped. He didn't like me. He didn't like me for his dad. I didn't know what to say, but he continued.

"Seeing him with you, I know that he wasn't happy before, but I think he is now." He paused, and I swallowed hard. He gave me his eyes, and they were full of trepidation. "Please don't hurt him."

At that precise moment, George took his rightful place in my heart.

I reached out and brushed his hair out of his eyes. "I won't. I promise."

Chapter 41 - Dirty

Ruby

Vander was beyond excited for Jace and me to move in. We planned to move Yiayia into Gus and Amber's house on Sunday, then Jace and I would move in with Vander over the course of the following week. It thrilled me how excited he was, but at the same time, it reminded me of how alone he'd been all these years, and that hurt my heart.

After the family dinner, where Yiayia, in true form decided where everybody would live, Vander readily agreed to look for a new house in the same neighbourhood as Gus and Amber so Jace could stay in the same school as Alex. It would be a fresh start for all of us.

Could it really be this easy? Only a few weeks ago, my future goals comprised of franchising Spuds. Now, I wasn't even sure I wanted that anymore. I'm not sure I ever did.

I wanted something more than what I had, and franchising seemed like the only 'more' I could safely reach for. The world seemed so much bigger with Vander in it. Possibilities that didn't exist before, presented themselves to me on all sides.

Travel, something I ruled out as an impossibility, seemed possible, even probable, with Vander. Knowing he and I both needed to get to the same home, eased the fear that, on my own, I wouldn't be able to get back.

I dreamed of taking Jace to Greece, and even more, taking Yiayia back to Greece! It had been fifteen years since she'd been back. I started to investigate honeymoon destinations although we didn't yet have a wedding date.

I suppose we would have to talk about that at some point. The church recognized a second marriage, but not in the same way it regarded the first. Our ceremony would begin with prayers of repentance for his failed marriage, and I wasn't sure if Vander knew that.

I told myself it didn't matter, and in the grand scheme of things, it didn't. But I'd be lying to myself if I pretended it didn't dull the shine off our big day for me.

Vander took up a lot of my free time, time I happily gave to him. He said he planned to scale back at his work to prioritize me and our family. Did I really want to get into a situation where I was the one shackled to work?

Time for things like reading, and bookstagram, would necessarily take a backseat if I started with this new venture.

I had to think it over, but that was for another day.

Not that reading mattered at the moment. I left my book in Blue Mountain. Someone would be treated to a very informative read, I snickered to myself. I downloaded the electronic version and ordered the paperback so Amber and Minty wouldn't know I lost it.

Vander was on his way to pick me up. I didn't know where we were going, but I knew where we'd end up and I looked forward to having the house to ourselves where I wouldn't have to worry about anyone hearing us.

He must have had the same idea because he picked up food and headed straight to his house. We laughed and ate at the table. I pulled the box of pictures down from his closet to look for the ones I wanted to frame. We were going to make our place a home, and a home needed pictures.

Later, lying on our bed, he undressed me slowly, uncovering me bit by bit, kissing each inch of skin as he exposed me.

"So," he murmured, his voice low in my ear.

He covered my naked body with his, his thighs resting on the outside of mine, keeping me from opening under him. He kissed me behind my ear, ran his teeth along the juncture of my neck and my shoulder, and brushed his lips across mine.

Propping himself up on his elbows, he arched a brow, his eyes heated.

"So, what?" I prodded him softly.

"I found your book."

"What?" I cocked my head in question. "What book?"

"The one you had with you at Blue Mountain."

"Oh! You have it? That's good. I thought I'd lost it."

"Mm-hmm. 'Oh'."

I froze and stared at him. "You didn't read it, did you?"

His lips curled up wickedly at the corner. "You want to be tied down, koukla mou?"

"Uhh..."

He dropped a hard kiss on my mouth. "You want to be blindfolded?"

"Oh, God... you read it." I couldn't tell if he was angry or turned on.

He rolled me on top of him and grabbed handfuls of my ass. "You want to be spanked? You want me to take your ass?"

I panted. Rolled my pelvis over his.

He grasped my hips and held me still. "You want to sit on my face? You want me to fuck your mouth?"

I let out an involuntary moan and his face darkened.

"Is that okay? You seem angry."

"I'm not angry that you want it. I'm pissed that I didn't know what you like."

I huffed. "How could you know when I don't even know? It's not like I've done any of that stuff."

His anger cleared and only heat remained. He grasped my hips and dragged my pussy over his cock.

"Okay," I breathed, rubbing my clit over the swollen head of his cock. "But, uh, about the, um, ass part? That's strictly an exit."

He stared at me for half a frozen second before bursting into laughter.

"Vander!" I snapped. "This is not an appropriate time to laugh at me!"

"I'm not, I'm not," he protested, his eyes dancing. "Let's just see how things go, hmm? You might change your mind."

"I won't," I assured him.

"Don't make it a challenge, woman," he warned, rolling his hips against me. "Even talking about it has you soaked."

"Stop talking and make me feel good," I snapped.

He chuckled low in his chest. With his hands at my ribs, he heaved me up to straddle his chest.

Uh, oh. He wasn't wasting any time. "Up you come, koukla. Sit on my face."

"Sit on your face?" I froze.

He chuckled. The vibrations reverberated through his chest to my pussy, and I had the urge to grind down on him.

"Yeah." He tipped his chin down to look at me and took a deep breath in, his eyes closed.

"Sit? Like actually sit? Or, like, hover?"

His eyes popped open, and his chest jerked with suppressed laughter.

I narrowed my eyes at him in warning, and his face turned serious.

"Get up here and do what feels good. When I need to breathe, I'll tap out for a minute. Don't hold back."

"I'm not sure about this..." I said even as I swung one thigh over his shoulder, placing my knee beside his head.

He wasn't laughing anymore. He turned his head and licked the inside of my upper thigh.

"I can taste you," he whispered.

Wet flooded from my core and he groaned. "You're slick. Come on, baby. Get up here."

I placed my other knee on the other side of his head and held myself over him.

"Tell you what," he muttered. "You're in control. You want my mouth, you bring your pussy down here and I'll lick and suck and fuck you with my tongue. When you need a break, you raise yourself up."

I let myself sink down towards his mouth. His tongue came out and licked me from my opening all the way to my clit. My head fell back. The pleasure of the first touch always shocked me.

I angled my hips to give him my clit. He teased the little bud, circling it with the tip of his tongue, before sucking it into his mouth.

I pulled back to give him a minute and he turned his head and licked the inside of my thigh. I lowered myself again.

This time his hands came up around my thighs and he tugged me down over his face and devoured me.

I cried out, part surprise, all wicked pleasure. His tongue entered me, fluttering along my walls, and I spasmed. He groaned. Digging his fingers into my thighs, he plunged his tongue inside me again and again before coming back up to my clit, his bearded chin brushing against my opening.

I ground down onto his chin, the guttural groans coming from between my legs making me hotter. He let go of one thigh, and I watched as he squeezed the head of his cock, a bead of pre-cum dripping down the side.

That sight tipped me over. I grabbed his hair and rubbed over his face, the pleasure mounting. He reached up and tweaked my nipples, hard.

A harsh moan escaped my lips as the first spasm rocked through me and he carried me through to the end, his tongue circling and lapping gently at my clit.

I slumped with my release, and he pushed me up.

"Turn," he ordered.

"What?" I asked, dazed.

"Knees either side of my head and face my feet."

I hesitated and he responded with a sharp crack on my ass. "You want to suck my cock?"

"I do," I breathed.

"Then, turn. I want your pussy in my face while you do it. I want to see you slick and dripping."

329

I turned quickly, more turned on than I'd ever been in my life. I wrapped my hand around his cock and licked the tip just as he plunged two fingers inside me, searching for my g-spot. I cried out, then took his cock to the back of my throat. I heard him grunt and his hips flexed, pressing in further. I pulled back to breathe.

He curled his fingers inside me. The first stirrings of my orgasm fluttered. I wasn't going alone this time.

"You go, I go," Vander asserted.

I took him deep in my throat while Vander worked his magic. I no longer cared that my ass hung over his face. I aimed all my attention towards hollowing out my cheeks around his swollen member and the spasms beginning to rock my pussy.

I swirled my tongue around his head, sucked gently at the tip, ran my tongue along the thick vein on the underside, cupped his balls in my hand, took him to the back of my throat and swallowed.

"Get there, Ruby," he growled.

His voice hit me like an aphrodisiac. My hips began moving of their own accord, riding his fingers.

A low moan came from my throat, and I swallowed him as I came around his fingers.

He grunted and the first hot spurt of semen hit the back of my tongue. I sucked him back and swallowed around the head as he pulsed with his release.

As soon as I swallowed the last drop, I carefully slid him out of my mouth, then spun quickly around. I stared Vander in the face, slightly aghast at my previous position.

He looked back at me steadily. His voice sounded gruff when he spoke. "You alright, there, Ruby-mine?"

He lay splayed out on the bed in front of me, his beautiful body sated, eyes at half mast, his heart on his sleeve. He liked what we did.

Hell, I liked what we did.

A lot.

I wanted to do it again.

The realization of what I nearly missed, the laughter, the sex, giving Jace a father, the future we mapped out, it all hit me in that moment. We were getting a second chance. Actually, a third chance. Who gets a third chance? My entire body relaxed.

"Yeah, baby. I'm good."

"Come." He lifted his arm in invitation. "Lie down with me and have a nap."

Two hours later, I stretched awake.

Vander lay beside me, on his side, curled around my back.

This.

This was happiness.

I lay still for as long as I could, then eased out from under his arm. He rolled to his back and let out a huge snore.

I smiled. Charming.

My book, The Naughty Pine, lay on the bedside table on my side. I slid it over and opened it looking for my bookmark and had to stifle a laugh.

Sticky tabs.

Sticky tabs all throughout with happy faces drawn onto them.

"I thought we'd start at the beginning and work our way through."

His deep, sleepy voice made me jump.

I looked at him and laughed, then hit him with my book.

He wrestled me to the bed.

"You can't hit me!" He laughed and grabbed the book from my hands. "You're not the Dom, I'm the Dom!" He pinned my wrists over my head and hovered over me. "I get to spank you on your gorgeous ass, you don't get to hit me with a book! That's abuse!"

I smiled up at him and he smiled back. I waited until he shifted his weight off me before I pounced.

"Gotcha!" I screamed.

I felt his hand jerk under my knee.

He arched, yelling, "Ow! My finger! I think you broke my finger!"

I jumped off him and reached for his hand.

"Oh no!" I cried. "Which one? Not the good one!"

"The good one?" He huffed, shaking out his hand. "Which one, exactly, is the good one?"

I chortled. "The good one. You know, my favourite. The one that makes me feel good."

His mouth fell open and he grabbed me once again, pulling me under him. "I think I'll have to introduce you to all my fingers. What do you think of that?"

"I'll host a meet and greet."

Vander chuckled deep in his chest and covered my laughing mouth with his.

Minty canceled our Bookstagram meeting for Saturday. She had last minute plans for a spa weekend with the girls she worked with, Willa and Junie. She seemed excited about it and told us she'd tell us the story at our next meeting.

With Bookstagram night canceled, Amber and I decided to pack up all Yiayia's things on Saturday while Vander and Gus took the boys out, then Jace and I planned to sleep at Vander's.

What I really wanted to do, was stay in my house with my Yiayia on our last night, but Yiayia would not have it.

"Oxi, koukla. I gonna go to bed early and you need to get Jace used to sleeping at Vander's, with you. You go. Have a fun." When I went to argue further, she lay her hand against my cheek. "Koukla mou. I need time by myself to say goodbye to this old house."

This made sense to me, and I would not deny her. "Okay, Yiayia. If that's what you want, that's what you're going to have."

"Ah, bravo. Good girl."

Which is how I found myself cuddled up with Vander on one couch, Jace lying full out on the other, eating popcorn and watching a movie.

I couldn't stop looking at them together. How did I not realize Jace was Vander's son? Their mannerisms were the same, the way they smiled, the way they walked, the way they looked.

Jace blossomed under Vander's attention. He called Vander 'dad' easily, and while he didn't offer hugs the way he did to me, I noticed that he would position himself beside and just a little in front of Vander often, and Vander never failed to rest his hand on the nape of Jace's neck. As soon as Vander made contact, Jace relaxed back and leaned in.

The first time I saw Jace lean in like that, the mixture of grief and gratitude on Vander's face forced me to turn away. Every time I saw Jace do it, Vander's face reflected his gratitude and adoration, but Jace? Jace lit up like a beacon.

As the movie credits rolled, Jace stretched and rolled off the couch. He leaned over me and gave me a hug.

"Goodnight, Momma," he muttered tiredly. "I love you."

"Goodnight, agapimeno mou." I cupped his cheek. "I love you, too."

He turned to Vander and held out a limp fist bump.

Vander chuckled and bumped him, then Jace leaned over and hugged him.

The smile fell off Vander's face as his arm came up to embrace his son. "Goodnight, Dad. I love you."

Vander's voice sounded strained. "Goodnight, buddy. I love you, too."

Jace stumbled off to his room, his footsteps light on the stairs.

Vander and I sat unmoving. I reached for his hand and winced at the pain on his face. He swallowed hard and squeezed my hand.

"Sometimes the sadness sneaks up on me," he admitted softly.

I swung around to straddle his lap and wrapped my arms around him. His arms around my back crushed me to him painfully like bands of steel. "I'm sorry, Ruby-mine."

I sighed. "I'm sorry, too, agapimeno mou. I should have figured it out."

He tucked his face in my neck. "I'm so damn sorry. I hate that you were alone."

I tunneled my fingers gently through his thick hair, lightly scratching his scalp. "I'm not alone now. Neither are you. Vander, agapimeno, we need to let the guilt go."

His chest heaved with his inhale, my ribs ached from his hold on me, and despair rolled off him in waves. Instead of pulling away from the pain of his hold, I melted against him. He spread his arms out, splaying his big hands across my back, and I took a breath.

"I'm selling my company."

I jolted with the information. "What? What do you mean?"

He leaned back and rubbed the tops of my thighs. "I don't need to work if I don't want to. I'll have enough to set us up, take care of both boys' education, look after your Yiayia, and my parents if need be. I'll need something to do, though. I might work on a consultancy basis. But I think we need to step things up with your franchising project. I'd like to get that sorted while I'm still heading the company."

I didn't want to talk about franchising. Not tonight, and being honest with myself, at least, not at all.

What I did want, was to take him out of the dark place full of grief and despair. I spread my hands over his chest and flicked his nipple through his t-shirt, then brushed my mouth softly across his.

"Can we talk about that later," I teased softly. "At a time when I'm not straddling your lap?"

He grinned. "Oh, yeah? Is this a problem for you?" He smoothed his hands up my thighs firmly and rounded to my ass, yanking me forward.

"Well, yes," I said primly. "It makes me feel dirty. Like I'm screwing the boss for favours."

I quelled my smile and maintained my prim demeanour as his eyes lit up.

"You are screwing the boss."

His lips tugged up at one side and he smiled into my eyes, then he cupped his hand around the back of my neck and tugged my face closer to his.

Looking into my eyes, he murmured softly, "And I'll give you all the favours you'd never think to ask for, including getting you as dirty as you want to be."

Chapter 42 - Tag-A-Long

<u>Vander</u>

My cell buzzed on the bedside table.

I stretched to get it, trying not to disturb my barnacle. I kissed the top of her messy head. During the day she pushed and pulled, seesawing between sweet and fiery. At night she turned into a barnacle and couldn't get close enough.

She wasn't like this when we used to sleep together when we were younger. She liked to spread out and usually had an arm or a leg spilling off the bed. I wondered if it would change in a few months when she gained more confidence in us.

The time on my cell read seven oh-eight. My whole body went on alert and Ruby startled.

"What is it?" She whispered worriedly.

I opened the message. Fuck. I glanced at Ruby quickly. I could think of no way to soften this, so I'd help her by taking charge.

I shot off a text, then turned to Ruby and took hold of her jaw. "That was Gus. Yiayia fell. She's fully conscious and talking. They are taking her to the hospital to get her checked out."

Ruby's eyes glazed over. "What?"

I gave her jaw a gentle squeeze. "Ruby, eyes on me."

She sharpened her gaze on mine, and I saw the fear behind them. "That was Gus. Yiayia fell. She is conscious and talking. They are taking her to the hospital to get her checked out. I'm going to wake Jace and tell him to get dressed. You start getting ready. I'll be right back. Okay?"

Her face had taken on a look of horror.

"Don't go there, Ruby-mine. Let's just put all suppositions on the back burner until we see what we're dealing with. I'll be with you every step of the way."

She nodded and moved to get out of the bed. Then turned quickly and hugged me tightly, her body trembling.

I splayed my hand over her back. "It'll be okay, koukla mou."

Yiayia arrived by ambulance, and the hospital staff immediately whisked her off into a room.

Amber and Gus arrived shortly after Yiayia, and Amber raised hell until one of the nurses brought her back to her. Some of these fucking people followed their rules in the absence of common sense at times. Amber came out and collected Ruby to take her back as well.

Gus, both boys, and I hung out in the waiting room. After an hour and a half, the two boys sat slumped against the chairs. There was no help for it. Neither Gus nor I were willing to leave, not until we got news of Yiayia's condition.

I checked the time.

"One of us has got to get them some breakfast soon."

Gus and I stood staring at one another. Two men who understood the depths of their failures. Gus wanted to be there for Amber just as much as I needed to be there for Ruby.

"Boys," a soft voice called softly from behind me.

Jace and Alex sat straight up, then went flying out of their chairs into the arms of the cool blond standing behind us.

Gus looked at the floor for a moment before looking up at Minty who stood with an arm around each of them.

336

Minty met Gus's eyes and smiled at him sweetly. "It's good to see you, Angus. Truly."

He nodded, then cleared his throat gruffly. "Did Amber call you?"

She shook her head, her long, blond ponytail swinging behind her. "Ruby called. She asked me to come and get the boys for the day. Is that alright with you?"

"Of course," he murmured.

I wasn't sure what went on between them, but I was uncomfortably aware of it.

"You have my cell number memorized, agori mou?" I asked Jace.

He stepped away from Minty and stepped towards me before stopping, unsure of himself.

I held out my arm and he came into my side. "You okay, buddy?"

"Shouldn't I stay with you, Dad? Wait to find out if Yiayia is okay?"

I ran my hand over his curls. "I think it's best that you go with Minty, honestly. How about I take Minty's cell phone number and I'll update Minty whenever we know anything?"

He stood looking at the floor, unconvinced.

"Come on, boys. We have work to do," Minty said softly.

Jace's head came up. "What? What work do we have to do?"

"First, we need to eat some breakfast to keep our strength up, then we have to get food to bring back to your parents. Then we are going to head to Yiayia's house to tidy up and make some meals for everybody. Okay?"

Jace nodded slowly. He leaned his head against my bicep. I cupped my hand around the back of his neck and kissed the top of his head.

Angus wrapped Alex up tight in his arms and Minty stood waiting patiently, her eyes shiny.

"Thank you, Minty." She nodded in response to me than walked over to Gus, placing a cool hand on his arm.

"I'm so glad you're here, Gus. Let me take Alex so you can do what you need to do."

Gus nodded and kissed Alex's head.

I felt suddenly bereft watching the boys leave with Minty.

"She seems like a good woman."

"The best," Gus said softly, and I looked at him sharply.

He caught it and smiled wryly. "No. Nothing like that. She's pure-hearted and as good as gold. You can't help but love her once she lets you in." He paused. "Besides, she's always been there for Amber, especially when I wasn't. She's been there for both of us."

"Let me know if I can ever help, Gus. I know how it is to royally fuck up."

By silent mutual agreement, we let the subject drop and headed for two empty chairs to wait.

Ruby

"Keep your cool when you see her, Ruby," my sister coached as we walked through the doors to the emergency department. "It's not as bad as it looks."

I looked up quickly to question Amber, but she was busy staring daggers at the poor nurse who didn't realize who she was and gave her a hard time about getting back to our Yiayia.

Amber slipped into the room one step ahead of me, then reached a hand back to grasp mine and squeezed it reassuringly. No matter, nothing could have prepared me for seeing Yiayia lying still and pale in the hospital bed.

Blood pooled purple under the fragile skin of her right arm, visible past the short sleeve of her hospital gown. Wires that led to a long needle in her left hand lay taped to her left arm. A tube snaked out from under the blankets and wires connected her to a machine that monitored her heart rate and oxygen levels.

Her eyes were closed, the blue lines visible beneath the thin skin.

With no makeup, no flowery blouse, and no jewelry, Yiayia looked her age, and it was not a comforting sight.

"Where's Yiayia's ruby ring? It's not on her hand."

"I don't know, Ruby. I don't know if she was wearing it when Gus found her this morning."

"What was he doing there so early?"

She looked at me sideways. "Apparently they have a standing date for breakfast on Sunday mornings. He said he went early because you weren't there, and he knew she gets up at five most mornings."

"Thank, God," I whispered.

Amber's eyes looked betrayed. I lay my hand on her arm. "I didn't know."

She nodded shortly. Believing.

Truthfully, it would not be unlike me to walk past a party in the dining room and miss it, lost in my own head.

"He does love you, Amber." I held up my hand to forestall the protestation poised on her lips. "I'm not telling you what to do. I don't know enough facts to even offer an opinion. But a blind man could see that he loves you and I know what it is to live separated from the one that you love. It's got to be killing him."

"You think it's not killing me?" Amber hissed.

I took half a step back. Amber didn't usually lose her cool.

"Then, why, Amber? Why deny yourselves?"

She looked away. "In this, Ruby, you need to mind your own business. You're right, you don't know the facts," she swung back to look at me and her cognac-coloured eyes were flat, "and I don't owe you them."

I swallowed hard and nodded, realizing that while Minty seemed to be more aware about what happened between Amber and Gus, I was not.

God, I really was a third wheel to them, even after all these years.

I stepped back and turned to face Yiayia's small form in the bed. I snorted to myself. Never thought I'd see a day when facing Yiayia still and quiet in a hospital bed was preferable to facing my sister.

I pulled a chair up to her left side and slipped my hand under hers, closed my eyes, and prayed.

Amber sat down on the other side and after a few minutes, when I could successfully hide my hurt, I spoke to her.

"The doctor's been in?"

"Yes." Amber glanced at me warily and cleared her throat. "She has a hairline fracture in her right arm and a possible concussion. They still need to run more tests, and they are concerned about her right hip."

I swallowed hard. "I hope it's not her hip," I whispered.

I'd heard the stories, we both had, about elderly people going into the hospital with a broken hip and never coming out. Being stuck in a hospital bed did funny things to people and the elderly were particularly susceptible.

"Just pray that it's not her hip, and that her concussion isn't bad, so we can bring her home."

"I think she should come home to her own house. Now is not the time to move her."

If I had been there, this would not have happened. She wouldn't have been lying there with no one to help her, no one to find her for hours.

Shitfuckdamn.

If she fell at five and Gus didn't get there until seven? Did she lose consciousness? Is it bad that we don't know that?

Did she fall because she was upset? Of course, she was upset. She wanted to be by herself to say goodbye to the home she shared with Pappou, the only home she'd ever known here in Canada.

Oh, God! What if she fell last night and waited all night, cold and alone, on the floor?

"Ruby, don't fall down any rabbit holes. You've waited a long time to be with Vander and you are doing the right thing."

There was Amber slipping into her role as my big sister, giving advice she wouldn't take herself. I wondered if Minty saw me the same way.

"Look after your own problems, Amber. You're hardly in a position to be giving me advice."

I heard her quick intake of breath and regret for my harsh words hit me immediately, but Yiayia's small hand fluttered over mine and drew my attention.

"Yiayia?"

"Don't look so worried, poulaki mou. Yiayia is strong. I not gonna die today. Or tomorrow either."

I laughed roughly and she gave me a gentle squeeze then looked at me. "Don't talk to your sister like that poulaki mou. You don't know the whole story."

"You're right. I don't."

I turned to Amber. She looked worried. "I'm sorry I spoke to you like that, Amber."

She smiled tentatively, and I smiled back, but something had shifted between us. While she didn't know what it was, I did. I would forever be the tagalong.

"What the doctor said?" Yiayia asked Amber.

Amber placed her hand on Yiayia's leg. "Broken arm and concussion. They want to take a closer look at your hip and then they'll tell us when we can take you home."

"Okay, koukla mou. Don't worry. Yiayia is strong."

Yiayia turned to me. "You don't put your life on hold for me no more, koukla. I be okay. I want you to be okay. Life is adventure, koritzaki mou, and life is happening whether you scared or brave. The world is in your little hands! Don't throw it away."

Her voice sounded scratchy, and I reached for the water to give her a sip.

She turned to Amber. "I have headache, koukla. Gus is not a perfect man, he is only human, but he is a good man. Don't lose that."

Amber smiled tightly. "Okay, Yiayia."

"Don't say 'okay' and not do anything about it. I see more than you think I do. I know more than you all tell me." She tried to wave away Amber's next words and gasped at the pain in her arm. Amber jumped up, alarmed.

"Is okay, koukla. I forgot about my arm. Go ask the nurse for something for my head, koritzi mou."

Just then, the nurse opened the door to check Yiayia's vitals. By the time she finished, Yiayia was asleep, and the nurse reassured us she would be back in an hour to check on her again.

341

"I'm sorry, Ruby," Amber murmured. "I shouldn't have spoken to you like that."

"It's okay, Amber." I tried to smile at her reassuringly. "I understand."

I did.

Changes were coming hard and fast and I felt lost and displaced.

First Vander showed up, then I gave into my feelings for him, after which I was hit with the revelation that Vander was Jace's father.

Quick on those heels, I met George and accepted him into my life with the plan to combine our households. This necessitated leaving Yiayia and losing the only home I'd had since I was ten years old.

The first night away from her, she fell and hurt herself, and all I could think about was eventually losing her for good.

To top it all off, I realized that my place in Amber's life had not really changed since those early days when I dropped out of university, when she and Minty pulled me into their fold.

Maybe Yiayia was right, and I didn't have my own life. I'd even shelved my franchising idea. It was a lot to think about.

Amber and I took turns giving Vander and Gus updates, as well as touching base with Minty and the boys. After several hours, the doctor admitted Yiayia into a ward. They decided to keep her overnight for observation and confirmed that she did in fact have a concussion. They hoped to release her in the morning.

There was nothing left for us to do, so we headed home.

I tried to convince Vander I was fine at home alone with Jace, but he insisted.

Too tired to argue, I nodded.

I could use his big arms around me while I slept.

Chapter 43 - Meddling

Ruby

Walking into the house last night, I felt Yiayia's absence acutely. Rarely, over the past ten years, had I arrived home to an empty house. Without her, the house was a brittle shell with only memories echoing off the walls.

I held it together, ordered pizza for dinner, even pulled out a board game to play with Jace and Vander. But as soon as Jace headed to bed, I dropped the façade. Standing in the kitchen, I stared out the window into the night until Vander led me upstairs by the hand.

Slipping into my bed, I folded in on myself. Vander curled around my back with one arm around my waist, holding me close, the other under my head, his hand wrapped around my wrist, tethering me to him tightly, and surprisingly, I slept.

First thing in the morning, I called the hospital for an update, then called Amber. She had two patients she couldn't reschedule in the afternoon but planned to go to the hospital in the morning. I agreed to go in the afternoon. Hopefully by then, we'd be allowed to bring Yiayia home, well, to Amber and Gus's house. I still believed the familiarity of home might be better.

Vander left for work, hugging me tightly and kissing me deeply before he left, dropping Jace off to school on his way. He planned to pick Jace and Alex up from school and keep them at his place for the night. Gus would take the following night. The goal was to keep the boys in the loop but distracted. The comfort of each others' presence would help them cope with the uncertainty of Yiayia's health.

At Spuds, I found little to do. I put a sign up on the door stating we were closed due to a family emergency, cleaned out the fridge of all perishables, and disinfected the surfaces. Locking the door, I headed to the hospital only to find out that Yiayia's blood oxygen levels were dropping dramatically for no known reason, and she'd be staying another night.

Amber left to meet her appointments and I sat in the world's most uncomfortable chair and watched Yiayia breathe, my anxiety spiking with every alert from the machines that monitored her vitals.

When awake, Yiayia spoke clearly, her thought process lucid, but she wasn't awake a whole lot.

By late afternoon, Amber returned, and we waited together for the doctor to show up. A short while later, a brisk knock on the door announced her arrival.

"Hi, ladies. I'm Dr. Galena. I'm your grandmother's physician here at the hospital," she said with a ready smile.

"Nice to meet you. I'm Amber and this is Ruby. What can you tell us about our grandmother's condition?"

She flipped through the file, murmuring, "Nothing has changed since this morning, that's good..." She looked up at us. "Okay. Her hip is fine. The break in her arm is going to take a while to heal. She cannot use that hand for six weeks. It should heal if she doesn't try to use it. As for the concussion, there are certain things for you to watch for like dizziness, confusion, headaches, anything out of the ordinary. I'd like her to have a seated walker with her at all times so that if a dizzy spell comes, she can sit until it passes."

"Um, we were in the process of moving her when this happened," I interjected. "Would it be better to just keep her in the home where she's lived all her life?"

"Hmm. Where was she moving to?"

"My house," Amber replied. "We have a granny suite on the main floor. Her house is a two story."

"I would think she'll be much better off in the one floor plan. How are the bathing facilities?"

"My husband is outfitting her bathroom with safety bars and seating today."

"That sounds good."

Whatever else they said escaped my notice.

Yiayia stirred but didn't wake.

The walls closed in, thinning the air around me, and I needed to escape before I embarrassed myself. Standing, I thanked the doctor, told Amber I'd check in with her later, pulled back my shoulders to open my chest, and walked out as calmly as I could.

Breaking through the front doors of the hospital, I sucked in a breath of cool air. I walked the perimeter of the parking lot, taking deep breaths and repeating my mantras, but the overarching urge to get home swelled up within me pushing me to beeline to my car.

I concentrated on the drive. The need to focus offered a welcome respite from my rising anxiety. I mentally traced the routes in my head, choosing the one with less traffic while not going into those isolated stretches of road I'd deemed unsafe.

Okay, okay, okay. You're doing good. Almost home.

The relief I expected would greet me once home embraced me within its walls, was conspicuously absent. I wandered the first floor, searching for something to anchor me, something to make me feel safe.

The silence acted as a greenscreen for the noise in my head.

I plodded upstairs, my head floating above my body, my legs jellied, my pulse pounding in my ears.

Working to keep my breaths long and even, I dug Vander's university sweatshirt out of the back of my closet and pulled it on over my t-shirt. With stiff, bloodless fingers, I struggled to release the button of my jeans and exchanged them for pyjama pants. Digging through my drawer, I found a pair of warm, fuzzy socks and put them on with shaking hands.

Seeing Yiayia at the hospital, so small and frail, shook me. She would never come home to me, we no longer shared a home, and this separation marked the beginning of a painfully long goodbye.

345

My tiny house ballooned around me in an anti-Alice in Wonderland phenomenon.

I closed my bedroom door against the threat and turned the lock. Crossing to the window, I yanked open the curtains as wide as they could go. Then, sitting back against my headboard, with Vander's pillow in my arms, lost in my thoughts, I dozed off and on while the afternoon sky darkened to night.

Hunger pains rumbled, reminding me I hadn't eaten since that morning.

I slipped out of my room, turning on every light in the house as I made my way to the kitchen. My cell phone buzzed on the counter where I'd dropped it when I got home.

So many missed calls. I called Vander back immediately, apologizing, telling him I'd fallen asleep.

"You're okay, koukla mou? Do you want me to head over there with the boys?" He spoke quickly, his voice laced with worry.

I looked at the time. Eight-thirty. The time they should be settling down to go to bed. They still had school tomorrow and they needed their sleep.

"I'm okay, moro mou."

"You're sure?" He didn't sound convinced.

"As okay as I can be at this time."

"Ruby. Should I come?" Vander's voice deepened and he spoke almost harshly.

"No," I insisted firmly. "I don't want the boys disrupted."

"They're not in bed yet. They just got their jammies on."

"It's okay. They'll still be alarmed if you pull them out of the house right now."

"I'll be there first thing in the morning, Ruby-mine. I'll drop the boys off at school and head straight over."

"Okay, honey. I love you, Vander."

"I love you, too, Ruby-mine. It's going to be okay, koukla. I promise you'll be okay."

I warmed up some leftovers and ate while I called Amber and Minty back. Their voices held back the silence from encroaching too closely.

After I hung up, I put my dishes in the dishwasher and tidied up the house, ghosts of memories following me from room to room.

My dad standing behind Yiayia in the kitchen while she cooked, reaching around her to steal food, and laughing when she pretended to scold him.

Pappou sitting at the small kitchen table, his reading glasses perched on his nose, poring over bank statements and order forms for Spuds, while Yiayia stood at the stove making him Greek coffee.

Amber and I standing on stools at the counter, learning to cook with Yiayia.

In the family room, my mother, when my dad was still with us, curled up in the corner of the couch reading a romance novel, Yiayia beside her, studying cookbooks and occasionally asking for an explanation.

Then, after my mother left, Amber and I at the dining room table with a younger Yiayia and Pappou, doing our homework, eating dinner, hearing the gossip from the Greek community.

In the hallway, Yiayia welcoming guests who came to celebrate Pappou's name day, heading out the door with Amber on the weekends to help at Spuds, getting ready for church, Yiayia threatening to boil us if we didn't hurry up.

Yiayia putting homemade lunches in schoolbags by the door, a limo out front ready to carry the three of us who were left to the church, Yiayia so enormously proud to walk Amber down the aisle.

Yiayia putting the new sheets on the crib in Jace's nursery.

Yiayia chasing Alex and Jace when they were toddlers, coaxing them to eat, do their homework, be careful, forever telling them to be careful.

Countless family dinners took place in that dining room, and a parade of apparition-like Ambers and Rubys passed from the kitchen to the dining room, carrying thousands upon thousands of platters overflowing with food made with Yiayia's love.

Yiayia.

Always Yiayia.

347

My constant.

My anchor.

My safe harbour from the storm.

I stopped in front of the fireplace and picked up the framed, yellowed, photograph of Pappou and Yiayia on board the ship that carried them to this country, full of hope, full of plans, full of my father. I wondered what dreams they had, how it must have felt to see them shatter.

I saw myself in the hospital saying goodbye to the unconscious shell of my father.

I heard Amber screaming on the driveway, her nails curling into the flesh of my arms, leaving me with two different kinds of scars from the day we lost our mom.

Arriving home to a Yiayia clothed head to toe in black, never to hear my Pappou's booming voice again.

Saying goodbye as Vander went back to B.C.

Seeing the Facebook post proving he moved on, I heard once again the awful, keening sounds erupting from the bottomless pit of my grief.

Watching Drew's handsome, sweet face go from happiness to confusion to resignation over the weeks following Jace's birth as I froze him out. Looking back, I could have loved him. I was too afraid he wouldn't love me.

Waiting for Vander's text after the conference.

Yiayia at the hospital.

The empty house.

Alone.

I gently replaced the photograph on the mantle. Lifting Yiayia's afghan from the couch, I curled up into my Pappou's old chair, imagined his strong arms around me, and fell asleep.

"Ruby."

A deep voice came as if from far away. In my sleepy state, I dreamed it was Pappou. I heard a deep sigh.

"Ruby."

I opened my eyes to find Vander leaning over me. "Vander."

"Why aren't you in bed? You're freezing," he said as he ran his warm hands over my arms.

"Too lonely up there. The house feels too big with nobody in it."

He scooped one arm under my knees and the other around my back, then lifted me up before turning to sit in the chair with me on his lap. The muscles in his thighs bunched and flexed under my butt as he shifted to get more comfortable, then tugged me close to his chest.

"You need your sleep," he murmured. "We've got a big day today."

"I know. There's no help for it now. I'll be okay, moro mou."

I moved to get up, but he smoothed one big hand down my back and cupped the back of my head with his other one, tucking me under his chin. "Just sit for a while, Ruby-mine."

I settled into his lap, his strong arms around me, and slept easy.

A few hours later, at Gus and Amber's, Yiayia smiled to find her own bedroom suite in her new room. Even her jewelry box, picture frames, and knickknacks were laid out across the dresser. They were in the wrong places, and the jewelry box faced the wrong way, but Vander and Gus set it up as best as they could.

"Agoria mou! Thank you! Is perfect!"

Yiayia settled into her bed, fatigued after the excitement of the past few days.

"Ruby, koritzi mou, give me my ring from my jewelry box, please," Yiayia asked.

I turned the box right way round and retrieved her ring. Slipping it on her finger, I rubbed the pad of my thumb over the stones.

She sighed. "Better."

"We've arranged for a night nurse to stay with you overnight for the next several nights, okay, Yiayia?" Amber asked.

"Yes, koritzi mou."

"We've also arranged for VON nursing to come in daily to help you with bathing and to check your injuries," I added.

Amber's head snapped up, realizing, I think, that with Yiayia here needing so much assistance, she would need to be here too, which meant she'd be with Gus much more often than she was maybe ready for.

"I think we can handle the cleaning and the cooking together, right Amber?" I continued.

Gus cleared his throat. "Uh, I have a service coming in every two weeks. I can schedule them to come more often if you think it's necessary."

Amber narrowed her eyes at him. "I thought you said we didn't need a cleaning service?"

Gus flushed but his eyes remained steady on his wife's face. "I was wrong. I should not have expected you to look after all the housework on top of all your other responsibilities. I didn't help nearly enough."

"You did all the outside work," she murmured, dropping her eyes.

"Yes," he conceded, "but I enjoy that. This," he swept a hand indicating the house, "is not fun."

She studied him for a moment longer then turned away.

I realized, in that moment, that Yiayia was a meddling genius. I wondered, for just a moment, if she and Gus were in cahoots from the beginning.

Better not to ask.

This way I wasn't an accomplice.

Chapter 44 – The Glass Wall

Ruby

I lay in bed staring into space, Vander's side already cool, long past the time I should have gotten up to go to Spuds.

I rolled over and went back to sleep. One more hour wouldn't hurt.

When I next woke, I flew through my morning routine, dually driven to make it to Spuds with enough time to prep and to escape the emptiness of the house. The familiarity of Spuds offered little respite, and the hand that reached to remove the closed sign trembled like a leaf in the wind. The stress from the last few days visibly catching up to me.

I moved into the back room and began putting away the delivery before beginning preparations for the lunch rush. A vague sense of something being slightly off teased the edges of my consciousness. I checked the locks on the back door, double-checked the front door, and went back to my prep. Still not comfortable, I turned the music on, then turned it off again. Neither helped, and I had to force myself to finish up. I prepared half the options as usual, but for today it would have to do. Tomorrow would be better.

Between customers I paced back and forth. I watched the clock. I called Yiayia to check in. I gathered my papers for franchising into a large pile and placed them on my desk when what I really wanted to do was pitch them into the trash can.

My skin felt too tight and the urge to flee intensified. As soon as the clock reached two-thirty, I closed up shop. I sent out a text then drove to the school to pick up the boys. I'd drop Alex off at home and visit Yiayia.

She was sitting, disgruntled, in the family room when I arrived.

"Hi, Yiayia," I called out.

Her face lit up. "Koritzaki mou! Agoria!"

The boys bussed her on the cheek and headed into the kitchen to get themselves a snack. Gus kept two drawers in the fridge filled with ready snacks for the boys. His system was genius. I tried to get Yiayia to incorporate it but she wanted to prepare their snack when they got home from school.

I leaned over and kissed her soft cheek. "How are you, Yiayia?"

She scowled. "How you say... bored? I so bored!"

I thought for a moment. "You know, Yiayia, I might have something to help with that. I'll be back."

I ran home and grabbed the tablet that I rarely used. Back at Amber's, I curled up on the couch on Yiayia's left side, away from her sore arm.

"Okay, Yiayia. Let's introduce you to Pinterest and get your Instagram set up on this bigger screen."

By the end of the hour, I had written out instructions for her explaining how to navigate onto Pinterest, Instagram, the Greek news for her hometown, Greek radio, and Spotify.

She loved Greek radio.

The music sounded tinny coming from the tablet so I ordered a portable Bluetooth speaker that would arrive the next day. Gus or Alex would set it up for her.

I prepared dinner for them, leaving Minty's meals in the freezer for the next day when I wouldn't be off work so early. As five-thirty rolled around, I called Jace, and we headed for home where Vander would meet us.

Puttering around my own tiny kitchen, preparing dinner for the three of us, tickled me. This would be the first of many hours making dinner for my little family. And George, too, when he came home, I conceded happily.

352

The three of us ate in the tiny kitchen, Vander's knee butting up against mine under the table. Jace regaled us with tales of his day, Vander told a funny story from his, and I caught them up on Yiayia's success with the iPad. I smiled a lot over dinner. There would be more happy memories made in this house.

The next morning Vander drove Jace to school while I got ready for work. Stepping out of the shower, the silence of the house roared.

Did they lock the front door?

Did Jace remember his lunch? His coat?

I heard a noise and my stomach hollowed out. I placed my palm over it and breathed in deeply.

I crept towards my bedroom door, carefully closed and locked it, then got dressed.

Silly.

I took a deep breath and laughed a little as my stomach settled. I glanced into the bathroom. Today, I needed a little pill. I swallowed one down with water from the tap. I gathered up my phone and my purse and headed downstairs.

In the kitchen I ate my standard piece of toast and drank a cup of coffee while reading the last few chapters of my book. It was a good one. The main characters reminded me of Vander and me, the way their lack of communication kept them apart. It made me happy to have the paperback version. I snickered to myself. More so because of Vander's smiley face sticky tabs than anything else.

I put my dishes in the dishwasher, wiped off the counter, and swept my keys off the hook. Grabbing my coat, I pushed my arms through the holes, opened the front door, and came to a full stop.

No matter how I tried, I could not make my foot take one step over the threshold.

Shitfuckdamn!

I closed the door and paced back and forth in the small hallway. I was having a good morning! Better than yesterday, I even took my pill, what the hell?

I returned to the kitchen and spun in a slow circle, thinking. I wasn't afraid, exactly. Not like before with the shaking and sweating and heart pounding. No. This time my body simply refused to do what I bid it to do.

I looked at the time, rolled my neck, blew out a breath.

Okay.

I sat down with my hands resting loosely on my thighs, my feet flat on the floor. Breathe in for four, hold for five, out for six. Again.

Breathe in for four. Hold for five. *I breathe and live and move freely in my world.*

Breathe in for four. Hold for five. *I breathe and live and move freely in my world.*

Breathe in for four. Hold for five. *I breathe and live and move freely in my world.*

My shoulders dropped. The fist in my throat loosened its grip. My lungs filled with air. I stood slowly, breathing deeply.

I breathe and live and move freely in my world.

I picked up my keys and my purse,

I breathe and live and move freely in my world.

I opened the front door,

I breathe and live and move freely in my world.

and hit a glass wall.

I grabbed my cell phone.

"Minty?"

"Ruby? You okay?"

I snorted out a laugh. "Um. It's weird. I don't feel like I'm panicking but I can't make myself leave the house. Can you, um, can you go into Spuds and put a sign up on the door? I'll see if my part-timer is able to go in."

Minty, being the owner and landlord of the building, had access to all the downstairs shops.

"Sure. I can do that. You want some company?" She asked softly.

"Uh, no. I can manage," I replied. I relied on her and Amber too much in the beginning, and I did not want to be that person anymore.

"You sure, Rubes?" She sounded doubtful.

"Yes. I'm just going to take a break today. I'm sure I'll be fine tomorrow."

I was still standing motionless in the kitchen twenty minutes later when a soft knock sounded at the front door. I checked through the window to find Minty's car parked on the street outside.

I smiled ruefully when I let her in. She winked and hung up her coat.

"Offer me a cup of coffee or I'll tell your Yiayia that you sent me out into the cold."

I barked out a laugh and backed away into the kitchen, waving her in.

"Yiayia has cookies in the freezer, good ones. You want some?"

Minty dipped her chin and twisted her mouth. "Do you have to ask?"

I chortled and pulled them out. I breathed easier with her here and I felt a momentary stab of shame.

We carried the cookie plate and our coffees into the family room and settled in at either end of the couch.

"You know, Ruby, back when your agoraphobia first hit you, I could not help but think you could have gone so much further, so much faster, if you'd chosen to lean on Amber and me a little bit more than you did."

My mouth dropped open. "What are you talking about? I leaned on you guys constantly."

Minty cocked her head to the side. "No, no," she disagreed thoughtfully. "We were always asking you what you wanted to do, where we could take you, you never said."

I started to respond but she held up a smooth hand. "That conference is a prime example. Amber and I offered to drive you in. You said no. Fine. I understood you wanted to drive yourself. But when we offered to follow you in a couple of times so you could practice, you also said no. It took you six weeks to work up to that."

"What's wrong with that?" I cried indignantly.

She shrugged. "Nothing... if that's what you had to do. But it didn't have to be so hard. If you had allowed Amber or me to drive with you, or even follow you in once or twice, you would have been fine, and it wouldn't have been nearly so difficult for you."

"I didn't even break a sweat driving there!" I defended.

She smiled her small, enigmatic smile. "How about all the practice times? Were you sweating then?"

I swallowed.

I was.

There were times I had to pull over to the side of the road. The first time I tried I had a panic attack at the city border and had to turn back.

She leaned over and placed a cool hand on my arm. "Ruby, you're incredibly strong, and it's good that when you have to do something on your own that you can push through and get it done, but does it make sense to you to make everything three times as difficult just so you don't have to ask for help?"

I stared into her cool brown eyes, looking for judgement, finding none.

"You don't understand," I whispered.

She smiled. "Don't I? Have you seen my house? Do you ever see me looking less than ready to face the camera? How about those times when I cancel last minute with no explanation? The fact that I insist I only take the boys together and never just one of them? Or when we move Bookstagram night to my place even when it means pulling the boys out late in the evening to go home? How I hate having the boys take the bus and tell you constantly if they need a ride, I can drive them? How about my habitual lateness?"

"I never thought about it," I admitted. "I just thought you were a bit quirky, maybe a little controlling."

She laughed her tinkling laugh. "That's one way of thinking about it. You and Amber accommodate me without a second thought. Why will you not let me help you?"

"You've never asked me for help."

"I've never had to."

I looked down into my lap, shamed, and she reached a hand out immediately and placed it on my bent knee.

"No, Ruby, you misunderstand. I've never had to ask because you and Amber are naturally patient and tolerant. You are the only people I'm completely myself with."

"You have anxiety?"

She nodded. "I have O.C.D."

I slapped my hand over the side of my face. "Minty! I'm so sorry! I've been so wrapped up in myself I didn't even notice."

"There's nothing to be sorry about, Ruby. You're the most loving, accepting person I've ever met. I never even felt like I had to explain. Any time I told you I was uncomfortable with something or wanted to do something differently, you've only ever rolled with it."

"Still. I'd like to know more. I'd like to understand so I can be there better."

"I promise to be more transparent so you can understand. But I need you to understand that I've done years of therapy, I still go to therapy, and I have to be careful not to allow people to enable this disease. You, however," she smiled softly, "you just need a little assistance and then you fly on your own."

I heard the front door swing open and rose hesitantly to my feet to peek around the corner. Amber stood in the doorway, the morning sun spilling in behind her.

"Amber? What are you doing here?" I asked, surprised.

"I stopped into Spuds to see you and you weren't there. When I saw the sign on the door, I worried that you were having trouble."

"I'm not one of your patients, Amber," I snapped.

Her eyes widened and flew to mine. "Ruby," she whispered. "What's wrong?"

I threw my arm out at her. "You want to go all big sister on me, but when I try to be there for you, I'm just Ruby the flighty ass screwup little sister!"

"What? No!" Her eyebrows lowered suddenly, and she dipped her chin. "Is this about Angus again?"

357

I drew back slightly. "Not just about him, but yes. You want to help me, but you never ask for help. You try to give me advice, but you never want to take any."

Amber pulled in a deep breath and walked into the family room. She threw her purse on the chair and flopped down into it.

"I've never needed to ask for help, Ruby. You've always just given it."

Minty let out an unladylike snort and Amber's gaze swung to her.

"That's what I told her," she explained.

Amber waved nonchalantly at me. "You're the one who refuses to ask for help. You're the one who always has to do things the hard way. If you'd just accept a little help, you'd be much less stressed all the time and you'd have a much bigger life."

My jaw hit the floor and I sucked in a breath ready to give it to her.

Minty leaned forward into my line of vision, her face concerned. "You're both suffering and upset. You're both going through a lot right now. Take a breath before either of you say something you'll regret."

I paused and then turned back to Amber.

She sat forward in the chair, her hands clasped in front of her, tears rimming her eyes.

"He's my husband, Ruby," She whispered. "I can't betray him by revealing his sins to you or anyone. The only thing I'm able to take from you is exactly what you've given me, and I need it, Ruby. I need your calm acceptance. I need your shoulder bumping mine. I need you beside me while I work this out."

I stood and crossed the room to my sister and wrapped my arms around her. Her hands came around my back and she gripped me, hard. She felt thin, too thin, in my arms.

"I'm sorry, Amber. I'll be here. I promise. You don't have to say anything."

She nodded once, her slight figure trembling.

"I'm so sorry, Amber. I thought I was just a tagalong to you and Minty."

Amber drew back and swiped two fingers under her eyes.

"You've never understood what you've been to me, Ruby. You think I don't remember that day?" Her pained eyes followed her finger to the crescent-shaped scar on my inner arm. "You've always been there for me. Let me be there for you a little, too. Just because we don't need the same things from each other, doesn't mean we all don't need one another. Minty, too. We need each other. It's not easy out there." She laughed.

I pulled Amber off the chair and over to the couch where she took the middle seat, with Minty and I turning in toward her.

"Have I really been so averse to help?"

Amber and Minty looked at each other and laughed. "Yeah. You have. Why don't you accept help?"

I tilted my head to the side. "I don't even know. I think it's because I'm afraid if I'm too much of a burden, I'll run people off."

Amber linked her fingers with mine. "Not everybody leaves."

"I won't," Minty promised.

"Me neither," Amber and I said at once.

"I'm here for you guys through thick and thin," I promised.

"Thick and thin," Amber agreed.

Minty reached out to both of us, and we clasped her hands. She smiled. "Thick and thin, sick and sin."

Chapter 45 – Safe or Sabotaged

Ruby

Amber and Minty left together after lunch, with Minty reassuring me that she secured the emergency closure sign on the door at Spuds. I knew I couldn't stay closed indefinitely, there were bills to pay. I had to find my way through this.

I made a hot chocolate, full cream with whip on the top, and carried it into the family room. Amber and Minty left me with a lot to think about.

I'd totally missed how they saw me. I'd missed a lot of things. Most of those things direct results of my own decisions.

The last brave and fearless thing I'd done had been going to B.C. for university. After that, I played it safe, always, to protect myself.

But had I protected myself?

A perfect memory of Gus angling his wide shoulders through the hospital doorway, Gus with his forehead on Amber's, the look on Gus's face when Amber gave birth to Alex, unfolded in my mind.

Superimposed over that was Vander angling through his office doorway, his eyes on me. Vander pressing his forehead to mine, thanking me for Jace. The look of wonder on Vander's face, still, when he looked at Jace, the gratitude when he looked at me afterwards.

But Vander's gratitude was mixed with grief, shame, and sorrow, those things that my decisions played a part in purchasing for him.

Playing it safe meant narrowing my world down to thirty square kilometres, a fish tank world as Yiayia once called it. Playing it safe meant not telling Vander about my agoraphobia, not going to him that summer, not leaving a job I'd long since grown tired of, not traveling, not moving out of my childhood home, and not dating. It meant choosing to settle for the progress I'd made instead of continuing with therapy.

Playing it safe included not texting Vander after the conference, and that ensured that he missed out on doctor appointments, Jace's first tooth, first step, first day of school, first everything.

It bought Jace mentioning Gus being a good dad with that note of yearning in his voice that cut me so deeply.

It meant Vander not being there when Jace asked to do things, and my first instinct, which I eventually pushed past, to say no.

Safe? Or sabotaged?

I rinsed my mug and placed it in the dishwasher.

Walking through the kitchen to the front door I opened it tentatively. Maybe I'd just sit on the front step.

Nope! I laughed lightly.

Okay, then.

There would be no avoidance this time.

Back on the couch, I thought back over the past weeks with Vander and remembered, for the first time, that it had always been like that with us. Laughter, and fun, and togetherness, and yes, even then, he had the tendency to be bossy. All these years, I'd focussed on the pain of our parting, the losses between us, the negative space in the picture of what was us.

I did that with all my choices. I assessed every option, searching for every negative possibility so I could avoid it.

No matter how improbable.

Anytime I had to drive somewhere, I traced the routes on my mental road map, choosing the one with the least perceived risk.

Every time I refused to let Jace try something, every time I had an opportunity for a relationship, every decision I made, was a sacrifice made to the god of risk avoidance.

Every single time, I made the safe choice that suddenly didn't feel as though it kept me safe at all.

Jace would be home from school soon, and I needed to talk to Vander first.

I picked up my cell and dashed off a text before I could think too hard about it. Fifteen minutes later he barreled through the front door, his face pinched with concern.

"You okay, koukla mou?"

Without removing his coat, he moved towards me and pulled me out of the couch and into his arms.

His hands were heavy on my head as he clutched me against his chest, and I realized he was afraid. I pulled away and after a brief hesitation, he let me.

"Vander, honey, I'm okay. I'm not upset, just stuck."

His dark brows knit together, and he peered at me carefully. Turning, he shrugged out of his coat and draped it over the arm of the couch, then pulled me down to straddle his lap. He gripped my hips firmly then ran his hands down to my buttocks and pulled me closer, his worried eyes scanning my face.

I tangled my fingers in his hair that had grown just long enough to curl over his collar.

"Yesterday, when I went to Spuds, I felt a little jittery. It didn't alarm me overmuch because I'm aware that I've been struggling with all the recent changes."

He nodded, waiting for me to continue.

"I closed up early, picked up the boys from school, then headed over to see Yiayia. Here, at home, I was quite happy making dinner for us knowing it was the first of many."

He smiled at that, and his face began to relax. His fingers lost their death grip on my ass, and he began to knead my curves.

362

"Did you go in this morning?" He asked, his deep voice soothing.

"Nope." I shook my head. "As soon as I went to step through the door, I hit a glass wall. I must have looked like one of those mimes." I guffawed. "It was crazy. I did my calming routine, tried again, but couldn't do it. I called Minty and asked her to put the sign back up on the door, then she showed up here fifteen minutes later."

Vander's eyebrows rose. "She did? Wasn't she at work?"

"Yup."

He smiled. "She's a good friend to you, isn't she?"

Tears hit my eyes, and I sniffed. "Yeah, she is. I didn't realize how good a friend until today. And a little while after she got here, Amber showed up."

"She called her?"

"No!" I laughed. "Amber went by Spuds to see me and when she saw the sign she headed straight here."

"Why are you laughing?"

"I don't really know." I shrugged. "I guess I just don't feel alone."

His arms tightened around me, and he pressed his face between my breasts. His back expanded with his deep inhale. "You're never going to be alone."

I ran my hands through his curls and lightly scratched his scalp, then pressed my nose against his hair and breathed him in.

"They told me I need to ask for help, and not do everything the hard way. When they left, I did a lot of thinking about my choices, and how I always thought I chose the safe option. I didn't. I sabotaged myself."

He kissed my breastbone and leaned back against the couch again where he could meet my eyes.

"Then I tried to go out again, still couldn't do it, so, I called you." I finished simply, then shrugged a little self-consciously.

He looked at the time. "I'm glad you called me." With his hands on my hips, he pushed me up off his lap. "Grab your coat and we'll go pick up Jace and go out for dinner. We can swing by and check on Spuds if you want."

363

I grabbed my coat and purse.

"Do you want to go to West End Diner or take him somewhere else? Will we have Alex with us today?" Vander asked reaching for my hand.

With his hand in mine, I walked out the front door without a second thought.

Vander

She took my hand and walked straight out the front door with no hesitation. There was no doubt she'd been under stress the past few weeks, but I promised it would be short-lived, and me being here for things like this was a part of that.

An idea began to take shape in my head, but I'd wait until I fleshed it out before I broached the subject with her.

I called Gus on the way to the school to see if we could pick up Alex and take him out with us. Gus gave us the okay, so we headed out. The boys sat, delighted at the change in routine, in the back seat chatting.

Ruby sat beside me, smiling out the window, perfectly at ease. When she saw the turn-off we were taking, she turned to me.

"Are we-"

I shushed her quietly, and she grinned. "I'm not getting a cookie this time, am I?"

"You'll get a treat. Don't worry about that," I promised. I glanced at her sideways in time to see her telltale blush. I chuckled. I'd never get used to that.

Pulling into a parking spot, the boys stopped talking and looked around.

"Are we going go-karting? With Thia?" Alex yelled.

Ruby twisted around in her seat, jerking her thumb at me. "I beat him, and I'll beat you, too."

"Oh, it's on, Thia!" He cackled delightedly.

"You guys really went go-karting?" Jace asked.

"Yeah," I said.

"And she beat you?" Jace's voice went up with incredulity.

364

I smirked. "She cheated."

Alex laughed. "Yup! That sounds like Thia!"

Ruby laughed and didn't stop laughing until we were finished at the track. She won again, the same way she won the first time.

Ruby did what she could to revive her curly mop from helmet head before we grabbed burgers at The Works. Afterwards we dropped Alex home, and she got a chance to visit with Yiayia and Gus. It wasn't until we got back home that the tension returned to her frame.

Jace set himself up in the dining room to do his homework while Ruby puttered around the kitchen making us a coffee.

"Uh..."

"Oh, please don't tell me you're going to start calling me 'uh' now!"

She spun around with a laugh and threw an oven mitt at my head. I caught it midair and grinned back at her. "What were you going to say?"

"Well, today, I had fun. Lots of it," she reiterated. "It was exactly what I needed but what if I can't go to work tomorrow?"

I shook my head. "I took the rest of the week off. I'm going in with you."

Her mouth dropped open. "What?" She whispered.

I couldn't read her reaction. This could go in any direction, with my track record, it would probably be south.

Ah, hell. There was no turning back now.

"I'm going in with you. Consider it research for your franchising prospects."

Ruby carefully turned off the ring under the Greek coffee and walked over to me. Holding my face between her palms she whispered fervently, "I am so in love with you!"

I blew out a breath in relief and chuckled. Cupping her face in my palms, I pulled her forehead to mine.

"I love you, too, Ruby-mine."

Chapter 46 - Watching

Vander

In the morning, we dropped Jace off at school together, swung through Tim Horton's drive–thru for coffee, then headed to Spuds.

Unlike her home, Spuds had been updated over the years. Looking at it from a business perspective, I could see no glaring need for improvement. It had proven itself to be a viable business over the years, particularly with the controlled rent Ruby paid. Knowing that Minty owned the building, I understood now how that was the case.

Working at Spuds with Ruby reminded me of the first time we worked together more than two decades before. This time was just as much fun.

"Your grandparents, did they work well together?"

"Oh, yeah. Lots of teasing, lots of laughing, lots of sweating, too. They had their tough times, but they were happy working together." She smiled as she reminisced.

When the lunch rush hit, and Ruby's part-timer came in, I retreated to Ruby's table in the corner and went over my emails from work. Looked like I would have to go in after Spuds closed for an hour or two.

During clean up, I decided to broach the subject of franchising with her again.

"Ruby-mine, I'm going to go into work for a couple of hours after we pick up Jace and I drop you home."

Her face fell. "Oh, no, Vander! I'm so sorry!" She pressed her forefinger into the divot of her top lip. "I've caused you too much trouble today."

"Not at all," I rushed to reassure her. "It's not uncommon for me to work until eight or nine, sometimes even ten at night. Usually not on a Friday, but it happens. I need to go in for a meeting. This meeting would take place in the evening no matter what. You haven't caused any trouble."

She looked doubtful but hopeful.

"Truly, Ruby. I'm telling you the truth. In any case, I did tell you I'm selling my company, right? These kinds of hours cripple the kind of family life I want with you and Jace, and Georgie when he's here."

"You're sure?"

"Positive. But I do want to talk to you about franchising. Before I sell the company, I want to have your situation well in hand."

She shifted uncomfortably from foot to foot. "I'm not so sure I want to franchise anymore, Van."

My eyebrows hit my hairline. "What?"

This was a project over a decade in the making. Was she scared? Was this somehow taking her out of her comfort zone? How did I navigate this without making her situation worse?

Pacing back and forth, she began waving her hands around expressively as she explained.

"All these years, every time I got bored," she paused and looked at me pointedly, "which was often, I'd think about how I could shake things up a bit. When I went through all the possibilities, the only change I considered 'safe', was franchising Spuds." She stopped and faced me head-on. "Maybe I don't have to make the 'safe' choice anymore."

Excitement bubbled up in my chest thinking the Ruby of old might be taking back her life.

"Explain," I demanded.

"Okay, well, I did a lot of thinking after Minty and Amber left yesterday, and I determined that my safe choices actually sabotaged me. They led me away from what I really wanted. But because I was too afraid to admit what I really wanted, I substituted other things that would never really satisfy."

My breath stuck in my lungs. "What do you really want?"

"I want what my Yiayia had with my Pappou. I want you. I want our family. I want to do couple and family things like take vacations and buy new furniture and go out for dinner and take the kids to the pool. I want to spend time with my Yiayia, my sister and her family, and Minty." She put her hands on her hips defiantly. "I mean, I wouldn't mind seeing if there's something else I might like to do, instead of Spuds. Maybe even pick up a hobby." She threw her hands up into the air. "If I franchise, I'll be super busy doing something that's only ever been a substitute instead of enjoying you and the kids, my family, and Minty. I definitely won't have time to try anything new for myself. You'll be scaling back, and I'll be getting busier. I don't want that."

She finished by crossing her arms over her chest. Her declaration infused my system with joy. I grinned.

"Does this mean you accept my marriage proposal?"

She chortled. "You haven't proposed!" Her smile dropped away, and her mouth twisted to the side as she glanced at me out of the corner of her eye.

"What is it? You're practically chewing on the words. Spit it out." I was rabid for the rest of it. If I could ensure that she never held anything back again, I would.

"It's just that, our wedding, it's not going to be the same," she said softly.

"The same as what?"

"As Amber's." She swallowed and rolled her neck. "As your first wedding."

I knew what my first wedding was like but had no idea about Amber's. I couldn't imagine any reality in which they would be similar.

"What are you talking about? You're not making any sense."

She huffed. "Our wedding ceremony. It won't be the same as Amber's, or as your first marriage. Our ceremony will be one of repentance because of your divorce." She paused. "Why are you smiling? You think this is funny?

368

You do know that the church doesn't recognize the second marriage the same way it does the first?"

Suddenly, I understood all her excuses and hesitations. I grinned.

"Oh, I know. It just doesn't apply. I got married at the courthouse the first time."

Ruby froze, gaping at me for a split second before her face screwed up and she burst into tears.

I pulled her, sobbing, into my arms.

Chuckling, I rubbed her back.

"Ruby-mine, you have got to learn to communicate. I couldn't tell you anything because you refused to talk about the past, but you have all these preconceived ideas that are just plain wrong."

"Okay." She hiccoughed. "Go ahead and book the church. I can do it now. I just wasn't ready to face the other ceremony."

"So," I grinned. "Are we engaged?"

She sniffed and side-eyed me. "Not officially. You haven't given me a ring or properly proposed."

I laughed and tucked her under my chin. I rested my cheek on top of her head.

The sweetness was almost painful.

Nothing beat the feeling of driving home from work later that night knowing she and Jace were waiting at the end of the day, at the end of a week, and that my weekend would be filled with them.

The meeting had gone well, better than I had expected. All three of my senior consultants wanted in, with the condition that I stay on in an advisory capacity for up to three years. That gave me a working salary for the next three years while slowly scaling back to part-time hours.

Dylan also met with me privately and gave me the results of the location search for Spuds. It was better than I hoped.

I stuck my head in Jace's bedroom door to find him asleep. Standing over his bed, it struck me how close I came to missing out on him entirely. I shuddered at the thought of what might have been, save for a chance encounter with an old friend, and my willingness to steamroll Ruby.

Thank you, God, for this child.

Quietly, I backed out of his room and headed to the master, anticipation a low burn in my gut.

Ruby sat up against the headboard with her knees drawn up wearing an oversized t-shirt. The smile she gave me lit up her whole face and warmed me from across the room.

I carefully closed and locked her bedroom door. When I turned back around, Ruby knelt on the bed in nothing but a pair of white lace panties, the t-shirt tossed onto the floor.

I let out a low whistle, then cocked an eyebrow at her and grinned.

"See, now that's how you should greet me every night," I declared.

Tilting her head, she lay down her challenge. "If you make it worth my while, I just might."

Moving towards her, I unbuttoned my shirt.

Her body was a wonder to me. If we had been together all these years, I probably would have taken her for granted by now. Considering all that we'd been through, I doubted the marvel of her would ever fade.

Heat and hunger flitted across her face as my hands went for my buckle. I whipped my belt off and her eyes widened. I ducked my head, so she didn't see my smile. There were so many things I wanted to do to her, with her, and tying her to the bed with my belt just got added to that lengthy list.

Kneeling onto the bed in only my boxers, I pulled her into my arms, her bare breasts against my chest.

She smiled up at me, her eyes happy.

"Hi."

I grinned. "Hi, yourself."

She wiggled against me. "I love it when all the body parts are lined up."

I laughed. "I know you do."

She pushed her fingers through my hair and lightly scratched my scalp. "How was your meeting?"

I thought for a moment. "Informative."

She raised her eyebrows. "That's it? One word answer?"

Half of me yearned to cradle her in my arms, discuss the meeting, confess the dreams and plans I had for us. The other half, the much more insistent half, wanted to fuck her into the mattress.

I kissed the corners of her mouth, and she smiled against my lips. I pressed my lips firmly against hers and lay down on my back, taking her with me.

She parted her thighs around my hips. I dragged my hand down her side and gripped the top of her thigh.

That area was a hotspot for her, and she hummed with pleasure.

With my other hand, I grabbed a fistful of her curls and tilted her head, angling her mouth to receive my kiss. I kissed her slowly, sweetly, methodically, holding back, waiting for her to give herself over to me.

Slowly, her body relaxed. Soft in all the right places, she melted against me with a little sigh.

Rolling my hips, I rubbed against her wet heat and plunged my tongue into her mouth.

She gasped and bowed her back, seeking more friction.

I squeezed her ass and pulled her firmly against me, rolling into her heat.

She reached down and hooked a finger in the waistband of my boxers and tore her mouth from mine.

"Off," she demanded.

I released her, and she backed down the bed between my legs, dragging my boxers down with her, then shimmied out of her panties. Crawling back up, she nestled between my legs and took hold of my cock for half a second before quickly swallowing me to the back of her throat.

I curled up off the bed with the shocking pleasure of her hot mouth. This was so not going according to plan. My eyes rolled back in my head as she hollowed out her cheeks, and I cursed myself for being all kinds of stupid, but I reached down, hauled her up my body, and slammed my mouth down on hers.

She dug her fingers into my shoulders and rubbed against me, dragging her wet over my cock.

371

I grasped her ass with both hands and pulled her down as I thrust up against her.

Her breath came in soft pants as she writhed on top of me. When she went to sheath me with her heat, I grasped her ribs to hold her off and sucked her nipple deep into my mouth. Arching her back, offering me her breasts, she moaned as I licked and nibbled at the stiff peaks.

"Please, Vander..."

Ah, fuck. I loved to hear her beg.

Grasping her hips, I positioned myself at her entrance.

"Don't bounce," I growled. "You're going to sit on my dick and play with your pussy until you come all over me."

Her mouth fell open and her face flamed. "What are you going to be doing?"

I nearly laughed out loud. I would have if not for the slick dripping down my cock.

"Watching."

I pulled her hips down and thrust up inside her then stilled.

She moaned into my mouth.

I kissed her soundly, with one hand squeezing the crease of her thigh, holding her still. With my other hand, I took hold of her wrist and nudged her hand in between our bodies.

"Touch yourself, baby," I urged. "I want to feel you come on my cock."

Her breath hitched and I felt her fingers in a vee around my cock, stroking the joining of our bodies.

"Oh, god, Vander," she moaned. "Feeling us together here..."

"I know, baby. Touch your pussy, baby. Make yourself come."

She moved her fingers to her little bud and stroked and circled and rubbed.

I kept hold of her ass with one hand and played with her breasts with the other, focussed on her face, watching her eyes glaze over, feeling the first ripple of her orgasm before she cried out and soaked me, thighs trembling, back bowing, her forehead pressed against my chest.

I gritted my teeth to hold back my own orgasm, my balls high and tight against my body, screaming for release.

I gently squeezed her breast and caressed up and down her sides while she slowly came down.

She lifted her head, her eyes dazed, sated, and confused.

She shimmied her hips. "What about you?"

"Give me a minute and I'll tell you what I want."

Her eyes lit with interest, and I chuckled, pressing my mouth against hers as I eased her off me.

After a few minutes, minutes I sorely needed, I turned her to face the foot of the bed and directed her to straddle my thighs. She looked back at me nervously.

"I think it's going to be hard to balance."

"I'll help you," I assured her, running my hands up and down her sides.

"Where do I put my hands?"

"You can brace yourself on my legs or lean back and put your hands on my chest."

She tried both ways and then pushed herself up straight and raised her arms over her head. "I think, um, I think it's better for balance if I just put them up here. That's better."

"Raise yourself up and tilt your ass back," I directed.

She hesitated then did as I asked.

I grasped my cock and notched it at her entrance.

She wiggled her hips, pressing down, and carefully lowered herself.

I stared at the curve of her beautiful back, the flare of her hips, the roundness of her ass as she held her arms up over her head and raised herself up experimentally.

I squeezed her hips as she lowered herself back down.

"Oh, Vander, this is not bad!"

I chuckled. "It's pretty good from my end too, baby."

She laughed and pushed herself up with her thighs and lowered with a grind of her hips. "Mmm..."

She started to ride me in earnest, arms wrapped around her head, head thrown back, back arched.

I grabbed hold of her ass and spread her, watching my dick disappear inside her sweet body.

She looked at me over her shoulder. "Vander?"

So beautiful. I squeezed her hips, prodding her to continue. "Yeah, baby?"

"You good?"

"Fuck, yeah."

"I'm not too heavy like this?"

"Fuck, no." I slapped her ass. "Stop talking and ride me like you fucking mean it."

She threw her head back and laughed then rode me until I came so hard I saw stars.

Chapter 47 – All Three, Always

Ruby

Saturday morning, I woke to the sound of a soft knock at my bedroom door.

"Come in, honey," I called to Jace.

He poked his head in the door but came no further.

I realized this was the first time he'd ever seen a man in my bed, and it must be weird for him. I could feel Vander waking up behind me. I bumped him with my butt.

"Move back, buster."

He chuckled low in his chest and shifted to give me more room.

I moved over and opened the covers to Jace. "Come cuddle for two minutes, agapimeno."

His eyes skittered to Vander then back to me as he took a hesitant step in.

I smiled at him, and Vander spoke. "Come lie down for a minute, agori mou, and we'll plan the day."

Jace's face broke into a smile. He ducked his head shyly, but jumped into our bed and cuddled in.

"We're going to FaceTime Georgie soon..."

I cuddled my son in my arms, my lover's warmth against my back, and closed my eyes to better hear the sweet sound of my son's father making plans with him for our weekend.

Vander and Gus took the boys rock climbing, then met Amber and me back at Amber's house for dinner.

On Sunday, Jace insisted that Vander come with us for breakfast and so we replaced an old tradition with a new one, one that would include Georgie when he visited.

Family dinner took place at Amber's house where she and Gus stumbled around each other, trying to figure out their places in this new dynamic.

Late Sunday night when we were in bed, Vander brought up Spuds.

"I'll go with you to Spuds tomorrow, but I need to take my own car."

The heat of shame warmed my face. "I might be okay tomorrow..." Even as I said it my heart started pounding in my chest.

His big hand rubbed a slow circle over my back. "Just the same," he murmured, "I think I'll follow you in and work with you for a couple of hours. If you're okay with it, I might run to the office to pick up some papers, but then I'll be back."

I sighed. "Vander...I can't keep taking you away from your work."

"The meeting on Friday, I didn't tell you about it yet."

"You said it was 'informative'," I teased.

He squeezed me and chuckled. "I approached my senior consultants a couple of weeks ago about buying me out. Friday night they accepted my offer."

I swallowed hard. What did this mean for us? Where would he look for work?

"Ruby." He gave me a little shake. "Don't start freaking out."

I narrowed my eyes at him. "Don't tell me what to do."

"Alright." He lifted his head off the pillow to look at me. "Just listen to the rest."

I nodded for him to continue.

"The agreement states that I stay on as a consultant for up to three years. This means I'll have a salary for the next three years while I slowly scale back to part-time hours. In the meantime, we have to decide what to do about franchising."

"I really don't think I want to do that anymore, Vander." I murmured. "I don't want to be busier than I already am while you're becoming freer. I'd rather leave things the way they are."

He took a deep breath, his eyes watching me closely.

"What if I bought into the business and we expanded instead of franchising? One of the locations that came up as ideal was Bayview Village. Also, expanding into school catering may be a lucrative offshoot. If we expand, you can get out from behind the counter most days. There will be times when we'll both have to work behind the counter, but we can schedule it that we work together most of the time. It'll be fun."

My thoughts bounced around erratically in my head. Giving over half of Spuds meant giving up my independence. If something happened between us, I could lose it. I didn't think anything would happen, but I'd been wrong before. Spuds gave me financial security and provided for Jace. Spuds had been mine and mine alone for so long, I'd never even considered sharing it, not since Amber said she was happy to let it go.

"Can I think about it?"

He turned on his side, pushed me forward, and tucked his long legs behind mine. His chest warming my back, our heartbeats aligned. He reached around me and interlocked his fingers with mine before kissing the side of my face and bowing his face into my neck.

"For as long as you need to."

Monday morning, we turned up the music. When Rubylove came on, Vander serenaded me with his terrible voice while he chased me around the produce table in the back. This is what Yiayia and Pappou had.

This was joy.

This was family.

This was everything.

Just before the lunch rush, Vander slipped out to pick up his papers. The time passed quickly and being busy left me no time to worry.

377

When the influx of customers trickled to a stop, I considered Vander's idea for Spuds.

Expanding with Vander meant I would get out from behind the counter, and have something new with someone I trusted to guide the process. I had never considered partnering with anyone else with my business, but I could share Spuds with Vander.

With business issues, I trusted him implicitly. I still harboured the tiniest of doubts over how I would cope if we ever fell apart, but with Spuds, I knew he could take us to the next level.

As a father, I also knew that he would not let Jace down.

Partnering with him with Spuds would not be a huge change, not much different than what I planned to do with franchising. Expanding Spuds with Vander's help, while a change, did not feel like a scary one.

We still needed to decide what to do about the house. With Yiayia moved in with Amber and Gus, there were enough bedrooms for our family. Staying in Yiayia's house would keep Jace in his same school and in his same home. That was important.

And I didn't want to leave.

Tuesday morning, I went to work by myself with Vander on standby if needed.

He wasn't needed.

Wednesday evening, I broached the subject of him selling his house, and us renovating Yiayia's house instead. He'd been staying there with Jace and me, and I loved it. Anyways, it would be much easier for him to move his few things here than for Jace and I to move to his house. He was practically living here already.

At first, he hesitated, but when I told him how much it meant to me, he agreed.

"If that's what it'll take to make you happy, I'll do it. I'm not crazy about bringing George into Jace's space, but if that's what you need, we'll renovate the house, make it new, and make it work."

Thursday after work I went to visit Yiayia and pick Jace up from Gus's house. Yiayia sat on the couch, Jace and Alex on either side of her, the iPad on her lap. Every few seconds they burst into highly contagious, raucous laughter.

I chortled. "What are you guys laughing at?"

Jace looked up, his eyes alight. Alex answered, his mouth stretched wide in a grin. "We're showing Yiayia funny videos and seeing her reaction!"

I sat down with them and immediately saw the joke. Yiayia's reactions ranged from shock to disapproval to glee, and sometimes all three within one video.

"Okay, agoria, you go do homework or something before I put you to work in the kitchen. I teach your Mommas how to cook and I teach you, too!"

Jace and Alex laughingly got up and scooted out of the room.

"You want a coffee, Yiayia?" I asked.

"Yes, koritzaki mou," she answered. "Help me get up. I never knew I need my hands to stand up!"

I helped her up and got her settled in the kitchen where she caught me up on all the Greek news: who died, who was sick, who got married, who got a divorce, and who had a baby.

"I have really good news, Yiayia." I smiled as I sat down with coffee and cookies.

"Tell me, koukla mou. I need some good news today."

"Vander and I have decided to sell his house and renovate ours to live in!" I exclaimed.

Yiayia sat quietly, her head cocked gently to the side.

"Did you hear me, Yiayia? We're going to live in your house! We're not going to sell it!" I explained again.

"I hear you, koukla. I just don't know if is good idea."

My mouth dropped open. "Why?" I asked, astonished.

"I think is time you moved on, made your own place, a new place with Vander and your boys," she stated. "In fact, that is what I wish for you. I think is better for everybody to start fresh."

379

I was flabbergasted. I thought she'd be happy, delighted even, that her house would be staying in the family.

Disappointment hit me in the gut, followed quickly by a sharp stab of anger.

"I thought you'd be happy," I accused.

"I'm happy if you're happy, koukla. Is just a house. Is you and Vander and the boys who are important.

I tamped down my feelings. Yiayia didn't know what she was saying. It wasn't just a house, it held all my memories, it was my safe place.

I couldn't let it go.

Saturday, we FaceTimed George. His mother and stepfather were out with his younger sisters at an event at their school, so he took advantage of the privacy to indulge in a long call. We set him up on the dining room table with all of us. After a while, George asked Vander for help with a school project, so Vander picked up the iPad and took it into the kitchen.

Jace went upstairs to do his homework before we went to visit Yiayia.

I stood up to make myself a cup of tea when I heard George say my name. I stopped just outside the kitchen doorway. A voice in the back of my head warned me I was being rude, but curiosity overruled it.

"I really like her dad. I think she makes you happy."

"She does. George, I was never unhappy when you were with me, but Ruby is the love of my life, and it was a different kind of lonely without her."

"I'm glad you have her. It's a little, uh, weird, I guess, for me..." George stated.

"How do you mean?"

I could hear the anxiety in Vander's tone.

"Well, here, there's a mom and a dad and their kids, and then me. Now, over there, there's a mom and a dad and their kid, and then me. I kind of don't fit entirely anywhere now."

I pressed my palm over my heart and Vander's cross. *Poulaki mou.*

"You belong with me, agori mou. Always with me."

380

"I know, I know, I guess it's just hard to explain."

"How do you feel about having a brother?"

"Oh, fuck, Dad, don't even go there! Jace is awesome. And, Dad, Ruby's awesome, too. Don't get everything twisted. It's just two sides, you know?"

"You feel uncomfortable with the change and you're happy that you have a brother."

"Hm. More like I am happy I have a brother, and that Ruby is with us, and I feel like the odd man out. Does that make sense?"

I stepped away from the door.

My heart ached.

Vander

George's words played over and over in my head all night. I hated that he felt like the odd man out. I couldn't even deny it. While he always belonged with me, no matter where I was or who I was with, I saw his point. Moving him into Jace and Ruby's house was not optimal, but I'd put Ruby last for so many years, she had to come first this time.

Not just this time.

All the time.

Still.

It hurt.

The next morning, before heading to work, I popped in to talk to Yiayia.

"Ela, agori mou. Come in, come in," she exclaimed. She threw her good arm up in the air. "I can't even offer you a coffee!"

"It's okay, Yiayia. I brought you a coffee from Tim Horton's."

She shuffled her way into the kitchen, opened the fridge with her good hand, and retrieved a container of cookies. She placed them on the table and brought me a plate. She watched me quietly while I sipped my coffee.

"I'm here on an official capacity today, Yiayia." I smiled.

Tears came to her eyes. "You gonna ask for my Ruby's hand?"

I shook my head. "No. Not asking for her hand. That, I'm taking. I'm asking for your blessing."

She shook her finger at me. "Ech, I boil you!"

I laughed.

She leaned forward and placed her hand softly on the side of my face. "She wait so long for you. You take good care of her, agori mou."

I nodded. "I promise, Yiayia."

"I have something for you." She stood. "I be right back."

She went to her room and came back with a worn velvet box in her hand. "I don't know if you buy a ring yet, but I want to give you this. You take this for my Ruby."

I opened the box to find her ruby ring nestled inside. I glanced at her hand to see a plain wedding band where her ruby used to be.

"You sure, Yiayia? Isn't this your engagement ring?"

"No. Pappou, he bought it for me for twenty-five years. Is three stones." She rubbed the tip of her finger over the stones. "Past, present, future. You give it to Ruby so she remember she have all three, always."

Chapter 48 – Faking It

Ruby

Sunday morning, after breakfast at West End Diner, I escaped to my bedroom and called Gus. He picked up immediately.

"Everything alright, Ruby?"

I fiddled with the cuff of my sweater.

"Yeah, Gus. Everything is okay. Can we meet to discuss selling Vander's house?"

"Uh, he already called me, Ruby. He told me to look for a buyer for his house. He told me he's moving in with you."

I blew out a breath. That made it both harder and easier. Harder because he made it difficult to resist. Easier because he gave it to me so freely.

"That's just the thing, Gus. I'd like to keep this a secret for now, but do you think you could show me some houses in the area? I don't want Vander to know I'm looking, but I'd like to see if I can find something new for us. A fresh start for us and the boys together."

Gus was quiet for a moment. "I can absolutely do that for you, Rubes. Tell me exactly what you're looking for."

Gus assured me he'd get back to me the next day or two with the best he could find.

True to his word, he called me just after the lunch rush died down on Monday afternoon.

"Hey, Rubes. I've got three for you to look at, two of which are move-in ready and have everything you wanted."

"So soon? That's awesome, Gus! When can I see them?"

"I'm going to forward the listings to your email. Take a look and call me back."

I flipped open my laptop excitedly. Huh. I thought I'd be dreading this whole process, but my brain buzzed with excitement!

The first house seemed like an excellent prospect. The second house I eliminated immediately, but the third was perfect. I called him back.

"Gus, have you been in these homes? Are they as perfect as they look?" My voice rang loudly with excitement.

He laughed. "Two of them are, one needs some work."

We determined that the one I eliminated needed too much work, and I asked if we could go see the other two.

"One is empty, we can go see it after you close today if you want. The other I'll have to see if it's available. Want to meet me over there?"

"Yes, definitely, and if the other one is available, can we go see it after?"

"Absolutely."

My stomach flipped and spun as I pulled into the driveway of the first home. I told Vander I was going to visit Minty and would be home late. Then, because I felt guilty for lying, I called Minty and asked her to go with me.

Gus's car was already there when we got there. Walking through, the house was perfect, just as I suspected, and I hated it.

"You don't like this one, Ruby," Minty commented.

I threw my hands up. "I know! And there's zero reason to not like it! It's perfect. You agree, don't you?" I asked them.

Feeling discouraged, I started questioning the wisdom of what I was doing. Then I remembered the hollow sound of George's voice.

"It lacks the character you're used to, Ruby," Gus commented. "It's a new home and doesn't have the quirks and idiosyncrasies you're used to."

"Let's go see the other one, Gussie," I said.

"I'm not a grandmother," Gus grumbled in his deep, gritty, voice, and Minty laughed her tinkling laugh.

At the next house, the little hope I had left, sputtered and died. If anything, this house was better than the first. Granite countertops, modern bathrooms, open concept kitchen and family room, and move-in ready. But if a house had a taste, I'd say this one needed salt.

"You don't like this one, either," Gus guessed. "Probably for the same reasons."

I sighed. "I'm sorry, Gus."

"What are you sorry for?" Gus asked, surprised.

"Wasting your time."

He snorted. "No, Ruby, it's fine. In fact, why don't you humour me and come see the other house, the one we eliminated?"

The third house needed work.

Lots of it.

The kitchen cabinetry was solid wood which we could refinish, but that was the only thing it had going for it. It needed new flooring, new countertops, sinks, toilets, bathtubs, and appliances. The walls appeared to have been builder's beige a couple of decades ago and now looked almost camo with all their marks and smudges.

None of it mattered.

Wide, gorgeous trim ran along the baseboards and framed the doors. A solid wood staircase with its square, carved newel post led to the upstairs. Nooks and crannies and ledges were built into the walls, and the woodburning fireplace took my breath away. Stained glass transom windows graced the top of the interior doors, and both the kitchen and the family room boasted a brick wall. Vintage glass ceiling fixtures lit the kitchen, and the chandelier in the dining room swung from a beautifully intricate ceiling medallion.

I turned to Gus and spread my hands wide. "I am in love."

Minty laughed her tinkling laugh, and Gus grinned.

"The good thing about this home, Ruby, is you and Vander and the boys can make it how you want it. It'll be your first big project as a family," Gus rumbled.

I pulled in a breath, a deep sense of satisfaction pervading my system.

"The other good thing is that it's walking distance to our place. Jace and Alex will take the same bus to school, and it'll be easier for them to meet up."

"When can we show Vander?" I asked excitedly.

"You don't want to think about it over night, Ruby?" Minty checked.

I shook my head. "I don't think so, Minty. I think, if Vander likes it, this is the one."

"Before you get excited, let me pull up all the information I have on this house. There should be a recent inspection, but you'll want to hire your own guy. Actually, I have a guy I can call for you guys."

"Okay!" I clapped my hands excitedly and Minty laughed. "You do your research and call your guy. If it's good, can we meet back here tomorrow with Vander and Jace?"

Gus threw a beefy arm over my shoulders. "I'll be happy to."

I made a mental note to make sure George could join us for the house inspection through the magic of FaceTime. I'd get Jace to do that. A niggling doubt wiggled into my consciousness. What if Jace was not on board with the move?

Vander

Something was up with Ruby. I didn't think it was anything bad because Jace was obviously in on it, and he seemed excited.

I waited until we were in bed before I confronted her. I turned on my side to face her and took the book out of her hand.

"What are you up to, Ruby-mine?"

Her eyes widened comically, and her face flushed. "What do you mean?"

I laughed, loud. "Ruby, you are a terrible liar, and you are even worse at keeping secrets. What's going on?"

She narrowed her eyes at me and blew out a breath.

"Okay! You're right, I have a secret but it's not a bad one, and I'll probably be able to tell you tomorrow. So, don't ask me anything. You know I have a bucket mouth, and I don't want to let anything slip."

"I'll make you a wager," I offered.

"What kind of wager?" She asked suspiciously.

"If you come first, you have to tell me. If I come first, you can keep your secret until tomorrow."

She laughed and snapped her fingers, pointing me to the bed.

"You make it too easy! Lie down, big boy. I'll have this settled in seven minutes."

She pushed my shoulders back on the bed, but I held her back. "Not so fast. You only have four minutes before we switch turns, and I'm going first."

She smirked and lay back on the bed.

A little over eleven minutes later she clamped her thighs around my head and shoved her fist in her mouth to hold back her cries. I took her through to the end, gently lapping at her sensitive clit until the last tremor died.

I climbed up over her and smiled down at her sated face.

"I win."

She smiled slyly, stretching like a cat underneath me.

"I faked it."

My mouth fell open, and I laughed. "You are such a cheater!"

She laughed, and I flipped her onto her belly.

"What are you doing?" She whispered harshly.

I rubbed my hand firmly over her ass. "Having my way with you."

I pulled her hips up and pushed my palm down firmly on the centre of her back when she moved to push up on her hands.

"Relax, Ruby-mine. Let's see if I can get you to fake another one."

She laughed, tilted her hips, and I slid home.

Chapter 49 - Home

<u>Ruby</u>

Gus came through as promised with the information about the house.

The reports on the house showed good bones. Despite the dilapidated look of the interior, the previous owners replaced the furnace, installed new windows, shingled the roof, and updated the plumbing and electrical. Most of what needed doing was cosmetic. As it turned out, it was his guy who did the inspection on the house and Gus trusted him implicitly.

I sent a brief text to Vander asking him to pick Jace up and meet me at Spuds after close. Then I texted Jace to make sure he had George on standby. While Jace knew about the house, we decided to make it a surprise for Vander and George.

Jace agreed that it was the right thing to do. While I didn't tell Jace about the conversation I overheard between his brother and his dad, he seemed to understand intuitively that George might find it difficult to move into Yiayia's house.

"You know, Momma, he and Dad have been a little family just the same as you and I have been a little family. I felt a little weird about moving into Dad and George's house even though I knew Dad bought that house for you. Imagine how George must feel? Besides, it's kind of exciting to make a change!"

I laughed.

Jace grabbed life by the horns and hung on for the ride. Always had. I should have known he'd be on board for a little adventure.

Amber walked in the door an hour before Vander and Jace were set to arrive.

I went to her and hugged her, tight.

She chuckled. "What was that for?"

I shrugged. "For coming over the other day. You and Minty helped me sort my head out."

"Oh," She waved me off. "That's okay, Ruby. I'm just glad you're moving ahead."

"Yeah," I answered. "I realized a few things."

She raised one perfect eyebrow. "You want to share?"

We sat down at my table. "I figured if I asked for help that made me a burden, and people would want to get away from me. I was afraid of being rejected so I didn't allow myself to ever be in that position. I never gave anybody a chance."

Amber nodded. She knew that part. "You know where that comes from, right?"

I nodded, then continued.

"Another thing I realized is that I coped with my restlessness by making plans for the distant future, things I'd have to work towards. This gave me hope for change and excitement, but because it was in the distant future, it didn't trigger my anxiety. Franchising is a perfect example. The other thing I did was make substitutes for what I really wanted, because what I really wanted scared me. Again, franchising is the perfect example of a substitute. As soon as it was in my hand, I didn't want it."

"What did you really want?" Amber murmured.

"I want what Yiayia and Pappou had: a love, a family, a life intertwined. That scared me because it meant I had to accept the risk of trusting someone not to leave. Worse, I had to trust myself to be able to cope if it all fell apart. I couldn't even admit what I really wanted until now."

Amber reached across the table. "I'm so proud of you, Rubes," she whispered. "I'm so happy for you, and proud of you."

389

Happy tears sprung to my eyes. "You want to know where I'm going in an hour?"

"Where?"

"I went to see a few houses with Gus yesterday. I found one I liked. I'm going to surprise Vander with it."

She squeezed my hand tightly. "Ruby, I'm so damn proud of you! I'm in awe of your strength."

Amber's eyes shone with admiration, and I flushed. "Thank you, Amber. I've always looked up to you. Your admiration means the world to me."

"Ah, Ruby," she waved me off. "You've always had it. You've always been so strong, even though I wished you'd ask for help, I always admired your strength."

"Vander wants to partner with me with Spuds," I blurted out.

Amber's eyebrows hit her hairline. "Really? Are you going to do it?"

I nodded decisively. "I am. I haven't told him, yet, but I am. He's going to help me take it to the next level. You know he went to work with me for only two days, and I got past that block I had last week? You were right. You and Minty both. I'll ask for help from now on when I get stuck." I took a deep breath. "I want to move forward. I'm going back to therapy, too. I'm going to travel!" I squealed and Amber laughed.

Vander

Jace remained tight-lipped the whole way to Spuds. I wondered if he suffered from Bucket Mouth syndrome like his mother, so I decided not to tease him. I didn't want him to feel bad if he let something slip.

Ruby reminded me of Tigger from Winnie the Pooh when we walked into Spuds. Flushed and bright-eyed, she barely contained her energy.

"Hi, agapimeno mou!" She hugged Jace tightly, and he laughed.

"Hi, Momma. You excited about your surprise?"

Ruby placed her finger over his lips. "Shh! Don't spill! Bucket mouth!"

I laughed. "Don't worry. He didn't say one word to me, about anything, the whole way here. I felt like a taxi driver with an antisocial passenger."

Ruby laughed and clapped her hands together once. "Okay! Let's take your car, but I'll drive."

"Fair enough." I grinned and handed her the keys.

"There's someone I want you to meet, but I don't want you to figure it out until we get there."

I raised my eyebrows. I had no idea what, or who, she was hiding. Ten minutes later, she pulled into the driveway of a house a few blocks away from Gus and Amber's place.

Jace's tablet buzzed. He must be logged onto either mine or Ruby's wifi. I peeked over the seat at him. "Don't take that right now, buddy. Mom has something important going on."

"It's George," Jace explained. "I have to take it."

"It's okay, it's okay!" Ruby waved my concerns away. "I want George to see, too."

We got out of the car, and it suddenly struck me what this was all about. I reached out and nabbed her elbow.

"You didn't," I warned.

"Didn't what?" She asked, her eyes wide.

"A puppy?" I whispered.

I didn't think bringing a puppy into the mix was a good idea just yet. There were things I wanted to do with Ruby and the boys, and a puppy at this point would only tie us down.

She laughed then gave me a scathing once over. "What kind of monster doesn't want a puppy?"

"Ruby," I warned, but she skipped away from me and grabbed Jace's hand.

Looking back, she said over her shoulder, "You'll just have to wait and see!"

Peering at the screen, she said, "Hi Georgie! Are you ready for my surprise?"

George grinned at her, then laughed. "I hope so, Ruby!"

She led us up the overgrown front walk, opened the front door, and stepped inside. We followed her into the front hall.

"Turn the camera around so George can see, agapimeno," Ruby directed Jace.

"Is anybody home?" I asked. The house appeared to be empty save for a few pieces of furniture.

"That depends," Ruby answered, her hands clasped together at her chest.

"On what?" I asked.

Instead of answering, Ruby spun around and walked into the kitchen, then through to the dining room, living room, and family room. At the stairs, she put her foot on the bottom step.

"Ruby, is anybody home here? We can't just go traipsing around someone's house."

"I'm pretty sure the person we're looking for is upstairs. You got the camera turned around for Georgie, agapimeno?"

"Yup!" Jace answered happily.

At the top of the stairs, Ruby opened the first door and stepped inside. I heard her greet someone, then followed her in.

"Gus? What the hell are you doing here?"

My brain worked feverishly to catch up to what my heart already guessed as Gus grinned at me wryly.

Ruby turned to face me, Jace, and George. The first hint of trepidation flickered over her face.

"You asked if there was anybody home. Well, we're here. We might be home. If you like it. You and the boys." She nodded towards Jace and George.

I stared at her, dumbfounded. She took my silence for confusion and continued.

"Uh, I called Gus the other day and asked him to look for a house for us. We, uh, we went out yesterday and looked at a few houses, including this one. I didn't like the other ones, even though they were perfect. I know this one needs work, but I thought it would be a good project for us." She waved her hand to encompass me and the boys. "All of us. We could make it what we want."

George spoke first, sounding young and unsure. "I thought we were moving into your house, Ruby?"

Ruby met his eyes through the magic of technology, and answered, "We're making a new family, you, your dad, your brother, and me. I thought we should have a new house, too."

"Cool," George whispered.

All my senses tuned into Ruby, and the rest of the world slipped away. She shifted from one foot to the other, fidgeting with my cross. I slipped past Jace and cupped her face in my hands. She stilled. Resting my forehead on hers, I silently thanked God for bringing her back to me.

"Thank you, Ruby."

"Do you like it, Van?" She whispered.

"You like it?"

She nodded. "I do. But I want you and the boys to like it, too."

I knew I'd buy it for her no matter what, but I wanted her to have the pleasure of selling it to us.

I turned to look at George to see his reaction. He stared at Ruby with something akin to adoration.

"Alright, Georgie?" I asked.

His eyes swung to me. "Fuck, yeah!"

"George!" Ruby yelled and threw her hands up in the air.

Gus chuckled, Jace laughed, and George mumbled a non-repentant, grinning, 'sorry'.

"Jace? You want to go first? Follow Thio Gus and make sure George gets a good look?"

I tucked Ruby's hand tightly inside mine and tipped her chin up to look at me. Her eyes shone with happiness, and she smiled widely.

I couldn't smile, I just took her in. Tugging her closer, I wrapped my arm around her back and pressed my mouth to hers.

I cupped the back of her head in my palm and held her still. "I don't deserve you, but I promise, I'll do whatever it takes until I do."

"I have another surprise for you..." She whispered.

"Give it to me," I demanded.

"I'm all in if you want to partner with Spuds." Her eyes held a hint of fear mixed in with her elation at that declaration.

"I am in awe of all you give me," I whispered. "I won't let you down."

The fear left her eyes and she smiled at me softly.

"Momma? Dad? Come on!" Jace yelled.

Gus took us through the four bedrooms, ran down the list of completed renovations as well as those still needed, detailed the findings on the inspection, took us through the kitchen, family room, living room, and dining room. Pointed out what needed doing in the bathrooms and finished up by taking a quick peek at the unfinished basement and the backyard.

"It's a big yard," Gus commented. "You'll be able to build a kickass deck back here, and with all these trees, you'll have lots of privacy."

I could hear the boys discussing which bedrooms they wanted and how they planned to set up the extra bedroom as a games room. I'd have to nip that in the bud. That room sat next to the master, and nobody would be in there.

"The room next to the master is going to be our office. We're going to be expanding Spuds together and we'll need office space." Both boys' faces dropped. "However, you two can design the basement however you'd like to be your games room. We'll put a big tv down there, bean bag chairs, a couple of couches, maybe a foosball table, an air hockey table, even a pool table if you prefer. That'll be your space."

Whoops of excitement floated back to us as they made their way downstairs and quickly checked out the basement.

Gus, Ruby, and I caught up with the boys at the front door.

"Well, Ruby-mine? Should we put in an offer?"

She turned to the boys. "Do you guys like it?"

She got two enthusiastic thumbs up. She then turned to me.

"You like it?" She searched my eyes for my answer.

"I do. There's just one thing that has to happen first."

Her eyebrows knit together, and she drew back, confused. I didn't blame her. She'd given so much already.

"What's that?"

I lifted her left hand and slipped Yiayia's ring onto her finger. She gasped in surprise and looked at me in question.

"I asked Yiayia for her blessing, and she gave me this to give to you."

Tears sprung to her eyes as she ran the pad of her thumb over the smooth stones.

I lifted her hand to my lips and kissed the back, then turned her hand in mine and pressed a kiss into her palm before closing her fingers around it. I gently pulled her into my arms and kissed her lightly, then crushed her to my chest. I couldn't get close enough to her, but I'd have to wait until later to fulfil that craving. I tilted her chin up to look at me and gave her my promise.

"I love you, Ruby-mine."

She sniffed and nodded, swallowing hard, and I chuckled.

Turning, I lifted her hand and showed the boys. "We're officially engaged, agoria mou."

Ruby snapped out of her daze. "What?" She snapped, snatching her hand back. "You haven't proposed!"

I shoved my hands deep into my pockets.

"What are you talking about? I just did!" I exclaimed, laughing.

"No," she argued. "You steamrolled!"

I looked to the boys who were both grinning at me. "Did I propose?"

George shrugged. "You gave her a ring, she accepted," George replied with a sly grin. "Looked like a proposal to me."

"Jace?"

"I agree!" He chortled like his mom.

Ruby's mouth fell open and she threw up her hands. "Lavender! Lavender tuxedos for all of you!"

Epilogue

<u>Ruby</u>

I stood and looked out my bedroom window, watching the antics of my boys outside. What they were supposed to be doing was getting ready for this afternoon. What they were doing was pelting each other with snowballs.

As if he could feel me, Vander suddenly turned and looked up at my window. I lurched backwards so that he couldn't see me, then stood on my tiptoes to peer out at him from three feet away from the window.

I could just barely see his face.

He stood still, a half smile tipping his beautiful lips up on one side. He broke into a laugh and raised his hand in a wave. How could he see me?

"I can't see you, but I know you're peeking!" He yelled.

Whoever bought this house needed to put in new windows right away.

He continued hollering. "Isn't it bad luck to see the groom on the wedding day?"

Vander's parents flew in the same day George did. They cried when they met Jace and hugged me fiercely. The first few days with them had been emotional, but they were starting to settle down.

Vander, George, Jace, and Gus had a boys' night last night at Amber and Gus's house, that included Yiayia because she needed the comfort of her own bed.

Amber stayed here with me for my last night as a single woman. Gus brought Yiayia over early this morning, and the three of us ate the breakfast she made for us.

The itinerary Amber and I drew up did not include Vander and the boys having a snowball fight on the morning of our wedding.

Yiayia puttered around downstairs in the kitchen. Her arm had fully healed, and she suffered no lasting effects from the mild concussion she sustained from her fall two months ago.

I heard the front door open, and my yiayia's voice carried up to me.

"You gonna have bad luck you try to see Ruby before the church today! Go get ready! And bring Jace back here for twelve-thirty!"

"Five more minutes, Yiayia, just five more minutes. We're making something for Ruby."

That was George. I smiled. Yiayia could never withstand the charms of any of her boys.

"Kala, agori mou, five minutes only... then you go get ready!" The front door slammed shut again.

I heard a soft knock on my bedroom door. I twisted around and called, "Come in."

Amber stuck her head in the door, took one look at my semi-proximity to the window, and laughed.

"You just cannot resist, can you?"

I smiled. "I'm curious! Aren't you curious about what they're doing?"

She smirked. "No, I saw what they're doing, and you'll see, too, if you ever finish getting ready."

I sat down on my bed in my bathrobe that I put on after my shower, and Amber sat down beside me.

She smiled and bumped me with her shoulder.

"You ready for today?"

398

I bumped her back. "I've never been more ready."

"So! Something old," she touched Yiayia's ruby on my hand, "something new," she pointed to my dress hanging on the back of the door, "something borrowed, and something blue." With that, she gave me two boxes.

"What's this?" I exclaimed.

She looked at me drily. "I just told you, something borrowed and something blue," she deadpanned.

I chortled, she snickered, and we bumped shoulders.

She extended one delicate finger and touched the square box. "Open this one first."

I pulled the tail of the ribbon and it fell away from the box. I lifted the lid to reveal a pile of pale blue lace. The first piece was a delicate lacey bra.

"Oh, Amber, it's lovely!"

Underneath the bra I found a lacy triangle attached to a few strings. "Well, at least I won't have panty lines," I said drily.

Not that my dress would show panty lines. Never having been one for dresses, no one was more surprised than me at my choice. The top boasted a lace overlay over the deep vee bodice and long, lacy, fitted sleeves. The skirt gathered gently at the waist under a thin waistband, then fell to the floor in soft, voluminous folds. And those folds, thankfully, hid pockets!

She snickered. "There's one more thing."

I lifted the tissue paper to find a delicate, matching garter.

"Amber, it's so pretty! Not gaudy at all!"

She sighed, a small smile on her pretty face. "It is, isn't it."

I placed the delicate lingerie back in the box. "Vander's going to love this," I snickered.

"That's the idea," she wagged her eyebrows at me.

This was honeymoon calibre lingerie. Our real honeymoon was still in the planning stages, part of that planning included some intensive therapy that Vander periodically attended with me to prepare for air travel.

We still hadn't decided if we were bringing the boys with us. If I had it my way, we would. I could not imagine being so far away from Jace. Even the thought of George traveling gave me palpitations.

The boys were sleeping over at Amber's tonight, but with George only here for two weeks, we didn't want to take more than one night. We were working up to a weekend away without Jace, probably to Blue Mountain, in just a few weeks.

I was glad we had tonight, and I knew Vander would love my something blue.

"Now, this one," Amber said, handing me the smaller box. "Your something borrowed is from Minty, not me."

I opened the lid to see the sparkle of diamond solitaire earrings. "Oh, my goodness! These are beautiful!"

Amber sniffed. "Not only that, but they are her most prized possession. These were her mother's."

I felt the blood drain from my face. "Oh, no, Amber. I can't wear these! You know how I lose things!"

Amber smiled softly. "She knew you'd say that. She told me to tell you the backs screw on and it's impossible for them to accidentally fall out. She also gave me strict instructions to be the one to put them in your ears and screw on the backs so you would not have responsibility for them for even a second."

I laughed. "She knows me pretty well!"

"She does. And you're very important to her. Wear them, okay?"

I sniffed. "Okay. Put them in."

Amber slid the posts through my holes and secured the backs. I looked in the mirror. "I already look like a million dollars."

Amber and I did our make-up. She helped me tame my hair, then we carried our dresses downstairs to Yiayia. Minty's soft knock came at the front door, and Amber rushed to let her in.

Together, the three of us, with Yiayia supervising, finished getting ready. While I chose the black velvet material, and the lavender for accent, Amber and Minty chose their own style of dress.

Minty wore a black, long-sleeved, V-neck, fitted sheath that fell straight to the floor. In the front, a thigh-high slit revealed the deep lavender lining with her every step. It was elegant, as she was.

Amber's dress, also long sleeved, featured a crossover top creating a deep Vee in the front, leading to a cinched crossover waist that met in a twist in the front, leading to a draped split right down the middle, showcasing her legs as well as the purple lining. It boasted a seventies vibe which suited her perfectly.

Amber helped Yiayia on with her dress, and Minty put the barest touches of make-up on her face. We got Yiayia a long-sleeve, gentle scoop neck, black velvet dress with an empire waist that hit her at her knee. We found a belt in the exact same shade of lavender to replace the belt that came with the dress.

"Yiayia, you look beautiful!"

I stood with my hands clasped to the side of my face, staring at all three of them. They were strong, kind, loyal, beautiful, and they were mine. For as long as God granted them time, they were mine.

"Your turn," Minty said huskily while Amber swiped a finger beneath her eye.

Amber and Minty helped me step into my dress, and Minty made short work of the buttons going up the back.

"Do not let him rip this," she directed me firmly.

Amber laughed, but Minty continued seriously. "In fact, I'll tell him myself."

I laughed knowing she would.

They stepped back and Amber turned the full-length mirror Minty brought over from her house so I could see myself.

I stared, speechless, at my reflection.

"You clean up good, kid," Minty whispered.

"Yiayia is very proud!" Yiayia sniffed, and Amber and I burst out laughing.

"This would be a good time to show her your shoes, Rubes," Amber snickered.

Minty opened the shoebox to reveal my rich lavender heels. They were the highest heels I'd ever worn, and I'd been practicing for a month. By this point, I could run in them.

"Purple?" Yiayia did her cross over her chest. "What I'm going to do with you? Purple shoes in the church!"

Amber slid the other boxes towards Minty and Minty smiled her enigmatic smile. She knew her role in this.

Opening all three lids, she slipped hers on first, then passed Amber her pair which she promptly put on, then turned to Yiayia.

"These ones are for you, Yiayia." She lifted out a very low-heeled, classy pump in the exact shade of lavender as ours.

Yiayia's eyes lit up. She always loved a good shoe. "We gonna be matching!"

Minty laughed her tinkling laugh and helped her put them on.

At that moment, Jace opened the door and walked in.

My heart stopped. Despite my threats of powder blue, then lavender, then pink tuxedos, we chose classic black for all the men to wear.

Gus, Alex, Jace, and George were in the wedding party.

Gus and Amber accepted the role of koumbari and would both be active participants during the wedding ceremony.

Minty would stand as my maid of honor.

Jace would walk me down the aisle, then take his position next to his dad and his brother on the altar.

It was a little unorthodox, with Jace doing double duty, but with the way we finally came together, how could it not be?

"Yiayia is very proud!" The tears were thick in her voice, and we all sniffed.

"You will not ruin your make-up, Ruby," Minty said softly but firmly, and Yiayia laughed.

The limo pulled up outside.

Getting married from this house that had sheltered me for so long felt right.

Vander's house sold immediately, and he moved in here with Jace and me while we renovated our new house. It would be ready by the time George came back for March Break. Over the Christmas holidays, they planned to pick out the furniture, décor, and pool table for their games room in the basement. Vander and I had chosen everything else already.

I was glad it wasn't ready. Of all the milestones and heartaches this house had witnessed and comforted me through, I wanted to meet this one here, too.

Vander and the boys had cleared a wide pathway from the house to the road so we would not slip on our way to the limo.

Just before I got into the car, Amber gently touched my elbow and nodded back to the house. I turned to find a lopsided snowman wearing a tacky, plaid, suit jacket and matching bow tie.

I screamed with laughter, my Yiayia, my sister, and my best friend laughing with me. I turned to Jace to find him recording my reaction.

I spread my arms wide. "I love him! I never thought to threaten you with plaid!"

"They did such good job!" Yiayia praised. "They work so hard to make it. They came very early, poulaki." Then she grumbled, "I nearly boil Vander when he try to look on you."

The limo took us to the church, and Jace wandered off to find his dad, his brother, and his uncle. He came back in time to lead Yiayia to her seat, then returned to walk me down the aisle.

The men waited at the front.

The music began, and Amber and Minty walked down together.

"You look so beautiful, Momma," Jace whispered as he crooked his arm to escort me down the aisle.

"Agapimeno mou," I whispered back.

He laughed. "No crying! Minnie warned me not to make you cry and I'm afraid of what she'll do to me if you mess up your make-up!"

I could barely see the top of Vander's head with the number of people who stood at my entrance.

403

I easily picked Elisavet and Yanni out in the crowd. Both had tears in their eyes.

Maria sat with her husband and pretended to spit on me for luck. I don't know what to tell you. It's a Greek thing.

Voula gave me a huge grin and a double thumbs-up.

Vander's mom held tightly to her husband, their eyes shiny and bright.

Jace puffed out his chest proudly as he passed his new grandparents, his serious face showing just how much his role meant to him.

Vander compressed his lips in a straight line but couldn't stop the single tear from rolling down his handsome face.

Jace placed my hand in Vander's, and Vander wrapped his other hand around the back of Jace's neck and kissed his forehead.

In that moment, a case of the sniffles ran through the church.

Gus, Alex, and George looked gorgeous in their tuxedos. Of all of them, George was the only one who thought I was the slightest bit serious about lavender tuxes. Finally, I had to put his mind at ease and let him off the hook by showing him what we'd ordered.

When it came time for the rings, Gus stepped forward. He slipped our rings on the ring fingers of our right hands, then put my ring on the tip of Vander's finger, and his on mine, then switched back, signifying the intertwining of our lives, before sliding the rings on completely.

I had not yet seen the rings Vander had chosen for us as he wanted it to be a surprise. It wasn't until Gus slid the ring onto my finger that I saw mine for the first time. I sucked in a breath at the sight. A band of rose cut diamonds, alternating between two sizes, encircled my finger. I looked up to find him anxiously awaiting my reaction. I offered him a shaky, watery, smile, and he relaxed.

At this point in the service, the priest joined our right hands. For the rest of the service, we had to hang onto each other and not let go. This signified the unity of our marriage, and at this point, we were officially married.

We hung on tight.

Gus stepped forward once again to perform the ceremony with the crowns. He placed Vander's crown over his head, and mine over mine, then switched them back.

Amber tied a ribbon between the two crowns, and Gus placed them on our heads, signifying that our lives would be forever intertwined and our union unbreakable.

Amber and Gus accompanied us on our first walk as a married couple around the altar, signifying their willingness to walk beside us as we walked through life together, and then the priest delivered his blessing and presented us to our guests, inviting Yiayia and Vander's parents to be the first to congratulate us.

We turned and smiled. So many faces, shiny with tears, beamed back at us.

Vander laughed out loud, turned me in his arms, and kissed me.

Stepping off the altar, all our men, weirdly, gathered in a little huddle. With their backs to us, they fiddled with their jackets. As one, they turned.

They each had one hand stuffed in their pants pocket, holding their jackets open. With the other hand, they jacked up their pant leg, showing me their deep lavender waistcoats, that I did not order, and matching socks.

I slapped my hands over my face and Amber snickered with laughter, holding onto her sides. Yiayia tsked beside me, and I opened my arm to bring her in close. Her shoulders shook with the laughter she tried to suppress. Her boys could do nothing wrong, not really.

They grinned at me, and I chortled. "How did you pull this off?"

George tilted his head in Minty's direction. "It was my idea, but Minnie helped."

I looked at Minty and noted a well of tears in her eyes. I knew she would be taking George under her wing as well.

"Don't ruin your make-up," I murmured softly with a smile.

She laughed, and touched an elegant finger to each eye, sweeping the moisture away.

Vander held his hand out to me, and I took it. He crooked his elbow for Yiayia and dipped to kiss his mother's cheek.

Surrounded by those we loved most in this world, we stepped into the future.

The End

Thank you for reading Broken Road.
I hope Ruby and Vander's love story touched your heart the same way it did mine.
Read on for a sneak peak at Amber and Gus' story,

Chosen Road.

Chapter 1: The Old Days

Amber

This kid was going to fall through the cracks. I could feel it.

I turned away from Mallory's file to go back to my internet searching, but knew it was pointless. I'd exhausted every community and governmental resource I could to try to help her. Short of a Harry Potter truth serum, there was nothing I could do until she talked to me.

And she wasn't going to.

I recognized her pain, though I had little right. Her mother was an addict who had dipped in and out of her life since she was a toddler.

Unlike me, she did not have a loving family for the first ten years of her life.

Unlike me, she had no grandparents who stepped in when she was abandoned.

Unlike me, she bounced from foster home to foster home and was now looking at a group home because she was no longer small and cute.

Well, that and the fact that her rage could level a room in under ten minutes. Her emotions were out of control.

Unlike me, Mallory hadn't yet learned to lock them down.

Alex's bouncing step sounded on the stairs. I forced myself to set the file down on the desk Gus bought me for the family room. It was a couple of years ago when I first accepted this position and we realized how much extra work it entailed. He said if I had to bring work home, he at least wanted me to have the option of being in the same room as him and Alex.

At the time it exemplified everything that I loved most about him. Why it irritated me now, I could not explain, but then, everything he did irritated me lately.

Nothing made me happy.

You're just like me.

I shuddered at the thought. My mother walked out on us when I was twelve years old and Ruby only ten. As if that wasn't bad enough, she did it only one year after we lost my dad to a five-year battle with colon cancer.

He wasn't desperately ill the entirety of the five years. There were six really terrible months after his diagnosis. Ruby and I were only four and six and, thankfully, we didn't understand most of what was going on.

After that, he got well. When I thought back, those were the years I counted as the happiest of my childhood. Back then our home was filled with laughter. Mom took me everywhere with her, and every outing was an adventure.

I could hear her, still.

"Ruby's a daddy's girl, but you're mommy's girl, aren't you my little jewel?" She would say, tucking me against her side.

She smelled like the rich mix of spices and fragrances she used to make her homemade candles, potpourri, and perfume oils. She wore soft fabrics that caressed my cheek like a whisper, and I closed my eyes as I nestled in. I heard the tinkle of her earrings as she dipped her face down to brush a kiss across my forehead and gave me another gentle squeeze before releasing me.

"Come on, my jewel. Let's pop into The Treasure Trove and see if there's anything weird or wonderful."

The Treasure Trove was a common stop for us. A vintage clothing slash secondhand store that often lived up to its name. Silk scarves, one-of-a-kind jewelry, flowing skirts and dresses, embroidered purses, beaded clutches, as well as some truly horrendous pieces. The collection was eclectic.

My father's eyes lit up at the sight of Mom's smile when we walked through the door. "What new bauble did you pick up, koukla?" His question was always the same, the love in his eyes warm and bright.

"I bought three silk scarves for me and my beautiful girls." She pulled them from her bag, giving one to me and one to Ruby.

Ruby looked bemused by the gift and ran it through her hands. She lifted it to cover her face and peered through it. "It turns the world purple, Momma."

"You're supposed to wear it, darling," Momma advised her, then turned to me. "Come here, little jewel." She took my scarf, a golden yellow, and looped it around my neck before wrapping the matching one around her own throat. "There. We're twins!"

By the time I was eleven, before my dad got sick again, I was well versed in all manner of combining spices and fragrances. While she didn't allow me to make the candles on my own, I made loads of potpourri, and the perfumes I created rivalled hers. When we did blind smell tests with Ruby, Dad, and Yiayia, mine won the popular vote as often as hers.

She would laugh when that happened and hold me close, her whispered words for my ears alone. "My jewel, It's you and me, baby, my mini-me, my partner in crime."

I took after her in coloring as well, having the same dirty blond hair and light brown eyes. I also shared her same slender build, and apparently the same taste in clothing and accessories. It took me awhile to accept our similarities.

She was the last person I wanted to take after.

Looking back through adult eyes, Mom was oddly dismissive of Ruby. She hugged her, kissed her, and tucked her in at night. She bought her something whenever she bought something for me, although it was what we liked, never anything that might appeal to Ruby. She didn't take her out with her the way she did with me. She didn't teach Ruby about essential oils and fragrances. As far as I knew, Ruby never asked. Still. It was odd.

I remember feeling a vague sense of guilt that she never included Ruby, mostly because I liked having Mom to myself, but Ruby never seemed bothered. She had Dad. I had Dad, too. He treated us equally, but he spent more time with Ruby, probably because Mom was always with me.

And I *wanted* to be with her. It got to the point where I sensed her mood. I could tell when she started getting restless, and I remembered the sensation of anticipation that pooled in my belly. She made me feel special, loved, and important.

Until she didn't.

Over the year after my dad passed, Mom became more and more irritable with Ruby and me. At night she sometimes let me come into her bed and she cuddled me like she used to, but the time between those sweet moments stretched further and further apart.

I felt her rising restlessness. I could barely contain my excitement, knowing there would soon be a mommy-and-me adventure.

Ruby and I came home from school to find her standing on the driveway with her coat on and I thrilled at the knowledge that the time had come.

She opened her arms to us, and I went to her readily. I wondered why she was ready to go so early. Yiayia wasn't home yet, and we couldn't leave Ruby home by herself.

"Go on into the house, my jewels," she ordered us.

Her eyes glittered in a way I'd never seen before. I couldn't read her, and it frightened me.

"Mommy?" I questioned. I hadn't called her Mommy for years, but something about the moment made me feel younger and uncertain.

"My jewel, I love you so much," she said softly, then smiled. A real smile, a genuine smile, the kind we hadn't gotten from her in so long. "Go on into the house."

That time when she told me to go inside, I listened.

I shrugged out of my coat and had just hung up my backpack when I heard the car start.

My heart skipped in my chest, understanding instinctively that which my brain denied. I flung open the front door and stood in the archway, wondering why she was moving the car. She stared at me for a moment and my body went cold.

"Mommy?" I asked, though she could not hear me.

She stretched her arm over the back of the seat and quickly pulled out onto the street.

I stepped out onto the porch and yelled her name. "Mommy!"

She paused; I know she did. I saw her look down at her lap, and I ran. I ran down the driveway because I knew if I could get to her in time she'd change her mind.

She'd come back into the house and wait for Yiayia to come home.

She'd nestle me into her side and take me to Treasure Trove.

She'd call me her jewel and remind me that I was just like her.

My stockinged feet hit the edge of the sidewalk as the car rolled faster and faster away from me. I screamed, "Mommy! Mommy, no! Mommy, come back!" I screamed as loud as I could because if she heard me, if she heard me, she'd come back.

Ruby met me on the driveway, her pigtails bouncing around her pale face, her skinny arms reaching for me, and I lashed out at her like a wild animal. And like a wild animal she hung onto me through my incoherent screaming and clawing, fighting against the arms that held me back from where I wanted to go.

The neighbor called Yiayia at work and she came home right away, but it was too late.

The bottom had dropped out of my world. I lost my sense of self. We were best friends, I was her mini-me, we were partners in crime. I was just like her. Losing her was like losing a limb. There was no earth beneath my feet, my foundation: erased.

Even now, whenever memories of her snuck past my barriers, I found myself back on that driveway, clinging to Ruby and screaming for my mom to come back for me. I could still feel Ruby's strong arms holding me. I could still feel her flesh give way beneath my nails.

She bore those scars still.

For the longest time, I believed she'd come back for me. Not for Ruby, I somehow knew she wouldn't be back for Ruby, but I could not fathom her leaving me. I was Mommy's girl; Ruby was Daddy's girl.

At the time, it made a sick sort of sense to me. Looking back through adult eyes, I could see it was all kinds of fucked up, but in my mind, it was normal. I was her mini me. Our relationship was special, she'd be back for me.

For weeks, I waited.

411

As time passed, I accepted that she was gone although I continued to look for her. Even now I searched for her every time I looked in the mirror. Only now, I worried that I'd find her.

With Yiayia and Pappou gently pushing me, and Ruby holding my hand, I carried on with the business of living. The shock of her betrayal slowly receded into the background to lay dormant inside me. When triggered, it was a terrible thing.

My mother snuck into my thoughts more and more often lately. I wasn't so obtuse that I did not understand the reason. Alex was the age I was when my dad died, which also marked the beginning of my mother's withdrawal.

And this girl. Mallory. The one who was destined for the cracks. Mallory was a projectile slamming into my brittle heart, sending ripples and streams of spiderweb-like cracks along its surface.

And all along those fissures leaked thoughts of my mother.

Alex's stockinged feet hit the bottom of the staircase. Taking a running leap, he slid across the wood floors towards me.

"Momma! Are you going to play Lego with me and Dad?"

"Yes, agori mou, of course I am." He continued on down to the basement without waiting for my answer, confident that I would be right behind him.

Gus was already down there, turning on the overhead lights and plugging in the lighting around the Lego table. Two years ago, when we accepted the fact that Lego would never, ever, leave our home, Gus built a giant U-shaped table with shelves and built-in lighting along three walls. It was a Lego lover's dream.

"I turned the gas fireplace on for you, beautiful," Gus murmured in passing, dragging his hand along the back of my hips. "Do you want to build today, or relax and watch?"

"I can look after myself, you know. I don't need you to cater to me all the time," I muttered.

He stopped in his tracks, his eyes narrowed as he studied me. "I'm sorry?" he asked, taken aback and more than a little pissed.

In the old days, he would have crowded me even more and told me that he was born to take care of me. He would have wrapped me in a blanket and tickled me until I peed or begged him to stop. In the old days, he would have turned me over his knee, spanked my 'sassy ass' and finger-fucked me into submission. In the old days he would have pushed, I would have laughed, and we would have gotten past the blip in my normally polite persona and carried on.

Momentarily chagrined, but then, against my own judgement, I doubled down. "I don't need you to baby me. I can look after myself."

These were not the old days, because he simply closed his eyes in disgust and muttered, "Have at it."

Gus

We played with Alex, and God help me, I touched Amber every opportunity I could though I knew it irritated her. It seemed I could do no right in her eyes. She denied that anything was wrong, begged off going to counseling, but had been pulling away from me by infinitesimal degrees for the past two years.

Since she got that damn job.

I'd known from the beginning that I would always come second to Yiayia and Ruby. I understood that you don't go through what those three ladies went through together and not come out of it bonded as a unit.

I understood it, was in awe of it, accepted it, even supported it.

When Alex came, I willingly slipped into third place. It was okay because we were a team. Amber and Gus, rooting together for Alex.

Then her work picked up. Contract after contract, bigger and bigger projects, and longer hours. I stepped up as much as I could. I made dinner, arranged to pick up Alex whenever possible, got Yiayia to her appointments, and occupied Alex on the weekends for several hours so she could work. And she brought home lots of work, coming in the door barely in time to sit down for dinner, balancing her purse and her laptop and the ever-growing clutch of files.

I tried, many times, to talk to her about it to no avail. The last time was over three months ago. Alex had gone upstairs to have his nightly shower and I approached her.

"I'd like to talk to you after Alex goes to bed," I stated calmly.

She looked at me with barely repressed impatience. "I don't have time tonight." She indicated the files on her desk with a sweep of her hand. "I've got too much to do."

"Amber, is it possible you could hire an assistant? You barely have any free time."

"Maybe Jacqueline would be willing to step up. I'm sure she'd love to spend more time with you," she snapped.

The sudden souring of her attitude towards Jacqueline bewildered me. Jacqueline was a happily married woman with a child. She had no interest in me. "What does Jacqueline have to do with this? Although, you're absolutely right, someone like her would be excellent."

"Oh, really? You think she could do a better job than I do?"

I huffed in exasperation. "I didn't say that! I don't think she *could* do what you do. I simply said you have no free time and maybe you could get an assistant to take on whatever you don't have to do yourself!" My temper flared and I swore to myself I wouldn't tonight. I took a deep breath. "I miss you, honey."

"Gus," her shoulders fell, defeated. "I can't not do my job. These kids have nobody."

"I hear you. I do," I reiterated seeing her doubtful glance. "But we need you, too."

Her shoulders tensed up again and she spoke carefully and evenly. "I've never not been there for Alex."

"I never said you haven't," I agreed, but left out the obvious fact that it had been a long time since she'd been there for me. It wasn't all her fault. The more she pulled away, the less I did to ease her way. That was something I could rectify.

"What can I do to make things easier for you, honey?"

"Don't try to save me, Gus. I don't need saving," she retorted.

That was rich coming from her, and my frustration boiled over. "Me saving you? What are you talking about? You're the one who's on a mission to save the fucking world, Amber, and there's no room for me, for us, in your goddamn plans!"

414

I hadn't brought it up since, but it was always on my mind.

I turned off the fireplace and refocused on Alex.

He stood with his legs akimbo. "Dad, I was thinking, if we moved all the Star Wars Lego to one place," he waved his arms around and then pressed his palms together, "we could make Lego planets!"

Internally, I groaned. I caught Amber's smirk directed at me. It made me smile that we could share that small moment. We had only just finished spreading the Star Wars Lego out over the table so they could fly to different galaxies.

"I think that's a great idea, buddy. Before we start moving things, why don't you come up with a plan for all the Lego planets and where they will be?"

The three of us spent the next hour sitting down with paper and markers, a U-shaped map in front of us, while Alex ran back and forth between us and the table, cataloguing his collections into planets.

Finally, he yawned and stretched.

"Time for bed, agori mou." Amber stroked his silky hair off his forehead.

"Not yet, Momma," he protested.

"C'mon," I interrupted. "I'll race you. See if you can get your jammies on before I close everything up down here."

He leapt to his feet and pointed at me. "You're on! I get a ten second head start!"

Amber turned and followed him upstairs, counting out his ten second start.

I watched them leave, and the loneliness that hovered all day on the fringes of my consciousness rolled in to fill the vacuum created by Amber and Alex's absence. I wondered when that had become a daily occurrence.

By the time I finished up, Amber was back to sitting at her desk, steam rising from the cup of tea beside her. Upstairs, Alex waited for me to tuck him into bed.

This was the time of day Amber and I used to cherish, turned toward each other in our bed, getting caught up on each other's days. An hour

415

later, she'd be wrapped around me, moaning into my neck, her hands running up and down my spine.

I checked the locks, set the alarm, and grabbed a bottle of water.

As I did most every night, I headed upstairs by myself. I paused on the staircase. The light from her monitor illuminated her pretty face. She looked tired. I wondered if she was lonely or if she missed me at all.

I called to her softly, "Goodnight, baby."

She didn't look up from her computer. "Mm-hmm."

I wondered how much longer I could go on like this.

Special Acknowledgements

Oh, boy, where to start...

The bookstagram community has been so good to me. So many people, who wouldn't know me if they passed me on the street, have supported me because they believe in my work. That's astounding to me. And so incredibly validating.

I've come to depend on a few special souls, specifically Nola Marie, @authornolamarie, Sionna Trenz, @sionnatrenz, and Anita of @anita_thebookaddict. These three ladies support me on the daily and make me wheeze with laughter while they're doing it! I hope I give back what you give me.

Rachel, @bookaddictblog, and Amara, @amararaeauthor, thank you for beta reading Ruby and Vander's story for me. Don't ever doubt how crucial your input is to me.

Torie, @the_insomniacreader, and Anna, @annapsbooknook, thank you for giving me such valuable feedback. I appreciate you!

To my entire Street Team, as well as the Steam Queens, thank you for posting and sharing all my reels, graphics, and stories. Sorry about all the technical difficulties!

To my ARC readers, I can't thank you enough for reading my work and encouraging me with your wonderful reviews. Your words mean so much to me.

Nola Marie, thank you for helping me with Canva and sharing your expertise with me.

Sionna, thank you for helping me with blurbs and newsletters. You have a gift for gab!

Anita, thank you for being my PA. I appreciate you so much. You do all the things I'm too uncomfortable or too disorganized to do well myself. And you do it all with a smile.

Sibylla Matilde, @sibyllamatilde, for writing a book that touched my heart, and allowing me to mention your book in mine.

Selena Moore, @selenamooreromance, for helping me with the Greek/English translations. It's been a long time since my husband has been in Greek school and he appreciated the backup. He was also delighted every time you proved him right!

My eldest daughter, Brianna, for encouraging me while I grapple with writing, and for channeling her inner romance writer to give me that fantastic line when Amber gives romance writing a go. We laughed hard that night, didn't we, darling!

My youngest daughter, Alicia, for drawing the icon of Ruby for the chapter headings. Thank you, my joy.

My eldest son, Bryce, for encouraging me to carve out time for myself, for making me believe it's okay to go for it.

My youngest son, Dominick, for tech support and being 'proud'. You're not that easy to impress which only makes it that much more valued.

I love you guys so very much.

My husband and kids, always, for respecting my time and being proud of my writing, for encouraging me when imposter syndrome barges in, and for being happy for me while I type away at my laptop alternately laughing, scowling, and crying.

About the Author

I live in a small town in Southern Ontario. I married my husband a million years ago in 1993, and we built a family consisting of 4 kids, a handful of doggos over the years, and even a couple of kittycats. We live in the house my husband's father built.

My father-in-law immigrated from Greece in 1965 with no education, little money, and a pregnant wife. Pappou, as my children call him, is truly a legend. He worked tirelessly for his family and his heart is as generous as they come. Yiayia is no slouch either. As of this moment, I'm lying on my couch after foot surgery waiting for them to drop off our homemade dinner. I love my big, fat, Greek family, even when they drive me nuts.

And there are times when they definitely do. I'm sure that works both ways as I haven't always been the compliant Xeni they wish me to be.

This work is a love letter for people who will never read it.

But you'll know.

And that's enough for me right now.

Also by Devin Sloane

Find me here: devinsloane.ca

__The Bridgewater Novels__

Live Again

Breathe Again

Feel Again

__The Milltown Novels__

Broken Road

Chosen Road

Mountain Road

__The Sage Ridge Novels__

A Lifetime of Afters

__The Mulberry Place Novels__

Sweet Everythings

9 798223 881018

Āzijas virtuves grāmata
Eksotiskas garšas un ēdienu tradīcijas no Āzijas valstīm

Keita Dukure

Saturs

4

5

6

Saldskābā karpa

Pasniedz 4

1 liela karpa vai līdzīga zivs

300g/11oz/¬œ tase kukurūzas miltu (kukurūzas ciete)

250 ml/8 fl oz/1 glāze augu eļļas

30 ml/2 ēdamkarotes sojas mērces

5 ml/1 tējkarote sāls

150 g / 5 unces / uzkrāta ¬Ω glāze cukura

75 ml/5 ēdamkarotes vīna etiķa

15 ml/1 ēdamkarote rīsu vīna vai sausā šerija

3 lociņi, smalki sagriezti

1 šķēle ingvera saknes, smalki sagriezta

250 ml / 8 fl oz / 1 glāze verdoša ūdens

Notīriet zivis, atkaļķojiet un vairākas stundas iemērciet aukstā ūdenī. Nosusiniet un nosusiniet, pēc tam dažas reizes pārvelciet katru pusi. Rezervē 30 ml/2 ēdamkarotes kukurūzas miltu, pēc tam pakāpeniski iemaisiet pietiekami daudz ūdens atlikušajos kukurūzas miltos, lai izveidotu stingru mīklu. Pārklājiet zivis mīklā. Uzkarsē eļļu līdz ļoti karstai un cep zivi, līdz ārpuse kļūst kraukšķīga, tad samazini uguni un turpina cept, līdz zivs ir mīksta. Tikmēr sajauc atlikušos kukurūzas miltus, sojas mērci, sāli, cukuru, vīna etiķi,

vīns vai šerijs, sīpols un ingvers. Kad zivs izcepusies, pārliek to uz silta pasniegšanas šķīvja. Pievienojiet eļļai mērces maisījumu un ūdeni un labi samaisiet, līdz tā vārās, līdz mērce sabiezē. Pārlej zivi un pasniedz uzreiz.

Karpas ar tofu

Pasniedz 4

1 karpu

60 ml/4 ēdamkarotes zemesriekstu eļļas

225g/8oz tofu, kubiņos

2 lociņi, smalki sagriezti

1 ķiploka daiviņa, smalki sagriezta

2 ingvera saknes šķēles, smalki sagrieztas

15 ml/1 ēdamkarote čili mērces

30 ml/2 ēdamkarotes sojas mērces

500 ml / 16 fl unces / 2 tases buljona

30 ml/2 ēdamkarotes rīsu vīna vai sausā šerija

15 ml/1 ēdamkarote kukurūzas miltu (kukurūzas ciete)

30 ml/2 ēdamkarotes ūdens

Izgrieziet, izķidājiet un notīriet zivis un ievelciet 3 diagonālās līnijas katrā pusē. Uzkarsē eļļu un viegli apcep tofu līdz zeltaini brūnai. Izņem no pannas un labi notecina. Pievienojiet zivis pannā un cepiet līdz zeltaini brūnai, pēc tam izņemiet no pannas. Nolejiet visu eļļu, izņemot 15 ml/1 ēdamkarote, pēc tam apcepiet sīpolus, ķiplokus un ingveru 30 sekundes. Pievienojiet čili mērci, sojas mērci, buljonu un vīnu un uzvāra. Uzmanīgi ievietojiet zivis pannā

tofu un vāra uz lēnas uguns, bez vāka, apmēram 10 minūtes, līdz zivs ir gatava un mērce ir samazinājusies. Pārliek zivis uz sasildīta servēšanas šķīvja un pa virsu uzliek tofu ar karoti. Kukurūzas miltus un ūdeni samaisa biezenī, iemaisa mērcē un maisot vāra uz lēnas uguns, līdz mērce nedaudz sabiezē. Liek virsū zivīm un nekavējoties pasniedz.

Mandeļu zivju rullīši

Pasniedz 4

100 g/4 unces/1 tase mandeles

450 g/1 mārciņa mencas fileja

4 šķēles kūpināta šķiņķa

1 lociņš, sasmalcināts

1 šķēle ingvera saknes, sasmalcināta

5 ml/1 tējk kukurūzas milti (kukurūzas ciete)

5 ml/1 tējk cukurs

2,5 ml/¬Ω tējkarote sāls

15 ml/1 ēdamkarote sojas mērces

15 ml/1 ēdamkarote rīsu vīna vai sausā šerija

1 ola, viegli sakulta

eļļa dziļai cepšanai

1 citrons, sagriezts šķēlēs

Mandeles blanšē verdošā ūdenī 5 minūtes, pēc tam nokāš un sasmalcina. Sagrieziet zivis 9 cm/3¬Ω kvadrātos un šķiņķi 5 cm/2 kvadrātos. Sajauc sīpolu, ingveru, kukurūzas miltus, cukuru, sāli, sojas mērci, vīnu vai šeriju un olu. Iemērciet zivis maisījumā, pēc tam novietojiet zivis uz darba virsmas. Virsū uzber mandeles, tad liek šķiņķa šķēli. Sarullē zivi un sasien ar šefpavāru, Uzkarsē eļļu un apcep zivju ruļļus dažas minūtes līdz zeltaini brūnai. Nokāš uz virtuves papīra un pasniedz ar citronu.

Menca ar bambusa dzinumiem

Pasniedz 4

4 žāvētas ķīniešu sēnes
900 g mencas filejas, kubiņos
30 ml/2 ēdamkarotes kukurūzas miltu (kukurūzas ciete)
eļļa dziļai cepšanai
30 ml/2 ēdamkarotes zemesriekstu eļļas
1 lociņš, sagriezts
1 šķēle ingvera saknes, sasmalcināta
sāls
100g/4oz bambusa dzinumi, sasmalcināti
120 ml / 4 fl oz / ¬Ω tase zivju buljona
15 ml/1 ēdamkarote sojas mērces
45 ml / 3 ēdamkarotes ūdens

Sēnes 30 minūtes iemērc siltā ūdenī, pēc tam nokāš. Izmetiet kātus un nogrieziet vāciņus. Pārkaisa pusi zivs kukurūzas milti. Uzkarsē eļļu un apcep zivis līdz zeltaini brūnai. Nokāš uz virtuves papīra un turi siltumu.

Tikmēr uzkarsē eļļu un apcep sīpolu, ingveru un sāli, līdz tie ir viegli brūni. Pievienojiet bambusa dzinumus un maisot apcepiet 3 minūtes. Pievieno buljonu un sojas mērci, uzvāra un vāra uz lēnas uguns 3 minūtes. Pārējos kukurūzas miltus sajauc ar ūdeni, pievieno pannā un maisot vāra uz lēnas uguns, līdz mērce sabiezē. Pārlej zivi un pasniedz uzreiz.

Zivis ar pupiņu kāpostiem

Pasniedz 4

450 g/1 mārciņa pupiņu asnu

45 ml/3 ēdamkarotes zemesriekstu eļļas

5 ml/1 tējkarote sāls

3 šķēles ingvera saknes, sasmalcinātas

450g/1lb zivs fileja, sagriezta

4 lociņi, sagriezti šķēlēs

15 ml/1 ēdamkarote sojas mērces

60 ml/4 ēdamkarotes zivju buljona

10 ml / 2 tējkarotes kukurūzas miltu (kukurūzas ciete)

15 ml/1 ēdamkarote ūdens

Pupiņu asnus 4 minūtes blanšē verdošā ūdenī, pēc tam labi nokāš. Uzkarsē pusi eļļas un apcep sāli un ingveru 1 minūti. Pievienojiet zivis un vāriet, līdz tās ir viegli brūnas, pēc tam izņemiet no pannas. Uzkarsē atlikušo eļļu un apcep lociņus 1 minūti. Pievieno sojas mērci un buljonu un uzvāra. Liek zivis atpakaļ uz pannas, uzliek vāku un vāra uz lēnas uguns 2 minūtes, līdz zivs ir gatava. Kukurūzas miltus un ūdeni samaisa pastu, pievieno pannā un maisot vāra, līdz mērce ir dzidra un sabiezējusi.

Zivs fileja brūnā mērcē

Pasniedz 4

450 g/1 mārciņa mencas filejas, biezi sagrieztas

30 ml/2 ēdamkarotes rīsu vīna vai sausā šerija

30 ml/2 ēdamkarotes sojas mērces

3 lociņi, smalki sagriezti

1 šķēle ingvera saknes, smalki sagriezta

5 ml/1 tējkarote sāls

5 ml/1 tējkarote sezama eļļas

30 ml/2 ēdamkarotes kukurūzas miltu (kukurūzas ciete)

3 olas, sakultas

90 ml/6 ēdamkarotes zemesriekstu eļļas

90 ml/6 ēdamkarotes zivju buljona

Ievietojiet zivju fileju bļodā. Sajauc vīnu vai šeriju, sojas mērci, sīpolus, ingveru, sāli un sezama eļļu, pārlej zivīm, pārklāj un atstāj marinēties 30 minūtes. Izņemiet zivis no marinādes un iemetiet kukurūzas miltos, pēc tam iemērciet sakultajā olā. Uzkarsē eļļu un apcep zivis līdz zeltaini brūnai no ārpuses. Eļļu notecina un iemaisa buljonu un atlikušo marinādi. Uzkarsē līdz vārīšanās temperatūrai un vāra uz lēnas uguns apmēram 5 minūtes, līdz zivs ir gatava.

Ķīniešu zivju kūkas

Pasniedz 4

450 g/1 mārciņa malta (malta) menca
2 lociņi, smalki sagriezti
1 ķiploka daiviņa, sasmalcināta
5 ml/1 tējkarote sāls
5 ml/1 tējk cukurs
5 ml/1 tējk sojas mērce
45 ml/3 ēdamkarotes augu eļļas
15 ml/1 ēdamkarote kukurūzas miltu (kukurūzas ciete)

Sajauc mencu, lociņus, ķiplokus, sāli, cukuru, sojas mērci un 10 ml/2 tējk. eļļas. Rūpīgi samaisa, ik pa laikam uzkaisot nedaudz kukurūzas miltu, līdz maisījums ir mīksts un elastīgs. Veido 4 zivju kūkas. Uzkarsē eļļu un cep zivju pīrādziņus apmēram 10 minūtes, līdz tie kļūst zeltaini, cepšanas laikā tos piespiežot plakaniski. Pasniedziet karstu vai aukstu.

Kraukšķīgi cepta zivs

Pasniedz 4

450 g/1 mārciņa zivju filejas, sagrieztas strēmelēs
30 ml/2 ēdamkarotes rīsu vīna vai sausā šerija
sāls un svaigi malti pipari
45 ml/3 ēdamkarotes kukurūzas miltu (kukurūzas ciete)
1 olas baltums, viegli saputots
eļļa dziļai cepšanai

Pievienojiet zivis vīnam vai šerijam un pievienojiet sāli un piparus. Viegli apkaisa ar kukurūzas miltiem. Atlikušos kukurūzas miltus saputo olu baltumā līdz stingrībai, pēc tam iemērciet zivis mīklā. Uzkarsē eļļu un apcep zivju strēmelītes dažas minūtes līdz zeltaini brūnas.

Cepta menca

Pasniedz 4

900 g mencas filejas, kubiņos

sāls un svaigi malti pipari

2 olas, sakultas

100 g/4 unces/1 glāze vienkāršu (universālu) miltu

eļļa dziļai cepšanai

1 citrons, sagriezts šķēlēs

Garšojiet mencu ar sāli un pipariem. Sakuļ olas un miltus mīklā un pievieno sāli. Iemērciet zivis mīklā. Uzkarsē eļļu un apcep zivis dažas minūtes, līdz tās kļūst zeltainas un gatavas. Nokāš uz virtuves papīra un pasniedz ar citrona daiviņām.

Piecu garšvielu zivs

Pasniedz 4

4 mencas filejas

5 ml/1 tējk piecu garšvielu pulveris

5 ml/1 tējkarote sāls

30 ml/2 ēdamkarotes zemesriekstu eļļas

2 ķiploka daiviņas, sasmalcinātas

2,5 ml/1 ingvera sakne, sasmalcināta

30 ml/2 ēdamkarotes rīsu vīna vai sausā šerija

15 ml/1 ēdamkarote sojas mērces

dažus pilienus sezama eļļas

Zivi ierīvē ar piecu garšvielu pulveri un sāli. Uzkarsē eļļu un apcep zivis no abām pusēm, līdz tās ir viegli brūnas. Izņem no pannas un pievieno atlikušās sastāvdaļas. Maisot uzkarsē, pēc tam ielieciet zivis atpakaļ pannā un pirms pasniegšanas viegli uzkarsējiet.

Smaržīgi zivju nūjiņas

Pasniedz 4

30 ml/2 ēdamkarotes rīsu vīna vai sausā šerija

1 lociņš, smalki sagriezts

2 olas, sakultas

10 ml/2 tējk karija pulveris

5 ml/1 tējkarote sāls

450g/1lb baltās zivs filejas, sagrieztas strēmelītēs

100 g/4 unces rīvmaizes

eļļa dziļai cepšanai

Iemaisa vīnu vai šeriju, sīpolu, olas, karija pulveri un sāli. Iemērciet zivis maisījumā, lai vienmērīgi pārklātu gabalus, pēc tam iespiediet tos rīvmaizē. Uzkarsē eļļu un cep zivis dažas minūtes, līdz tā kļūst kraukšķīga un zeltaini brūna. Labi nokāš un nekavējoties pasniedz.

Zivis ar kornišoni

Pasniedz 4

4 baltās zivs filejas

75 g / 3 unces mazi kornišoni

2 lociņi (sīpoli)

2 šķēles ingvera saknes

30 ml/2 ēdamkarotes ūdens

5 ml/1 tējkarote zemesriekstu eļļas

2,5 ml/¬Ω tējkarote sāls

2,5 ml/¬Ω tējkarote rīsu vīna vai sausa šerija

Liek zivis uz karstumizturīga šķīvja un pārkaisa ar pārējām sastāvdaļām. Liek uz restēm tvaikonī, vāku un vāra uz lēnas uguns apmēram 15 minūtes virs verdoša ūdens, līdz zivs ir mīksta. Pārlieciet uz sasildīta šķīvja, izmetiet ingveru un lociņus un pasniedziet.

Menca ar ingvera garšvielām

Pasniedz 4

225 g/8 unces tomātu biezenis (pasta)

30 ml/2 ēdamkarotes rīsu vīna vai sausā šerija

15 ml/1 ēdamkarote rīvētas ingvera saknes

15 ml/1 ēdamkarote čili mērces

15 ml/1 ēdamkarote ūdens

15 ml/1 ēdamkarote sojas mērces

10 ml/2 tējk cukurs

3 ķiploka daiviņas, sasmalcinātas

100 g/4 unces/1 glāze vienkāršu (universālu) miltu

75 ml/5 ēdamkarotes kukurūzas miltu (kukurūzas ciete)

175 ml / 6 fl oz / ¬œ tase ūdens

1 olas baltums

2,5 ml/¬Ω tējkarote sāls

eļļa dziļai cepšanai

450 g/1 mārciņa mencas fileja, nomizota un sagriezta kubiņos

Lai pagatavotu mērci, sajauciet tomātu biezeni, vīnu vai šeriju,
ingveru, čili mērci, ūdeni, sojas mērci, cukuru un ķiplokus.
Uzkarsē līdz vārīšanās temperatūrai, tad maisot vāra 4 minūtes.

Saputojiet miltus, kukurūzas miltus, ūdeni, olu baltumu un sāli līdz gludai. Uzkarsē eļļu. Iemērciet zivju gabalus mīklā un apcepiet apmēram 5 minūtes, līdz tie ir gatavi un zeltaini brūni. Nokāš uz virtuves papīra. Nolejiet visu eļļu un ieliec iet zivis un mērci atpakaļ pannā. Viegli karsējiet apmēram 3 minūtes, līdz zivs ir pilnībā pārklāta ar mērci.

Menca ar mandarīnu mērci

Pasniedz 4

675 g/1¬Ω lb mencas fileja, sagriezta strēmelēs

30 ml/2 ēdamkarotes kukurūzas miltu (kukurūzas ciete)

60 ml/4 ēdamkarotes zemesriekstu eļļas

1 lociņš, sasmalcināts

2 ķiploka daiviņas, sasmalcinātas

1 šķēle ingvera saknes, sasmalcināta

100g/4oz sēnes, sagrieztas

50g/2oz bambusa dzinumi, sagriezti sloksnēs

120 ml / 4 fl oz / ¬Ω tase sojas mērces

30 ml/2 ēdamkarotes rīsu vīna vai sausā šerija

15 ml/1 ēdamkarote brūnā cukura

5 ml/1 tējkarote sāls

250 ml / 8 fl oz / 1 tase vistas buljona

Iemērciet zivis kukurūzas miltos, līdz tās ir viegli pārklātas. Uzkarsē eļļu un apcep zivis no abām pusēm līdz zeltaini brūnai. Noņemiet to no pannas. Pievienojiet sīpolus, ķiplokus un ingveru un apcepiet, līdz tie ir viegli brūni. Pievienojiet sēnes un bambusa dzinumus un maisot apcepiet 2 minūtes. Pievieno pārējās sastāvdaļas un uzvāra

29

maisot uzvāra. Liek zivis atpakaļ uz pannas, uzliek vāku un vāra uz lēnas uguns 20 minūtes.

Zivis ar ananāsiem

Pasniedz 4

450 g/1 mārciņa zivju fileja

2 lociņi, sasmalcināti

30 ml/2 ēdamkarotes sojas mērces

15 ml/1 ēdamkarote rīsu vīna vai sausā šerija

2,5 ml/¬Ω tējkarote sāls

2 olas, viegli sakultas

15 ml/1 ēdamkarote kukurūzas miltu (kukurūzas ciete)

45 ml/3 ēdamkarotes zemesriekstu eļļas

225 g/8 unces konservētu ananāsu gabaliņi sulā

Sagrieziet zivis 2,5 cm/1 sloksnēs pāri graudiem un ievietojiet bļodā. Pievienojiet sīpolus, sojas mērci, vīnu vai šeriju un sāli, labi samaisiet un ļaujiet nostāvēties 30 minūtes. Nosusiniet zivis, izmetiet marinādi. Sakuļ olas un kukurūzas miltus mīklā un iemērciet zivis mīklā, lai tās pārklātu, notecinot lieko. Uzkarsē eļļu un apcep zivis no abām pusēm, līdz tās ir viegli brūnas. Samaziniet siltumu un turpiniet gatavot, līdz tas ir mīksts. Tikmēr sajauciet 60 ml/4 ēdamkarotes ananāsu sulas ar atlikušo mīklu un ananāsu gabaliņiem. Liek pannā uz mazas uguns un vāra, nepārtraukti maisot, līdz uzkarsē. Sakārtot pagatavotas zivis uz sasildīta servēšanas šķīvja un pārlej ar mērci, lai pasniegtu.

Zivju rullīši ar cūkgaļu

Pasniedz 4

450 g/1 mārciņa zivju fileja

100 g / 4 unces vārīta cūkgaļa, malta (malta)

30 ml/2 ēdamkarotes rīsu vīna vai sausā šerija

15 ml/1 ēdamkarote cukura

eļļa dziļai cepšanai

120 ml / 4 fl oz / ¬Ω tase zivju buljona

3 lociņi, sasmalcināti

1 šķēle ingvera saknes, sasmalcināta

15 ml/1 ēdamkarote sojas mērces

15 ml/1 ēdamkarote kukurūzas miltu (kukurūzas ciete)

45 ml / 3 ēdamkarotes ūdens

Sagrieziet zivis 9 cm/3¬Ω kvadrātos. Sajauc cūkgaļu ar vīnu vai šeriju un pusi cukura, izklāj uz zivju kvadrātiem, sarullē un nostiprina ar auklu. Uzkarsē eļļu un apcep zivis līdz zeltaini brūnai. Nokāš uz virtuves papīra. Tikmēr uzkarsē buljonu un pievieno sīpolus, ingveru, sojas mērci un atlikušo cukuru. Uzkarsē līdz vārīšanās temperatūrai un vāra uz lēnas uguns 4 minūtes. Sajauc kukurūzas miltus un ūdeni līdz viendabīgai masai, ielej pannā un uz lēnas uguns vāra.

maisot, līdz mērce kļūst dzidra un sabiezē. Pārlej zivi un pasniedz uzreiz.

Zivis rīsu vīnā

Pasniedz 4

400 ml / 14 fl unces / 1¬œ tases rīsu vīna vai sausā šerija

120 ml / 4 fl unces / ¬Ω tase ūdens

30 ml/2 ēdamkarotes sojas mērces

5 ml/1 tējk cukurs

sāls un svaigi malti pipari

10 ml / 2 tējkarotes kukurūzas miltu (kukurūzas ciete)

15 ml/1 ēdamkarote ūdens

450 g/1 mārciņa mencas fileja

5 ml/1 tējkarote sezama eļļas

2 lociņi, sasmalcināti

Vīnu, ūdeni, sojas mērci, cukuru, sāli un piparus uzvāra un vāra, līdz tas samazinās uz pusi. Kukurūzas miltus sajauc ar ūdeni, pievieno pannā un maisot vāra uz lēnas uguns 2 minūtes. Garšojiet zivis ar sāli un apslakiet ar sezama eļļu. Pievienojiet pannai un ļoti maigi sautējiet apmēram 8 minūtes, līdz tas ir gatavs. Pasniedz ar sīpoliem.

Ātri cepta zivs

Pasniedz 4

450 g/1 mārciņa mencas filejas, sagrieztas strēmelēs

sāls

sojas mērce

eļļa dziļai cepšanai

Apkaisiet zivis ar sāli un sojas mērci un ļaujiet tai nostāvēties 10 minūtes. Uzkarsē eļļu un apcep zivis dažas minūtes, līdz tās kļūst gaiši zeltainas. Nokāš uz virtuves papīra un pirms pasniegšanas bagātīgi pārlej ar sojas mērci.

Sezama sēklu zivs

Pasniedz 4

450 g/1 mārciņa zivju filejas, sagrieztas strēmelēs

1 sīpols, sasmalcināts

2 šķēles ingvera saknes, sasmalcinātas

120 ml/4 fl oz/¬Ω tase rīsu vīna vai sausā šerija

10 ml/2 tējk brūnā cukura

2,5 ml/¬Ω tējkarote sāls

1 ola, viegli sakulta

15 ml/1 ēdamkarote kukurūzas miltu (kukurūzas ciete)

45 ml/3 ēdamkarotes vienkāršu (universālu) miltu

60 ml/6 ēdamkarotes sezama sēklu

eļļa dziļai cepšanai

Ielieciet zivis bļodā. Sajauc sīpolu, ingveru, vīnu vai šeriju, cukuru un sāli, pievieno zivīm un ļauj marinēties 30 minūtes, ik pa laikam apgriežot. Sakuļ olu, kukurūzas miltus un miltus, lai izveidotu mīklu. Iemērciet zivis mīklā, pēc tam iespiediet sezama sēklas. Uzkarsē eļļu un cep zivju strēmelītes apmēram 1 minūti, līdz tās kļūst zeltainas un kraukšķīgas.

Tvaicētas zivju bumbiņas

Pasniedz 4

450 g/1 mārciņa malta (malta) menca

1 ola, viegli sakulta

1 šķēle ingvera saknes, sasmalcināta

2,5 ml/¬Ω tējkarote sāls

šķipsniņa svaigi maltu piparu

15 ml/1 ēd.k. kukurūzas milti (kukurūzas ciete) 15 ml/1 ēd.k. rīsu

vīns vai sausais šerijs

Visas sastāvdaļas labi samaisa un veido valrieksta lieluma bumbiņas. Ja nepieciešams, apkaisa ar nedaudz miltiem. Liek seklā cepeškrāsns necaurlaidīgā traukā.

Novietojiet trauku uz grila tvaicētājā, pārklājiet un vāriet uz lēnas uguns uz lēnas uguns apmēram 10 minūtes, līdz tas ir gatavs.

Marinētas saldskābās zivis

Pasniedz 4

450 g/1 mārciņa zivju filejas, sagrieztas gabalos

1 sīpols, sasmalcināts

3 šķēles ingvera saknes, sasmalcinātas

5 ml/1 tējk sojas mērce

sāls un svaigi malti pipari

30 ml/2 ēdamkarotes kukurūzas miltu (kukurūzas ciete)

eļļa dziļai cepšanai

saldskābo mērci

Ielieciet zivis bļodā. Sajauc sīpolu, ingveru, sojas mērci, sāli un piparus, pievieno zivīm, pārklāj un ļauj nostāvēties 1 stundu, ik pa laikam apgriežot. Izņem zivis no marinādes un pārkaisa ar kukurūzas miltiem. Uzkarsē eļļu un apcep zivis līdz kraukšķīgai un zeltaini brūnai. Nokāš uz virtuves papīra un liek uz sasildīta servēšanas šķīvja. Tikmēr pagatavo mērci un pārlej zivij, lai pasniegtu.

Zivis ar etiķa mērci

Pasniedz 4

450 g/1 mārciņa zivju filejas, sagrieztas strēmelēs

sāls un svaigi malti pipari

1 olas baltums, viegli saputots

45 ml/3 ēdamkarotes kukurūzas miltu (kukurūzas ciete)

15 ml/1 ēdamkarote rīsu vīna vai sausā šerija

eļļa dziļai cepšanai

250 ml / 8 fl oz / 1 glāze zivju buljona

15 ml/1 ēdamkarote brūnā cukura

15 ml/1 ēdamkarote vīna etiķa

2 šķēles ingvera saknes, sasmalcinātas

2 lociņi, sasmalcināti

Garšojiet zivis ar nedaudz sāli un pipariem. Saputo olu baltumus ar 30 ml/2 ēdamk. kukurūzas miltiem un vīnu vai šeriju. Iemērciet zivis mīklā, līdz tās ir pārklātas. Uzkarsē eļļu un apcep zivis dažas minūtes līdz zeltaini brūnai. Nokāš uz virtuves papīra.

Tikmēr uzvāra buljonu, cukuru un vīna etiķi. Pievienojiet ingveru un sīpolu un sautējiet 3 minūtes. Atlikušos kukurūzas miltus samaļ ar nedaudz ūdens un samaisa

uz pannas un maisot vāra, līdz mērce ir dzidra un sabiezējusi.
Pasniedz virs zivīm.

Cepts zutis

Pasniedz 4

450g/1lb zutis

250 ml / 8 fl oz / 1 tase zemesriekstu (zemesriekstu) eļļas

30 ml/2 ēd.k. tumšās sojas mērces

30 ml/2 ēdamkarotes rīsu vīna vai sausā šerija

15 ml/1 ēdamkarote brūnā cukura

šķipsniņa sezama eļļas

Nomizo zuti un sagriež gabaliņos. Uzkarsē eļļu un apcep zuti līdz zeltainam. Izņem no pannas un notecina. Nolejiet visu eļļu, izņemot 30 ml/2 ēdamkarotes. Uzkarsē eļļu un pievieno sojas mērci, vīnu vai šeriju un cukuru. Uzkarsē, tad pievieno zuti un maisot vāra, līdz zutis ir labi pārklāts un lielākā daļa šķidruma iztvaikojusi. Apslaka ar sezama eļļu un pasniedz.

Sauss vārīts zutis

Pasniedz 4

5 kaltētas ķīniešu sēnes

3 lociņi (sīpoli)

30 ml/2 ēdamkarotes zemesriekstu eļļas

20 ķiploka daiviņas

6 šķēles ingvera saknes

10 ūdens kastaņi

900g/2lb zutis

30 ml/2 ēdamkarotes sojas mērces

15 ml/1 ēdamkarote brūnā cukura

15 ml/1 ēdamkarote rīsu vīna vai sausā šerija

450 ml/¬œ pt/2 tases ūdens

15 ml/1 ēdamkarote kukurūzas miltu (kukurūzas ciete)

45 ml / 3 ēdamkarotes ūdens

5 ml/1 tējkarote sezama eļļas

30 minūtes iemērciet sēnes siltā ūdenī, pēc tam noteciniet un izmetiet stublājus. 1 sīpolu sagriež gabaliņos un otru sasmalcina. Uzkarsē eļļu un apcep sēnes, sīpolu gabaliņus, ķiplokus, ingveru un kastaņus 30 sekundes. Pievieno zušus un maisot cep 1 minūti. Pievieno sojas mērci, cukuru, vīnu vai

šeriju un ūdeni, uzvāra, uzliek vāku un vāra uz lēnas uguns 1¬Ω stundas, gatavošanas laikā pēc vajadzības pievienojot nedaudz ūdens. Kukurūzas miltus un ūdeni samaisa biezenī, pievieno pannā un maisot vāra uz lēnas uguns, līdz mērce sabiezē. Pasniedziet pārslakātus ar sezama eļļu un sasmalcinātiem sīpoliem.

Zutis ar seleriju

Pasniedz 4

350 g / 12 unces zutis

6 selerijas kāti

30 ml/2 ēdamkarotes zemesriekstu eļļas

2 lociņi, sasmalcināti

1 šķēle ingvera saknes, sasmalcināta

30 ml/2 ēdamkarotes ūdens

5 ml/1 tējk cukurs

5 ml/1 tējkarote rīsu vīna vai sausā šerija

5 ml/1 tējk sojas mērce

svaigi malti pipari

30 ml/2 ēdamkarotes sasmalcinātu svaigu pētersīļu

Nomizo zuti un sagriež strēmelītēs. Selerijas sagriež strēmelītēs. Uzkarsē eļļu un apcep sīpolus un ingveru 30 sekundes. Pievieno zuti un maisot apcep 30 sekundes. Pievienojiet seleriju un maisot apcepiet 30 sekundes. Pievienojiet pusi ūdens, cukuru, vīnu vai šeriju, sojas mērci un piparus. Uzkarsē līdz vārīšanās temperatūrai un vāra uz lēnas uguns dažas minūtes, līdz selerijas ir mīkstas, bet joprojām kraukšķīgas un šķidrums ir samazinājies. Pasniedz pārkaisītu ar pētersīļiem.

Ar pikšu pildītie pipari

Pasniedz 4

225 g pikšas fileja, malta (malta)

100 g / 4 unces mizotas garneles, maltas (maltas)

1 lociņš, sasmalcināts

2,5 ml/¬Ω tējkarote sāls

pipari

4 zaļie pipari

45 ml/3 ēdamkarotes zemesriekstu eļļas

120 ml / 4 fl unces / ¬Ω tase vistas buljona

10 ml / 2 tējkarotes kukurūzas miltu (kukurūzas ciete)

5 ml/1 tējk sojas mērce

Sajauc pikšas, garneles, sīpolus, sāli un piparus. Nogrieziet
piparam kātu un izņemiet vidu. Piepildiet piparus ar jūras velšu
maisījumu. Uzkarsē eļļu un pievieno piparus un buljonu. Uzkarsē
līdz vārīšanās temperatūrai, uzliek vāku un vāra uz lēnas uguns
15 minūtes. Pārliek papriku uz sasildīta pasniegšanas šķīvja.
Sajauc kukurūzas miltus, sojas mērci un nedaudz ūdens un
iemaisa pannā. Uzkarsē līdz vārīšanās temperatūrai un maisot
vāra uz lēnas uguns, līdz mērce ir dzidra un sabiezējusi.

Pikša melno pupiņu mērcē

Pasniedz 4

15 ml/1 ēdamkarote zemesriekstu eļļas

2 ķiploka daiviņas, sasmalcinātas

1 šķēle ingvera saknes, sasmalcināta

15 ml/1 ēdamkarote melno pupiņu mērces

2 sīpoli, sagriezti

1 selerijas nūjiņa, sasmalcināta

450 g pikšas filejas

15 ml/1 ēdamkarote sojas mērces

15 ml/1 ēdamkarote rīsu vīna vai sausā šerija

250 ml / 8 fl oz / 1 tase vistas buljona

Uzkarsē eļļu un apcep ķiploku, ingvera un melno pupiņu mērci, līdz tie ir viegli brūni. Pievienojiet sīpolus un seleriju un maisot apcepiet 2 minūtes. Pievienojiet pikšu un cepiet apmēram 4 minūtes no katras puses vai līdz zivs ir gatava. Pievieno sojas mērci, vīnu vai šeriju un vistas buljonu, uzvāra, uzliek vāku un vāra uz lēnas uguns 3 minūtes.

Zivis brūnajā mērcē

Pasniedz 4

4 pikšas vai līdzīgas zivis

45 ml/3 ēdamkarotes zemesriekstu eļļas

2 lociņi, sasmalcināti

2 šķēles ingvera saknes, sasmalcinātas

5 ml/1 tējk sojas mērce

2,5 ml/¬Ω tējkarote vīna etiķa

2,5 ml/¬Ω tējkarote rīsu vīna vai sausa šerija

2,5 ml/¬Ω tējkarote cukura

svaigi malti pipari

2,5 ml/¬Ω tējkarote sezama eļļas

Nogrieziet zivis un sagrieziet to lielos gabaliņos. Uzkarsē eļļu un apcep sīpolus un ingveru 30 sekundes. Pievienojiet zivis un cepiet, līdz tās ir viegli brūnas no abām pusēm. Pievienojiet sojas mērci, vīna etiķi, vīnu vai šeriju, cukuru un piparus un vāriet uz lēnas uguns 5 minūtes, līdz mērce sabiezē. Pasniedz, pārslaka ar sezama eļļu.

Piecu garšvielu zivs

Pasniedz 4

450 g pikšas filejas

5 ml/1 tējk piecu garšvielu pulveris

5 ml/1 tējkarote sāls

30 ml/2 ēdamkarotes zemesriekstu eļļas

2 ķiploka daiviņas, sasmalcinātas

2 šķēles ingvera saknes, sasmalcinātas

30 ml/2 ēdamkarotes rīsu vīna vai sausā šerija

15 ml/1 ēdamkarote sojas mērces

10 ml/2 tējk sezama eļļa

Pikšas fileju ierīvē ar piecu garšvielu pulveri un sāli. Uzkarsē eļļu un apcep zivis no abām pusēm, līdz tās ir viegli brūnas, tad izņemam no pannas. Pievienojiet ķiplokus, ingveru, vīnu vai šeriju, sojas mērci un sezama eļļu un apcepiet 1 minūti. Liek zivis atpakaļ uz pannas un lēni vāra, līdz zivs ir mīksta.

Pikša ar ķiploku

Pasniedz 4

450 g pikšas filejas

5 ml/1 tējkarote sāls

30 ml/2 ēdamkarotes kukurūzas miltu (kukurūzas ciete)

60 ml/4 ēdamkarotes zemesriekstu eļļas

6 ķiploka daiviņas

2 šķēles ingvera saknes, sasmalcinātas

45 ml / 3 ēdamkarotes ūdens

30 ml/2 ēdamkarotes sojas mērces

15 ml/1 ēdamkarote dzelteno pupiņu mērces

15 ml/1 ēdamkarote rīsu vīna vai sausā šerija

15 ml/1 ēdamkarote brūnā cukura

Apkaisa pikšu ar sāli un pārkaisa ar kukurūzas miltiem. Uzkarsē eļļu un apcep zivis no abām pusēm līdz zeltaini brūnai, tad izņem no pannas. Pievienojiet ķiplokus un ingveru un vāriet 1 minūti. Pievieno pārējās sastāvdaļas, uzvāra, uzliek vāku un vāra uz lēnas uguns 5 minūtes. Liek zivis atpakaļ uz pannas, pārklāj un vāra uz lēnas uguns, līdz tās ir mīkstas.

Zivis ar pikantām garšvielām

Pasniedz 4

450 g pikšas filejas, sagriezta kubiņos

1 citrona sula

30 ml/2 ēdamkarotes sojas mērces

30 ml/2 ēdamkarotes austeru mērces

15 ml/1 ēdamkarote rīvētas citrona miziņas

šķipsniņa malta ingvera

sāls un pipari

2 olu baltumi

45 ml/3 ēdamkarotes kukurūzas miltu (kukurūzas ciete)

6 kaltētas ķīniešu sēnes

eļļa dziļai cepšanai

5 lociņi, sagriezti sloksnēs

1 selerijas nūjiņa, sagriezta strēmelēs

100g/4oz bambusa dzinumi, sagriezti sloksnēs

250 ml / 8 fl oz / 1 tase vistas buljona

5 ml/1 tējk piecu garšvielu pulveris

Ielieciet zivis bļodā un apkaisa ar citronu sulu. Sajauc kopā sojas mērci, austeru mērci, citrona miziņu, ingveru, sāli, piparus, olu baltumus un visu kukurūzas miltu, izņemot 5 ml/1 tējkaroti.

aiziet

marinē 2 stundas, ik pa laikam apmaisot. Sēnes 30 minūtes iemērc siltā ūdenī, pēc tam nokāš. Izmetiet kātus un nogrieziet vāciņus. Uzkarsē eļļu un apcep zivis dažas minūtes, līdz tās kļūst zeltainas. Izņem no pannas. Pievienojiet dārzeņus un vāriet, līdz tie ir mīksti, bet joprojām kraukšķīgi. Izlejiet eļļu. Vistas buljonu sajauc ar atlikušajiem kukurūzas miltiem, ielej to dārzeņos un uzvāra. Liek zivis atpakaļ uz pannas, apkaisa ar piecu garšvielu pulveri un pirms pasniegšanas uzkarsē.

Ingvera pikša ar Pak Soi

Pasniedz 4

450 g/1 mārciņa pikšas filejas

sāls un pipari

225g/8oz pak soi

30 ml/2 ēdamkarotes zemesriekstu eļļas

1 šķēle ingvera saknes, sasmalcināta

1 sīpols, sasmalcināts

2 kaltēti sarkanie čili pipari

5 ml/1 tējkarote medus

10 ml/2 tējk tomātu kečups (catsup)

10 ml/2 tējk iesala etiķis

30 ml/2 ēdamkarotes sausā baltvīna

10 ml/2 tējk sojas mērce

10 ml/2 tējk zivju mērce

10 ml/2 tējk austeru mērce

5 ml/1 tējkarote garneļu pastas

Mencai nomizojiet ādu, pēc tam sagrieziet to 2 cm/¬æ gabaliņos.
Pārkaisa ar sāli un pipariem. Kāpostus sagriež mazos gabaliņos.
Uzkarsē eļļu un apcep ingveru un sīpolu 1 minūti. Pievienojiet

53

kāpostus un čili un apcepiet 30 sekundes. Pievieno medu, tomātus

kečups, etiķis un vīns. Pievienojiet pikšu un vāriet uz lēnas uguns 2 minūtes. Iemaisa sojas, zivju un austeru mērces un garneļu pastu un viegli sautē, līdz pikša ir gatava.

Melni plankumi pazudīs

Pasniedz 4

450 g/1 mārciņa pikšas filejas, nodīrātas

sāls

5 ml/1 tējk piecu garšvielu pulveris

2 citronu sula

5 ml/1 tējkarote anīsa, malta

5 ml/1 tējk svaigi malti pipari

30 ml/2 ēdamkarotes sojas mērces

30 ml/2 ēdamkarotes austeru mērces

15 ml/1 ēdamkarote medus

60 ml/4 ēdamkarotes malta ķiploka

8-10 spinātu lapas

45 ml/3 ēdamkarotes vīna etiķa

Zivi sagriež garās plānās strēmelītēs un veido bizītes, pārkaisa ar sāli, piecu garšvielu pulveri un citrona sulu un lej bļodā. Sajauc anīsu, piparus, sojas mērci, austeru mērci, medu un maurlokus, pārlej zivīm un ļauj marinēties vismaz 30 minūtes. Izklājiet tvaicētāja grozu ar spinātu lapām, uzlieciet bizes uz augšu, pārklājiet un vāriet viegli verdošā ūdenī ar etiķi apmēram 25 minūtes.

Tvaicēti zivju ruļļi

Pasniedz 4

450 g/1 mārciņa pikšas filejas, nomizotas un sagrieztas kubiņos

1 citrona sula

30 ml/2 ēdamkarotes sojas mērces

30 ml/2 ēdamkarotes austeru mērces

30 ml/2 ēdamkarotes plūmju mērces

5 ml/1 tējkarote rīsu vīna vai sausā šerija

sāls un pipari

6 kaltētas ķīniešu sēnes

100 g/4 unces pupiņu asni

100 g/4 unces zaļie zirnīši

50 g/2 unces/¬Ω glāze valriekstu, sasmalcināti

1 ola, sakulta

30 ml/2 ēdamkarotes kukurūzas miltu (kukurūzas ciete)

225g/8oz Ķīnas kāposti, blanšēti

Ielieciet zivis bļodā. Sajauc citronu sulu, sojas, austeru un plūmju mērces, vīnu vai šeriju, sāli un piparus. Pārlej zivīm un ļauj marinēties 30 minūtes. Pievienojiet dārzeņus, riekstus, olu un kukurūzas miltus un labi samaisiet. Novietojiet 3 ķīniešu lapas vienu virs otras, ar karoti uzlieciet kādu zivju maisījumu un vērpjot. Turpiniet, līdz ir izlietotas visas sastāvdaļas. Ievietojiet ruļļus tvaicētāja grozā, pārklājiet un vāriet uz lēnas uguns 30 minūtes.

Paltuss ar tomātu mērci

Pasniedz 4

450 g paltusa filejas

sāls

15 ml/1 ēdamkarote melno pupiņu mērces

1 ķiploka daiviņa, sasmalcināta

2 lociņi, sasmalcināti

2 šķēles ingvera saknes, sasmalcinātas

15 ml/1 ēdamkarote rīsu vīna vai sausā šerija

15 ml/1 ēdamkarote sojas mērces

200g/7oz konservētu tomātu, nosusināti

30 ml/2 ēdamkarotes zemesriekstu eļļas

Otus bagātīgi apkaisa ar sāli un atstāj uz 1 stundu. Nomazgājiet sāli un nosusiniet. Ievietojiet zivis cepeškrāsnī necaurlaidīgā bļodā un samaisiet ar melno pupiņu mērci, ķiplokiem, sīpoliem, ingveru, vīnu vai šeriju, sojas mērci un tomātiem. Novietojiet bļodu uz grila tvaicētājā, pārklājiet un vāriet 20 minūtes virs verdoša ūdens, līdz zivs ir gatava. Uzkarsē eļļu līdz gandrīz kūpināšanai un pirms pasniegšanas pārlej zivīm.

Jūras velnis ar brokoļiem

Pasniedz 4

450 g/1 mārciņa jūrasvelnu aste, kubiņos

sāls un pipari

45 ml/3 ēdamkarotes zemesriekstu eļļas

50g/2oz sēnes, sagrieztas

1 mazs burkāns, sagriezts sloksnēs

1 ķiploka daiviņa, sasmalcināta

2 šķēles ingvera saknes, sasmalcinātas

45 ml / 3 ēdamkarotes ūdens

275g/10oz brokoļu ziediņi

5 ml/1 tējk cukurs

5 ml/1 tējk kukurūzas milti (kukurūzas ciete)

45 ml / 3 ēdamkarotes ūdens

Jūras velni labi apkaisa ar sāli un pipariem. Uzkarsē 30 ml/2 ēdamkarotes eļļas un apcep jūrasvelnu, sēnes, burkānus, ķiplokus un ingveru, līdz tie ir viegli brūni. Pielej ūdeni un turpina vārīt bez vāka uz mazas uguns. Tikmēr blanšējiet brokoļus verdošā ūdenī, līdz tie kļūst mīksti, pēc tam labi noteciniet. Uzkarsē atlikušo eļļu un maisot apcep brokoļus un cukuru ar šķipsniņu sāls, līdz brokoļi ir kārtīgi pārklāti eļļā. Kārto ap sasildīto pasniegšanas šķīvis. Kukurūzas miltus un ūdeni samaisa līdz biezenim, pievieno zivīm un maisot cep, līdz mērce sabiezē. Pārlej ar brokoļiem un pasniedz uzreiz.

Kefales ar biezu sojas mērci

Pasniedz 4

1 sarkanā kefale

eļļa dziļai cepšanai

30 ml/2 ēdamkarotes zemesriekstu eļļas

2 lociņi, sagriezti šķēlēs

2 šķēles ingvera saknes, sasmalcinātas

1 sarkanais čili pipars, sasmalcināts

250 ml / 8 fl oz / 1 glāze zivju buljona

15 ml/1 ēdamkarote biezas sojas mērces

15 ml/1 ēdamkarote svaigi malta balta

pipari

15 ml/1 ēdamkarote rīsu vīna vai sausā šerija

Izgrieziet zivis pa diagonāli no abām pusēm. Sildiet eļļu un apcepiet zivis līdz pusei. Izņem no eļļas un labi notecina.

Uzkarsē eļļu un apcep sīpolus, ingveru un čili piparus 1 minūti.

Pievienojiet pārējās sastāvdaļas, labi samaisiet un uzvāra.

Pievieno zivi un vāra uz lēnas uguns, bez vāka, līdz zivs ir gatava un šķidrums gandrīz iztvaikojis.

Pasniedz 4

1 kefale

30 ml/2 ēdamkarotes zemesriekstu eļļas

4 lociņi, sasmalcināti

1 sarkanais čili pipars, sasmalcināts

4 ingvera saknes šķēles, sasmalcinātas

45 ml/3 ēdamkarotes brūnā cukura

30 ml/2 ēdamkarotes sarkanvīna etiķa

30 ml/2 ēdamkarotes ūdens

30 ml/2 ēdamkarotes sojas mērces

svaigi malti pipari

Notīriet un sagrieziet zivis un veiciet 2 vai 3 iegriezumus pa diagonāli katrā pusē. Uzkarsē eļļu un maisot apcep pusi sīpolu, čili un ingveru 30 sekundes. Pievienojiet zivis un cepiet, līdz tās ir viegli brūnas no abām pusēm. Pievieno cukuru, vīna etiķi, ūdeni, sojas mērci un piparus, uzvāra, uzliek vāku un vāra uz lēnas uguns apmēram 20 minūtes, līdz zivs ir gatava un mērce ir samazinājusies. Pasniedz, dekorējot ar atlikušajiem sīpoliem.

Cepta plekste

Pasniedz 4

4 plekstes filejas
sāls un svaigi malti pipari
30 ml/2 ēdamkarotes zemesriekstu eļļas
1 šķēle ingvera saknes, sasmalcināta
1 ķiploka daiviņa, sasmalcināta
salātu lapas

Apkaisiet pleksti ar sāli un pipariem. Uzkarsē eļļu un apcep ingveru un ķiplokus 20 sekundes. Pievienojiet zivis un vāriet, līdz tās ir gatavas un zeltaini brūnas. Labi nokāš un pasniedz uz salātu gultas.

Tvaicēta plekste ar ķīniešu sēnēm

Pasniedz 4

4 žāvētas ķīniešu sēnes

450 g/1 mārciņa butes filejas, kubiņos

1 ķiploka daiviņa, sasmalcināta

1 šķēle ingvera saknes, sasmalcināta

15 ml/1 ēdamkarote sojas mērces

15 ml/1 ēdamkarote rīsu vīna vai sausā šerija

5 ml/1 tējkarote brūnā cukura

350g/12oz vārīti garengraudu rīsi

Sēnes 30 minūtes iemērc siltā ūdenī, pēc tam nokāš. Izmetiet kātus un nogrieziet vāciņus. Sajauc ar butēm, ķiplokiem, ingveru, sojas mērci, vīnu vai šeriju un cukuru, uzliek vāku un atstāj marinēties 1 stundu. Ievietojiet rīsus tvaika katlā un uzlieciet zivis. Tvaicējiet apmēram 30 minūtes, līdz zivs ir gatava.

Butes ar ķiploku

Pasniedz 4

350g/12oz plekstes fileja

sāls

45 ml/3 ēdamkarotes kukurūzas miltu (kukurūzas ciete)

1 ola, sakulta

60 ml/4 ēdamkarotes zemesriekstu eļļas

3 ķiploka daiviņas, sasmalcinātas

4 lociņi, sasmalcināti

15 ml/1 ēdamkarote rīsu vīna vai sausā šerija

5 ml/1 tējkarote sezama eļļas

Butes nomizo un sagriež strēmelītēs. Apkaisa ar sāli un ļauj nostāvēties 20 minūtes. Apkaisiet zivis ar kukurūzas miltiem, pēc tam iemērciet olā. Uzkarsē eļļu un apcep zivju sloksnes apmēram 4 minūtes līdz zeltaini brūnai. Izņem no pannas un notecina uz virtuves papīra. Izlejiet no pannas visu eļļu, izņemot 5 ml/1 tējkaroti, un pievienojiet pārējās sastāvdaļas. Uzkarsē līdz vārīšanās temperatūrai, maisot, tad vāra uz lēnas uguns 3 minūtes. Pārlej zivi un pasniedz uzreiz.

Butes ar ananāsu mērci

Pasniedz 4

450 g/1 mārciņa plekstes filejas

5 ml/1 tējkarote sāls

30 ml/2 ēdamkarotes sojas mērces

200 g/7 unces konservētu ananāsu gabaliņi

2 olas, sakultas

100 g/4 unces/¬Ω tase kukurūzas miltu (kukurūzas ciete)

eļļa dziļai cepšanai

30 ml/2 ēdamkarotes ūdens

5 ml/1 tējkarote sezama eļļas

Butes sagriež strēmelītēs un liek bļodā. Apkaisa ar sāli, sojas
mērci un 30ml/2 ēd.k. ananāsu sulas un ļauj nostāvēties 10
minūtes. Sakuļ olas ar 45 ml/3 ēdamk. kukurūzas miltu līdz
mīklai un iemērc mīklā zivis. Uzkarsē eļļu un apcep zivis līdz
zeltaini brūnai. Nokāš uz kajēnas pipariem. Nelielā katliņā ielej
atlikušo ananāsu sulu. Sajauc 30 ml/2 ēd.k. kukurūzas miltus ar
ūdeni un iemaisa pannā. Uzkarsē līdz vārīšanās temperatūrai un
maisot vāra uz lēnas uguns, līdz sabiezē. Pievienojiet pusi
ananāsu gabaliņu un uzkarsējiet. Pirms pasniegšanas iemaisa
sezama eļļu. Novietojiet pagatavoto zivi uz sasildītās porcijas

šķīvi un izrotājiet ar rezervētu ananāsu. Pārlej ar karstu mērci un pasniedz nekavējoties.

Lasis ar tofu

Pasniedz 4

120 ml/4 fl oz/¬Ω tase zemesriekstu (zemesriekstu) eļļas

450 g/1 mārciņa kubiņos sagriezta tofu

2,5 ml/¬Ω tējkarote sezama eļļas

100g/4oz laša fileja, sasmalcināta

šķipsniņa čili mērces

250 ml / 8 fl oz / 1 glāze zivju buljona

15 ml/1 ēdamkarote kukurūzas miltu (kukurūzas ciete)

45 ml / 3 ēdamkarotes ūdens

2 lociņi, sasmalcināti

Uzkarsē eļļu un apcep tofu, līdz tas ir viegli brūns. Izņem no pannas. Uzkarsē eļļu un sezama eļļu un apcep laša un čili mērci 1 minūti. Pievienojiet buljonu, uzkarsē līdz vārīšanās temperatūrai, pēc tam atgrieziet tofu pannā. Viegli vāra bez vāka, līdz sastāvdaļas ir gatavas un šķidrums ir samazinājies. Sajauc kukurūzas miltus un ūdeni līdz pastai. Mazliet maisot un maisot vāra, līdz maisījums sabiezē. Jums var nebūt vajadzīga visa kukurūzas miltu pasta, ja esat ļāvis šķidrumam samazināties. Pārliek uz sasildīta servēšanas šķīvja un pārkaisa ar maurlokiem.

Cepta marinēta zivs

Pasniedz 4

450 g/1 mārciņa brētliņas vai citas mazas zivis, iztīrītas

3 šķēles ingvera saknes, sasmalcinātas

120 ml / 4 fl oz / ¬Ω tase sojas mērces

15 ml/1 ēdamkarote rīsu vīna vai sausā šerija

1 krustnagliņa zvaigžņu anīsa

eļļa dziļai cepšanai

15 ml/1 ēdamkarote sezama eļļas

Ielieciet zivis bļodā. Sajauc ingveru, sojas mērci, vīnu vai šeriju un anīsu, pārlej zivij un ļauj nostāvēties 1 stundu, ik pa laikam apgriežot. Nosusiniet zivis, izmetiet marinādi. Uzkarsē eļļu un pa daļām apcep zivis līdz kraukšķīgai un zeltaini brūnai. Nosusiniet uz virtuves papīra un pasniedziet, aplejotu ar sezama eļļu.

Forele ar burkāniem

Pasniedz 4

15 ml/1 ēdamkarote zemesriekstu eļļas
1 ķiploka daiviņa, sasmalcināta
1 šķēle ingvera saknes, sasmalcināta
4 foreles
2 burkāni, sagriezti strēmelēs
25 g/1 unce bambusa dzinumu, kas sagriezti sloksnēs
25 g/1 unce ūdens kastaņi, sagriezti sloksnēs
15 ml/1 ēdamkarote sojas mērces
15 ml/1 ēdamkarote rīsu vīna vai sausā šerija

Uzkarsē eļļu un apcep ķiplokus un ingveru, līdz tie ir viegli
brūni. Pievienojiet zivis, pārklājiet un vāriet, līdz zivs ir
necaurspīdīga. Pievienojiet burkānus, bambusa dzinumus,
kastaņus, sojas mērci un vīnu vai šeriju, viegli samaisiet,
pārklājiet un vāriet uz lēnas uguns apmēram 5 minūtes.

Cepta forele

Pasniedz 4

4 foreles, iztīrītas un ķidātas

2 olas, sakultas

50 g/2 unces/¬Ω glāzes vienkāršu (universālu) miltu

eļļa dziļai cepšanai

1 citrons, sagriezts šķēlēs

Vairākas reizes nogrieziet zivis pa diagonāli no abām pusēm.
Iemērciet sakultās olās, pēc tam pievienojiet miltus, lai tas
pilnībā pārklātu. Nokratiet lieko. Uzkarsē eļļu un cep zivis
apmēram 10-15 minūtes, līdz tās ir gatavas. Nokāš uz virtuves
papīra un pasniedz ar citronu.

Forele ar citronu mērci

Pasniedz 4

450 ml / ¬œ pt / 2 tases vistas buljona

5 cm/2 kvadrātveida citrona mizas gabals

150 ml / ¬° pt / bagātīga ¬Ω glāze citrona sulas

90 ml/6 ēdamkarotes brūnā cukura

2 ingvera saknes šķēles, sagrieztas strēmelēs

30 ml/2 ēdamkarotes kukurūzas miltu (kukurūzas ciete)

4 foreles

375 g/12 unces/3 glāzes vienkāršu (universālu) miltu

175 ml / 6 fl oz / ¬œ tase ūdens

eļļa dziļai cepšanai

2 olu baltumi

8 lociņi, plānās šķēlēs

Lai pagatavotu mērci, sajauc buljonu, citrona miziņu un sulu, cukuru un 5 minūtes. Noņem no uguns, izkāš un liek atpakaļ pannā. Kukurūzas miltus sajauc ar nedaudz ūdens, tad iemaisa pannā. Vāra uz lēnas uguns 5 minūtes, bieži maisot. Noņem no uguns un turi mērci siltu.

Zivi no abām pusēm viegli apkaisa ar miltiem. Atlikušos miltus saputo ar ūdeni un 10 ml/2 tējk eļļas līdz gludai. Saputo olu baltumus līdz stingrībai, bet ne sausai un iecilā mīklā. Uzkarsē atlikušo eļļu. Iemērciet zivis mīklā tā, lai tā būtu pilnībā pārklāta. Gatavojiet zivis apmēram 10 minūtes, vienu reizi apgriežot, līdz tās ir gatavas un zeltainas. Nokāš uz virtuves papīra. Novietojiet zivis uz sasildīta servēšanas šķīvja. Siltajā mērcē iemaisa sīpolus, pārlej zivi un pasniedz uzreiz.

Ķīnas tuncis

Pasniedz 4

30 ml/2 ēdamkarotes zemesriekstu eļļas

1 sīpols, sasmalcināts

200g/7oz konservēta tunča, nosusināta un sasmalcināta

2 selerijas kāti, sasmalcināti

100 g / 4 unces sēnes, sasmalcinātas

1 zaļā paprika, sasmalcināta

250 ml / 8 fl oz / 1 tase buljona

30 ml/2 ēdamkarotes sojas mērces

100g/4oz smalkas olu nūdeles

sāls

15 ml/1 ēdamkarote kukurūzas miltu (kukurūzas ciete)

45 ml / 3 ēdamkarotes ūdens

Uzkarsē eļļu un apcep sīpolus līdz mīkstam. Pievienojiet tunci un samaisiet, līdz tas ir labi pārklāts ar eļļu. Pievieno seleriju, sēnes, piparus un maisot apcep 2 minūtes. Pievieno buljonu un sojas mērci, uzvāra, uzliek vāku un vāra uz lēnas uguns 15 minūtes. Pa to laiku makaronus vāra verdošā sālītā ūdenī apmēram 5 minūtes, līdz tie ir mīksti, pēc tam kārtīgi nokāš un liek uz sasildītas porcijas.

plāksne. Kukurūzas miltus sajauc ar ūdeni, iemaisa maisījumu tunča mērcē un maisot vāra, līdz mērce kļūst dzidra un sabiezē.

Marinēti zivju steiki

Pasniedz 4

4 merlanga vai pikšas steiki

2 ķiploka daiviņas, sasmalcinātas

2 šķēles ingvera saknes, sasmalcinātas

3 lociņi, sasmalcināti

15 ml/1 ēdamkarote rīsu vīna vai sausā šerija

15 ml/1 ēdamkarote vīna etiķa

sāls un svaigi malti pipari

45 ml/3 ēdamkarotes zemesriekstu eļļas

Ielieciet zivis bļodā. Sajauc ķiplokus, ingveru, lociņus, vīnu vai šeriju, vīna etiķi, sāli un piparus, pārlej zivij, pārklāj un atstāj marinēties vairākas stundas. Izņem zivis no marinādes. Uzkarsē eļļu un apcep zivis no abām pusēm, līdz tās ir brūnas, tad izņemam no pannas. Ielejiet marinādi pannā, uzkarsē līdz vārīšanās temperatūrai, pēc tam ielieciet zivis atpakaļ pannā un vāriet uz lēnas uguns, līdz tās ir gatavas.

Garneles ar mandelēm

Pasniedz 4

100 g/4 unces mandeles

225g/8oz lielas nemizotas garneles

2 šķēles ingvera saknes, sasmalcinātas

15 ml/1 ēdamkarote kukurūzas miltu (kukurūzas ciete)

2,5 ml/¬Ω tējkarote sāls

30 ml/2 ēdamkarotes zemesriekstu eļļas

2 ķiploka daiviņas

2 selerijas kāti, sasmalcināti

5 ml/1 tējk sojas mērce

5 ml/1 tējkarote rīsu vīnu vai sausā šerija

30 ml/2 ēdamkarotes ūdens

Sausā pannā apgrauzdē mandeles, līdz tās ir viegli grauzdētas, pēc tam noliek malā. Garneles nomizo, atstāj astes un pārgriež uz pusēm gareniski līdz astei. Sajauc ar ingveru, kukurūzas miltiem un sāli. Sildiet eļļu un apcepiet ķiplokus, līdz tie ir viegli brūni, pēc tam izmetiet ķiplokus. Pievienojiet seleriju, sojas mērci, vīnu vai šeriju un ūdeni pannā un uzvāra. Pievienojiet garneles un maisot apcepiet, līdz tās uzkarsē. Pasniedz ar grauzdētām mandelēm.

Anīsa garneles

Pasniedz 4

45 ml/3 ēdamkarotes zemesriekstu eļļas

15 ml/1 ēdamkarote sojas mērces

5 ml/1 tējk cukurs

120 ml / 4 fl oz / ¬Ω tase zivju buljona

šķipsniņa malta anīsa

450 g/1 mārciņa nomizotas garneles

Uzkarsē eļļu, pievieno sojas mērci, cukuru, buljonu un anīsa sēklas un uzvāra. Pievienojiet garneles un sautējiet dažas minūtes, līdz tās ir sasilušas un mīkstas.

Garneles ar sparģeļiem

Pasniedz 4

450 g/1 mārciņa sparģeļi, sagriezti gabaliņos

45 ml/3 ēdamkarotes zemesriekstu eļļas

2 šķēles ingvera saknes, sasmalcinātas

15 ml/1 ēdamkarote sojas mērces

15 ml/1 ēdamkarote rīsu vīna vai sausā šerija

5 ml/1 tējk cukurs

2,5 ml/¬Ω tējkarote sāls

225 g/8 unces mizotas garneles

Sparģeļus 2 minūtes blanšē verdošā ūdenī, pēc tam labi nokāš. Uzkarsē eļļu un apcep ingveru dažas sekundes. Pievienojiet sparģeļus un samaisiet, līdz tie ir labi pārklāti ar eļļu. Pievieno sojas mērci, vīnu vai šeriju, cukuru un sāli un karsē. Pievienojiet garneles un maisiet uz lēnas uguns, līdz sparģeļi ir mīksti.

Garneles ar bekonu

Pasniedz 4

450 g/1 mārciņa lielas nemizotas garneles

100 g / 4 unces bekona

1 ola, viegli sakulta

2,5 ml/¬Ω tējkarote sāls

15 ml/1 ēdamkarote sojas mērces

50 g/2 unces/¬Ω tase kukurūzas miltu (kukurūzas ciete)

eļļa dziļai cepšanai

Nomizojiet garneles, atstājot astes neskartas. Pārgriež uz pusēm gareniski līdz astei. Sagrieziet bekonu mazos kvadrātiņos. Katras garneles centrā iespiež gabaliņu bekona un saspiež kopā abas puses. Sakuļ olu ar sāli un sojas mērci. Iemērciet garneles olā, pēc tam apkaisa ar kukurūzas miltiem. Uzkarsē eļļu un apcep garneles, līdz tās ir kraukšķīgas un zeltainas.

Garneļu bumbiņas

Pasniedz 4

3 kaltētas ķīniešu sēnes

450 g/1 mārciņa garneļu, smalki maltas

6 ūdens kastaņi, smalki samalti

1 sīpols (smalki sagriezts).

1 šķēle ingvera saknes, smalki samalta

sāls un svaigi malti pipari

2 olas, sakultas

15 ml/1 ēdamkarote kukurūzas miltu (kukurūzas ciete)

50 g/2 unces/¬Ω glāzes vienkāršu (universālu) miltu

zemesriekstu (zemesriekstu) eļļa cepšanai

Sēnes 30 minūtes iemērc siltā ūdenī, pēc tam nokāš. Izmetiet kātus un smalki sagrieziet vāciņus. Sajauc ar garnelēm, ūdens kastaņiem, sīpoliem un ingveru, pārkaisa ar sāli un pipariem. Sajauc 1 olu un 5 ml/1 tējkarotes kukurūzas miltu rullīti bumbiņās apmēram tējkarotes lielumā.

Sakuļ atlikušo olu, kukurūzas miltus un miltus un pievieno pietiekami daudz ūdens, lai izveidotu biezu, gludu mīklu. Sarullējiet bumbiņas mīklu Uzkarsē eļļu un apcep dažas minūtes līdz gaiši zeltaini brūnai.

Grilētas garneles

Pasniedz 4

450 g/1 mārciņa lielas nomizotas garneles

100 g / 4 unces bekona

225 g / 8 unces vistas aknas, sagrieztas kubiņos

1 ķiploka daiviņa, sasmalcināta

2 šķēles ingvera saknes, sasmalcinātas

30 ml/2 ēdamkarotes cukura

120 ml / 4 fl oz / ¬Ω tase sojas mērces

sāls un svaigi malti pipari

Nogrieziet garneles gar muguru, negriežot cauri, un nedaudz saplaciniet. Sagrieziet bekonu gabaliņos un pievienojiet bļodā ar garnelēm un vistas aknām. Sajauc pārējās sastāvdaļas, pārlej garnelēm un ļauj nostāvēties 30 minūtes. Uzvelciet garneles, bekonu un aknas uz iesmiem un grilējiet vai grilējiet apmēram 5 minūtes, bieži apgriežot, līdz tās ir gatavas, laiku pa laikam aplejot ar marinādi.

Garneles ar bambusa dzinumiem

Pasniedz 4

60 ml/4 ēdamkarotes zemesriekstu eļļas

1 ķiploka daiviņa, sasmalcināta

1 šķēle ingvera saknes, sasmalcināta

450 g/1 mārciņa nomizotas garneles

30 ml/2 ēdamkarotes rīsu vīna vai sausā šerija

225g/8oz bambusa dzinumi

30 ml/2 ēdamkarotes sojas mērces

15 ml/1 ēdamkarote kukurūzas miltu (kukurūzas ciete)

45 ml / 3 ēdamkarotes ūdens

Uzkarsē eļļu un apcep ķiplokus un ingveru, līdz tie ir viegli brūni. Pievieno garneles un maisot cep 1 minūti. Pievienojiet vīnu vai šeriju un labi samaisiet. Pievienojiet bambusa dzinumus un maisot apcepiet 5 minūtes. Pievieno pārējās sastāvdaļas un maisot cep 2 minūtes.

Garneles ar pupiņu kāpostiem

Pasniedz 4

4 žāvētas ķīniešu sēnes

30 ml/2 ēdamkarotes zemesriekstu eļļas

1 ķiploka daiviņa, sasmalcināta

225 g/8 unces mizotas garneles

15 ml/1 ēdamkarote rīsu vīna vai sausā šerija

450 g/1 mārciņa pupiņu asnu

120 ml / 4 fl unces / ¬Ω tase vistas buljona

15 ml/1 ēdamkarote sojas mērces

15 ml/1 ēdamkarote kukurūzas miltu (kukurūzas ciete)

sāls un svaigi malti pipari

2 lociņi, sasmalcināti

Sēnes 30 minūtes iemērc siltā ūdenī, pēc tam nokāš. Izmetiet kātus un nogrieziet vāciņus. Uzkarsē eļļu un apcep ķiplokus, līdz tie ir viegli brūni. Pievieno garneles un maisot cep 1 minūti. Pievienojiet vīnu vai šeriju un apcepiet 1 minūti. Iemaisa sēnes un pupiņu kāpostus. Apvienojiet buljonu, sojas mērci un kukurūzas miltus un samaisiet pannā. Uzkarsē līdz vārīšanās temperatūrai, tad maisot vāra, līdz mērce ir dzidra un sabiezējusi. Garšojiet ar sāli un pipariem pēc garšas. Pasniedz ar sīpoliem.

86

Garneles ar melno pupiņu mērci

Pasniedz 4

30 ml/2 ēdamkarotes zemesriekstu eļļas

5 ml/1 tējkarote sāls

1 ķiploka daiviņa, sasmalcināta

45 ml/3 ēdamkarotes melno pupiņu mērces

1 zaļā paprika, sasmalcināta

1 sīpols, sasmalcināts

120 ml / 4 fl oz / ¬Ω tase zivju buljona

5 ml/1 tējk cukurs

15 ml/1 ēdamkarote sojas mērces

225 g/8 unces mizotas garneles

15 ml/1 ēdamkarote kukurūzas miltu (kukurūzas ciete)

45 ml / 3 ēdamkarotes ūdens

Uzkarsē eļļu un maisot apcep sāli, ķiploku un melno pupiņu mērci 2 minūtes. Pievieno piparus un sīpolus un maisot apcep 2 minūtes. Pievieno buljonu, cukuru un sojas mērci un uzvāra. Pievienojiet garneles un sautējiet 2 minūtes. Kukurūzas miltus un ūdeni samaisa viendabīgā masā, lej pannā un maisot vāra, līdz mērce kļūst dzidra un sabiezē.

Garneles ar seleriju

Pasniedz 4

45 ml/3 ēdamkarotes zemesriekstu eļļas

3 šķēles ingvera saknes, sasmalcinātas

450 g/1 mārciņa nomizotas garneles

5 ml/1 tējkarote sāls

15 ml/1 ēdamkarote šerija

4 selerijas kāti, sasmalcināti

100 g/4 unces mandeles, sasmalcinātas

Uzkarsē pusi eļļas un apcep ingveru, līdz tas ir viegli brūns. Pievienojiet garneles, sāli un šeriju un apcepiet eļļā, līdz tās ir labi brūnas, pēc tam izņemiet no pannas. Uzkarsē atlikušo eļļu un maisot apcep selerijas un mandeles dažas minūtes, līdz selerijas ir mīkstas, bet joprojām kraukšķīgas. Atgrieziet garneles uz pannas, labi samaisiet un pirms pasniegšanas uzkarsējiet.

Ceptas garneles ar vistu

Pasniedz 4

30 ml/2 ēdamkarotes zemesriekstu eļļas

2 ķiploka daiviņas, sasmalcinātas

225 g / 8 unces vārīta vistas gaļa, plānās šķēlēs

100g/4oz bambusa dzinumi, sasmalcināti

100g/4oz sēnes, sagrieztas

75 ml/5 ēdamkarotes zivju buljona

225 g/8 unces mizotas garneles

225 g / 8 unces mangetout (sniega zirņi)

15 ml/1 ēdamkarote kukurūzas miltu (kukurūzas ciete)

45 ml / 3 ēdamkarotes ūdens

Uzkarsē eļļu un apcep ķiplokus, līdz tie ir viegli brūni.
Pievienojiet vistu, bambusa dzinumus un sēnes un apcepiet eļļā,
līdz tās ir labi brūnas. Ielej buljonu un uzvāra. Pievienojiet
garneles un mangetout, pārklājiet un vāriet uz lēnas uguns 5
minūtes. Kukurūzas miltus un ūdeni samaisa pastu, pievieno
pannā un maisot vāra, līdz mērce ir dzidra un sabiezējusi.
Nekavējoties pasniedziet.

Čili garneles

Pasniedz 4

450 g/1 mārciņa nomizotas garneles

1 olas baltums

10 ml / 2 tējkarotes kukurūzas miltu (kukurūzas ciete)

5 ml/1 tējkarote sāls

60 ml/4 ēdamkarotes zemesriekstu eļļas

25 g/1 unce žāvēti sarkanie čili, apgriezti

1 ķiploka daiviņa, sasmalcināta

5 ml/1 tējk svaigi malti pipari

15 ml/1 ēdamkarote sojas mērces

5 ml/1 tējkarote rīsu vīna vai sausā šerija

2,5 ml/¬Ω tējkarote cukura

2,5 ml/¬Ω tējkarote vīna etiķa

2,5 ml/¬Ω tējkarote sezama eļļas

Ielieciet garneles bļodā ar sakultu olu, kukurūzas miltiem un sāli un atstājiet marinēties 30 minūtes. Uzkarsē eļļu un apcep čili piparus, ķiplokus un piparus 1 minūti. Pievienojiet garneles un pārējās sastāvdaļas un maisot apcepiet dažas minūtes, līdz garneles ir izkarsētas un labi sajauktas.

Garneles Suey

Pasniedz 4

60 ml/4 ēdamkarotes zemesriekstu eļļas

2 lociņi, sasmalcināti

2 ķiploka daiviņas, sasmalcinātas

1 šķēle ingvera saknes, sasmalcināta

225 g/8 unces mizotas garneles

100 g/4 unces saldētu zirņu

100 g sēņu, pārgrieztas uz pusēm

30 ml/2 ēdamkarotes sojas mērces

15 ml/1 ēdamkarote rīsu vīna vai sausā šerija

5 ml/1 tējk cukurs

5 ml/1 tējkarote sāls

15 ml/1 ēdamkarote kukurūzas miltu (kukurūzas ciete)

Uzkarsē 45 ml/3 ēdamkarotes eļļas un apcep sīpolus, ķiplokus un ingveru, līdz tie ir viegli brūni. Pievieno garneles un maisot cep 1 minūti. Izņem no pannas. Uzkarsē atlikušo eļļu un maisot apcep zirņus un sēnes 3 minūtes. Pievienojiet garneles, sojas mērci, vīnu vai šeriju, cukuru un sāli un maisot apcepiet 2 minūtes. Kukurūzas miltus sajauc ar nedaudz ūdens, sakrata pannā un maisot vāra, līdz mērce kļūst dzidra un sabiezē.

Garneles Chow Mein

Pasniedz 4

450 g/1 mārciņa nomizotas garneles

15 ml/1 ēdamkarote kukurūzas miltu (kukurūzas ciete)

15 ml/1 ēdamkarote sojas mērces

15 ml/1 ēdamkarote rīsu vīna vai sausā šerija

4 žāvētas ķīniešu sēnes

30 ml/2 ēdamkarotes zemesriekstu eļļas

5 ml/1 tējkarote sāls

1 šķēle ingvera saknes, sasmalcināta

100g/4oz Ķīnas kāpostu, sasmalcinātu

100g/4oz bambusa dzinumi, sasmalcināti

Mīksti cepti makaroni

Sajauciet garneles ar kukurūzas miltiem, sojas mērci un vīnu vai šeriju un ļaujiet nostāvēties, laiku pa laikam apmaisot. Sēnes 30 minūtes iemērc siltā ūdenī, pēc tam nokāš. Izmetiet kātus un nogrieziet vāciņus. Uzkarsē eļļu un apcep sāli un ingveru 1 minūti. Pievienojiet kāpostus un bambusa dzinumus un samaisiet, līdz tie ir pārklāti ar eļļu. Uzliek vāku un vāra uz lēnas uguns 2 minūtes. Iemaisa garneles un marinādi un maisot cep 3 minūtes. Iemaisa notecinātos makaronus un pirms pasniegšanas uzkarsē.

Garneles ar cukini un ličiem

Pasniedz 4

12 karaliskās garneles

sāls un pipari

10 ml/2 tējk sojas mērce

10 ml / 2 tējkarotes kukurūzas miltu (kukurūzas ciete)

15 ml/1 ēdamkarote zemesriekstu eļļas

4 ķiploka daiviņas, sasmalcinātas

2 sarkanie čili pipari, sasmalcināti

225 g/8 unces cukini (cukini), kubiņos

2 lociņi, sasmalcināti

12 liči, bez kauliņiem

120 ml / 4 fl oz / ¬Ω tase kokosriekstu krējuma

10 ml/2 tējk maiga karija pulveris

5 ml/1 tējk zivju mērce

Nomizojiet garneles, atstājot astes. Apkaisa ar sāli, pipariem un sojas mērci, pēc tam pārkaisa ar kukurūzas miltiem. Uzkarsē eļļu un apcep ķiplokus, čili piparus un garneles 1 minūti. Pievienojiet kabačus, lociņus un ličijas un maisot apcepiet 1 minūti. Izņem no pannas. Pannā ielej kokosriekstu krēmu, uzvāra un vāra uz lēnas uguns 2 minūtes, līdz tas sabiezē. Iemaisa kariju pulveri un zivju mērci, pievieno sāli un piparus. Atgrieziet garneles un dārzeņus mērcē, lai pirms pasniegšanas uzsildītu.

Garneles ar krabjiem

Pasniedz 4

45 ml/3 ēdamkarotes zemesriekstu eļļas

3 lociņi, sasmalcināti

1 sagriezta ingvera sakne, sasmalcināta

225g/8oz krabju gaļas

15 ml/1 ēdamkarote rīsu vīna vai sausā šerija

30 ml/2 ēdamkarotes vistas vai zivju buljona

15 ml/1 ēdamkarote sojas mērces

5 ml/1 tējkarote brūnā cukura

5 ml/1 tējkarote vīna etiķa

svaigi malti pipari

10 ml / 2 tējkarotes kukurūzas miltu (kukurūzas ciete)

225 g/8 unces mizotas garneles

Uzkarsē 30 ml/2 ēdamkarotes eļļas un apcep sīpolus un ingveru, līdz tie ir viegli brūni. Pievienojiet krabju gaļu un maisot apcepiet 2 minūtes. Pievienojiet vīnu vai šeriju, buljonu, sojas mērci, cukuru un etiķi un pēc garšas pievienojiet piparus. Maisot apcep 3 minūtes. Kukurūzas miltus sajauc ar nedaudz ūdens un iemaisa mērcē. Vāra uz lēnas uguns, maisot, līdz mērce sabiezē. Tikmēr atsevišķā pannā uzkarsē atlikušo eļļu un apcep garneles, pāris reizes apmaisot

minūtes, lai uzsildītu. Novietojiet krabju maisījumu uz sasildītas pasniegšanas šķīvja un uzlieciet garneles.

Garneles ar gurķiem

Pasniedz 4

225 g/8 unces mizotas garneles

sāls un svaigi malti pipari

15 ml/1 ēdamkarote kukurūzas miltu (kukurūzas ciete)

1 gurķis

45 ml/3 ēdamkarotes zemesriekstu eļļas

2 ķiploka daiviņas, sasmalcinātas

1 sīpols, smalki sagriezts

15 ml/1 ēdamkarote rīsu vīna vai sausā šerija

2 šķēles ingvera saknes, sasmalcinātas

Garneles apkaisa ar sāli un pipariem un pārkaisa ar kukurūzas miltiem. Gurķi nomizo, izņem sēklas un sagriež biezās šķēlēs. Uzkarsē pusi eļļas un apcep ķiplokus un sīpolus, līdz tie ir viegli brūni. Pievienojiet garneles un šeriju un maisot apcepiet 2 minūtes, pēc tam izņemiet sastāvdaļas no pannas. Uzkarsē atlikušo eļļu un apcep ingveru 1 minūti. Pievieno gurķi un maisot apcep 2 minūtes. Ievietojiet garneļu maisījumu atpakaļ pannā un maisot māriet, līdz tas ir labi sajaukts un uzkarsēts.

Garneļu karijs

Pasniedz 4

45 ml/3 ēdamkarotes zemesriekstu eļļas

4 lociņi, sagriezti šķēlēs

30 ml/2 ēdamkarotes karija pulvera

2,5 ml/¬Ω tējkarote sāls

120 ml / 4 fl unces / ¬Ω tase vistas buljona

450 g/1 mārciņa nomizotas garneles

Uzkarsē eļļu un apcep lociņus 30 sekundes. Pievienojiet karija pulveri un sāli un maisot apcepiet 1 minūti. Ielej buljonu, uzvāra un maisot vāra uz lēnas uguns 2 minūtes. Pievienojiet garneles un viegli karsējiet.

Garneļu un sēņu karijs

Pasniedz 4

5 ml/1 tējk sojas mērce

5 ml/1 tējkarote rīsu vīna vai sausā šerija

225 g/8 unces mizotas garneles

30 ml/2 ēdamkarotes zemesriekstu eļļas

2 ķiploka daiviņas, sasmalcinātas

1 šķēle ingvera saknes, smalki sagriezta

1 sīpols, sagriezts šķēlēs

100 g/4 unces sēņu

100 g/4 unces svaigu vai saldētu zirņu

15 ml/1 ēdamkarote karija pulvera

15 ml/1 ēdamkarote kukurūzas miltu (kukurūzas ciete)

150 ml / ¬° pt / dāsna ¬Ω glāze vistas buljona

Sajauc sojas mērci, vīnu vai šeriju un garneles. Uzkarsē eļļu ar ķiplokiem un ingveru un apcep, līdz tie kļūst viegli brūni. Pievienojiet sīpolus, sēnes un zirņus un maisot apcepiet 2 minūtes. Pievienojiet karija pulveri un kukurūzas miltus un maisot apcepiet 2 minūtes. Pamazām iemaisa buljonā, uzvāra, uzliek vāku un vāra uz lēnas uguns 5 minūtes, ik pa laikam apmaisot. Pievieno garneles un marinādi, uzliek vāku un vāra uz lēnas uguns 2 minūtes.

Ceptas garneles

Pasniedz 4

450 g/1 mārciņa nomizotas garneles
30 ml/2 ēdamkarotes rīsu vīna vai sausā šerija
5 ml/1 tējkarote sāls
eļļa dziļai cepšanai
sojas mērce

Ielejiet garneles vīnā vai šerija un apkaisa ar sāli. Ļaujiet nostāvēties 15 minūtes, pēc tam noteciniet un nosusiniet. Uzkarsē eļļu un apcep garneles dažas sekundes, līdz tās kļūst zeltaini brūnas. Pasniedz pārslaktu ar sojas mērci.

Sautētas garneles

Pasniedz 4

50 g/2 unces/¬Ω glāzes vienkāršu (universālu) miltu
2,5 ml/¬Ω tējkarote sāls
1 ola, viegli sakulta
30 ml/2 ēdamkarotes ūdens
450 g/1 mārciņa nomizotas garneles
eļļa dziļai cepšanai

Miltus, sāli, olu un ūdeni sakuļ mīklā, ja nepieciešams,
pievienojot vēl nedaudz ūdens. Pārlej ar garnelēm, līdz tās ir labi
brūnas. Uzkarsē eļļu un apcep garneles dažas minūtes, līdz tās
kļūst kraukšķīgas un zeltainas.

Garneļu klimpas ar tomātu mērci

Pasniedz 4

900 g/2 mārciņas nomizotas garneles

450 g/1 mārciņa malta (malta) menca

4 olas, sakultas

50 g/2 unces/¬Ω tase kukurūzas miltu (kukurūzas ciete)

2 ķiploka daiviņas, sasmalcinātas

30 ml/2 ēdamkarotes sojas mērces

15 ml/1 ēdamkarote cukura

15 ml/1 ēdamkarote zemesriekstu eļļas

Mērcei:

30 ml/2 ēdamkarotes zemesriekstu eļļas

100 g/4 unces lociņu, sasmalcināti

100 g / 4 unces sēnes, sasmalcinātas

100g/4oz šķiņķis, sasmalcināts

2 selerijas kāti, sasmalcināti

200 g/7 unces tomātu, nomizoti un sasmalcināti

300 ml/¬Ω pt/1¬° tases ūdens

sāls un svaigi malti pipari

15 ml/1 ēdamkarote kukurūzas miltu (kukurūzas ciete)

Garneles smalki sagriež un sajauc ar mencu. Iemaisa olas, kukurūzas miltus, ķiplokus, sojas mērci, cukuru un eļļu. Uzvāra lielu katlu ar ūdeni un katlā ielej karotes maisījuma. Vēlreiz uzvāra un vāra uz lēnas uguns dažas minūtes, līdz kotletes uzpeld virspusē. Labi notecina. Mērcei uzkarsē eļļu un apcep lociņus, līdz tie ir mīksti, bet nav gatavi. Pievienojiet sēnes un apcepiet 1 minūti, pēc tam pievienojiet šķiņķi, seleriju un tomātus un apcepiet 1 minūti. Pielej ūdeni, uzvāra un pievieno sāli un piparus. Uzliek vāku un vāra uz lēnas uguns 10 minūtes, ik pa laikam apmaisot. Kukurūzas miltus sajauc ar nedaudz ūdens un iemaisa mērcē. Vāra uz lēnas uguns dažas minūtes, maisot, līdz mērce ir dzidra un sabiezējusi. Pasniedz ar klimpām.

Garneļu un olu kausi

Pasniedz 4

15 ml/1 ēdamkarote sezama eļļas

8 nomizotas karaliskās garneles

1 sarkanais čili pipars, sasmalcināts

2 lociņi, sasmalcināti

30 ml/2 ēdamkarotes sasmalcinātas pērļgliemenes (pēc izvēles)

8 olas

15 ml/1 ēdamkarote sojas mērces

sāls un svaigi malti pipari

daži plakanu pētersīļu zariņi

Eļļojiet 8 ramekīnus ar sezama eļļu. Pievienojiet katram ēdienam vienu garneļu ar nedaudz čili, lociņiem un pērļgliemenes, ja lietojat. Katrā bļodā ielauž olu un pievieno sojas mērci, sāli un piparus. Liek ramekīnus uz cepešpannas un cep uzkarsētā cepeškrāsnī 200 ¬∞ C/400 ¬∞ F/gāzes atzīme 6 apmēram 15 minūtes, līdz olas ir sacietējušas un no ārpuses ir nedaudz brūnas. Uzmanīgi paceliet tos uz sasildīta pasniegšanas šķīvja un izrotājiet ar pētersīļiem.

Garneļu olu rullīši

Pasniedz 4

225 g/8 unces pupiņu asni

30 ml/2 ēdamkarotes zemesriekstu eļļas

4 selerijas kāti, sasmalcināti

100 g / 4 unces sēnes, sasmalcinātas

225g/8oz nomizotas garneles, sasmalcinātas

15 ml/1 ēdamkarote rīsu vīna vai sausā šerija

2,5 ml/¬Ω tējkarote kukurūzas miltu (kukurūzas ciete)

2,5 ml/¬Ω tējkarote sāls

2,5 ml/¬Ω tējkarote cukura

12 olu ruļļu ādas

1 ola, sakulta

eļļa dziļai cepšanai

Pupiņu asnus 2 minūtes blanšē verdošā ūdenī, pēc tam nokāš.
Uzkarsē eļļu un maisot apcep seleriju 1 minūti. Pievieno sēnes un
maisot apcep 1 minūti. Pievienojiet garneles, vīnu vai šeriju,
kukurūzas miltus, sāli un cukuru un maisot apcepiet 2 minūtes.
Atstāj atdzist.

Katras mizas centrā liek nedaudz pildījuma un malas apsmērē ar sakultu olu. Saloka malas, tad olu rullīti atrit prom no sevis, malas aizlīmē ar olu. Uzkarsē eļļu un apcep līdz zeltaini brūnai.

Tālo Austrumu stila garneles

Pasniedz 4

16,Äì20 nomizotas karaliskās garneles

1 citrona sula

120 ml/4 fl oz/¬Ω tase sausa baltvīna

30 ml/2 ēdamkarotes sojas mērces

30 ml/2 ēdamkarotes medus

15 ml/1 ēdamkarote rīvētas citrona miziņas

sāls un pipari

45 ml/3 ēdamkarotes zemesriekstu eļļas

1 ķiploka daiviņa, sasmalcināta

6 lociņi, sagriezti sloksnēs

2 burkāni, sagriezti strēmelēs

5 ml/1 tējk piecu garšvielu pulveris

5 ml/1 tējk kukurūzas milti (kukurūzas ciete)

Apkaisiet garneles ar citronu sulu, vīnu, sojas mērci, medu un citrona miziņu un pievienojiet sāli un piparus. Nosedziet un marinējiet 1 stundu. Uzkarsē eļļu un apcep ķiplokus, līdz tie ir viegli brūni. Pievieno dārzeņus un maisot cep, līdz tie mīksti, bet joprojām kraukšķīgi. Garneles nokāš, pievieno pannā un maisot cep 2 minūtes. Lai sasprindzinātu marinādi un sajauc ar piecu garšvielu pulveri un kukurūzas miltiem. Pievienojiet vokpannai, labi samaisiet un uzvāra.

Garneles Foo Yung

Pasniedz 4

6 olas, sakultas

45 ml/3 ēdamkarotes kukurūzas miltu (kukurūzas ciete)

225 g/8 unces mizotas garneles

100g/4oz sēnes, sagrieztas

5 ml/1 tējkarote sāls

2 lociņi, sasmalcināti

45 ml/3 ēdamkarotes zemesriekstu eļļas

Iecilā olas, tad iemaisa kukurūzas miltos. Pievienojiet visas pārējās sastāvdaļas, izņemot eļļu. Uzkarsē eļļu un pamazām ielej maisījumu pannā, lai izveidotu pankūkas apmēram 7,5 cm/3 diametrā. Cepiet, līdz apakšdaļa ir zeltaina, pēc tam apgrieziet un apcepiet otru pusi.

Garneļu kartupeļi

Pasniedz 4

12 lielas nevārītas garneles

1 ola, sakulta

30 ml/2 ēdamkarotes kukurūzas miltu (kukurūzas ciete)

šķipsniņa sāls

šķipsniņa piparu

3 maizes šķēles

1 cieti vārīts (cieti vārīts) olas dzeltenums, sasmalcināts

25 g/1 unce vārīta šķiņķa, sasmalcināta

1 lociņš, sasmalcināts

eļļa dziļai cepšanai

Noņemiet garnelēm čaumalas un muguras vēnas, atstājot astes neskartas. Nogrieziet garneļu aizmuguri ar asu nazi un viegli piespiediet tās uz leju. Sakuļ olu, kukurūzas miltus, sāli un piparus. Ieliec iet garneles maisījumā, līdz tās ir pilnībā pārklātas. No maizes noņemiet garozu un sagrieziet to ceturtdaļās. Uz katra gabala novietojiet vienu garneļu ar griezuma pusi uz leju un nospiediet uz leju. Katru garneļu apsmērē ar nedaudz olu maisījuma, tad apkaisa ar olas dzeltenumu, šķiņķi un sīpoliem.

Uzkarsē eļļu un pa daļām apcep garneļu maizes gabaliņus, līdz tie kļūst zeltaini. Nokāš uz virtuves papīra un pasniedz karstu.

Ceptas garneles mērcē

Pasniedz 4

75 g / 3 unces / uzkrāta ¬° tase kukurūzas miltu (kukurūzas ciete)

¬Ω ola, sakulta

5 ml/1 tējkarote rīsu vīna vai sausā šerija

sāls

450 g/1 mārciņa nomizotas garneles

45 ml/3 ēdamkarotes zemesriekstu eļļas

5 ml/1 tējkarote sezama eļļas

1 ķiploka daiviņa, sasmalcināta

1 šķēle ingvera saknes, sasmalcināta

3 lociņi, sagriezti šķēlēs

15 ml/1 ēdamkarote zivju buljona

5 ml/1 tējkarote vīna etiķa

5 ml/1 tējk cukurs

Sajauciet kukurūzas miltus, olu, vīnu vai šeriju un šķipsniņu sāls, lai izveidotu mīklu. Iemērciet garneles mīklā, lai tās viegli pārklātu. Uzkarsē eļļu un apcep garneles ārā, līdz tās kļūst kraukšķīgas. Izņemiet tos no pannas un noteciniet eļļu. Pannā sakarsē sezama eļļu, pievieno garneles, ķiplokus, ingveru un sīpolus un maisot apcep 3 minūtes. Pievienojiet buljonu, vīna

ctiķi un cukuru, labi samaisiet un pirms pasniegšanas uzkarsējiet.

Vārītas garneles ar šķiņķi un tofu

Pasniedz 4

30 ml/2 ēdamkarotes zemesriekstu eļļas

225g/8oz tofu, kubiņos

600 ml/1 pt/2¬Ω tases vistas buljona

100g/4oz kūpināts šķiņķis, kubiņos

225 g/8 unces mizotas garneles

Uzkarsē eļļu un apcep tofu, līdz tas ir viegli brūns. Izņem no pannas un notecina. Uzkarsē buljonu, pievieno tofu un šķiņķi un uz lēnas uguns vāra apmēram 10 minūtes, līdz tofu ir gatavs. Pievienojiet garneles un vāriet uz lēnas uguns vēl 5 minūtes, līdz tās ir sasilušas. Pasniedz dziļos traukos.

Garneles omāru mērcē

Pasniedz 4

45 ml/3 ēdamkarotes zemesriekstu eļļas

2 ķiploka daiviņas, sasmalcinātas

5 ml/1 tējk maltas melnās pupiņas

100 g maltas (maltas) cūkgaļas

450 g/1 mārciņa nomizotas garneles

15 ml/1 ēdamkarote rīsu vīna vai sausā šerija

300 ml/¬Ω pt/1¬° tases vistas buljona

30 ml/2 ēdamkarotes kukurūzas miltu (kukurūzas ciete)

2 olas, sakultas

15 ml/1 ēdamkarote sojas mērces

2,5 ml/¬Ω tējkarote sāls

2,5 ml/¬Ω tējkarote cukura

2 lociņi, sasmalcināti

Uzkarsē eļļu un apcep ķiplokus un melnās pupiņas, līdz ķiploki ir viegli brūni. Pievienojiet cūkgaļu un cepiet, līdz tā kļūst brūna. Pievieno garneles un maisot cep 1 minūti. Pievieno šeriju, pārklāj un vāra uz lēnas uguns 1 minūti. Ielej buljonu un kukurūzas miltus, maisot uzvāra, uzliek vāku un vāra uz lēnas uguns 5 minūtes. Nepārtraukti maisot iecilā olas, veidojot pavedienus. Pievieno soju

mērci, sāli, cukuru un lociņus un pirms pasniegšanas vāra uz lēnas uguns dažas minūtes.

Garneles ar ličī mērci

Pasniedz 4

50g/2oz/¬Ω tase vienkārša (universāla)
milti
2,5 ml/¬Ω tējkarote sāls
1 ola, viegli sakulta
30 ml/2 ēdamkarotes ūdens
450 g/1 mārciņa nomizotas garneles
eļļa dziļai cepšanai
30 ml/2 ēdamkarotes zemesriekstu eļļas
2 šķēles ingvera saknes, sasmalcinātas
30 ml/2 ēdamkarotes vīna etiķa
5 ml/1 tējk cukurs
2,5 ml/¬Ω tējkarote sāls
15 ml/1 ēdamkarote sojas mērces
200g/7oz konservēti liči, nosusināti

Sajauc miltus, sāli, olu un ūdeni, lai izveidotu mīklu, ja
nepieciešams, pievienojot vēl nedaudz ūdens. Pārlej ar garnelēm,
līdz tās ir labi pārklātas. Uzkarsē eļļu un apcep garneles dažas
minūtes, līdz tās kļūst kraukšķīgas un zeltainas. Nokāš uz
virtuves papīra un liek uz sasildīta servēšanas šķīvja. Tikmēr
uzkarsē eļļu un apcep ingveru 1 minūti. Pievienojiet vīna etiķi,

cukuru, sāli un sojas mērci. Pievienojiet ličus un samaisiet, līdz tie ir sasildīti un pārklāti ar mērci. Pārlej garnelēm un nekavējoties pasniedz.

Mandarīnā ceptas garneles

Pasniedz 4

60 ml/4 ēdamkarotes zemesriekstu eļļas

1 ķiploka daiviņa, sasmalcināta

1 šķēle ingvera saknes, sasmalcināta

450 g/1 mārciņa nomizotas garneles

30 ml/2 ēd.k. rīsu vīns vai sausais šerijs 30 ml/2 ēd.k. sojas

mērce

15 ml/1 ēdamkarote kukurūzas miltu (kukurūzas ciete)

45 ml / 3 ēdamkarotes ūdens

Uzkarsē eļļu un apcep ķiplokus un ingveru, līdz tie ir viegli brūni. Pievieno garneles un maisot cep 1 minūti. Pievienojiet vīnu vai šeriju un labi samaisiet. Pievienojiet sojas mērci, kukurūzas miltus un ūdeni un maisot apcepiet 2 minūtes.

118

Garneles ar Mangetout

Pasniedz 4

5 kaltētas ķīniešu sēnes

225 g/8 unces pupiņu asni

60 ml/4 ēdamkarotes zemesriekstu eļļas

5 ml/1 tējkarote sāls

2 selerijas kāti, sasmalcināti

4 lociņi, sasmalcināti

2 ķiploka daiviņas, sasmalcinātas

2 šķēles ingvera saknes, sasmalcinātas

60 ml / 4 ēdamkarotes ūdens

15 ml/1 ēdamkarote sojas mērces

15 ml/1 ēdamkarote rīsu vīna vai sausā šerija

225 g / 8 unces mangetout (sniega zirņi)

225 g/8 unces mizotas garneles

15 ml/1 ēdamkarote kukurūzas miltu (kukurūzas ciete)

Sēnes 30 minūtes iemērc siltā ūdenī, pēc tam nokāš. Izmetiet kātus un nogrieziet vāciņus. Pupiņu asnus 5 minūtes blanšē verdošā ūdenī, pēc tam labi nokāš. Uzkarsē pusi eļļas un 1 minūti apcep sāli, seleriju, sīpolu un pupiņu dīgstus, tad izņem no pannas. Uzkarsē atlikušo eļļu un apcep ķiplokus un ingveru, līdz tie ir viegli brūni. Pievienojiet pusi ūdens, sojas mērci, vīnu vai šeriju, mangetout un garneles, uzkarsē līdz vārīšanās temperatūrai un vāra uz lēnas uguns 3 minūtes. Kukurūzas miltus un atlikušo ūdeni samaisa viendabīgā masā, pievieno pannā un maisot vāra uz lēnas uguns, līdz mērce sabiezē. Atgrieziet dārzeņus uz pannas, vāriet uz lēnas uguns, līdz tie ir uzkarsēti. Nekavējoties pasniedziet.

Garneles ar ķīniešu sēnēm

Pasniedz 4

8 žāvētas ķīniešu sēnes
45 ml/3 ēdamkarotes zemesriekstu eļļas
3 šķēles ingvera saknes, sasmalcinātas
450 g/1 mārciņa nomizotas garneles
15 ml/1 ēdamkarote sojas mērces
5 ml/1 tējkarote sāls
60 ml/4 ēdamkarotes zivju buljona

Sēnes 30 minūtes iemērc siltā ūdenī, pēc tam nokāš. Izmetiet kātus un nogrieziet vāciņus. Uzkarsē pusi eļļas un apcep ingveru, līdz tas ir viegli brūns. Pievienojiet garneles, sojas mērci un sāli un maisot apcepiet, līdz tie ir pārklāti eļļa, pēc tam izņemiet no pannas. Uzkarsē atlikušo eļļu un maisot apcep sēnes, līdz tās ir pārklātas ar eļļu. Pievieno buljonu, uzvāra, pārklāj un vāra uz lēnas uguns 3 minūtes. Ieliecet garneles atpakaļ pannā un samaisiet, līdz tās ir sasilušas.

Garneles un zirņus, maisot apcep

Pasniedz 4

450 g/1 mārciņa nomizotas garneles
5 ml/1 tējkarote sezama eļļas
5 ml/1 tējkarote sāls
30 ml/2 ēdamkarotes zemesriekstu eļļas
1 ķiploka daiviņa, sasmalcināta
1 šķēle ingvera saknes, sasmalcināta
225g/8oz blanšēti vai saldēti zirņi, atkausēti
4 lociņi, sasmalcināti
30 ml/2 ēdamkarotes ūdens

sāls un pipari

Garneles sajauc ar sezama eļļu un sāli. Uzkarsē eļļu un maisot apcep ķiplokus un ingveru 1 minūti. Pievieno garneles un maisot apcep 2 minūtes. Pievieno zirņus un maisot apcep 1 minūti. Pievienojiet sīpolus un ūdeni, pievienojiet sāli un piparus un, ja vēlaties, vēl nedaudz sezama eļļas. Pirms pasniegšanas uzkarsē, rūpīgi maisot.

Garneles ar mango čatniju

Pasniedz 4

12 karaliskās garneles

sāls un pipari

1 citrona sula

30 ml/2 ēdamkarotes kukurūzas miltu (kukurūzas ciete)

1 mango

5 ml/1 tējkarote sinepju pulvera

5 ml/1 tējkarote medus

30 ml/2 ēdamkarotes kokosriekstu krējuma

30 ml/2 ēdamkarotes maiga karija pulvera

120 ml / 4 fl unces / ¬Ω tase vistas buljona

45 ml/3 ēdamkarotes zemesriekstu eļļas

2 ķiploka daiviņas, sasmalcinātas

2 lociņi, sasmalcināti

1 fenheļa spuldze, sasmalcināta

100g/4oz mango čatnijs

Nomizojiet garneles, atstājot astes neskartas. Apkaisa ar sāli, pipariem un citrona sulu, tad pārkaisa ar pusi kukurūzas miltu. Mango nomizo, no kauliņa nogriež mīkstumu, tad sagriež kubiņos. Sajauc sinepes, medu, kokosriekstu krējumu, karija pulveri, atlikušos kukurūzas miltus un buljonu. Uzkarsē pusi eļļas un apcep ķiplokus, sīpolus un fenheli 2 minūtes. Ielejiet buljona maisījumu, uzkarsē līdz vārīšanās temperatūrai un vāra uz lēnas uguns 1 minūti. Pievienojiet mango kubiņus un čatniju un viegli karsējiet, pēc tam pārnesiet uz uzsildītas pasniegšanas šķīvja. Uzkarsē atlikušo eļļu un maisot apcep garneles 2 minūtes. Kārto tos virsū dārzeņiem un pasniedz uzreiz.

Ceptas garneļu bumbiņas ar sīpolu mērci

Pasniedz 4

3 olas, viegli sakultas

45 ml/3 ēdamkarotes vienkāršu (universālu) miltu

sāls un svaigi malti pipari

450 g/1 mārciņa nomizotas garneles

eļļa dziļai cepšanai

15 ml/1 ēdamkarote zemesriekstu eļļas

2 sīpoli, sasmalcināti

15 ml/1 ēdamkarote kukurūzas miltu (kukurūzas ciete)

30 ml/2 ēdamkarotes sojas mērces

175 ml / 6 fl oz / ¬œ tase ūdens

Sajauc olas, miltus, sāli un piparus. Pievienojiet garneles mīklai. Uzkarsē eļļu un apcep garneles līdz zeltaini brūnai. Tikmēr uzkarsē eļļu un apcep sīpolus 1 minūti. Pārējās sastāvdaļas sasmalcina, iemaisa sīpolus un maisot vāra, līdz mērce sabiezē. Garneles notecina un liek uz sasildīta servēšanas šķīvja. Pārlej ar mērci un pasniedz nekavējoties.

Mandarīnu garneles ar zirņiem

Pasniedz 4

60 ml/4 ēdamkarotes zemesriekstu eļļas

1 ķiploka daiviņa, sasmalcināta

1 šķēle ingvera saknes, sasmalcināta

450 g/1 mārciņa nomizotas garneles

30 ml/2 ēdamkarotes rīsu vīna vai sausā šerija

225 g/8 unces saldētu zirņu, atkausētu

30 ml/2 ēdamkarotes sojas mērces

15 ml/1 ēdamkarote kukurūzas miltu (kukurūzas ciete)

45 ml / 3 ēdamkarotes ūdens

Uzkarsē eļļu un apcep ķiplokus un ingveru, līdz tie ir viegli brūni. Pievieno garneles un maisot cep 1 minūti. Pievienojiet vīnu vai šeriju un labi samaisiet. Pievieno zirņus un maisot apcep 5 minūtes. Pievieno pārējās sastāvdaļas un maisot cep 2 minūtes.

Pekinas garneles

Pasniedz 4

30 ml/2 ēdamkarotes zemesriekstu eļļas

2 ķiploka daiviņas, sasmalcinātas

1 šķēle ingvera saknes, smalki sagriezta

225 g/8 unces mizotas garneles

4 lociņi, biezi sagriezti

120 ml / 4 fl unces / ¬Ω tase vistas buljona

5 ml/1 tējkarote brūnā cukura

5 ml/1 tējk sojas mērce

5 ml/1 tējk hoisin mērce

5 ml/1 tējk tabasko mērce

Uzkarsē eļļu kopā ar ķiplokiem un ingveru un vāra, līdz ķiploki ir viegli brūni. Pievieno garneles un maisot cep 1 minūti. Pievieno sīpolus un maisot apcep 1 minūti. Pievieno pārējās sastāvdaļas, uzvāra, uzliek vāku un vāra uz lēnas uguns 4 minūtes, ik pa laikam apmaisot. Pārbaudiet garšvielas un, ja vēlaties, pievienojiet nedaudz vairāk Tabasco mērces.

Garneles ar pipariem

Pasniedz 4

30 ml/2 ēdamkarotes zemesriekstu eļļas

1 zaļā paprika, sagriezta gabaliņos

450 g/1 mārciņa nomizotas garneles

10 ml / 2 tējkarotes kukurūzas miltu (kukurūzas ciete)

60 ml / 4 ēdamkarotes ūdens

5 ml/1 tējkarote rīsu vīna vai sausā šerija

2,5 ml/¬Ω tējkarote sāls

45 ml/2 ēdamkarotes tomātu biezeņa (pastas)

Uzkarsē eļļu un maisot apcep papriku 2 minūtes. Pievienojiet garneļu un tomātu biezeni un labi samaisiet. Kukurūzas miltu ūdeni, vīnu vai šeriju un sāli sasmalcina pastu, pievieno pannā un maisot vāra uz lēnas uguns, līdz mērce ir dzidra un sabiezējusi.

Ceptas garneles ar cūkgaļu

Pasniedz 4

225 g/8 unces mizotas garneles

100 g liesas cūkgaļas, sasmalcinātas

60 ml/4 ēdamkarotes rīsu vīna vai sausā šerija

1 olas baltums

45 ml/3 ēdamkarotes kukurūzas miltu (kukurūzas ciete)

5 ml/1 tējkarote sāls

15 ml/1 ēdamkarote ūdens (pēc izvēles)

90 ml/6 ēdamkarotes zemesriekstu eļļas

45 ml/3 ēdamkarotes zivju buljona

5 ml/1 tējkarote sezama eļļas

Novietojiet garneles un cūkgaļu atsevišķos traukos. Sajauc 45 ml/3 ēd.k vīna vai šerija, olas baltumu, 30 ml/2 ēd.k. kukurūzas miltus un sāli, lai izveidotu irdenu mīklu, ja nepieciešams, pievienojot ūdeni. Sadaliet maisījumu starp cūkgaļu un garnelēm un labi samaisiet, lai vienmērīgi pārklātu. Uzkarsē eļļu un apcep cūkgaļu un garneles dažas minūtes līdz zeltaini brūnai. Noņemiet no pannas un nolejiet visu eļļu, izņemot 15 ml/1 ēdamkarote. Pievienojiet buljonu pannā ar atlikušo vīnu vai šeriju un kukurūzas miltiem. Uzkarsē līdz vārīšanās temperatūrai un maisot vāra uz lēnas uguns, līdz mērce sabiezē. Pārlejiet garnelēm un cūkgaļu un pasniedziet, aplejotu ar sezama eļļu.

Ceptas garneles ar šerija mērci

Pasniedz 4

50 g/2 unces/¬Ω glāzes vienkāršu (universālu) miltu
2,5 ml/¬Ω tējkarote sāls
1 ola, viegli sakulta
30 ml/2 ēdamkarotes ūdens
450 g/1 mārciņa nomizotas garneles
eļļa dziļai cepšanai

15 ml/1 ēdamkarote zemesriekstu eļļas

1 sīpols, smalki sagriezts

45 ml/3 ēdamkarotes rīsu vīna vai sausā šerija

15 ml/1 ēdamkarote sojas mērces

120 ml / 4 fl oz / ¬Ω tase zivju buljona

10 ml / 2 tējkarotes kukurūzas miltu (kukurūzas ciete)

30 ml/2 ēdamkarotes ūdens

Sajauc miltus, sāli, olu un ūdeni, lai izveidotu mīklu, ja nepieciešams, pievienojot vēl nedaudz ūdens. Pārlej ar garnelēm, līdz tās ir labi pārklātas. Uzkarsē eļļu un apcep garneles dažas minūtes, līdz tās kļūst kraukšķīgas un zeltainas. Nokāš uz virtuves papīra un liek uz sasildīta servēšanas trauka. Tikmēr uzkarsē eļļu un apcep sīpolus līdz mīkstam. Pievienojiet vīnu vai šeriju, sojas mērci un buljonu, uzkarsē līdz vārīšanās temperatūrai un vāra uz lēnas uguns 4 minūtes. Kukurūzas miltus un ūdeni samaisa pastu, pievieno pannā un maisot vāra, līdz mērce ir dzidra un sabiezējusi. Garnelēm pārlej mērci un pasniedz.

Ceptas sezama garneles

Pasniedz 4

450 g/1 mārciņa nomizotas garneles

¬Ω olu baltums

5 ml/1 tējk sojas mērce

5 ml/1 tējkarote sezama eļļas

50 g/2 unces/¬Ω tase kukurūzas miltu (kukurūzas ciete)

sāls un svaigi malti baltie pipari

eļļa dziļai cepšanai

60 ml/4 ēdamkarotes sezama sēklu

salātu lapas

Garneles sajauc ar sakultu olu, sojas mērci, sezama eļļu, kukurūzas miltiem, sāli un pipariem. Pievienojiet nedaudz ūdens, ja maisījums ir pārāk biezs. Uzkarsē eļļu un apcep garneles dažas minūtes, līdz tās kļūst gaiši zeltainas. Tikmēr sausā pannā īsi apgrauzdē sezama sēklas, līdz tās kļūst zeltainas. Garneles notecina un sajauc ar sezama sēklām. Pasniedziet uz salātu gultas.

Ceptas garneles ar čaumalām

Pasniedz 4

60 ml/4 ēdamkarotes zemesriekstu cļļas

750 g/1 mārciņa nemizotas garneles

3 lociņi, sasmalcināti

3 šķēles ingvera saknes, sasmalcinātas

2,5 ml/¬Ω tējkarote sāls

15 ml/1 ēdamkarote rīsu vīna vai sausā šerija

120 ml / 4 fl unces / ¬Ω tase tomātu kečups (catsup)

15 ml/1 ēdamkarote sojas mērces

15 ml/1 ēdamkarote cukura

15 ml/1 ēdamkarote kukurūzas miltu (kukurūzas ciete)

60 ml / 4 ēdamkarotes ūdens

Sildiet eļļu un apcepiet garneles 1 minūti, ja tās ir pagatavotas, vai līdz tās kļūst sārtas, ja tās nav vārītas. Pievienojiet sīpolus, ingveru, sāli un vīnu vai šeriju un maisot apcepiet 1 minūti. Pievienojiet tomātu kečupu, sojas mērci un cukuru un maisot apcepiet 1 minūti. Sajauc kukurūzas miltus un ūdeni, pievieno pannā un maisot vāra, līdz mērce ir dzidra un sabiezēta.

Mīksti ceptas garneles

Pasniedz 4

75 g / 3 unces / uzkrāta ¬° tase kukurūzas miltu (kukurūzas ciete)
1 olas baltums
5 ml/1 tējkarote rīsu vīna vai sausā šerija
sāls
350g/12oz nomizotas garneles
eļļa dziļai cepšanai

Saputo kukurūzas miltus, olu baltumu, vīnu vai šeriju un šķipsniņu sāls, lai izveidotu biezu mīklu. Iemērciet garneles mīklā, līdz tās ir labi pārklātas. Uzkarsē eļļu uz vidējas uguns un apcep garneles dažas minūtes, līdz tās kļūst zeltaini brūnas. Izņem no eļļas, uzkarsē līdz karstumam, tad atkal apcep garneles, līdz tās ir kraukšķīgas un brūnas.

Garneles Tempura

Pasniedz 4

450 g/1 mārciņa nomizotas garneles
30 ml/2 ēd.k. vienkāršu (universālu) miltu

132

30 ml/2 ēdamkarotes kukurūzas miltu (kukurūzas ciete)

30 ml/2 ēdamkarotes ūdens

2 olas, sakultas

eļļa dziļai cepšanai

Nogrieziet garneles līdz pusei iekšējā izliekumā un izklājiet, lai izveidotu tauriņu. Sajauc miltus, kukurūzas miltus un ūdeni līdz mīklai, tad iemaisa olas. Uzkarsē eļļu un apcep garneles līdz zeltaini brūnai.

Zem gumijas

Pasniedz 4

30 ml/2 ēdamkarotes zemesriekstu eļļas

2 lociņi, sasmalcināti

1 ķiploka daiviņa, sasmalcināta

1 šķēle ingvera saknes, sasmalcināta

100 g / 4 oz vistas krūtiņa, sagriezta sloksnēs

100g/4oz šķiņķis, sagriezts sloksnēs

100g/4oz bambusa dzinumi, sagriezti sloksnēs

100g/4oz ūdens kastaņi, sagriezti sloksnēs

225 g/8 unces mizotas garneles

30 ml/2 ēdamkarotes sojas mērces

30 ml/2 ēdamkarotes rīsu vīna vai sausā šerija

5 ml/1 tējkarote sāls

5 ml/1 tējk cukurs

5 ml/1 tējk kukurūzas milti (kukurūzas ciete)

Uzkarsē eļļu un apcep sīpolus, ķiplokus un ingveru, līdz tie ir viegli brūni. Pievieno vistu un maisot cep 1 minūti. Pievienojiet šķiņķi, bambusa dzinumus un ūdens kastaņus un maisot apcepiet 3 minūtes. Pievieno garneles un maisot cep 1 minūti. Pievieno sojas mērci, vīnu vai šeriju, sāli un cukuru un maisot apcep 2 minūtes. Kukurūzas miltus sajauc ar nedaudz ūdens, pievieno pannā un maisot vāra uz lēnas uguns 2 minūtes.

Garneles ar tofu

Pasniedz 4

45 ml/3 ēdamkarotes zemesriekstu eļļas

225g/8oz tofu, kubiņos

1 lociņš, sasmalcināts

1 ķiploka daiviņa, sasmalcināta

15 ml/1 ēdamkarote sojas mērces

5 ml/1 tējk cukurs

90 ml/6 ēdamkarotes zivju buljona

225 g/8 unces mizotas garneles

15 ml/1 ēdamkarote kukurūzas miltu (kukurūzas ciete)

45 ml / 3 ēdamkarotes ūdens

Uzkarsē pusi eļļas un apcep tofu, līdz tas ir viegli brūns, tad izņem no pannas. Uzkarsē atlikušo eļļu un maisot apcep lociņus un ķiplokus, līdz tie ir viegli brūni. Pievieno sojas mērci, cukuru un buļjonu un uzvāra. Pievienojiet garneles un maisiet uz lēnas uguns 3 minūtes. Kukurūzas miltus un ūdeni samaisa biezenī, pievieno pannā un maisot vāra uz lēnas uguns, līdz mērce sabiezē. Ielejiet tofu atpakaļ pannā un viegli sautējiet, līdz tas ir sasildīts.

Garneles ar tomātiem

Pasniedz 4

2 olu baltumi

30 ml/2 ēdamkarotes kukurūzas miltu (kukurūzas ciete)

5 ml/1 tējkarote sāls

450 g/1 mārciņa nomizotas garneles

eļļa dziļai cepšanai

30 ml/2 ēdamkarotes rīsu vīna vai sausā šerija

225 g / 8 unces tomātu, nomizoti, bez serdes un sasmalcināti

Sajauc olu baltumus, kukurūzas miltus un sāli. Samaisiet garneles, līdz tās ir labi pārklātas. Uzkarsē eļļu un apcep garneles, līdz tās ir gatavas. Nolej visu, izņemot 15 ml/1 ēd.k., un uzkarsē. Pievienojiet vīnu vai šeriju un tomātus un uzvāra. Pirms pasniegšanas iemaisa garneles un ātri uzsilda.

Garneles ar tomātu mērci

Pasniedz 4

30 ml/2 ēdamkarotes zemesriekstu eļļas
1 ķiploka daiviņa, sasmalcināta
2 šķēles ingvera saknes, sasmalcinātas
2,5 ml/¬Ω tējkarote sāls
15 ml/1 ēdamkarote rīsu vīna vai sausā šerija
15 ml/1 ēdamkarote sojas mērces
6 ml/4 ēdamkarotes tomātu kečups (catsup)
120 ml / 4 fl oz / ¬Ω tase zivju buljona
350g/12oz nomizotas garneles
10 ml / 2 tējkarotes kukurūzas miltu (kukurūzas ciete)
30 ml/2 ēdamkarotes ūdens

Uzkarsē eļļu un maisot apcep ķiplokus, ingveru un sāli 2 minūtes. Pievieno vīnu vai šeriju, sojas mērci, tomātu kečupu un buljonu un uzvāra. Pievieno garneles, uzliek vāku un vāra uz lēnas uguns 2 minūtes. Kukurūzas miltus un ūdeni samaisa pastu,

pievieno pannā un maisot vāra, līdz mērce ir dzidra un
sabiezējusi.

Garneles ar tomātu un čili mērci

Pasniedz 4

60 ml/4 ēdamkarotes zemesriekstu eļļas

15 ml/1 ēdamkarote malta ingvera

15 ml/1 ēdamkarote malta ķiploka

15 ml/1 ēdamkarote sasmalcinātu sīpolu

60 ml/4 ēdamkarotes tomātu biezeņa (pastas)

15 ml/1 ēdamkarote čili mērces

450 g/1 mārciņa nomizotas garneles

15 ml/1 ēdamkarote kukurūzas miltu (kukurūzas ciete)

15 ml/1 ēdamkarote ūdens

Uzkarsē eļļu un maisot apcep ingveru, ķiplokus un sīpolus 1
minūti. Pievienojiet tomātu biezeni un čili mērci un labi
samaisiet. Pievieno garneles un maisot apcep 2 minūtes.
Kukurūzas miltus un ūdeni sasmalcina biezenī, pievieno pannā
un vāra uz lēnas uguns, līdz mērce sabiezē. Nekavējoties
pasniedziet.

Ceptas garneles ar tomātu mērci

Pasniedz 4

50 g/2 unces/¬Ω glāzes vienkāršu (universālu) miltu

2,5 ml/¬Ω tējkarote sāls

1 ola, viegli sakulta

30 ml/2 ēdamkarotes ūdens

450 g/1 mārciņa nomizotas garneles

eļļa dziļai cepšanai

30 ml/2 ēdamkarotes zemesriekstu eļļas

1 sīpols, smalki sagriezts

2 šķēles ingvera saknes, sasmalcinātas

75 ml/5 ēdamkarotes tomātu kečupa (catsup)

10 ml / 2 tējkarotes kukurūzas miltu (kukurūzas ciete)

30 ml/2 ēdamkarotes ūdens

Sajauc miltus, sāli, olu un ūdeni, lai izveidotu mīklu, ja nepieciešams, pievienojot vēl nedaudz ūdens. Pārlej ar garnelēm, līdz tās ir labi pārklātas. Uzkarsē eļļu un apcep garneles dažas minūtes, līdz tās kļūst kraukšķīgas un zeltainas. Nokāš uz virtuves papīra.

Tikmēr uzkarsē eļļu un apcep sīpolu un ingveru, līdz tie mīksti. Pievienojiet tomātu kečupu un vāriet uz lēnas uguns 3 minūtes. Kukurūzas miltus un ūdeni samaisa viendabīgā masā, pievieno pannā un maisot vāra uz lēnas uguns, līdz mērce sabiezē. Pievienojiet garneles pannā un vāriet, līdz tās uzkarsē. Nekavējoties pasniedziet.

Garneles ar dārzeņiem

Pasniedz 4

15 ml/1 ēdamkarote zemesriekstu eļļas
225 g/8 unces brokoļu ziediņi
225 g/8 unces sēnes
225 g/8 unces bambusa dzinumi, sasmalcināti
450 g/1 mārciņa nomizotas garneles
120 ml / 4 fl unces / ¬Ω tase vistas buljona
5 ml/1 tējk kukurūzas milti (kukurūzas ciete)

5 ml/1 tējkarote austeru mērce

2,5 ml/¬Ω tējkarote cukura

2,5 ml/¬Ω tējkarote rīvētas ingvera saknes

šķipsniņa svaigi maltu piparu

Uzkarsē eļļu un maisot apcep brokoļus 1 minūti. Pievienojiet sēnes un bambusa dzinumus un maisot apcepiet 2 minūtes. Pievieno garneles un maisot apcep 2 minūtes. Apvienojiet atlikušās sastāvdaļas un iemaisiet garneļu maisījumā. Uzkarsē līdz vārīšanās temperatūrai, maisot, tad vāra 1 minūti, nepārtraukti maisot.

Garneles ar ūdens kastaņiem

Pasniedz 4

60 ml/4 ēdamkarotes zemesriekstu eļļas

1 ķiploka daiviņa, sasmalcināta

1 šķēle ingvera saknes, sasmalcināta

450 g/1 mārciņa nomizotas garneles

30 ml/2 ēdamkarotes rīsu vīna vai sausa šerija 225 g/8 unces

ūdens kastaņi, sagriezti

30 ml/2 ēdamkarotes sojas mērces

15 ml/1 ēdamkarote kukurūzas miltu (kukurūzas cietc)

45 ml / 3 ēdamkarotes ūdens

Uzkarsē eļļu un apcep ķiplokus un ingveru, līdz tie ir viegli brūni. Pievieno garneles un maisot cep 1 minūti. Pievienojiet vīnu vai šeriju un labi samaisiet. Pievienojiet ūdens kastaņus un maisot apcepiet 5 minūtes. Pievieno pārējās sastāvdaļas un maisot cep 2 minūtes.

Garneles Wontons

Pasniedz 4

450 g/1 mārciņa lobītas garneles, sasmalcinātas

225 g/8 unces jaukti dārzeņi, sasmalcināti

15 ml/1 ēdamkarote sojas mērces

2,5 ml/¬Ω tējkarote sāls

dažus pilienus sezama eļļas

40 wonton ādas

eļļa dziļai cepšanai

Sajauc garneles, dārzeņus, sojas mērci, sāli un sezama eļļu.

Lai salocītu wontonus, turiet ādu kreisās rokas plaukstā un ar karoti ielieciet centrā. Samitriniet malas ar olu un salokiet ādu trijstūrī, noslēdzot malas. Saslapiniet stūrus ar olu un sarullējiet.

Sildiet eļļu un apcepiet vontonus pa dažiem, līdz tie kļūst zeltaini brūni. Pirms pasniegšanas labi nokāš.

Abalone ar vistu

Pasniedz 4

400g/14oz konservēta pērļgliemene

30 ml/2 ēdamkarotes zemesriekstu eļļas

100 g / 4 unces vistas krūtiņa, sagriezta kubiņos

100g/4oz bambusa dzinumi, sasmalcināti

250 ml / 8 fl oz / 1 glāze zivju buljona

15 ml/1 ēdamkarote rīsu vīna vai sausā šerija

5 ml/1 tējk cukurs

2,5 ml/¬Ω tējkarote sāls

15 ml/1 ēdamkarote kukurūzas miltu (kukurūzas ciete)

45 ml / 3 ēdamkarotes ūdens

Nokāš āliņģi un sagriež šķēlēs, sulu paturot. Uzkarsē eļļu un maisot apcep vistu, līdz tā kļūst gaiša. Pievienojiet pērļgliemenes un bambusa dzinumus un maisot apcepiet 1 minūti. Pievienojiet pērļgliemenes buljonu, buljonu, vīnu vai šeriju, cukuru un sāli, uzkarsē līdz vārīšanās temperatūrai un vāra uz lēnas uguns 2 minūtes. Sajauc kukurūzas miltus un ūdeni līdz pastai un maisot vāra, līdz mērce ir dzidra un sabiezēta. Nekavējoties pasniedziet.

Abalone ar sparģeļiem

Pasniedz 4

10 kaltētas ķīniešu sēnes

30 ml/2 ēdamkarotes zemesriekstu eļļas

15 ml/1 ēdamkarote ūdens

225 g / 8 unces sparģeļu

2,5 ml/¬Ω tējkarote zivju mērces

15 ml/1 ēdamkarote kukurūzas miltu (kukurūzas ciete)

225 g / 8 unces konservēta pērļgliemene, sagriezta

60 ml/4 ēdamkarotes buljona

¬Ω mazi burkāni, sagriezti šķēlēs

5 ml/1 tējk sojas mērce

5 ml/1 tējkarote austeru mērce

5 ml/1 tējkarote rīsu vīna vai sausā šerija

Sēnes 30 minūtes iemērc siltā ūdenī, pēc tam nokāš. Izmetiet kātus. Uzkarsē 15 ml/1 ēdamkarote eļļas ar ūdeni un apcep sēņu cepurītes 10 minūtes. Tikmēr vāriet sparģeļus verdošā ūdenī ar zivju mērci un 5 ml/1 tējk kukurūzas miltiem, līdz tie ir mīksti. Kārtīgi nokāš un kārto uz sasildīta pasniegšanas šķīvja ar sēnēm. Turiet tos siltus. Uzkarsē atlikušo eļļu un dažas sekundes apcep āliņģi, tad pievieno buljonu, burkānus, sojas mērci, austeru mērci, vīnu vai šeriju un atlikušos kukurūzas miltus. Vāra apmēram 5 minūtes, līdz tie ir gatavi, tad ar karoti pārliek sparģeļiem un pasniedz.

Abalone ar sēnēm

Pasniedz 4

6 kaltētas ķīniešu sēnes
400g/14oz konservēta pērļgliemene
45 ml/3 ēdamkarotes zemesriekstu eļļas
2,5 ml/¬Ω tējkarote sāls
15 ml/1 ēdamkarote rīsu vīna vai sausā šerija
3 lociņi, biezi sagriezti

Sēnes 30 minūtes iemērc siltā ūdenī, pēc tam nokāš. Izmetiet kātus un nogrieziet vāciņus. Nokāš āliņģi un sagriež šķēlēs, sulu paturot. Uzkarsē eļļu un maisot apcep sāli un sēnes 2 minūtes. Pievieno āliņģu buljonu un šeriju, uzvāra, uzliek vāku un vāra uz lēnas uguns 3 minūtes. Pievieno āliņģi un lociņus un sautē, līdz tie ir sasiluši. Nekavējoties pasniedziet.

Abalone ar austeru mērci

Pasniedz 4

400g/14oz konservēta pērļgliemene

15 ml/1 ēdamkarote kukurūzas miltu (kukurūzas ciete)
15 ml/1 ēdamkarote sojas mērces
45 ml/3 ēdamkarotes austeru mērces
30 ml/2 ēdamkarotes zemesriekstu eļļas
50 g/2 oz kūpināts šķiņķis, malts

Iztukšojiet pērļgliemenes kannu un rezervējiet 90 ml/6 ēdamkarotes šķidruma. Sajauc to ar kukurūzas miltiem, sojas mērci un austeru mērci. Uzkarsē eļļu un maisot apcep notecināto āliņģi 1 minūti. Iemaisa mērces maisījumu un maisot vāra, līdz uzkarsē, apmēram 1 minūti. Pārliek uz sasildīta pasniegšanas šķīvja un pasniedz, dekorētu ar šķiņķi.

Tvaicēti gliemenes

Pasniedz 4

24 gliemenes

Gliemenes rūpīgi notīriet, pēc tam vairākas stundas iemērciet sālītā ūdenī. Noskalo zem tekoša ūdens un novieto uz sekla, cepeškrāsnī necaurlaidīga šķīvja. Liek uz grila tvaikonī, uzliek vāku un vāra virs lēnas uguns ūdens apmēram 10 minūtes, līdz visas gliemenes ir atvērušās. Izmetiet visus, kas paliek aizvērti. Pasniedz ar mērcēm.

Gliemenes ar pupiņu kāpostiem

Pasniedz 4

24 gliemenes

15 ml/1 ēdamkarote zemesriekstu eļļas

150 g/5 unces pupiņu asni

1 zaļā paprika, sagriezta sloksnēs

2 lociņi, sasmalcināti

15 ml/1 ēdamkarote rīsu vīna vai sausā šerija

sāls un svaigi malti pipari

2,5 ml/¬Ω tējkarote sezama eļļas

50 g/2 unces kūpināts šķiņķis, sasmalcināts

Gliemenes rūpīgi notīriet, pēc tam vairākas stundas iemērciet sālītā ūdenī. Noskalo zem tekoša ūdens. Katliņā uzvāra ūdeni, pievieno gliemenes un vāra uz lēnas uguns dažas minūtes, līdz tās atveras. Iztukšojiet un izmetiet to, kas paliek aizvērts. Noņemiet gliemenes no čaumalām.

Uzkarsē eļļu un apcep pupiņu kāpostus 1 minūti. Pievieno piparus un sīpolus un maisot apcep 2 minūtes. Pievienojiet vīnu vai šeriju un pievienojiet sāli un piparus. Uzkarsē, pēc tam iemaisa gliemenes un maisa, līdz labi saplūst un izkarsē. Pārliek uz sasildīta pasniegšanas šķīvja un pasniedz, pārslaka ar sezama eļļu un šķiņķi.

Gliemenes ar ingveru un ķiploku

Pasniedz 4

24 gliemenes

15 ml/1 ēdamkarote zemesriekstu eļļas

2 šķēles ingvera saknes, sasmalcinātas

2 ķiploka daiviņas, sasmalcinātas

15 ml/1 ēdamkarote ūdens

5 ml/1 tējkarote sezama eļļas

sāls un svaigi malti pipari

Gliemenes rūpīgi notīriet, pēc tam vairākas stundas iemērciet sālītā ūdenī. Noskalo zem tekoša ūdens. Uzkarsē eļļu un apcep ingveru un ķiplokus 30 sekundes. Pievienojiet gliemenes, ūdeni un sezama eļļu, pārklājiet un vāriet apmēram 5 minūtes, līdz gliemenes atveras. Izmetiet visus, kas paliek aizvērti. Viegli apkaisa ar sāli un pipariem un pasniedz nekavējoties.

Cepti gliemenes

Pasniedz 4

24 gliemenes

60 ml/4 ēdamkarotes zemesriekstu eļļas

4 ķiploka daiviņas, sasmalcinātas

1 sīpols, sasmalcināts

2,5 ml/¬Ω tējkarote sāls

Gliemenes rūpīgi notīriet, pēc tam vairākas stundas iemērciet sālītā ūdenī. Noskalo zem tekoša ūdens, pēc tam nosusina. Uzkarsē eļļu un apcep ķiplokus, sīpolus un sāli, līdz tie mīksti. Pievienojiet gliemenes, pārklājiet un vāriet uz lēnas uguns apmēram 5 minūtes, līdz atveras visas čaumalas. Izmetiet visus, kas paliek aizvērti. Pagatavojiet vēl 1 minūti, viegli aplejot ar eļļu.

Krabju kūkas

Pasniedz 4

225 g/8 unces pupiņu asni

60 ml/4 ēdamkarotes zemesriekstu eļļas 100 g/4 unces bambusa

dzinumi, sagriezti sloksnēs

1 sīpols, sasmalcināts

225 g/8 unces krabju gaļa, sasmalcināta

4 olas, viegli sakultas

15 ml/1 ēdamkarote kukurūzas miltu (kukurūzas ciete)

30 ml/2 ēdamkarotes sojas mērces

sāls un svaigi malti pipari

Pupiņu asnus 4 minūtes blanšē verdošā ūdenī, pēc tam nokāš.
Uzkarsē pusi eļļas un maisot apcep pupiņu asnus, bambusa
dzinumus un sīpolus, līdz tie kļūst mīksti. Noņemiet no karstuma
un sajauciet ar pārējām sastāvdaļām, izņemot eļļu. Tīrā pannā

uzkarsē atlikušo eļļu un apcep karotes krabju gaļas maisījuma, veidojot mazus pīrādziņus. Cepiet, līdz tie ir viegli brūni no abām pusēm, pēc tam nekavējoties pasniedziet.

Krabju krēms

Pasniedz 4

225g/8oz krabju gaļas
5 olas, sakultas
1 lociņš (smalki sagriezts).
250 ml / 8 fl oz / 1 tase ūdens
5 ml/1 tējkarote sāls
5 ml/1 tējkarote sezama eļļas

Visas sastāvdaļas labi samaisa. Ielieciet bļodā, pārklājiet un novietojiet uz dubultā katla virs karsta ūdens vai uz tvaikoņa plaukta. Vāra uz lēnas uguns apmēram 35 minūtes, ik pa laikam apmaisot, līdz kļūst krēmīga. Pasniedz ar rīsiem.

Krabju gaļa ar ķīniešu lapām

Pasniedz 4

450 g Ķīnas lapas, sasmalcinātas

45 ml/3 ēdamkarotes augu eļļas

2 lociņi, sasmalcināti

225g/8oz krabju gaļas

15 ml/1 ēdamkarote sojas mērces

15 ml/1 ēdamkarote rīsu vīna vai sausā šerija

5 ml/1 tējkarote sāls

Ķīnas lapas blanšē verdošā ūdenī 2 minūtes, pēc tam kārtīgi nokāš un noskalo aukstā ūdenī. Uzkarsē eļļu un apcep lociņus, līdz tie ir viegli brūni. Pievienojiet krabju gaļu un maisot apcepiet 2 minūtes. Pievieno ķīniešu lapas un maisot cep 4 minūtes. Pievieno sojas mērci, vīnu vai šeriju, sāli un labi samaisa. Pievieno buljonu un kukurūzas miltus, uzvāra un maisot vāra uz lēnas uguns 2 minūtes, līdz mērce ir dzidra un sabiezējusi.

Krabls Foo Yung ar pupiņu kāpostiem

Pasniedz 4

6 olas, sakultas

45 ml/3 ēdamkarotes kukurūzas miltu (kukurūzas ciete)

225g/8oz krabju gaļas

100 g/4 unces pupiņu asni

2 lociņi, smalki sagriezti

2,5 ml/¬Ω tējkarote sāls

45 ml/3 ēdamkarotes zemesriekstu eļļas

Iecilā olas, tad iemaisa kukurūzas miltos. Sajauc pārējās sastāvdaļas, izņemot eļļu. Uzkarsē eļļu un maisījumu pamazām lej pannā, veidojot mazas pankūkas, apmēram 7,5 cm/3 diametrā. Cepiet, līdz apakša kļūst brūna, pēc tam apgrieziet un apcepiet otru pusi.

Krabis ar ingveru

Pasniedz 4

15 ml/1 ēdamkarote zemesriekstu eļļas

2 šķēles ingvera saknes, sasmalcinātas

4 lociņi, sasmalcināti

3 ķiploka daiviņas, sasmalcinātas

1 sarkanais čili pipars, sasmalcināts

350g/12oz krabju gaļa, pārslas

2,5 ml/¬Ω tējkarote zivju pastas

2,5 ml/¬Ω tējkarote sezama eļļas

15 ml/1 ēdamkarote rīsu vīna vai sausā šerija

5 ml/1 tējk kukurūzas milti (kukurūzas ciete)

15 ml/1 ēdamkarote ūdens

Uzkarsē eļļu un apcep ingveru, sīpolus, ķiplokus un čili 2
minūtes. Pievienojiet krabju gaļu un samaisiet, līdz tā ir labi
pārklāta ar garšvielām. Iemaisa zivju pastu. Sajauc pārējās
sastāvdaļas līdz viendabīgai masai, tad pievieno pannā un maisot
cep 1 minūti. Nekavējoties pasniedziet.

Krabis Lo Meins

Pasniedz 4

100 g/4 unces pupiņu asni
30 ml/2 ēdamkarotes zemesriekstu eļļas
5 ml/1 tējkarote sāls
1 sīpols, sasmalcināts
100g/4oz sēnes, sagrieztas
225 g/8 unces krabju gaļa, sasmalcināta
100g/4oz bambusa dzinumi, sasmalcināti
Pievieno makaronus
30 ml/2 ēdamkarotes sojas mērces
5 ml/1 tējk cukurs
5 ml/1 tējkarote sezama eļļas
sāls un svaigi malti pipari

Pupiņu asnus 5 minūtes blanšē verdošā ūdenī, pēc tam nokāš.
Uzkarsē eļļu un apcep sāli un sīpolus, līdz tie mīksti. Pievieno
sēnes un maisot apcep līdz mīkstas. Pievienojiet krabju gaļu un
maisot apcepiet 2 minūtes. Pievieno pupiņu kāpostus un bambusa
dzinumus un maisot cep 1 minūti. Pievienojiet pannā notecinātus
makaronus un viegli samaisiet. Sajauc sojas mērci, cukuru un
sezama eļļu, pievieno sāli un piparus. Samaisiet pannā līdz
karstai.

Cepti krabji ar cūkgaļu

Pasniedz 4

30 ml/2 ēdamkarotes zemesriekstu eļļas

100 g maltas (maltas) cūkgaļas

350g/12oz krabju gaļa, pārslas

2 šķēles ingvera saknes, sasmalcinātas

2 olas, viegli sakultas

15 ml/1 ēdamkarote sojas mērces

15 ml/1 ēdamkarote rīsu vīna vai sausā šerija

30 ml/2 ēdamkarotes ūdens

sāls un svaigi malti pipari

4 lociņi, sagriezti sloksnēs

Uzkarsē eļļu un maisot apcep cūkgaļu līdz gaišai krāsai. Pievienojiet krabju gaļu un ingveru un maisot apcepiet 1 minūti. Sakuļ olas. Pievienojiet sojas mērci, vīnu vai šeriju, ūdeni, sāli un piparus un maisot apcepiet apmēram 4 minūtes. Pasniedz, dekorējot ar lociņiem.

Cepta krabju gaļa

Pasniedz 4

30 ml/2 ēdamkarotes zemesriekstu eļļas
450 g/1 mārciņa krabju gaļas, pārslu veidā
2 lociņi, sasmalcināti
2 šķēles ingvera saknes, sasmalcinātas
30 ml/2 ēdamkarotes sojas mērces
30 ml/2 ēdamkarotes rīsu vīna vai sausā šerija
2,5 ml/¬Ω tējkarote sāls
15 ml/1 ēdamkarote kukurūzas miltu (kukurūzas ciete)
60 ml / 4 ēdamkarotes ūdens

Uzkarsē eļļu un maisot apcep krabju gaļu, sīpolus un ingveru 1 minūti. Pievieno sojas mērci, vīnu vai šeriju un sāli, uzliek vāku un vāra uz lēnas uguns 3 minūtes. Kukurūzas miltus un ūdeni samaisa pastu, pievieno pannā un maisot vāra, līdz mērce ir dzidra un sabiezējusi.

Ceptas sēpiju bumbiņas

Pasniedz 4

450 g/1 mārciņa sēpiju

50 g/2 unces speķis, kausēts

1 olas baltums

2,5 ml/¬Ω tējkarote cukura

2,5 ml/¬Ω tējkarote kukurūzas miltu (kukurūzas ciete)

sāls un svaigi malti pipari

eļļa dziļai cepšanai

Sagrieziet sēpiju un samaisiet vai sasmalciniet to biezenī. Sajauc ar bekonu, olu baltumu, cukuru un kukurūzas miltiem un apkaisa ar sāli un pipariem. Saspiediet maisījumu mazās bumbiņās. Uzkarsē eļļu un apcep sēpiju bumbiņas, ja nepieciešams, pa daļām, līdz tās uzceļas uz eļļas augšdaļas un kļūst zeltaini brūnas. Labi nokāš un nekavējoties pasniedz.

Kantonas omārs

Pasniedz 4

2 omāri

30 ml/2 ēdamkarotes eļļas

15 ml/1 ēdamkarote melno pupiņu mērces

1 ķiploka daiviņa, sasmalcināta

1 sīpols, sasmalcināts

225g/8oz malta (malta) cūkgaļa

45 ml/3 ēdamkarotes sojas mērces

5 ml/1 tējk cukurs

sāls un svaigi malti pipari

15 ml/1 ēdamkarote kukurūzas miltu (kukurūzas ciete)

75 ml / 5 ēdamkarotes ūdens

1 ola, sakulta

Salaužam omārus, izņemam gaļu un sagriežam 2,5 cm/1 kubiņos. Uzkarsē eļļu un apcep melno pupiņu mērci, ķiplokus un sīpolus, līdz tie ir viegli brūni. Pievienojiet cūkgaļu un cepiet, līdz tā kļūst brūna. Pievieno sojas mērci, cukuru, sāli, piparus un omāru, uzliek vāku un vāra uz lēnas uguns apmēram 10 minūtes. Kukurūzas miltus un ūdeni sasmalcina biezenī, pievieno pannā un maisot vāra, līdz mērce ir dzidra un sabiezējusi. Pirms pasniegšanas nogriež uguni un iecilā olu.

Cepts omārs

Pasniedz 4

450 g/1 mārciņa omāra gaļas

30 ml/2 ēdamkarotes sojas mērces

5 ml/1 tējk cukurs

1 ola, sakulta

30 ml/3 ēdamkarotes vienkāršu (universālu) miltu

eļļa dziļai cepšanai

Omāra gaļu sagriež 2,5 cm/1 kubiņos un pārlej ar sojas mērci un cukuru. Atstājiet iedarboties 15 minūtes, pēc tam nosusiniet. Sakuļ olu un miltus, tad pievieno omāru un kārtīgi samaisa, lai tas pārklātos. Uzkarsē eļļu un apcep omārus līdz zeltaini brūnai. Pirms pasniegšanas nokāš uz virtuves papīra.

Pasniedz 4

4 olas, viegli sakultas

60 ml / 4 ēdamkarotes ūdens

5 ml/1 tējkarote sāls

15 ml/1 ēdamkarote sojas mērces

450 g/1 mārciņa omāra gaļa, pārslas

15 ml/1 ēdamkarote sasmalcināta kūpināta šķiņķa

15 ml/1 ēdamkarote sasmalcinātu svaigu pētersīļu

Sakuļ olas ar ūdeni, sāli un sojas mērci. Lej cepeškrāsnī izturīgā bļodā un pārkaisa ar omāra gaļu. Novietojiet bļodu uz grila tvaicētājā, pārklājiet un vāriet 20 minūtes, līdz olas ir sacietējušas. Pasniedz, dekorējot ar šķiņķi un pētersīļiem.

Omārs ar sēnēm

Pasniedz 4

450 g/1 mārciņa omāra gaļas

15 ml/1 ēdamkarote kukurūzas miltu (kukurūzas ciete)

60 ml / 4 ēdamkarotes ūdens

30 ml/2 ēdamkarotes zemesriekstu eļļas

4 lociņi, biezi sagriezti

100g/4oz sēnes, sagrieztas

2,5 ml/¬Ω tējkarote sāls

1 ķiploka daiviņa, sasmalcināta

30 ml/2 ēdamkarotes sojas mērces

15 ml/1 ēdamkarote rīsu vīna vai sausā šerija

Sagrieziet omāra gaļu 2,5 cm/1 kubiņos. Sajauciet kukurūzas miltus un ūdeni līdz pastai un iemetiet maisījumā omāra kubiņus, lai tie pārklātu. Uzkarsē pusi eļļas un apcep omāra kubiņus, līdz tie ir viegli brūni, izņem tos no pannas. Uzkarsē atlikušo eļļu un apcep lociņus, līdz tie ir viegli brūni. Pievienojiet sēnes un maisot apcepiet 3 minūtes. Pievienojiet sāli, ķiplokus, sojas mērci un vīnu vai šeriju un maisot apcepiet 2 minūtes. Ievietojiet omārus atpakaļ pannā un maisot vāriet, līdz tas ir uzkarsēts.

Omāru astes ar cūkgaļu

Pasniedz 4

3 kaltētas ķīniešu sēnes

4 omāra astes

60 ml/4 ēdamkarotes zemesriekstu eļļas

100 g maltas (maltas) cūkgaļas

50g/2oz ūdens kastaņi, smalki sagriezti

sāls un svaigi malti pipari

2 ķiploka daiviņas, sasmalcinātas

45 ml/3 ēdamkarotes sojas mērces

30 ml/2 ēdamkarotes rīsu vīna vai sausā šerija

30 ml/2 ēdamkarotes melno pupiņu mērces

10 ml/2 ēdamkarotes kukurūzas miltu (kukurūzas ciete)

120 ml / 4 fl unces / ¬Ω tase ūdens

Sēnes 30 minūtes iemērc siltā ūdenī, pēc tam nokāš. Izmetiet kātus un nogrieziet vāciņus. Pārgrieziet omāra astes gareniski uz pusēm. Noņemiet gaļu no omāra astēm, atstājot čaumalas. Uzkarsē pusi eļļas un apcep cūkgaļu līdz gaiši brūnai. Noņemiet no karstuma un samaisiet ar sēnēm, omāra gaļu, ūdens kastaņiem, sāli un pipariem. Iespiediet gaļu atpakaļ omāra čaumalās un kārtojiet uz cepeškrāsns izturīga šķīvja. Liek uz grila tvaicētājā, pārklāj un vāra uz lēnas uguns apmēram 20 minūtes, līdz tie ir gatavi. Tikmēr uzkarsē atlikušo eļļu un apcep ķiploku, sojas mērci, vīnu vai šeriju un melno pupiņu mērci 2 minūtes. Kukurūzas miltus un ūdeni samaisa pastu, pievieno pannā un maisot vāra uz lēnas uguns, līdz mērce sabiezē.

Cepts omārs

Pasniedz 4

450 g/1 mārciņa omāru astes

30 ml/2 ēdamkarotes zemesriekstu eļļas

1 ķiploka daiviņa, sasmalcināta

2,5 ml/¬Ω tējkarote sāls

350 g/12 unces pupiņu asni

50 g/2 unces sēņu

4 lociņi, biezi sagriezti

150 ml / ¬° pt / dāsna ¬Ω glāze vistas buljona

15 ml/1 ēdamkarote kukurūzas miltu (kukurūzas ciete)

Uzkarsē katlu ar ūdeni līdz vārīšanās temperatūrai, pievieno omāra astes un vāra 1 minūti. Nokāš, atdzesē, noņem čaumalu un sagriež biezās šķēlēs. Uzkarsē eļļu kopā ar ķiplokiem un sāli un vāra, līdz ķiploki ir viegli brūni. Pievienojiet omāru un maisot apcepiet 1 minūti. Pievieno pupiņu kāpostus un sēnes un maisot cep 1 minūti. Iemaisa lociņus. Ielej lielāko daļu buljona, uzvāra, uzliek vāku un vāra uz lēnas uguns 3 minūtes. Kukurūzas miltus sajauc ar pārējo buljonu, pievieno pannā un maisot vāra, līdz mērce kļūst dzidra un sabiezē.

Omāru ligzdas

Pasniedz 4

30 ml / 2 ēdamkarotes zemesriekstu eļļas

5 ml / 1 tējkarote sāls

1 sīpols, smalki sagriezts

100g/4oz sēnes, sagrieztas

100 g bambusa dzinumu, sasmalcinātu 225 g/8 unces vārītas

omāra gaļas

15 ml/1 ēdamkarote rīsu vīna vai sausā šerija

120 ml / 4 fl unces / ¬Ω tase vistas buljona

šķipsniņa svaigi maltu piparu

10 ml / 2 tējkarotes kukurūzas miltu (kukurūzas ciete)

15 ml/1 ēdamkarote ūdens

4 makaronu grozi

Uzkarsē eļļu un apcep sāli un sīpolus, līdz tie mīksti. Pievienojiet sēnes un bambusa dzinumus un maisot apcepiet 2 minūtes. Pievieno omāra gaļu, vīnu vai šeriju un buljonu, uzvāra, uzliek vāku un vāra uz lēnas uguns 2 minūtes. Garšojiet ar pipariem. Kukurūzas miltus un ūdeni samaisa viendabīgā masā, pievieno pannā un maisot vāra uz lēnas uguns, līdz mērce sabiezē. Sakārtojiet makaronu ligzdas uz sasildīta pasniegšanas šķīvja un uzlieciet omārus.

Mīdijas melno pupiņu mērcē

Pasniedz 4

45 ml/3 ēdamkarotes zemesriekstu eļļas

2 ķiploka daiviņas, sasmalcinātas

2 šķēles ingvera saknes, sasmalcinātas

30 ml/2 ēdamkarotes melno pupiņu mērces

15 ml/1 ēdamkarote sojas mērces

1,5 kg/3 mārciņas mīdijas, nomizotas un izgrieztas

2 lociņi, sasmalcināti

Uzkarsē eļļu un apcep ķiplokus un ingveru 30 sekundes. Pievienojiet melno pupiņu mērci un sojas mērci un vāriet 10 sekundes. Pievienojiet mīdijas, pārklājiet un vāriet apmēram 6 minūtes, līdz mīdijas atveras. Izmetiet visus, kas paliek aizvērti. Pārliek uz sasildītu servēšanas trauku un pasniedz, pārkaisot ar lociņiem.

Pasniedz 4

45 ml/3 ēdamkarotes zemesriekstu eļļas

2 ķiploka daiviņas, sasmalcinātas

4 ingvera saknes šķēles, sasmalcinātas

1,5 kg/3 mārciņas mīdijas, nomizotas un izgrieztas

45 ml / 3 ēdamkarotes ūdens

15 ml/1 ēdamkarote austeru mērces

Uzkarsē eļļu un apcep ķiplokus un ingveru 30 sekundes. Pievienojiet mīdijas un ūdeni, pārklājiet un vāriet apmēram 6 minūtes, līdz mīdijas atveras. Izmetiet visus, kas paliek aizvērti. Pārliek uz uzsildītā servēšanas traukā un pasniedz, pārlejotu ar austeru mērci.

Tvaicētas mīdijas

Pasniedz 4

1,5 kg/3 mārciņas mīdijas, nomizotas un izgrieztas
45 ml/3 ēdamkarotes sojas mērces
3 lociņi, smalki sagriezti

Mīdijas liek uz grila tvaicētājā, uzliek vāku un tvaicē virs verdoša ūdens apmēram 10 minūtes, līdz visas mīdijas ir atvērušās. Izmetiet visus, kas paliek aizvērti. Pārliek uz uzsildītu servēšanas trauku un pasniedz, pārlejotu ar sojas mērci un lociņiem.

Ceptas austeres

Pasniedz 4

24 austeres, sagrautas

sāls un svaigi malti pipari

1 ola, sakulta

50 g/2 unces/¬Ω glāzes vienkāršu (universālu) miltu

250 ml / 8 fl oz / 1 tase ūdens

eļļa dziļai cepšanai

4 lociņi, sasmalcināti

Garšojiet austeres ar sāli un pipariem. Sakuļ olu ar miltiem un ūdeni mīklā un izmanto austeru pārklāšanai. Uzkarsē eļļu un apcep austeres līdz zeltaini brūnai. Nokāš uz virtuves papīra un pasniedz, dekorējot ar sīpoliem.

Austeres ar bekonu

Pasniedz 4

175 g / 6 unces bekona

24 austeres, sagrautas

1 ola, viegli sakulta

15 ml/1 ēdamkarote ūdens

45 ml/3 ēdamkarotes zemesriekstu eļļas

2 sīpoli, sasmalcinati

15 ml/1 ēdamkarote kukurūzas miltu (kukurūzas ciete)

15 ml/1 ēdamkarote sojas mērces

90 ml/6 ēdamkarotes vistas buljona

Sagrieziet bekonu gabaliņos un aptiniet vienu gabalu ap katru austeri. Sakuļ olu ar ūdeni, pēc tam iemērc austerēs, lai tās pārklātu. Uzkarsē pusi eļļas un apcep austeres no abām pusēm, līdz tās ir viegli brūnas, tad izņem no pannas un notecina taukus. Uzkarsē atlikušo eļļu un apcep sīpolus, līdz tie ir mīksti. Kukurūzas miltus, sojas mērci un buljonu sajauc līdz biezenim, lej pannā un maisot cep, līdz mērce kļūst dzidra un sabiezē. Pārlej ar austerēm un nekavējoties pasniedz.

Ceptas austeres ar ingveru

Pasniedz 4

24 austeres, sagrautas

2 šķēles ingvera saknes, sasmalcinātas

30 ml/2 ēdamkarotes sojas mērces

15 ml/1 ēdamkarote rīsu vīna vai sausā šerija

4 lociņi, sagriezti sloksnēs

100 g / 4 unces bekona

1 ola

50 g/2 unces/¬Ω glāzes vienkāršu (universālu) miltu

sāls un svaigi malti pipari

eļļa dziļai cepšanai

1 citrons, sagriezts šķēlēs

Ievietojiet austeres bļodā ar ingveru, sojas mērci un vīnu vai šeriju un labi samaisiet, lai tās pārklātu. Atstāj nostāvēties 30 minūtes. Katrai austerei uzlieciet dažas sīpola sloksnes. Sagrieziet bekonu gabaliņos un aptiniet pa gabalu katrai austerei. Sakuļ olu un miltus mīklā un pievieno sāli un piparus. Iemērciet austeres mīklā, līdz tās ir labi brūnas. Uzkarsē eļļu un apcep austeres līdz zeltaini brūnai. Pasniedz dekorētu ar citrona šķēlītēm.

Austeres ar melno pupiņu mērci

Pasniedz 4

350 g/12 unces noslaucītas austeres

120 ml/4 fl oz/¬Ω tase zemesriekstu (zemesriekstu) eļļas

2 ķiploka daiviņas, sasmalcinātas

3 lociņi, sagriezti šķēlēs

15 ml/1 ēdamkarote melno pupiņu mērces

30 ml/2 ēd.k. tumšās sojas mērces

15 ml/1 ēdamkarote sezama eļļas

šķipsniņa čili pulvera

Austeres blanšē verdošā ūdenī 30 sekundes, pēc tam nokāš. Uzkarsē eļļu un apmaisot apcep ķiplokus un sīpolus 30 sekundes. Pievienojiet melno pupiņu mērci, sojas mērci, sezama eļļu un austeres un pēc garšas pievienojiet čili pulveri. Cepiet maisot, līdz uzkarsē, un nekavējoties pasniedziet.

Ķemmes ar bambusa dzinumiem

Pasniedz 4

60 ml/4 ēdamkarotes zemesriekstu eļļas

6 lociņi, sasmalcināti

225g/8oz sēnes, sagrieztas ceturtdaļās

15 ml/1 ēdamkarote cukura

450 g/1 mārciņa lobītas ķemmīšgliemenes

2 šķēles ingvera saknes, sasmalcinātas

225 g/8 unces bambusa dzinumi, sasmalcināti

sāls un svaigi malti pipari

300 ml/¬Ω pt/1 ¬° tases ūdens

30 ml/2 ēdamkarotes vīna etiķa

30 ml/2 ēdamkarotes kukurūzas miltu (kukurūzas ciete)

150 ml/¬° pt/liela ¬Ω glāze ūdens

45 ml/3 ēdamkarotes sojas mērces

Uzkarsē eļļu un apcep sīpolus un sēnes 2 minūtes. Pievieno cukuru, ķemmīšgliemenes, ingveru, bambusa dzinumus, sāli un piparus, pārklāj un vāra 5 minūtes. Pievieno ūdeni un vīna etiķi, uzvāra, uzliek vāku un vāra uz lēnas uguns 5 minūtes. Kukurūzas miltus un ūdeni samaisa biezenī, pievieno pannā un maisot vāra uz lēnas uguns, līdz mērce sabiezē. Garšojiet ar sojas mērci un pasniedziet.

Ķemmīšgliemenes ar olu

Pasniedz 4

45 ml/3 ēdamkarotes zemesriekstu eļļas

350 g/12 unces lobītas ķemmīšgliemenes

25 g/1 unce kūpināts šķiņķis, sasmalcināts

30 ml/2 ēdamkarotes rīsu vīna vai sausā šerija

5 ml/1 tējk cukurs

174

2,5 ml/¬Ω tējkarote sāls

šķipsniņa svaigi maltu piparu

2 olas, viegli sakultas

15 ml/1 ēdamkarote sojas mērces

Uzkarsē eļļu un maisot apcep ķemmīšgliemenes 30 sekundes. Pievieno šķiņķi un maisot cep 1 minūti. Pievienojiet vīnu vai šeriju, cukuru, sāli un piparus un maisot apcepiet 1 minūti. Pievienojiet olas un viegli maisiet uz lielas uguns, līdz sastāvdaļas ir labi pārklātas ar olu. Pasniedz pārslaktu ar sojas mērci.

Ķemmīšgliemenes ar brokoļiem

Pasniedz 4

350g/12oz ķemmītes, kubiņos

3 šķēles ingvera saknes, sasmalcinātas

¬Ω mazi burkāni, sagriezti šķēlēs

1 ķiploka daiviņa, sasmalcināta

45 ml/3 ēdamkarotes vienkāršu (universālu) miltu

175

2,5 ml/½ tējkarote sodas bikarbonāta (cepamā soda)

30 ml/2 ēdamkarotes zemesriekstu eļļas

15 ml/1 ēdamkarote ūdens

1 banāns, sagriezts

eļļa dziļai cepšanai

275 g/10 unces brokoļi

sāls

5 ml/1 tējkarote sezama eļļas

2,5 ml/½ tējkarote čili mērces

2,5 ml/½ tējkarote vīna etiķa

2,5 ml/½ tējkarote tomātu biezeņa (pastas)

Sajauc ķemmīšgliemenes ar ingveru, burkānu un ķiploku un atstāj nostāvēties. Sajauc miltus, cepamo sodu, 15 ml/1 ēdamkarote eļļas un ūdeni līdz viendabīgai masai un izmantojiet banānu šķēlīšu pārklāšanai. Uzkarsē eļļu un apcep banānu līdz zeltaini brūnai, tad nokāš un kārto ap sasildītu šķīvi. Tikmēr vāra brokoļus sālītā ūdenī, līdz tie ir mīksti, pēc tam nokāš. Uzkarsē atlikušo eļļu ar sezama eļļu un īsi apcep brokoļus, pēc tam kārto ap šķīvi ar banāniem. Pievienojiet pannā čili mērci, vīna etiķi un tomātu biezeni un maisot apcepiet ķemmīšgliemenes, līdz tās ir gatavas. Uzlieciet uz servēšanas šķīvja un nekavējoties pasniedziet.

Ķemmīšgliemenes ar ingveru

Pasniedz 4

45 ml/3 ēdamkarotes zemesriekstu eļļas

2,5 ml/¬Ω tējkarote sāls

3 šķēles ingvera saknes, sasmalcinātas

2 lociņi, biezi sagriezti

450 g/1 mārciņa lobītas ķemmīšgliemenes, pārgrieztas uz pusēm

15 ml/1 ēdamkarote kukurūzas miltu (kukurūzas ciete)

60 ml / 4 ēdamkarotes ūdens

Uzkarsē eļļu un apcep sāli un ingveru 30 sekundes. Pievienojiet sīpolus un maisot apcepiet, līdz tie ir viegli brūni. Pievienojiet ķemmīšgliemenes un maisot apcepiet 3 minūtes. Kukurūzas miltus un ūdeni samaisa viendabīgā masā, lej pannā un maisot vāra, līdz sabiezē. Nekavējoties pasniedziet.

Ķemmīšgliemenes ar šķiņķi

Pasniedz 4

450 g/1 mārciņa lobītas ķemmīšgliemenes, pārgrieztas uz pusēm
250 ml/8 fl oz/1 glāze rīsu vīna vai sausa šerija
1 sīpols, smalki sagriezts
2 šķēles ingvera saknes, sasmalcinātas
2,5 ml/¬Ω tējkarote sāls
100g/4oz kūpināts šķiņķis, sasmalcināts

Ievietojiet ķemmīšgliemenes bļodā un pievienojiet vīnu vai šeriju. Pārklājiet un atstājiet marinēties 30 minūtes, laiku pa
178

laikam apgriežot, pēc tam nosusiniet ķemmīšgliemenes un izmetiet marinādi. Ievietojiet ķemmīšgliemenes cepeškrāsnī izturīgā traukā kopā ar pārējām sastāvdaļām. Trauku liek uz grila tvaicētājā, pārklāj un tvaicē virs verdoša udens apmēram 6 minūtes, līdz ķemmīšgliemenes ir mīkstas.

Ķemmīšgliemeņu mīkla ar zaļumiem

Pasniedz 4

225g/8oz lobītas ķemmīšgliemenes
30 ml/2 ēdamkarotes sasmalcināta svaiga koriandra
4 olas, sakultas
15 ml/1 ēdamkarote rīsu vīna vai sausā šerija
sāls un svaigi malti pipari
15 ml/1 ēdamkarote zemesriekstu eļļas

Pievienojiet ķemmīšgliemenes tvaicētājam un tvaicējiet apmēram 3 minūtes, līdz tās ir gatavas, atkarībā no izmēra. Izņem no tvaicētāja un pārkaisa ar koriandru. Sakuļ olas ar vīnu vai šeriju un pēc garšas pievieno sāli un piparus. Sajauc ķemmīšgliemenes un koriandru. Uzkarsē eļļu un vāra olu-ķemmīšgliemeņu maisījumu, nepārtraukti maisot, līdz olas ir sacietējušas. Nekavējoties pasniedziet.

Ķemmīšgliemenes un sīpolus apcep maisot

Pasniedz 4

45 ml/3 ēdamkarotes zemesriekstu eļļas
1 sīpols, sasmalcināts
450 g/1 mārciņa pārslu ķemmīšgliemenes, sagrieztas ceturtdaļās
sāls un svaigi malti pipari
15 ml/1 ēdamkarote rīsu vīna vai sausā šerija

Uzkarsē eļļu un apcep sīpolus līdz mīkstam. Pievienojiet ķemmīšgliemenes un maisot apcepiet, līdz tās ir viegli brūnas. Garšojiet ar sāli un pipariem, pārlejiet ar vīnu vai šeriju un nekavējoties pasniedziet.

Ķemmīšgliemenes ar dārzeņiem

Pasniedz 4,Äì6

4 žāvētas ķīniešu sēnes

2 sīpoli

30 ml/2 ēdamkarotes zemesriekstu eļļas

3 selerijas kāti, sagriezti pa diagonāli

225 g/8 unces zaļās pupiņas, sagrieztas pa diagonāli

10 ml/2 tējk. rīvēta ingvera sakne

1 ķiploka daiviņa, sasmalcināta

20 ml/4 tējk kukurūzas milti (kukurūzas ciete)

250 ml / 8 fl oz / 1 tase vistas buljona

181

30 ml/2 ēdamkarotes rīsu vīna vai sausā šerija

30 ml/2 ēdamkarotes sojas mērces

450 g/1 mārciņa pārslu ķemmīšgliemenes, sagrieztas ceturtdaļās

6 lociņi, sagriezti

425 g/15 unces konservētas kukurūzas vālītes

Sēnes 30 minūtes iemērc siltā ūdenī, pēc tam nokāš. Izmetiet kātus un nogrieziet vāciņus. Sīpolus sagrieziet šķēlēs un atdaliet slāņus. Uzkarsē eļļu un apmaisot apcep sīpolus, seleriju, pupiņas, ingveru un ķiplokus 3 minūtes. Kukurūzas miltus sajauc ar nedaudz buljona, tad iemaisa atlikušo buljonu, vīnu vai šeriju un sojas mērci. Pievieno vokpannai un maisot uzvāra. Pievienojiet sēnes, ķemmīšgliemenes, sīpolus un kukurūzu un maisot apcepiet apmēram 5 minūtes, līdz ķemmīšgliemenes ir mīkstas.

Ķemmīšgliemenes ar pipariem

Pasniedz 4

30 ml/2 ēdamkarotes zemesriekstu eļļas

3 lociņi, sasmalcināti

1 ķiploka daiviņa, sasmalcināta

2 šķēles ingvera saknes, sasmalcinātas

2 sarkanie pipari, sagriezti kubiņos

450 g/1 mārciņa lobītas ķemmīšgliemenes

30 ml/2 ēdamkarotes rīsu vīna vai sausā šerija

15 ml/1 ēdamkarote sojas mērces

15 ml/1 ēdamkarote dzelteno pupiņu mērces

5 ml/1 tējk cukurs

5 ml/1 tējkarote sezama eļļas

Uzkarsē eļļu un maisot apcep sīpolus, ķiplokus un ingveru 30 sekundes. Pievieno papriku un maisot cep 1 minūti. Pievienojiet ķemmīšgliemenes un maisot apcepiet 30 sekundes, pēc tam pievienojiet pārējās sastāvdaļas un vāriet apmēram 3 minūtes, līdz ķemmīšgliemenes ir mīkstas.

Kalmāri ar pupiņu kāpostiem

Pasniedz 4

450 g / 1 mārciņa kalmāru

30 ml/2 ēdamkarotes zemesriekstu eļļas

15 ml/1 ēdamkarote rīsu vīna vai sausā šerija

100 g/4 unces pupiņu asni

15 ml/1 ēdamkarote sojas mērces

sāls

1 sarkanais čili pipars, sasmalcināts

2 šķēles ingvera saknes, sasmalcinātas

2 lociņi, sasmalcināti

Kalmāram noņem galvu, iekšas un membrānu un sagriež lielos gabaliņos. Katram gabalam izgrieziet krusta rakstu. Katliņā uzvāra ūdeni, pievieno kalmārus un vāra, līdz gabali saritinās, tad izņem un nokāš. Uzkarsē pusi eļļas un maisot ātri apcep kalmārus. Pārlej ar vīnu vai šeriju. Tikmēr uzkarsē atlikušo eļļu un maisot apcep pupiņu dīgstus, līdz tie kļūst mīksti. Sezona ar sojas mērci un sāli. Uz pasniegšanas šķīvja kārto čili piparus, ingveru un sīpolus. Centrā novietojiet pupiņu kāpostus un uzlieciet kalmārus. Nekavējoties pasniedziet.

Cepti kalmāri

Pasniedz 4

50 g/2 unces vienkāršu (universālu) miltu

25 g/1 unce/¬° tase kukurūzas miltu (kukurūzas ciete)

2,5 ml/¬Ω tējkarote cepamā pulvera

2,5 ml/¬Ω tējkarote sāls

1 ola

75 ml / 5 ēdamkarotes ūdens

15 ml/1 ēdamkarote zemesriekstu eļļas

450 g/1 mārciņa kalmāri, sagriezti gredzenos

eļļa dziļai cepšanai

Saputojiet miltus, kukurūzas miltus, cepamo pulveri, sāli, olu, ūdeni un eļļu, līdz izveidojas mīkla. Iemērciet kalmārus mīklā, līdz tie ir labi brūni. Uzkarsē eļļu un apcep kalmārus pa dažiem gabaliņiem līdz zeltaini brūnai. Pirms pasniegšanas nokāš uz virtuves papīra.

Kalmāru sūtījumi

Pasniedz 4

8 žāvētas ķīniešu sēnes

450 g / 1 mārciņa kalmāru

100g/4oz kūpināta šķiņķa

100g/4oz tofu

1 ola, sakulta

15 ml/1 ēdamkarote vienkāršu (universālu) miltu

2,5 ml/¬Ω tējkarote cukura

2,5 ml/¬Ω tējkarote sezama eļļas

sāls un svaigi malti pipari

8 wonton ādas

eļļa dziļai cepšanai

Sēnes 30 minūtes iemērc siltā ūdenī, pēc tam nokāš. Izmetiet kātus. Kalmāru sagriež un sagriež 8 daļās. Sagrieziet šķiņķi un tofu 8 daļās. Ielieciet tos visus bļodā. Olu sajauc ar miltiem, cukuru, sezama eļļu, sāli un pipariem. Pievienojiet sastāvdaļas bļodā un viegli samaisiet. Novietojiet sēņu cepuri un kalmāru, šķiņķa un tofu gabalu tieši zem katras Vontonas ādas vidus. Salieciet apakšējo stūri, salokiet sānos, pēc tam satiniet, saslapiniet malas ar ūdeni, lai to noslēgtu. Uzkarsē eļļu un apcep gabaliņus apmēram 8 minūtes, līdz tie kļūst zeltaini brūni. Pirms pasniegšanas labi nokāš.

Cepti kalmāru rullīši

Pasniedz 4

45 ml/3 ēdamkarotes zemesriekstu eļļas
225g/8oz kalmāru gredzeni
1 liela zaļā paprika, sagriezta gabaliņos
100g/4oz bambusa dzinumi, sasmalcināti
2 lociņi, smalki sagriezti
1 šķēle ingvera saknes, smalki sagriezta
45 ml/2 ēdamkarotes sojas mērces
30 ml/2 ēdamkarotes rīsu vīna vai sausā šerija
15 ml/1 ēdamkarote kukurūzas miltu (kukurūzas ciete)
15 ml/1 ēdamkarote zivju buljona vai ūdens

5 ml/1 tējk cukurs

5 ml/1 tējkarote vīna etiķa

5 ml/1 tējkarote sezama eļļas

sāls un svaigi malti pipari

Uzkarsē 15 ml/1 ēdamkarote eļļas un ātri apcep kalmāru gredzenus, līdz tie kļūst kraukšķīgi. Tikmēr atsevišķā pannā uzkarsē atlikušo eļļu un maisot apcep piparus, bambusa dzinumus, sīpolus un ingveru 2 minūtes. Pievienojiet kalmārus un maisot apcepiet 1 minūti. Iemaisa sojas mērci, vīnu vai šeriju, kukurūzas miltus, buljonu, cukuru, vīna etiķi un sezama eļļu, pievieno sāli un piparus. Vāra uz lēnas uguns, maisot, līdz mērce ir dzidra un sabiezējusi.

Squid Stir-Fry

Pasniedz 4

45 ml/3 ēdamkarotes zemesriekstu eļļas

3 lociņi, biezi sagriezti

2 šķēles ingvera saknes, sasmalcinātas

450 g/1 mārciņa kalmāru, sagriezti gabalos

15 ml/1 ēdamkarote sojas mērces

15 ml/1 ēdamkarote rīsu vīna vai sausā šerija

5 ml/1 tējk kukurūzas milti (kukurūzas ciete)

15 ml/1 ēdamkarote ūdens

Uzkarsē eļļu un apcep sīpolus un ingveru, līdz tie mīksti. Pievienojiet kalmārus un maisot apcepiet, līdz tie ir pārklāti eļļā. Pievieno sojas mērci un vīnu vai šeriju, uzliek vāku un vāra uz lēnas uguns 2 minūtes. Kukurūzas miltus un ūdeni samaisa pastu, pievieno pannā un maisot vāra, līdz mērce sabiezē un kalmāri mīksti.

Kalmāri ar kaltētām sēnēm

Pasniedz 4

50 g/2 unces kaltētas ķīniešu sēnes

450 g/1 mārciņa kalmāru gredzeni

45 ml/3 ēdamkarotes zemesriekstu eļļas

45 ml/3 ēdamkarotes sojas mērces

2 lociņi, smalki sagriezti

1 šķēle ingvera saknes, sasmalcināta

225g/8oz bambusa dzinumi, sagriezti sloksnēs

30 ml/2 ēdamkarotes kukurūzas miltu (kukurūzas ciete)

150 ml / ¬° pt / dāsna ¬Ω glāze zivju buljona

Sēnes 30 minūtes iemērc siltā ūdenī, pēc tam nokāš. Izmetiet kātus un nogrieziet vāciņus. Kalmāru gredzenus dažas sekundes blanšē verdošā ūdenī. Uzkarsē eļļu, tad pievieno sēnes, sojas mērci, sīpolus un ingveru un maisot apcep 2 minūtes. Pievienojiet kalmārus un bambusa dzinumus un maisot apcepiet 2 minūtes. Apvienojiet kukurūzas miltus un buljonu un samaisiet pannā. Vāra uz lēnas uguns, maisot, līdz mērce ir dzidra un sabiezējusi.

Kalmāri ar dārzeņiem

Pasniedz 4

45 ml/3 ēdamkarotes zemesriekstu eļļas

1 sīpols, sasmalcināts

5 ml/1 tējkarote sāls

450 g/1 mārciņa kalmāru, sagriezti gabalos

100g/4oz bambusa dzinumi, sasmalcināti

2 selerijas kāti, sagriezti pa diagonāli

60 ml / 4 ēdamkarotes vistas buljona

5 ml/1 tējk cukurs

100 g / 4 unces mangetout (sniega zirņi)

5 ml / 1 tējk kukurūzas milti (kukurūzas ciete)

15 ml/1 ēdamkarote ūdens

Uzkarsē eļļu un apcep sīpolu un sāli, līdz tie ir viegli brūni.

Pievienojiet kalmārus un vāriet, līdz tie ir pārklāti eļļā.

Pievienojiet bambusa dzinumus un seleriju un maisot apcepiet 3

minūtes. Pievieno buljonu un cukuru, uzvāra, uzliek vāku un vāra

uz lēnas uguns 3 minūtes, līdz dārzeņi ir mīksti. Iemaisa

mangetout. Kukurūzas miltus un ūdeni samaisa viendabīgā masā,

pievieno pannā un maisot vāra uz lēnas uguns, līdz mērce

sabiezē.

Sautēta liellopa gaļa ar anīsu

Pasniedz 4

30 ml/2 ēdamkarotes zemesriekstu eļļas

450 g/1 mārciņa steiks

1 ķiploka daiviņa, sasmalcināta

45 ml/3 ēdamkarotes sojas mērces

15 ml/1 ēdamkarote ūdens

15 ml/1 ēdamkarote rīsu vīna vai sausā šerija

5 ml/1 tējkarote sāls

5 ml/1 tējk cukurs

2 krustnagliņas zvaigžņu anīsa

Uzkarsē eļļu un apcep liellopu gaļu no visām pusēm, līdz tā kļūst brūna. Pievienojiet pārējās sastāvdaļas, uzkarsē līdz vārīšanās temperatūrai, uzliek vāku un uz lēnas uguns vāra apmēram 45 minūtes, pēc tam apgrieziet gaļu un pievienojiet vēl nedaudz ūdens un sojas mērci, ja gaļa izžūst. Vāra uz lēnas uguns vēl 45 minūtes, līdz gaļa ir mīksta. Pirms pasniegšanas izmetiet zvaigžņu anīsu.

Liellopu gaļa ar sparģeļiem

Pasniedz 4

450 g/1 mārciņa steiks, sagriezts kubiņos
30 ml/2 ēdamkarotes sojas mērces
30 ml/2 ēdamkarotes rīsu vīna vai sausā šerija
45 ml/3 ēdamkarotes kukurūzas miltu (kukurūzas ciete)
45 ml/3 ēdamkarotes zemesriekstu eļļas
5 ml/1 tējkarote sāls
1 ķiploka daiviņa, sasmalcināta
350g/12oz sparģeļu uzgaļi
120 ml / 4 fl unces / ¬Ω tase vistas buljona

15 ml/1 ēdamkarote sojas mērces

Ievietojiet steiku bļodā. Sajauc sojas mērci, vīnu vai šeriju un 30ml/2 ēd.k. kukurūzas miltus, pārlej steikam un kārtīgi samaisa. Atstāj marinēties 30 minūtes. Uzkarsē eļļu ar sāli un ķiplokiem un vāra, līdz ķiploki ir viegli brūni. Pievieno gaļu un marinādi un maisot cep 4 minūtes. Pievienojiet sparģeļus un viegli maisot apcepiet 2 minūtes. Ielej buljonu un sojas mērci, uzvāra un maisot cep 3 minūtes, līdz gaļa ir gatava. Atlikušos kukurūzas miltus sajauc ar nedaudz ūdens vai buljona un iemaisa mērcē. Vāra uz lēnas uguns dažas minūtes, maisot, līdz mērce ir dzidra un sabiezējusi.

Liellopu gaļa ar bambusa dzinumiem

Pasniedz 4

45 ml/3 ēdamkarotes zemesriekstu eļļas

1 ķiploka daiviņa, sasmalcināta

1 lociņš, sasmalcināts

1 šķēle ingvera saknes, sasmalcināta

225g/8oz liesa liellopa gaļa, sagriezta strēmelēs

100g/4oz bambusa dzinumi

45 ml/3 ēdamkarotes sojas mērces

15 ml/1 ēdamkarote rīsu vīna vai sausā šerija

5 ml/1 tējk kukurūzas milti (kukurūzas ciete)

Uzkarsē eļļu un apcep ķiplokus, sīpolus un ingveru, līdz tie ir viegli brūni. Pievienojiet liellopa gaļu un maisot apcepiet 4 minūtes, līdz tā ir viegli brūna. Pievienojiet bambusa dzinumus un maisot apcepiet 3 minūtes. Pievienojiet sojas mērci, vīnu vai šeriju un kukurūzas miltus un maisot apcepiet 4 minūtes.

Liellopu gaļa ar bambusa dzinumiem un sēnēm

Pasniedz 4

225g/8oz liesa liellopa gaļa

45 ml/3 ēdamkarotes zemesriekstu eļļas

1 šķēle ingvera saknes, sasmalcināta

100g/4oz bambusa dzinumi, sasmalcināti

100g/4oz sēnes, sagrieztas

45 ml/3 ēdamkarotes rīsu vīna vai sausā šerija

5 ml/1 tējk cukurs

10 ml/2 tējk sojas mērce

sāls un pipari

120 ml/4 fl oz/¬Ω glāze liellopu gaļas buljona

15 ml/1 ēdamkarote kukurūzas miltu (kukurūzas ciete)

30 ml/2 ēdamkarotes ūdens

Smalki sagrieziet liellopu gaļu no graudiem. Uzkarsē eļļu un maisot apcep ingveru dažas sekundes. Pievienojiet liellopa gaļu un maisot apcepiet, līdz tā ir tikko brūna. Pievienojiet bambusa dzinumus un sēnes un maisot apcepiet 1 minūti. Pievieno vīnu vai šeriju, cukuru un sojas mērci, pievieno sāli un piparus. Pievieno buljonu, uzvāra, pārklāj un vāra uz lēnas uguns 3 minūtes. Kukurūzas miltus sajauc ar ūdeni, pievieno pannā un maisot vāra, līdz mērce sabiezē.

Ķīniešu sautēta liellopa gaļa

Pasniedz 4

45 ml/3 ēdamkarotes zemesriekstu eļļas

900g/2lb steiks

1 lociņš, sagriezts

1 ķiploka daiviņa, sasmalcināta

1 šķēle ingvera saknes, sasmalcināta

60 ml/4 ēdamkarotes sojas mērces

30 ml/2 ēdamkarotes rīsu vīna vai sausā šerija

5 ml/1 tējk cukurs

5 ml/1 tējkarote sāls

šķipsniņa piparu

750 ml / 1¬° pts / 3 tases verdoša ūdens

Uzkarsē eļļu un ātri apcep liellopu gaļu no visām pusēm. Pievienojiet sīpolus, ķiplokus, ingveru, sojas mērci, vīnu vai šeriju, cukuru, sāli un piparus. Maisot uzvāra. Pievieno verdošu ūdeni, maisot vēlreiz uzvāra, tad uzliek vāku un vāra uz lēnas uguns apmēram 2 stundas, līdz liellopa gaļa ir mīksta.

Liellopu gaļa ar pupiņu kāpostiem

Pasniedz 4

450 g liesas liellopa gaļas, sagrieztas šķēlēs

1 olas baltums

30 ml/2 ēdamkarotes zemesriekstu eļļas

15 ml/1 ēdamkarote kukurūzas miltu (kukurūzas ciete)

15 ml/1 ēdamkarote sojas mērces

100 g/4 unces pupiņu asni

25 g/1 unce skābēti kāposti, sasmalcināti

1 sarkanais čili pipars, sasmalcināts

2 lociņi, sasmalcināti

2 šķēles ingvera saknes, sasmalcinātas

sāls

5 ml/1 tējkarote austeru mērce

5 ml/1 tējkarote sezama eļļas

Sajauciet liellopa gaļu ar sakultu olu, pusi eļļas, kukurūzas miltiem un sojas mērci un ļaujiet tai nostāvēties 30 minūtes. Blanšējiet pupiņu kāpostus verdošā ūdenī apmēram 8 minūtes, līdz tie ir gandrīz mīksti, pēc tam noteciniet. Uzkarsē atlikušo eļļu un maisot apcep liellopu gaļu, līdz tā ir viegli brūna, tad noņem no pannas. Pievienojiet skābos kāpostus, čili, ingveru, sāli, austeru mērci un sezama eļļu un maisot apcepiet 2 minūtes. Pievieno pupiņu kāpostus un maisot cep 2 minūtes. Ielieciet liellopu gaļu atpakaļ pannā un maisot vāriet, līdz tas ir labi sajaukts un uzkarsēts. Nekavējoties pasniedziet.

Liellopu gaļa ar brokoļiem

Pasniedz 4

450 g/1 mārciņa steiks, plānās šķēlēs

30 ml/2 ēdamkarotes kukurūzas miltu (kukurūzas ciete)

15 ml/1 ēdamkarote rīsu vīna vai sausā šerija

15 ml/1 ēdamkarote sojas mērces

30 ml/2 ēdamkarotes zemesriekstu eļļas

5 ml/1 tējkarote sāls

1 ķiploka daiviņa, sasmalcināta

225 g/8 unces brokoļu ziediņi

150 ml / ¬° pt / dāsna ¬Ω glāze liellopu gaļas buljona

Ievietojiet steiku bļodā. Sajauc 15 ml/1 ēdamkarote kukurūzas miltu ar vīnu vai šeriju un sojas mērci, iemaisa gaļā un atstāj marinēties 30 minūtes. Uzkarsē eļļu ar sāli un ķiplokiem un vāra, līdz ķiploki ir viegli brūni. Pievieno steiku un marinādi un maisot cep 4 minūtes. Pievienojiet brokoļus un maisot apcepiet 3 minūtes. Pievieno buljonu, uzvāra, uzliek vāku un vāra uz lēnas uguns 5 minūtes, līdz brokoļi ir mīksti, bet joprojām kraukšķīgi. Atlikušos kukurūzas miltus sajauc ar nedaudz ūdens un iemaisa mērcē. Vāra uz lēnas uguns, maisot, līdz mērce ir dzidra un sabiezējusi.

Sezama liellopu gaļa ar brokoļiem

Pasniedz 4

150g/5oz liesa liellopa gaļa, plānās šķēlītēs

2,5 ml/¬Ω tējkarotes austeru mērces

5 ml/1 tējk kukurūzas milti (kukurūzas ciete)

5 ml/1 tējkarote baltvīna etiķu

60 ml/4 ēdamkarotes zemesriekstu eļļas

100g/4oz brokoļu ziediņi

5 ml/1 tējk zivju mērce

2,5 ml/¬Ω tējkarote sojas mērces

250 ml / 8 fl oz / 1 glāze liellopu gaļas buljona

30 ml/2 ēdamkarotes sezama sēklu

Marinējiet liellopu gaļu ar austeru mērci, 2,5 ml/¬Ω tējkaroti kukurūzas miltu, 2,5 ml/¬Ω tējkaroti vīna etiķa un 15 ml/1 ēdamkarote eļļas 1 stundu.

Tikmēr uzkarsē 15 ml/1 ēdamkarote eļļas, pievieno brokoļus, 2,5 ml/¬Ω tējk zivju mērci, sojas mērci un atlikušo vīna etiķi un vienkārši pārlej ar verdošu ūdeni. Vāra uz lēnas uguns apmēram 10 minūtes, līdz tas ir mīksts.

Atsevišķā pannā uzkarsē 30 ml/2 ēd.k. eļļas un, maisot, īsi apcep liellopu gaļu, līdz tā sabiezē. Pievieno buljonu, atlikušos kukurūzas miltus un zivju mērci, uzvāra, uzliek vāku un vāra uz lēnas uguns apmēram 10 minūtes, līdz gaļa ir mīksta. Nokāš brokoļus un liek uz sasildīta pasniegšanas šķīvja. Virsū liek gaļu un bagātīgi pārkaisa ar sezama sēklām.

Grilēta liellopa gaļa

Pasniedz 4

450 g/1 mārciņa liess steiks, sagriezts

60 ml/4 ēdamkarotes sojas mērces

2 ķiploka daiviņas, sasmalcinātas

5 ml/1 tējkarote sāls

2,5 ml/¬Ω tējkarote svaigi maltu piparu

10 ml/2 tējk cukurs

Visas sastāvdaļas sajauc un ļauj marinēties 3 stundas. Grilējiet vai cepiet apmēram 5 minūtes katrā pusē.

Kantonas liellopu gaļa

Pasniedz 4

30 ml/2 ēdamkarotes kukurūzas miltu (kukurūzas ciete)

2 olu baltumi, saputoti

450 g/1 mārciņa steiks, sagriezts sloksnēs

eļļa dziļai cepšanai

4 selerijas kāti, sasmalcināti

2 sīpoli, sasmalcināti

60 ml / 4 ēdamkarotes ūdens

20 ml/4 tējk sāls

75 ml/5 ēdamkarotes sojas mērces

60 ml/4 ēdamkarotes rīsu vīna vai sausā šerija

30 ml/2 ēdamkarotes cukura

svaigi malti piņari

Sajauc pusi kukurūzas miltu ar olu baltumiem. Pievienojiet steiku un iemetiet, lai liellopu gaļa pārklātu mīklu. Uzkarsē eļļu un apcep steiku, līdz tas kļūst brūns. Izņem no pannas un notecina uz virtuves papīra. Uzkarsē 15 ml/1 ēdamkarote eļļas un maisot apcep seleriju un sīpolus 3 minūtes. Pievieno gaļu, ūdeni, sāli, sojas mērci, vīnu vai šeriju, cukuru un garšo ar pipariem. Uzkarsē līdz vārīšanās temperatūrai un maisot vāra uz lēnas uguns, līdz mērce sabiezē.

Liellopu gaļa ar burkāniem

Pasniedz 4

30 ml/2 ēdamkarotes zemesriekstu eļļas

450 g/1 mārciņa liesa liellopa gaļa, kubiņos

2 lociņi, sagriezti šķēlēs

2 ķiploka daiviņas, sasmalcinātas

1 šķēle ingvera saknes, sasmalcināta

250 ml / 8 fl oz / 1 tase sojas mērces

30 ml/2 ēdamkarotes rīsu vīna vai sausā šerija

30 ml/2 ēdamkarotes brūnā cukura

5 ml/1 tējkarote sāls

600 ml / 1 pt / 2¬Ω tases ūdens

4 burkāni, sagriezti pa diagonāli

Uzkarsē eļļu un apcep liellopu gaļu, līdz tā ir viegli brūna. Nolej lieko eļļu un pievieno sīpolus, ķiplokus, ingveru un anīsu un apcep 2 minūtes. Pievienojiet sojas mērci, vīnu vai šeriju, cukuru un sāli un labi samaisiet. Pievienu ūdeni, uzvāra, uzliek vāku un vāra uz lēnas uguns 1 stundu. Pievieno burkānus, uzliek vāku un vāra uz lēnas uguns vēl 30 minūtes. Noņem vāku un vāra uz lēnas uguns, līdz mērce ir samazinājusies.

Liellopu gaļa ar Indijas riekstiem

Pasniedz 4

60 ml/4 ēdamkarotes zemesriekstu eļļas

450 g/1 mārciņa steiks, plānās šķēlēs

8 lociņi, sagriezti gabaliņos

2 ķiploka daiviņas, sasmalcinātas

1 šķēle ingvera saknes, sasmalcināta

75 g/3 oz/¬œ tase grauzdētu Indijas riekstu

120 ml / 4 fl unces / ¬Ω tase ūdens

20 ml/4 tējk kukurūzas milti (kukurūzas ciete)

20 ml/4 tējk sojas mērce

5 ml/1 tējkarote sezama eļļas

5 ml/1 tējkarote austeru mērce

5 ml/1 tējk čili mērce

Uzkarsē pusi eļļas un maisot apcep gaļu, līdz tā ir viegli brūna. Izņem no pannas. Uzkarsē atlikušo eļļu un maisot apcep sīpolus, ķiplokus, ingveru un Indijas riekstus 1 minūti. Atgrieziet gaļu uz pannas. Sajauc pārējās sastāvdaļas un ielej maisījumu pannā. Uzkarsē līdz vārīšanās temperatūrai un maisot vāra uz lēnas uguns, līdz maisījums sabiezē.

Lēna liellopa gaļas sautējums

Pasniedz 4

30 ml/2 ēdamkarotes zemesriekstu eļļas

450g/1lb liellopa gaļas sautējums, kubiņos

3 šķēles ingvera saknes, sasmalcinātas

3 burkāni, sagriezti

1 rācenis, sagriezts kubiņos

15 ml/1 ēdamkarote melnie dateles, bez kauliņiem

15 ml/1 ēdamkarote lotosa sēklu

30 ml/2 ēdamkarotes tomātu biezeņa (pastas)

10 ml/2 ēdamkarotes sāls

900 ml/1¬Ω pts/3¬œ glāzes liellopu gaļas buljona

250 ml/8 fl oz/1 glāze rīsu vīna vai sausa šerija

Sildiet eļļu lielā cepeškrāsnī necaurlaidīgā katlā vai pannā un apcepiet liellopu gaļu no visām pusēm, līdz tā ir brūna.

Liellopu gaļa ar ziedkāpostu

Pasniedz 4

225 g/8 unces ziedkāpostu ziedi

eļļa dziļai cepšanai

225g/8oz liellopu gaļa, sagriezta strēmelēs

50g/2oz bambusa dzinumi, sagriezti sloksnēs

10 ūdens kastaņi, sagriezti strēmelēs

120 ml / 4 fl unces / ¬Ω tase vistas buljona

15 ml/1 ēdamkarote sojas mērces

15 ml/1 ēdamkarote austeru mērces

15 ml/1 ēdamkarote tomātu biezeņa (pastas)

15 ml/1 ēdamkarote kukurūzas miltu (kukurūzas ciete)

2,5 ml/¬Ω tējkarote sezama eļļas

Ziedkāpostu blanšē verdošā ūdenī 2 minūtes, pēc tam nokāš.
Uzkarsē eļļu un apcep ziedkāpostu, līdz tie ir viegli brūni. Izņem
un notecina uz virtuves papīra. Uzkarsē eļļu un apcep liellopu

gaļu, līdz tā ir viegli brūna, tad izņem un notecina. Nolejiet visu eļļu, izņemot 15 ml/1 ēdamkarote, un maisot apcepiet bambusa dzinumus un ūdens kastaņus 2 minūtes. Pievieno pārējās sastāvdaļas, uzvāra un maisot vāra uz lēnas uguns, līdz mērce sabiezē. Pievienojiet liellopa gaļu un ziedkāpostus atpakaļ pannā un viegli uzkarsējiet. Nekavējoties pasniedziet.

Liellopu gaļa ar seleriju

Pasniedz 4

100 g / 4 unces selerijas, sagrieztas sloksnēs
45 ml/3 ēdamkarotes zemesriekstu eļļas
2 lociņi, sasmalcināti
1 šķēle ingvera saknes, sasmalcināta
225g/8oz liesa liellopa gaļa, sagrieznta strēmelēs
30 ml/2 ēdamkarotes sojas mērces
30 ml/2 ēdamkarotes rīsu vīna vai sausā šerija
2,5 ml/¬Ω tējkarote cukura
2,5 ml/¬Ω tējkarote sāls

Selerijas blanšē verdošā ūdenī 1 minūti, pēc tam labi nokāš. Uzkarsē eļļu un apcep sīpolus un ingveru, līdz tie ir viegli brūni. Pievienojiet liellopa gaļu un maisot apcepiet 4 minūtes. Pievieno seleriju un maisot apcep 2 minūtes. Pievieno sojas mērci, vīnu vai šeriju, cukuru un sāli un maisot apcep 3 minūtes.

Cepti liellopa čipsi ar seleriju

Pasniedz 4

30 ml/2 ēdamkarotes zemesriekstu eļļas

450 g liesas liellopa gaļas, sagrieztas šķēlēs

3 selerijas kāti, sasmalcināti

1 sīpols, sasmalcināts

1 lociņš, sagriezts

1 šķēle ingvera saknes, sasmalcināta

30 ml/2 ēdamkarotes sojas mērces

15 ml/1 ēdamkarote rīsu vīna vai sausā šerija

2,5 ml/¬Ω tējkarote cukura

2,5 ml/¬Ω tējkarote sāls

10 ml / 2 tējkarotes kukurūzas miltu (kukurūzas ciete)

30 ml/2 ēdamkarotes ūdens

Sildiet pusi eļļas līdz ļoti karstai un pagatavojiet liellopu gaļu 1 minūti, līdz tā ir tikko brūna. Izņem no pannas. Uzkarsē atlikušo eļļu un apcep seleriju, sīpolu, pavasara sīpolu un ingveru, līdz tie ir nedaudz mīksti. Ielieciet liellopu gaļu atpakaļ pannā ar sojas mērci, vīnu vai šeriju, cukuru un sāli, uzkarsē līdz vārīšanās temperatūrai un maisot apcep, līdz tā ir uzkarsēta. Sajauc kukurūzas miltus un ūdeni, pievieno pannā un vāra uz lēnas uguns, līdz mērce sabiezē. Nekavējoties pasniedziet.

Sasmalcināta liellopa gaļa ar vistu un seleriju

Pasniedz 4

4 žāvētas ķīniešu sēnes

45 ml/3 ēdamkarotes zemesriekstu eļļas

2 ķiploka daiviņas, sasmalcinātas

1 sagriezta ingvera sakne, sasmalcināta

5 ml/1 tējkarote sāls

100 g liesas liellopu gaļas, sagrieztas strēmelēs

100g/4oz vistas, sagriezta strēmelēs

2 burkāni, sagriezti strēmelēs

2 selerijas kāti, sagriezti strēmelēs

4 lociņi, sagriezti sloksnēs

5 ml/1 tējk cukurs

5 ml/1 tējk sojas mērce

5 ml/1 tējkarote rīsu vīna vai sausā šerija

45 ml / 3 ēdamkarotes ūdens

5 ml/1 tējk kukurūzas milti (kukurūzas ciete)

Sēnes 30 minūtes iemērc siltā ūdenī, pēc tam nokāš. Izmetiet kātus un nogrieziet vāciņus. Uzkarsē eļļu un apcep ķiplokus, ingveru un sāli, līdz tie ir viegli brūni. Pievienojiet liellopa gaļu un vistu un pagatavojiet līdz brūnai. Pievieno seleriju, sīpolus, cukuru, sojas mērci, vīnu vai šeriju, ūdeni un uzvāra. Uzliek vāku un vāra uz lēnas uguns apmēram 15 minūtes, līdz gaļa ir mīksta. Kukurūzas miltus sajauc ar nedaudz ūdens, iemaisa mērcē un maisot vāra uz lēnas uguns, līdz mērce sabiezē.

Čili liellopu gaļa

Pasniedz 4

450 g/1 mārciņa steiks, sagriezts sloksnēs

45 ml/3 ēdamkarotes sojas mērces

15 ml/1 ēdamkarote rīsu vīna vai sausā šerija

15 ml/1 ēdamkarote brūnā cukura

15 ml/1 ēdamkarote smalki sagrieztas ingvera saknes

30 ml/2 ēdamkarotes zemesriekstu eļļas

50g/2oz bambusa dzinumi sagriezti sērkociņu kociņos

1 sīpols, sagriezts sloksnēs

1 selerijas kociņš, sagriezts sērkociņu kociņos

2 sarkanie čili pipari, bez kauliņiem un sagriezti strēmelēs

120 ml / 4 fl unces / ¬Ω tase vistas buljona

15 ml/1 ēdamkarote kukurūzas miltu (kukurūzas ciete)

Ievietojiet steiku bļodā. Sajauc sojas mērci, vīnu vai šeriju, cukuru un ingveru un iemaisa steikā. Atstāj marinēties 1 stundu. Izņem steiku no marinādes. Uzkarsē pusi eļļas un maisot apcep bambusa dzinumus, sīpolus, seleriju un čili 3 minūtes, pēc tam noņem no pannas. Uzkarsē atlikušo eļļu un maisot apcep steiku 3 minūtes. Iemaisa marinādi, uzvāra un pievieno apceptos dārzeņus. Maisot apcep 2 minūtes. Sajauc buljonu un kukurūzas miltus un ielej pannā. Uzkarsē līdz vārīšanās temperatūrai un maisot vāra uz lēnas uguns, līdz mērce ir dzidra un sabiezējusi.

Liellopu gaļa ar Pekinas kāpostiem

Pasniedz 4

225g/8oz liesa liellopa gaļa

30 ml/2 ēdamkarotes zemesriekstu eļļas

350g/12oz Ķīnas kāposti, sasmalcināti

120 ml/4 fl oz/¬Ω glāze liellopu gaļas buljona

sāls un svaigi malti pipari

10 ml / 2 tējkarotes kukurūzas miltu (kukurūzas ciete)

30 ml/2 ēdamkarotes ūdens

Smalki sagrieziet liellopu gaļu no graudiem. Uzkarsē eļļu un maisot apcep liellopu gaļu, līdz tā ir tikko brūna. Pievienojiet Ķīnas kāpostus un maisot apcepiet, līdz tie ir nedaudz mīksti. Ielejiet buljonu, uzvāra un pievienojiet sāli un piparus. Uzliek vāku un vāra uz lēnas uguns 4 minūtes, līdz liellopa gaļa ir mīksta. Kukurūzas miltus sajauc ar ūdeni, pievieno pannā un maisot vāra, līdz mērce sabiezē.

Liellopa gaļas karbonāde Suey

Pasniedz 4

3 selerijas kāti, sasmalcināti

100 g/4 unces pupiņu asni

100g/4oz brokoļu ziediņi

60 ml/4 ēdamkarotes zemesriekstu eļļas

3 lociņi, sasmalcināti

2 ķiploka daiviņas, sasmalcinātas

1 šķēle ingvera saknes, sasmalcināta

225g/8oz liesa liellopa gaļa, sagriezta strēmelēs

45 ml/3 ēdamkarotes sojas mērces

15 ml/1 ēdamkarote rīsu vīna vai sausā šerija

5 ml/1 tējkarote sāls

2,5 ml/¬Ω tējkarote cukura

svaigi malti pipari

15 ml/1 ēdamkarote kukurūzas miltu (kukurūzas ciete)

Seleriju, pupiņu kāpostus un brokoļus blanšē verdošā ūdenī 2 minūtes, pēc tam nokāš un notecina. Uzkarsē 45 ml/3 ēdamkarotes eļļas un apcep sīpolus, ķiplokus un ingveru, līdz tie ir viegli brūni. Pievienojiet liellopa gaļu un maisot apcepiet 4 minūtes. Izņem no pannas. Uzkarsē atlikušo eļļu un maisot apcep dārzeņus 3 minūtes. Pievienojiet liellopa gaļu, sojas mērci, vīnu vai šeriju, sāli, cukuru un šķipsniņu piparu un maisot apcepiet 2 minūtes. Kukurūzas miltus sajauc ar nedaudz ūdens, sakrata pannā un maisot vāra, līdz mērce kļūst dzidra un sabiezē.

Liellopu gaļa ar gurķiem

Pasniedz 4

450 g/1 mārciņa steiks, plānās šķēlēs
45 ml/3 ēdamkarotes sojas mērces
30 ml/2 ēdamkarotes kukurūzas miltu (kukurūzas ciete)
60 ml/4 ēdamkarotes zemesriekstu eļļas
2 gurķi, nomizoti, izņemti serdes un sagriezti šķēlēs
60 ml / 4 ēdamkarotes vistas buljona
30 ml/2 ēdamkarotes rīsu vīna vai sausā šerija
sāls un svaigi malti pipari

Ievietojiet steiku bļodā. Sajauc sojas mērci un kukurūzas miltus un iemaisa steikā. Atstāj marinēties 30 minūtes. Uzkarsē pusi eļļas un maisot apcep gurķus 3 minūtes, līdz tie kļūst necaurspīdīgi, pēc tam izņemam no pannas. Uzkarsē atlikušo eļļu un maisot apcep steiku, līdz tas kļūst brūns. Pievieno gurķus un maisot apcep 2 minūtes. Pievienojiet buljonu, vīnu vai šeriju un pievienojiet sāli un piparus. Uzkarsē līdz vārīšanās temperatūrai, uzliek vāku un vāra uz lēnas uguns 3 minūtes.

Liellopu čau Mein

Pasniedz 4

750 g / 1 ¬Ω lb steiks

2 sīpoli

45 ml/3 ēdamkarotes sojas mērces

45 ml/3 ēdamkarotes rīsu vīna vai sausā šerija

15 ml/1 ēdamkarote zemesriekstu sviesta

5 ml/1 tējkarote citrona sulas

350g/12oz olu makaroni

60 ml/4 ēdamkarotes zemesriekstu eļļas

175 ml / 6 fl oz / ¬œ tase vistas buljona

15 ml/1 ēdamkarote kukurūzas miltu (kukurūzas ciete)

30 ml/2 ēdamkarotes austeru mērces

4 lociņi, sasmalcināti

3 selerijas kāti, sasmalcināti

100g/4oz sēnes, sagrieztas

1 zaļā paprika, sagrieztu sloksnēs

100 g/4 unces pupiņu asni

Noņemiet un izmetiet taukus no gaļas. Graudu sagriež plānās šķēlēs. Sīpolus sagrieziet šķēlēs un atdaliet slāņus. Sajauc 15 ml/1 ēdamkarote sojas mērces ar 15 ml/1 ēdamkarote vīna vai šerija, zemesriekstu sviestu un citronu sulu. Iemaisa gaļu, pārklāj un ļauj nostāvēties 1 stundu. Pagatavojiet makaronus verdošā ūdenī apmēram 5 minūtes vai līdz tie ir mīksti. Labi notecina. Uzkarsē 15 ml/1 ēdamkarote eļļas, pievieno 15 ml/1 ēd.k. sojas mērci un nūdeles un apcep 2 minūtes, līdz tās ir viegli brūnas. Pārliek uz uzsildītas servēšanas šķīvja.

Atlikušo sojas mērci un vīnu vai šeriju sajauciet ar buljonu, kukurūzas miltiem un austeru mērci. Uzkarsē 15 ml/1 ēdamkarote eļļas un maisot apcep sīpolus 1 minūti. Pievienojiet seleriju, sēnes, piparus un pupiņu kāpostus un maisot apcepiet 2 minūtes. Izņem no wok pannas. Uzkarsē atlikušo eļļu un maisot apcep liellopu gaļu, līdz tā kļūst brūna. Pievieno buljonu, uzvāra, pārklāj un vāra uz lēnas uguns 3 minūtes. Dārzeņus liek atpakaļ wok pannā un maisot cep apmēram 4 minūtes, līdz tie ir uzkarsēti. Masu pārlej pāri makaroniem un pasniedz.

Gurķu steiks

Pasniedz 4

450 g/1 mārciņa steiks
10 ml / 2 tējkarotes kukurūzas miltu (kukurūzas ciete)
10 ml/2 tējk sāls
2,5 ml/¬Ω tējkarote svaigi maltu piparu
90 ml/6 ēdamkarotes zemesriekstu eļļas
1 sīpols, smalki sagriezts
1 gurķis, nomizots un sagriezts
120 ml/4 fl oz/¬Ω glāze liellopu gaļas buljona

Sagrieziet steiku sloksnēs, pēc tam plānās šķēlēs pāri graudiem. Liek bļodā un iemaisa kukurūzas miltus, sāli, piparus un pusi eļļas. Atstāj marinēties 30 minūtes. Uzkarsē atlikušo eļļu un apcep liellopu gaļu un sīpolus, līdz tie ir viegli brūni. Pievieno gurķus un buljonu, uzvāra, uzliek vāku un vāra uz lēnas uguns 5 minūtes.

Milton Keynes UK
Ingram Content Group UK Ltd.
UKHW020636230124
436534UK00016B/577